FAITHBREAKER

Also by Hannah Kaner

The Fallen Gods Trilogy
Godkiller
Sunbringer

FAITHBREAKER

HANNAH KANER

HARPER
Voyager

Harper*Voyager*
An imprint of HarperCollins*Publishers* Ltd
1 London Bridge Street
London SE1 9GF

www.harpercollins.co.uk

HarperCollins*Publishers*
Macken House,
39/40 Mayor Street Upper,
Dublin 1
D01 C9W8
Ireland

First published by HarperCollins*Publishers* Ltd 2025
1

A catalogue record for this book is available from the British Library.

ISBN: 978-0-00-852156-1 (HB)
ISBN: 978-0-00-852157-8 (TPB)

Typeset in Adobe Jenson Pro by Palimpsest Book Production Ltd, Falkirk, Stirlingshire

Printed and Bound in the UK using 100% Renewable Electricity
at CPI Group (UK) Ltd

*For my brothers and sister.
My fiercest defenders, and my oldest friends.*

PROLOGUE

HESTRA, GOD OF HEARTHS, FELT THE FLAME OF HSETH'S coming. A flesh beyond her flesh, a fire beyond her fire. Hseth was no longer a god of burning heather for the herds to graze, nor a god of furnace and forges. The fire god had been reborn for blood and brass and bone. For war.

And as the weeks passed, Hseth's power grew, feeding from fury and fear as the Talicians came over mountains and waves to claim Middren for their own.

Hestra, with her dwindling power, could sense the hearths of Daesmouth crumbling and falling as its people tried to hold off the sea invasion. She could feel the stones that had once been carved with her ancient symbols in the north, which cracked and cooled as Middrenites fled down the Bennite Mountains ahead of the Talicians' flaming raids. They left behind their homes, those few places that still held Hestra's twig-and-moss figurines buried beneath the hearthstones in return for her blessing.

So few still remembered that the hearts of their houses held fire god shrines.

And that did not stop them burning.

From the shadows of fireplaces, Hestra saw clouds of smoke rising over burning groves of ripening fruit. She saw wells blacken with the blood of the people who had drunk from them. She saw the poor folk who were caught. Their livestock, their children, dragged to be sacrifices at the feet of a god who would not remember what love could feel like when freely given. Not taken with blade and flame.

And Hseth's fire priests were happy to burn rich lands if it meant they could claim them more quickly and without a fight. They did not care that their own fighters were choking on their flames, their bellies empty and their clothes threadbare. They did not care that gods were not supposed to be used as weapons.

Hestra wondered if she should go to Hseth, speak from hearth to flame and remind the Talician god of the promises she had made. Remind her that she had been wise once, that she had known when to let flames burn, and when to let them die.

She did not. Hseth would not hear her; all she heard were the voices of her priests, and the screams of her victims.

There was only one person who wanted Hestra to speak, and she had no words for him.

'Will you not talk to me, hearth god?' Arren whispered in the rare moments he was alone, now he had negotiated himself free from confinement by the rebels and used his banner to summon armies to their defence. 'Will you be silent till all of our people are ash and dust?'

Our people?

'The Vittosk lands to the east are overrun, Hestra,' Arren pressed, the use of her name like a tug on her heart. What she knew by sight he learned through letters, pleas for help, promises of soldiers, guards, supplies. She could feel his voice in her twigs, in her body. She could feel his fear as if it were her own. 'They took Blenraden and hung its pilgrims and guards from the walls, like totems, flayed with fire.'

Hestra burrowed deeper into his heart, wishing his words could not find her. Burning faithful, delighting in pain; that was not what she wanted. Hestra wanted people to turn away from their bright cities and gods of fortune. She wanted them to leave their coin and silks and spices, and to come back to the hearth, come back to her. To seek out her warmth for fear of the dark.

'She has forgotten you, my heart.'

Hestra knew. Of course she knew. All promises had been broken with Hseth's death. Now, she was left to wonder if the other deity of fire had ever meant them at all.

Was it so wrong to help her? She just had to do one thing, rescue one little boy-king, gasping away his life on a stone floor, and manipulate him into her power, connect him with Hseth and her conniving. They had hoped to take root in the space where Middren's gods had been torn out.

It had been good, for a while. Hestra had gained life and strength, suffused with colour, in her binding to him. So many hopes, dreams, so many promises he gave to her.

All now on the brink of destruction.

Arren's fortress had been shattered and invaded, his beloved had tried to run him through, and he and Hestra both had been choked almost to death by the demigod, the Craier girl. He was a king of little, now. Lost pride and a losing war.

He had no power to offer, and she had nothing to say to him. Gods could hold the silence of centuries, and only the first boon she had granted him, etched black in his flesh, kept them together.

The promise to keep him alive.

Could she leave? She had used almost all of her old power to take Arren's double with his army to Lesscia, and then the rest bringing him back again to the fortress with his precious knight, the little god of white lies and the halfling girl who slipped with them to her hearth. Her prayers were so sparse now, so faint, her will so weak that if she left the king she was afraid she would lose her form, her shape, her very self. She would be nothing but nameless power, a malevolent spirit, a breath on the wind.

Perhaps she should do it. Disappear. What else was there? Staying in a land of the faithless, half-throned king, harassed by flames she could not command? Caught in the chest of a man who wanted all the love, the worship, everything for himself?

Our people.

'Will you leave me here alone,' said Arren, 'like everyone else?'

He spoke as if to himself, staring out of his window into the starry sky above the city of Sakre. Was he truly speaking to her? Or was it Elogast in his mind? She kept her thoughts close, giving neither comfort nor pain. He wanted love, like her. And power. War had caught them both between two worlds: flame and a future, a king and chaos.

God and human.

CHAPTER ONE

Kissen

KISSEN LAY IN THE PERFECT CROOK BETWEEN ELO'S SHOULDER and chest, sated and exhausted. The cabin she had been permitted was barely three strides across, and her small cot took up most of the room.

Still, she preferred it to a hammock in the belly of the ship, cheek to cheek with its crew that looked like they'd steal her teeth from her mouth and slit her throat with a smile. Despite Inara's assurances, Kissen didn't trust Lessa Craier, or her rebels. Her hand still ached from having to escape from the lady's chains through a cellar of blackfire.

It was nice to have a locking door between her and them. And, well, some privacy went a long way.

'How do you have so much energy?' she groaned, sitting up and reaching over to splash herself with cold water from the washstand. Elo hoisted himself on his elbows and grinned across at her, looking annoyingly pleased with himself.

'I didn't hear you complaining,' he said.

'I didn't say I was complaining.' She leaned back against the other side of the cot and regarded her friend in the thin light of the porthole.

He had changed. He was harder, wilder than he was when she met him. The burn scar across his chest that he had received from Hseth had healed well into a mottled pink hand, bright against the dark brown skin of his broad chest. It added to the hatchwork of scars from battles old and new.

'But,' she added, 'I know when I'm being used as a distraction.'

Elo tipped his head and smirked. He had a shadow of stubble, accentuating the sharp line of his jaw. 'I promise you, Kissenna, you had my full attention,' he said.

Bastard. No one used her full name. Not even Yatho and Telle.

He sat up straighter, his smile falling. 'Of course I need a distraction,' he said. 'We're on the losing side of war.'

It didn't feel like war in Sakre. It had been weeks since Kissen had stopped Lessa Craier's attempted coup, and the king was still lurking in the capital, gathering forces from local nobles, shoring up defences, supplies, weaponry. Most of this war was the tedium of waiting for it to happen.

But Kissen knew that the battle with Hseth wasn't the only one on Elo's mind. His own rebellion had failed, lost at the outset, and now he had been forced to unite again with the king he had tried to kill, who had tried to kill him.

'You should come with us to Irisia,' said Kissen, and he frowned. 'Fuck the king. Fuck all of this. Join the Craier mission and speak for Middren there, in your mothers' land.' She nudged him with her foot. 'Anyway, between Skedi, Inara, her mother and the gods, I don't know where I stand.' She lifted her shortened leg and wiggled it at him. 'Or hop.'

Elo laughed, closing his eyes, and Kissen pulled her leg back, rubbing her thumb over the severed end of her knee. She was most comfortable naked, scarred in all her glory, and it was rare that she had the luxury of the privacy and warmth that a ship's cabin afforded. After she had dragged herself through the rugged Talician highlands, she was going to make the most of it.

'Or . . .' she continued. 'If you want me to stay, I could fight—'

He opened his eyes again. 'No,' he said. 'Last word I could find of your sisters was that they made it to Weild. If there's any goodness in the world, they will have taken the first ship to Irisia.'

Kissen glanced out of the porthole towards the harbour wall, between the towers to the open sea, bright as glass and silver-tipped.

It was a big world, and her sisters could be anywhere. 'It's a fool's hope,' she said.

'But it's hope. You've given more than enough for this country.'

'And you haven't?'

He rubbed his brow. The early summer sun beat at the sides of the cabin, and heat prickled on their skin despite the slight breeze slipping beneath the door. The air was scented with the Irisian stew Elo had brought her in a thin pottery bowl from one of the harbourside stalls. His favourite. 'I can't leave,' he said. 'I won't. My place is here. Only a coward abandons the mess they made.'

'It's not your mess,' insisted Kissen. 'It's Arren's, it's the gods', it's Lessa Craier's. You tried to put things right.'

'And failed.' Elo laughed hollowly. 'Miserably. I almost broke our land on the brink of war. I almost lost Inara, got your family killed.' He touched the top of his hair; it had grown out in tight coils, nearly long enough to braid. 'I almost got you killed, Kissen.'

'Well, I contributed some arrogance to that, didn't I?' she said.

He laughed again. At least she could make him laugh. His smile was warm, but brief, and he swung his muscled legs out over the side of the narrow bed. She liked that he was comfortable around her, in his own skin. Honest. They were honest with each other. This was no love story between them, no romance. It was trust, unfettered. Need, without possession. She had the sudden urge to kiss him again.

'My time is marked by failure,' he said. 'I may as well accept it and fix my mistakes, or die trying.'

'Or, you could leave behind this land that has done nothing but hurt you.'

He looked at her then, and by the crease near his lip, the tension in his jaw, she knew he would not. Could not. He had given too much to Middren, to Arren, to let it all go.

'Do you think you'll come back?' he said instead of answering.

Kissen pushed her hair from her eyes and leaned back against the cabin wall. 'I don't know,' she said, honestly. 'There's not much left for me here apart from you. And I might have your attention, baker-knight,' she looked him up and down, 'and the rest of you. But . . . I know your heart lies elsewhere.'

Elo winced. Then he stood and grabbed his shirt from the pile he had made of his clothes. The rotten man had folded them as they were undressing. 'I'd better leave,' he said, pulling it over his head and the scar on his chest. 'Before the ship disembarks with me on it.'

Shit. Not her best choice of words. It was his heart, his life, that Hseth and the king had tried to take from him in exchange for power.

Arren. The core of Elo's hurt and bad humour. His betrayer, and the centre of his soul.

'He told you he loved you,' pressed Kissen, 'didn't he?'

'He was manipulating me,' said Elo, bending over to grab his trousers and giving Kissen a quite tasty view. 'While I tried to kill him.'

'And he succeeds in it because . . .' Because Elo's life was intertwined with Arren's, tangled, knotted, and painful. And ignoring that wasn't making it go away.

'We've never even kissed, Kissen.'

'If love were only kisses everyone would be in less trouble.'

'I hate him. Everything he has done. Everything he stands for.'

'Love and pain are not so different,' said Kissen. 'Why else would gods want blood and death as sacrifice?'

Elo sighed, lacing up his trews. 'He's not a good man.'

'No.' Kissen grabbed her own rumpled shirt and pulled it on. These stolen moments could not last long, not when they both walked the fine line between arrest and usefulness in this city. But perhaps it would have lasted longer had she some better skill in holding her tongue. 'But if you're fighting in his army, you're going to need to resolve your issues somehow.'

Her knight ignored her, sitting on the bed to pull his boots on.

'You could fuck,' she said brightly. 'That worked for us.'

Despite himself, Elo snorted, one boot on, one off. Kissen gave him a grin and leaned over to pick up her new prosthesis from the floor. Elo had helped navigate Sakre and paid for a new one from the funds he had stored in one of the city temples that had been repurposed as banks.

'Is it working all right for you?' he asked, noticing her adjusting the straps to put it on. It was a fine enough piece, with red leather for the kneecap and a wooden leg, but it was nowhere near as effective as the one that Yatho had made. Its base was already chipped and battered from use, and it hadn't been created for her, so she felt unsteady in it, as if her leg was a breath behind the rest of her. Still, it was an improvement on the twisted thing that her old one had become through all her trials.

'It's like losing a sword made for your hand, and being given a hammer to use instead,' said Kissen. A hammer that bit the hand; the agonising squeezing of her right shin and calf were worse when her leg didn't feel enough like her own body. 'But it's serviceable. The artificers have got better in the years since the God War, you should see the shit I wore as a kid.'

Elo put his warm hand on her shoulder, and she leaned into it for a second. Then he took a breath—

'If you say you're sorry again I'll punch you in the mouth,' she said, finishing her straps and shrugging him off. 'I made my choice to fight the fire god. And beat her too. And I'd do it again.'

Elo nodded, passed her her trews, then picked up his own tabard. This was a bright padded blue, striped in curling waves of gold, and he fastened it with his belt and a new sword. He had lost his old one in Lesscia, and this new blade had a plain hilt, no longer a reminder of the lion's head he had sacrificed.

'Only . . .' she pulled her trews over her prosthesis, the right leg adjusted and unlaced so it would slide on easily. 'She has briddite in her heart. I don't know if a veiga's tricks will harm her this time.'

'Do you think the reports are true?' said Elo, kneeling down without being asked to help her tie up the laces. 'That they can summon her to use as a weapon of war?'

Kissen sighed, and pulled her belt down from its hook from the wall. She had sourced a few throwing knives, one briddite, and a cutlass with a briddite edge. Not enough of the ore in her opinion, but she had to make do. Sakre was mostly still loyal to Arren, and most of their briddite stores had been melted down into useless talismans they wore to ward off bad gods and spirits.

'I've never seen a god's power like hers,' she said at last. Of course, gods sometimes manifested at their shrines when they were called, but not always. If they could summon Hseth at will, the god was either very naïve, or very greedy. Or both. 'Her priests lead the country, command the army. They use fear and pain as weapons, so I don't doubt that they can use the god too. I saw the shrines they made; if they carry them with their armies, they could summon her anywhere.'

'Their foot soldiers must be exhausted,' Elo murmured. 'Talicia hasn't run a ground war in nearly fifty years. Few of them will be trained, and you said half of them were farmhands, fisherfolk, younglings. Why would they put themselves through this?'

'Fear and power make people do stupid things,' said Kissen. 'Mad things.' She had told all she had seen in Talicia to Elo, Lessa and the king: the burning of children, of people, the zeal and the terror.

'I don't know how to stop this,' she admitted. 'Even if the Craiers get help from Irisia, even if you can hold them off in the north . . .'

'I'll think of something,' said Elo.

Infuriating. He was infuriatingly calm.

A rattle of knocking at the door, and their brief peace was broken. 'What?' Kissen barked.

'The tide is up,' said a familiar voice. 'And if we set sail, Elo might not wish to swim to shore.'

Kissen grabbed her staff, and slid open the door to see Inara standing in the warm, bright sunlight, with an intentionally innocent look. Her cropped hair suited her well, springing up into a thicket of curls around her neck and ears. Her thirteenth birthday had been and gone as the spring warmed, and she had also grown drastically in height in what felt like a bare few weeks since Kissen had first met her.

'How did you know I was here?' said Elo, grabbing the pottery bowls he had brought from the food vendor and sliding them back into his satchel, wiped clean with bread and ready to return in exchange for a copper.

'You were seen sneaking aboard in the wee hours,' said Inara. 'Like a thief in the night.'

Elo sucked his teeth, yet when he stepped out into the brightness and noise of the ship's deck, it was hard to imagine him thieving or haggling over petty coin. His skin glowed as if he had been born of the sun, and in his fine garb he looked more like a lord than a working knight, or even the baker he had called himself when they first met.

Inara was also well pranked up. She had forgone the Craier green and instead wore a stiff ochre undershirt with brushed wool leggings, and a long red tunic over both, dotted at the shoulders with droplets of tumbled glass. For a moment, in her rumpled shirt and patched trews, Kissen felt like a stranger. She was a foreign orphan, a guttersnipe and a mercenary, she wasn't meant to stand side by side with knights and nobles and kings.

Well, she had never been one to know her place.

'I'll bet the god ratted us out,' said Kissen, looking up. She was right, Skediceth, god of white lies, was perched on the highest of the three mainmasts that stabbed through Lessa Craier's ship, his wings outstretched as he bathed in the sun and the sea air. He had mostly recovered himself since the fights in Lesscia, but he had stayed smaller, quieter than she remembered. He often kept to the high perch when he wasn't on Inara's shoulder, a silent sentinel against would-be assassins seeking vengeance against the Craiers on their ship, the *Silverswift*.

Kissen had to admit, it was a beauteous vessel; its raised foredeck had gilt banisters up to the top, carved in flowing, twisting designs. This held Kissen's cabin side by side with the one belonging to Lessa's guard captain and fellow rebel, Tarin. The aftcastle where Lessa and Inara would stay was at the other side of the well-polished main deck, now empty of barrels and livestock but busy with crew who were preparing the sails for release.

There, between the upright panelling and doors, three small shrines were studded into the wood. Before the God War, every Middrenite ship would have had such shrines, to gods who might protect them on the seas. Now, these altars seemed preserved from another age.

One was clearly for Yusef, the god of safe haven. Inara's father. The totem carved for him was a statue, broad-shouldered and bearded, draped in a string of red glass beads. As with most of his shrines Kissen had seen before his death, he wore the travelling robes of the eastern tribes that had settled Restish centuries before, and a woven belt of what looked like sail rope.

The others weren't so familiar: one held a spiked conch and a crown of gold-dipped cowries, the other a winged totem of a gull carved from pale, smooth stone. The latter was probably some wind god, and Kissen resisted the urge to spit in its offering cup. She was not fond of wind gods of late.

'Everything's stowed,' said Inara, dragging her attention away. 'Apart from Legs.'

Kissen glanced overboard to see her horse, merrily eating hay from a bag, his tail swishing away the flies that clustered about him, oblivious to the noise of the harbour. He was still in the temporary stables beneath the pulleys they used to bring beasts aboard. She had stopped them, not wanting him to spend the night aboard in the cramped dark beneath the deck.

Kissen sighed. This was going to hurt.

'Elo, I have a gift for you,' she said, using her staff to ease herself onto the gangplank before carefully moving sideways down it. Better to feel like a crab than to fall and break her neck.

'What do you mean?' said Elo, following her. The main port of Sakre, north of the *Silverswift*, was teeming with folk – merchants, haulers, runners and crews – but the Craier ship had a privileged position in the nobles' docks, separate and in a pool of quiet, save for the pining cries of gulls. It was one of the few remaining hints, other than the stink of lye and blood in the Healers' streets, that the city had hung in the balance between king and rebels. That was until Lady Craier finally understood that destroying Arren meant splitting their country into factions that would fight each other instead of following her to war.

As Kissen reached the stones of the harbour, Legs nickered, coming forward to greet her. Kissen reached up a hand for his warm, strong nose and stroked the white streak that marked it. His arrow and thorn wounds had healed well but had left pale notches in his flanks.

'Shall I call the captain to bring him aboard?' Inara asked, her eyes also on his scars.

'No,' said Kissen. 'He's not coming.'

'Not coming?'

Inara climbed the fence of his pen so she could stroke him too, but he stamped his feet and shifted his face towards Elo, ignoring the girl. Her lips tugged downwards, but she held in her disappointment as Elo patted Legs's neck.

At last, he understood. 'You can't leave him,' he said. 'I went through great lengths to fetch him here for you.'

'I know,' said Kissen heavily. 'But I told you before: I owe him better than a slow death in a cage.'

'But he loves you,' said Inara, and didn't add *even if he has not forgiven me for riding him into a riot.* Kissen patted her arm in comfort.

'Sometimes, you need to let love go,' she said. 'He's a pathway horse, he knows this land. I can't close him in a stinking hull for weeks with no light and air. It would break his heart.'

She couldn't imagine Legs away from the green places, the trees and the mountains, the roads he had carried her through time and time again, the chestnut leaves and the bracken. She had bought him, barely a year old, from a woman too liberal with a whip and too stingy with her grazing. It had taken a long while for him to warm to her, but when he did, he became family.

Elo shook his head as Legs nuzzled his shoulder. 'We both owe him better than a long road to war.'

'Then don't take him into battle. He's loyal, steady on the way. And . . .' She clicked her tongue as her own bloody horse pressed his nose into Elo's hands. 'Bastard seems to like you.'

'You told me once to get the fuck away from him,' said Elo, now scratching Legs's white streak.

'Well, if I can't offer you my arms, baker-knight, at least I can offer my Legs.' She winked at him, and Inara snorted. 'There are packhorses in the army, he can be yours. A friend. One you can trust.'

Elo smiled so fully that his eyes crinkled, then turned and clasped her shoulders. 'I don't know what to say.'

'Say you'll look after him,' said Kissen, reaching to hold the back of his neck, somewhere between a warrior's clasp and a lover's embrace.

'I promise.'

Legs huffed, annoyed at being left, then gently, carefully, came back to Inara and put his nose to her shoulder, sniffing at the jewels there. He didn't move as she slowly raised a hand to his mane, and he let her hold him.

Kissen breathed out. She wished she could hold Elo together in her arms, hold the world together through her will alone. She was afraid that if she let him go he would disappear, run into war, die a hero, when she wanted him to live, wanted him to keep living.

'I hope we meet again, baker,' she said, instead of all that she felt. He knew. Of course he knew.

'We will,' said Inara, and she leaned over to put her arms around both of them. 'We're coming back with ships and weapons, from Irisia. Maybe their gods too.'

A flutter of wings, and as if summoned by the word 'gods', Skedi alighted on the fence beside Legs, the size of a small squirrel, his wings bright and dappled like an owl's. From his antlers dangled some odd objects: one of Inara's mother-of-pearl buttons, a piece of curling hair, wrapped tight, and a green beaded bracelet from one of the archivists who had helped Inara and Telle make off with the contents of the cloche. He also had a smudge on his brow which could have been dirt . . . or blood.

'Humans do like touching each other, don't they?' he said, his whiskers twitching.

'What do you want, godling?' said Kissen, stepping back from the others as Skedi cocked his head. She approximated that to a smile.

'Inara's mother is coming,' he said. He tightened the tuck of his wings and shifted his paws anxiously. 'And so is the king.'

CHAPTER TWO

Inara

NO SOONER HAD SKEDI SPOKEN THAN INARA'S HEART thrummed with unease. The warm feeling as she had held on to Elo and Kissen turned harder, twisted. Mother. King. Allies. Enemies.

Why would the king come? He and her mother had reached a tentative truce, his ability to unite Middren against the threat of Hseth against the certain knowledge that Lessa had almost overthrown him once, and could do it again if he failed. Inara had hated it, but unlike her mother, she had seen Hseth as she had once been, huge and terrifying. She had seen the distant fires of the first attack on Daesmouth. She had seen the way the army in Lesscia had glowed with faith in Arren, faith in his power.

But Inara did not want him here. Not on her mother's ship, even if she could barely bring herself to speak to the woman who had lied to her. Who had hidden her away, lost her and never found her again.

And now Inara didn't know where she belonged any more. She was tangled up in the clothes of an heir to a great House, the cloth heavy on her shoulders, her shorn hair light on her head. She strangely missed the sour smell of her waxwool cloak, the feel of a bow in her hands and fire in her belly. Was she a lady's heir? A child or a rebel? A god or a human?

Inara glanced back towards the ship, to the shrine of Yusef.

Restish, the homeland of her father, the source of his great shrines, had supplied Talicia with ships and weapons. They were the enemies of Middren, and the source of her heritage.

I can see the dimness in your colours, Inara, Skedi said softly into her mind through the link between them that no one else could overhear. She blinked, and turned to look at him, his familiar face, long ears, and wise, bird-like eyes. His horns looked brighter lately: he was more like himself.

Why is the king coming?

I do not know.

I wish never to see his face again.

Want to make that a prayer? His tone turned wry with humour. *I could make a good lie.*

Inara laughed.

'What's funny?' said Elo, straightening his jacket. At the mention of the king his colours had churned into potent medleys of blues and golds, silvers and reds. A storm in his heart that softened when he was around Kissen, but didn't disappear. The seed of it was still there, even at his most serene. They shared a look now, an understanding, and touched their blades for reassurance, despite the truce.

Inara had toyed with the idea that Kissen and Elo might run away together. Maybe she would run with them and hide in secret again for the rest of their lives, baking and hunting and fighting. It didn't fit, that dream. Not now. Maybe it never would.

'Skedi said something,' said Inara.

'Does Skedi want to share with the rest of us?' Kissen asked drily, and the hare-god flicked his wings.

'Skedi doesn't share anything with veiga if they don't have something nice to say back,' he returned pertly.

'You little—'

A rattle of hooves on cobbles silenced her retort, and Skedi flew to Inara's shoulder. His presence was known now, among the docks, on the ship, but he still went to her.

A horse rounded one of the narrow alleys that threaded to the harbour from the city centre, sparks kicking out from its hooves. On its back was Captain Tarin, her short hair flicking out behind her, dark against her green tabard.

She thundered to a halt by them, her face flushed. For all her childhood, Inara had never known Tarin to lose her calm. She had been so jealous of her as a younger child; her mother's steadiest shadow, her closest counsel, a cousin of a lesser House on the Craier lands.

That jealousy had faded with time. The captain brought her little gifts from their travels, and, when her mother was holding meetings in her study, she would cut Inara apricots from the tall waving branches that she couldn't reach. She would even let her sit with her and Tethis, the similarly stoic steward of the manor, while they picked nettle leaves for tea and told each other of their lives apart, themselves mother and daughter. Inara had dreamed that one day she and Lessa would be so close.

But Tethis had died on the night Tarin and Lessa had left the manor, warned that the king knew of their rebellion, but not thinking that he would attack their home. They had been halfway to Sakre when the message had found them, and had returned to ruin and ash. By then, Inara had been long gone.

And this Tarin who dismounted was not the calm and quiet guard Inara remembered. 'Veiga, make yourself useful and get back aboard,' she said. 'You'll be acting as Lady Craier's guard.'

Kissen spluttered. 'I'll what?'

'You too, Ser Elogast,' Tarin spoke over her. If she was surprised at seeing him here, she didn't show it in her face or her colours. Perhaps it didn't matter. 'We may need your sword.'

'I'm sorry, when did I say you could give me orders?' said Kissen. Tarin narrowed her eyes and shook a stray dark hair out of her face.

'Either you protect the Craiers,' she said, 'or you leave the ship. The choice is yours.'

Kissen tongued her gold tooth, glanced at Inara, then sniffed. 'Fine.'

Inara tried not to smirk. Kissen had once been furious at the idea of even pretending to be her bodyguard, but Tarin was commanding when she wanted to be, dragging everything into her wake. Even, it seemed, the obstinate godkiller.

'Good,' said Tarin. 'The king decided he wanted to parade with Lady Craier to the ship in a show of unity, but the crowd that's gathered looks more likely to riot. I don't know if they'll turn.' She turned to Inara. 'Ina, stay out of sight.'

Before she could protest a voice came from above.

'Battle stations, Tarin?' said Aleda, the first mate and the captain's wife. Tarin shook her head.

'I hope not, just have the crew go below, we don't need to remind them who smuggled in the blackfire that blew up the palace walls.'

Aleda grinned, then moved back on deck and began barking orders. Tarin looked back at Inara. 'Now, Ina. I won't tell you again.'

'She doesn't have to hide from him,' said Elo, his voice dark.

'I didn't ask your opinion.'

'Nor mine,' said Inara. Jealousy aside, Tarin had no right to tell her what to do. She had forfeited that right when she had helped Lessa lie to her for years. When she had left the manor, and let it burn.

'If I'm to protect the Craiers, then I protect Inara,' said Kissen. 'And she's spent enough of her life hiding from the world.' Inara felt a rush of warmth. Kissen and Elo, they were both on her side. 'Go get your bow, *liln*.'

Inara turned on her heel and ran up the gangplank, Skedi flying up from her shoulder and onto Elo's before Tarin could say another word.

As she raced across the deck to her cabin, the crew were dropping down from the masts, heading below as they had been told. They appeared at ease, joking, sweaty with the summer heat. Inara didn't like that they were being sent away. She wanted an army at her back. She wanted the king to see her unafraid.

She grabbed her stolen bow, her arrows, and came back out to see even the captain, Lertes, standing without a care in the world with Aleda's arm on his shoulder, while Kissen, Elo and Tarin had come back onto the deck, hands on their pommels. Lertes grinned as the first mate leaned over, kissing his ear beneath the salt-and-pepper plaits that he wore in western-style braids: three, thick woven and laced through with glass-green ribbon the same colour as his eyes. Aleda wore matching colours wrapped around her wrist as her marriage band. Her smile was like Kissen's, broken with gold.

However, unlike Kissen, neither of them hid their emotions: their colours were bright, gaudy, and changeable, amber, grey, amethyst, indigo, shifting between them as if they were one person.

Elo and Kissen, at least, seemed prepared for anything. Kissen, because she always had the air of someone ready for a fight, but Elo was tense, eyes on the harbour.

Inara, said Skedi into her mind, *look to the city.*

Inara tore her gaze away from the ship and looked instead towards the Sakrean hills. The winding cobbles disappeared between the customs houses, the stores, the weighing rooms, the harbour watch and the seagulls that wheeled over the covered market. The colours were cacophonous, clashing, shifting, bright and overwhelming.

But beyond, further into Sakre, she could see flickers of shades of blue and gold glimmering between the walls. Kings' colours. Many of them. Growing. The sound of the city was changing too, as the colours encroached, voices raised in rhythm and shouting. Inara had seen such a wave of emotions in Lesscia, before it turned violent. Her heart hammered faster in her chest, clawing upwards to her throat.

'Steady,' said Elo, perhaps sensing the rush of her terror, or feeling it too. The glimmers of gold in his shades had turned sharper with his fear.

'Looks like common folk,' said Aleda. 'Let them have their song and dance.'

'I've seen enough riots begin with marching,' muttered Kissen.

'I've seen plenty of marches in favour of peace,' said Lertes scornfully.

'Then I suggest you pray for it,' said Elo. He added something in a whisper to Skedi, who flew up towards the crow's nest to give them a better vantage. Inara felt the tug of their bond on her heart. Taut again. Once they had been parted over half a city; now he could barely climb a mainmast.

'Ina, keep your arrows in the quiver,' said Kissen. 'Some people don't need much of an excuse to start a fight.' How many faith-riots had she and Elo seen in Blenraden? Inara nodded, but kept her hands poised, her eyes on the colours slowly spreading down the hills.

There's a vanguard, said Skedi into Inara's mind. *Four, and one is your mother.* Inara passed this along to the others, to save them a god's mindspeak drilling into their heads. *Behind is the king, with ten guards, but there are over a hundred following.*

The horns blasted closer, and Inara saw her mother astride a charger that would have dwarfed her if she had any less certainty in her spine. Tarin softened with relief.

'Aren't those House Graiis colours on her guards?' said Lertes. He was right, none of the knights around Lessa wore her colours. They were just ahead of the crowd that was growing in their wake, and as they caught sight of the ship, they sped up, breaking free from the mass of people and putting distance between them as they hurried downhill. Inara tightened her hand on her bow.

'She sent her own guard east,' said Tarin. 'With the Vittosks.'

'The Vittosk lands are long gone,' said Elo, frowning.

'The House doesn't take defeat on their backs. And Lady Craier protects her allies.'

'How well will she be able to protect us?' muttered Aleda, her eyes on the crowd. Finally, they understood the danger they might be in. Lertes now had his hand lightly balanced on his sword. 'Should we call up the crew?'

'This isn't an attack,' said Elo. 'It's a show. He's proving that he still has power. That people still believe in him. He wants you to know this before you go to Irisia.'

Lertes eyed him. 'Are you a rebel or a knight these days *Ser* Elogast?'

Elo didn't answer. Perhaps he didn't know.

'He's not wrong,' said Tarin wearily. 'Some people still seem to love him, no matter what he's done.'

'Some people are fools,' said Aleda. 'We should let them all rot together in these torched and godless lands.'

That drew Inara out of watching the colours of the crowd, vivid and churning.

'These "torched and godless lands" are our home,' she said. '*Lady Craier's* home.' She laid the emphasis on thick, so they remembered whose ship this was: her mother's, not theirs. 'She already gave up everything, her rebellion, to fight for it.' Why was she defending her mother?

'The captain your mother once was would have cut off the king's head and taken the consequences later,' said Aleda. 'I've never known her to ally with an enemy she was so close to defeating.'

'Perhaps she has learned that running a country is more complex than running a ship,' Kissen muttered. Lertes scowled at her, his hand closing on his sword, but then Tarin cleared her throat.

'Funny,' she said, not taking her eyes off the harbour, where folk had stopped in their work to watch for what was coming, or were already running to join the parade. 'I've never known the woman to treat a mutinous tongue any better than a mutinous blade.'

Aleda blanched, and Lertes took his hand off the hilt as if it had burned him. 'I didn't mean—'

'I know,' Tarin added, 'you speak out of concern for the lady. But if she chooses to fight for Middren, sink with it, or abandon it, you swore the *Silverswift* to her command when she left it in your charge.'

Aleda controlled her glower, and nodded.

'Apologies,' said Lertes. 'No harm was meant.'

'And she won't abandon Middren,' Inara pressed, wanting them to agree with her. Elo and Kissen shared a glance, and Inara realised even they weren't sure. These people spoke about a mother she didn't know, had never known. Who had lied to her. Had abandoned *her*. Could she really trust her with any certainty?

'Of course she won't,' said Tarin, and put a hand on Inara's back, reassuring. For a moment, Inara remembered the days in the kitchen, the nettle tea. The child she used to be, all Tarin's kindnesses, and that she had lost her own mother. 'We'll bring allies from Irisia and win this war,' Tarin continued. 'Then, Inara, we'll go home, and rebuild.'

She sounded confident, but her colours were uncertain twists of lavender and primrose.

Inara . . . Skedi spoke into her head.

Don't tell me it's a white lie, she replied. *Let me believe it.* She wanted to cling on to her shaken faith in her mother, her childhood love of Tarin, just for a little longer.

Lessa reached the ship and dismounted. She did not wait for her armed escort to struggle down from their saddles, instead

leaving her charger to stand obediently by the stables and striding
to the bottom of the gangplank. She paused there, and looked up
at the ship, her mouth lifting in a slight smile. It quickly fell as she
saw Inara, Elo and Kissen standing along the railings.

'Permission to board, Captain Lertes?' she called up.

Inara glanced sideways at Lertes. Why should her mother ask
permission? *Our ship*, he had said. Lessa was trying to keep him sweet.

'The *Silverswift* is yours once more, Lady Craier,' Lertes replied
assuredly. 'Thirteen years, we have guarded her well. Now our
barque is your bite.'

Thirteen years since she had given it away. Thirteen was Inara's
age.

Lessa nodded and ascended the gangplank with only one more
wary glance towards the city. Inara could see the silvery shine of
armour now amidst the mob, the brocade of horses, and splashes
of blue cloth. The blast of horns was closer now, the clapping and
stamping feet. She could feel it in her bones.

'My thanks captain,' the lady said. She hadn't spared another
glance for Inara, but gave Lertes a respectful bow. The front of
her green cotton jacket was studded with embroidered birds
from the Craier crest: the tiflet, a mythical, legless swallow, always
seeking.

And, like the tiflet, she turned next to Elo, who was gazing in
the king's direction, his colours moving in swells and eddies of red
and blue. 'Lion of Lesscia,' she said. 'Are you here to pledge to me,
and follow us to Irisia?'

Elo's colours flickered, a glimmer of longing shining over them
like a light through stained glass. Irisia, where his own mother still
lived. But he smiled and shook his head. 'I am here for goodbyes,
my lady,' he said. 'Kissen is an able fighter and can offer you fair
wisdom.' Kissen looked as if she wanted to kick him.

'The godkiller,' said Lessa coldly, 'has been granted passage over
the Trade Sea at Inara's special request.'

Now, at last, Inara found herself reflected in the dark of her
mother's eyes as the lady's gaze turned to her. Inara didn't know
what she had hoped for. Perhaps the respect she had shown Lertes,
or the warmth she had shown Tarin. Even the appraisal given Elo

would have been better than the distance she had when she looked at her own daughter. Inara stared back.

They're coming.

They flinched as Skedi's voice pierced through them. The king's parade had broken fully into the harbour. Its crowd had grown larger still, spilling out around the phalanx of ten steeds in blue and gold barding. Two of the riders had drums, and two were, as Tarin promised, in the colours of other Houses; Crolle and Elemni. The rest were the remains of Arren's armoured guard, holding halberds with clubbed bases.

In the centre rode King Arren himself, his head bare save for a circlet of sunrays and antlers. He looked vulnerable, and young. Not a coward's double of twigs and flame this time. Instead, he wore a cuirass in a deep V down to his navel, exposing his open shirt and the dark, flickering maw of his chest and heart. The cuirass itself was painted, reds and oranges. Flames and fire. What was he trying to do? Claim the sun and now claim flame for himself as well? A challenge to Hseth?

Inara's blood boiled, and her fingers itched for an arrow. He had ordered the death of gods, of her mother, of her home, and here he was riding towards them as if he were the most innocent of innocents.

And the crowd trailed the horses like a brook of boiling water, flowing, gasping, churning out across the roads, frothing up from the main port.

'Sunbringer, Sunbringer!' they called.

So strange to see so much adulation, bright blues and golds of love for their monarch as they roared for their king's attention.

But there were others in the mix, greens and silvers threading through, and more: fears in red, and yellow. Skedi flew down from the mast and landed defensively on Inara's shoulder. *Faith brings fervour*, he whispered into her mind. *Or fury.*

As the crowd tumbled after the king's array they shoved each other, some trying to get close enough to Arren to throw flowers, or hear him speak.

'Sunbringer! Save us from the fire god!'

'Save us from Talicia!'

Kissen grumbled. 'What pompy nonsense is this, Elo?'

'Isn't this show of unity what you asked for, veiga?' said Lessa. 'Don't blame me for your messes, noble.'

The king approached the ship, and the Graiis guards looked to Lessa, wondering whether to stop him, but she shook her head slightly. Arren dismounted in one smooth motion, clearly a practised rider, then headed up the gangplank. His guards stayed behind on the harbour wall, but Elemni and Crolle joined him on the ship. Lady Crolle was a lean, fair woman with shrewd eyes. She did not wear armour, but a split tunic and wide trews that had allowed her to sit astride the horse. Elemni was a broad barrel of a woman, with curled gold-brown hair that cascaded around her shoulders.

Between them, Arren's quick blue eyes assessed Kissen, Lessa, Inara and Skedi. So many of his enemies. His eyes landed on Elo, and his colours flickered amber, sharp and painful.

'Lady Craier!' came a call from the crowd. 'Help us!'

'Traitor to the king,' screamed another.

'Take us with you!'

'Pirate scum!'

'Save Middren!'

Some fruit and a clump of mud came their way but broke on the gunwales.

'Bastards,' muttered Lertes, but fell silent when Lessa cast him a glance.

Arren tore his gaze from Elo's and smiled, beatific, but his colours were changeable: bright, then dim; certain, then fearful. Too many at once. Falsehoods and truths, terrors and hopes. A man in conflict. The flame in his chest was smaller than it had been when Inara had seen him last, but still, she had the distinct feeling the god who kept him alive was watching her.

Hestra, she greeted that god in her mind.

After a moment, Hestra whispered back to her. *I'm not speaking to you, halfling*, she said. *Half god, half mortal, halfwit.*

You have a lot to say for a god who is not speaking.

The fire in the king's chest flared with annoyance, and Arren's eyes found Inara. He stared, the corners of his mouth turning down before the briefest moment, and she stared back. Kissen, subtly, moved slightly in front of her, and the king gathered himself, brightening with his smile once more.

'I come to bless your voyage, my lady,' he said, turning his voice towards the crowd, loud and charming. 'And give gratitude for your important endeavour.' He bowed.

Liar, whispered Skedi, though Inara already knew. However, the baying of the crowd fell to a more respectful murmur as they hushed to listen. He played them well.

'Our previous entreaties have met with silence,' Arren continued. 'I only hope that a demonstration of our unity will convince Irisia to ally with us against the treacherous Talicians.'

Lessa kept her face impassive, and went to her knee. Tarin, Aleda and Lertes followed, then Elogast, but Kissen stayed by Inara and neither of them kneeled.

'My thanks to you, King Arren,' said Lessa. 'It is a long way to come down to the harbour. What shine you show to us, to join us as we make our leave on your behalf.' Her response, though perfectly courteous, dripped with barbs of reprimand and barely concealed hatred. Arren's jaw flexed. 'Please,' her voice gentled, like ice meeting spring sunlight. 'Guard our lands well till my return.'

Arren nodded, satisfied enough. The crowd seemed to hold its breath, and Inara relaxed a little. Perhaps it would be all right. Perhaps they would begin to believe that the rebels and the king would work together.

'I bring you this,' said Arren, and nodded at Crolle. She stepped forward holding a small box, her mouth narrow with disapproval, but opened it in front of Lessa to reveal a signet ring set with a red stone, marked with the stag-and-sun of Arren's insignia.

'This, Lady Craier, is proof of your collaboration with the king,' said Crolle, 'and his trust.'

The Crolle House was one of those loyal to the king, who had refused to align with the rebellion and preserved Arren's kingship. Tiamh, Yether, Movenna, Elemni, all powerful enough to refuse Lessa and align against her.

'The stone is new,' said Arren, 'but the band belonged to my mother and sister.' For a moment, his colours again shifted, turning dim and dark. The set of Lessa's shoulders softened, only slightly, but Inara frowned. If he felt pain for the loss of his mother, his sister, he deserved it. It was nothing to the burn of a hand on Elo's chest, to the pain of the gods who had lost their faithful, to the people of Craier manor, her people, who had died on his orders. For a breath, Inara imagined what would happen if Lessa drew her sword and ran him through. How much would it really change?

'Sunbringer, Sunbringer, Sunbringer.'

The crowd was whispering once more, clapping their hands. A pounding of certainty. A hope. Their colours shining. Green and blue. Faith. Unity.

Lessa reached out her hand and took the ring from the box. Then she lifted it high, so the crowd could see, and slid it onto her finger. It seemed such a paltry thing, but a House's signet was a symbol of their authority, a symbol to be obeyed. Arren had ceded some of his power to Lessa, in public, where people could see. The mob let out a roar of approval, the knights and Graiis guards at the dock relaxed.

But then, a hollering cut through the rest of the noise. Three women ran forward, their hair braided and plaited in crowns around their heads, looped in with deer antlers that had been affixed on bands of woven leather. Their quick movement surprised the king's guards, breaking through to the gangplank of the *Silverswift* in a breathless moment.

'Traitor!' they cried. They were dressed in white cotton, blue ribbons tied around their waists that draped down their skirts in ragged stripes. The Graiis guards crowded onto the gangway, drawing their swords.

'Don't kill our citizens!' cried Arren.

They hesitated, and it cost them. One woman put up a wild fight, clawing and biting, while another fell into the water, but the crowd took courage from the breakthrough, all of them now surging up the gangway past the bemused guards, and it turned into a melee. Two of the women managed to grapple through to the deck, the crowd like a wave shoving up behind them.

'Sunbringer! Sunbringer!'

The sound of the mob was everywhere, their colour, shaking through Inara's chest, her breath. She drew an arrow, but where to fire? They didn't look armed, they didn't look dangerous. Were they any less innocent than the people of Craier manor?

Elo, at least, had some presence of mind. He leapt for the gangplank before they were overrun. He obeyed Arren's instruction not to kill, but instead tore off his belt so he could hold his scabbarded longsword like a staff. One hand on the pommel and the other on the sheathed blade, he used it to ram the Sakrean mob back from the deck and down, shoving them overboard where he could. Lertes and Aleda joined him, defending their ship.

'Return to shore!' Elo bellowed. 'King's guard, hold off the base!'

'Protect the king!' yelled someone else, probably Crolle, who herself had no weapon and had backed up along the deck, standing slack-jawed by the mainmast. Elemni at least had drawn a sword, but was standing in front of Arren, doing little else. Three of the folk threw themselves at his feet, reaching to touch the king's tunic as he backed away.

But the women in white had another target. Inara felt a grab on her wrist as Kissen pulled her back, away from the madness, protecting her as she had promised. Tarin was running forward to block the two women as they ran. Not for Arren . . . for Lessa.

'For Sunbringer!'

Something glinted in the layers of cloth in their skirts, and Inara saw Kissen's colours for the briefest moment in yellow, unguarded fear.

'They're armed!'

Too late. Kissen ran for them, grabbing one woman by her arm and wrenching her off balance, throwing her into the capstan. Too late, Tarin reached for her own blade, when the attacker she faced already had a knife in her hand.

The barrage of stabs was overwhelming, quick, brutal, effective. The sharp edge of the blade sliced through Tarin's arm as she reached for her own, the second and third went into her chest and belly. She hadn't been wearing armour, she hadn't been ready. She hadn't been lucky in the three breaths it had taken for the tide to turn.

Inara nocked an arrow as the attacker tried to shove Tarin aside, moving for her final target: Lessa, who had unsheathed her blade.

But Tarin, bloodied, had drawn her knife. She would not be shoved aside. Instead, she grabbed the woman's neck, and held tight.

'Release me!' cried the assassin, stabbing Tarin again, again as Skedi flapped his wings in distress.

'Tarin stop!' screamed Lessa, as Inara loosed her arrow. It struck the antlered woman in the ribs, and she screamed, but it turned into a gurgle as Tarin drove her dagger up through her throat, and out the back of her neck.

Her death was instant, her colours went out, and the two of them collapsed. Lessa caught Tarin as she fell.

'Hold!' Arren cried, finding his voice. 'My people! Calm yourselves!'

The assassin Kissen had thrown stumbled up, scrabbling for the knife she had dropped. Lessa was holding Tarin. She was vulnerable.

But Kissen was ready. She grabbed the woman by her antlers, her other hand closing on her weapon-hand and twisting it with a crack that made her scream.

'Traitors must die!' the woman howled, dropping the knife as Kissen put her in a headlock. 'We fight for our god with his heart of fire.' Her voice was lost in the muscle of Kissen's arm.

'Shut the fuck up,' the veiga snarled.

The rest of the would-be mob had backed away from Elo, Lertes and Aleda, perhaps hearing Arren, perhaps realising that something had gone terribly wrong.

'Tarin,' Lessa said, her guard gathered in her arms. She had her hand pressed to one of her wounds. Only one. Of so many. Blood poured out around her fingers.

'It's nothing, my lady,' Tarin whispered. The blood was bright. There was too much of it. 'Just . . . just a scratch.' Tarin's colours were aflame with green in a hundred shades, tinged with yellow. Nettle leaves and apricots. A tear crept out of her eye, inching down towards the deck.

Don't look, said Skedi to Inara. But she had to look. She couldn't stop.

'Stay with me,' said Lessa. 'We'll get a healer. I'll call a god. We've done too much not to survive this.'

Inara looked up at Kissen, who returned helpless eyes, and

confirmed what she knew. No one could survive this. Only the king had survived anything close, and he stood now, hand over his chest as if to protect it. The fire in the wound that should have killed him. Inara clenched her hand around the bow.

'Bury me with my mother,' whispered Tarin at last, so quietly that even Inara could barely hear her. Her colours had softened, fainter yellow, like sunlight through the leaves of orchard trees. 'Please. Have me buried in the Craier lands.'

'No,' said Lessa. She was not crying, but her voice was tight. 'You'll live, Tarin. You're strong enough to live.'

Inara choked on a sob, and anger tightened on her throat, clawing up into her eyes, white hot and blinding. 'Why?' she whispered. Then, harder, hotter. 'Why!'

Why must she lose so much? Why must she feel this pain. She drew another arrow and nocked it, turning the weapon towards the woman Kissen held, who sounded as if she was singing now, murmuring songs under her breath.

'Fireheart, Sunbringer
Bravest king of kings'

This was her fault too. Inara couldn't kill Arren, but she could kill her. She could have *some* vengeance.

'No, Inara!' said Kissen. Even the wild woman stopped, her eyes staring, hateful. 'Don't.'

'She should be punished!' said Inara, tears welling hot up behind her eyes. Tarin was dying. Tarin who made her tea, who reached the high branches. Tarin who she would never be able to forgive for her lying, to love as a guard, to learn about the life she and her mother had led. 'They should be punished!'

'Not by you.'

'You punish gods!'

'Inara,' said Skedi, small and frightened on her shoulder. 'Gods can fight back, she can't. She's stopped. Kissen stopped her.'

Inara swallowed. She wasn't only pointing the arrow at the woman; she was pointing it at Kissen who looked . . . frightened. She dropped her bow, which clattered into the blood, and she fell to her knees beside Tarin. The red between Lessa's fingers was pulsing more slowly now.

The king was breathing heavily, pale with shock. Elemni had ushered away the citizens who had thrown themselves at his feet, and the knights and Graiis guards were pushing the crowd back, back, away from the ship. In a bare few heartbeats, tragedy had torn through them like a blast of wind.

It was Elo who spoke next.

'Is this faith, "*Sunbringer*"?' he said, spitting the epithet, his voice low but enough to be heard over the shouting of the citizens as they were shoved away from the ship, the shaky singing of the would-be assassin that Kissen held tightly. 'Is this the love you wanted so badly?'

Arren didn't answer.

This couldn't be faith. This bloody, frightening, appalling thing. This thing that washed decks with blood and killed good women who missed their home.

Inara was too angry to speak. She held Tarin's hand as she choked out her last breaths and died on the deck of her lady's ship. Those colours, so intense and beautiful, winked out.

Then, Inara heard the voice of Arren's god, Hestra, sidling into her mind.

Now you know how hopes are broken.

CHAPTER THREE

Elogast

'YOU DAMNED FOOL OF A MAN,' SNARLED ELOGAST, FOLLOWING Arren through the gates of his shattered Reach.

The blood of the coup had been washed from the Regnas' ancestral palace, but some evidence remained: a scratch of sword in stone, a dark space where a carpet had once been, a cracked panel of wood. Outside, the walls and gardens were a shattered mess, the bones of the old catacombs exposed to the salt air.

'You cannot speak to me that way, Ser Elogast,' Arren bit back as they reached the inner keep. Though he had dismissed his guards, the palace was still filled with people. Stewards, builders, engineers, all trying to clear the mess that had been made. Nobles, or their emissaries, and their trains of hangers-on, record keepers, lawmakers and guards. They muttered about the cloisters, staring.

Elo held his tongue. Barely. Arren led him up into the citadel proper, and along a cool and draughty corridor that still smelled faintly of blood and smoke. Back to the war room, with its dented brass door and blackened ceiling.

As they entered past the guards who kept station at the door, they disturbed two archivists in grey who looked aghast at the sight of the king in their midst. They were carefully separating the pieces of Arren's detailed map of Middren, unpicking the threads that bound each piece of vellum to the whole, and then rolling each one and packing it into labelled scrolls that would follow the king on their journey north. Elo had to admit the genius of Arren's work; in using the notation and drawing skills they had whipped into them as squires, he had given them one of their few advantages against the Talicians: knowledge of their own lands.

'May I address you now?' said Elo through gritted teeth. He had left Inara behind, grieving once more, and Kissen, with hurried and rough goodbyes so he could follow the king back up from the mayhem and blood of the shore, and the ship could set sail. He might never see them again.

'Sunbringer,' murmured one of the guards at the door. 'I can have him removed?'

'No,' said Arren quicky before Elo rounded on the man. 'Leave us.'

The knight cast Elo a filthy look but did as he was bidden. The archivists followed and the door was closed behind them.

'You as good as killed that woman,' said Elo when they were alone. 'We're losing control of our own citizens before we've even made it onto the field.'

'I did no such thing,' said Arren.

'You should not have come to the harbour, showing your arrogance to the masses. You knew this was their first sighting of you in weeks. You *knew* there could be blood. You should have stayed where you were put.'

Arren's expression flashed with anger, his jaw setting in a hard line. 'How dare you?' he said. 'She is the one to blame for the knife's edge this city walks. And so are you.'

'What did you expect?' said Elo. 'That you could burn noble families and take no consequences? Waste a fortune marching on a peaceful city to show your might? You are *exactly* the fool-boy you were. Sword first, head later.'

'You have *no* idea,' Arren said, and laughed hollowly. 'When I came to power this land had lost wealth, gods and faith. I held it together when the gods would have torn us apart. And they are still trying. I am *still* fighting for our freedom from their madness.'

'Yet you desire to be one of them,' growled Elo. 'What does that make you?'

Arren scoffed, flushed with fury. Elo, too, felt the anger within him, burning up his flesh, his throat, his skin. He wanted to throttle Arren, wanted to fight him again, beat him into the ground. He wanted to ask why, of all the things he could have said to hurt him, had he chosen to tell him he loved him?

'I desire to be the greatest king that Middren has ever known,' said Arren in a low voice, putting his hand on his chest. 'To break our reliance on gods and their games. Like that girl you have been harbouring.'

For a moment, Elo saw Inara, her face twisted with rage, her hand outstretched towards Arren, choking the life from his heart. He had seen Inara do terrifying things: summon gods through a city, acting as their shrine, kill a man in the dark with an arrow. But he shook the images away. He would speak none of it to Arren, who might use her whatever it cost her.

'Inara did not choose her birth,' he said. 'It is you who wants to burn like a god, demand like a god, sacrifice like a god.'

'I know all the sides of my own story, Elogast,' said Arren. 'I had to be ruthless to secure this throne.'

'The throne you all but lost weeks ago?' He laughed without humour. He could not hold it in. He wanted to lay every accusation at the altar of their broken trust and wound him as deeply as he had been wounded. 'Whatever you think you gain, Arren, you leave only blood and chaos in your wake.'

Arren winced as the blow landed. Elo recognised the expression of quiet, inward shattering he so often wore after facing his mother. What had happened to the man who said he had run out of tears at the first death her own pridefulness had caused? How had he seen the path she had walked blindly and then followed her, knowing that blood would be at its end?

Arren took in a breath, clearly willing himself to be calm. The fire in his heart was quiescent. Elo wondered if the god listened to their conversations, if she had used her will and power to turn him cruel. Perhaps he had wished it. But no. Every step Arren had taken had been his own.

'Elogast, I didn't know what would happen at the harbour,' he said. 'It would do me no good now to have Lady Craier dead. I'd lose the other Houses that sided with her, Vittosk, Graiis, Yesef . . . and any potential for Irisian aid.'

'If you didn't know you'd stoked madness enough in your followers that they'd kill for you, then you are stupider than I thought.'

They stood, staring at each other. The afternoon sun, casting light through the glass trellis doors, was briefly scattered by a cloud of swifts wheeling past, screaming.

There was too much said and unsaid between them, and the silence was full of embers and dying flame.

'I mean to name you commander of the standing army,' said Arren at last. He reached up and lifted the circlet from his head, then placed it on the table by his map.

'You . . .' Elo floundered. 'What?'

'You are to be reinstated, since our previous commander general failed in his duties.'

Failed in his duties? Arren had killed him when Elo made a laughing stock of him.

'You will receive a commander's pay,' added Arren, as if that was incentive. 'And join my war council when we gather mornings and evenings on the trail.'

'You can't buy me.'

'Your *country* needs you,' Arren growled, then he paused, his voice lowering, softening. 'And so do I.'

'You have plenty of nobles to choose from.'

'I don't want a noble who's been tilting at fixed targets since they were five years old,' said Arren. 'I need the boy who read every strategic treatise because he could. The one who worked to be better than everyone even though he started fighting later. The one who helped me win the God War, recruited a whole country to my side. I need your strategic mind, your level head, and your ability to challenge me.' He grimaced. 'Though perhaps not quite so fiercely.'

Elo wouldn't let Arren sway him. 'I made my stance clear years ago,' he said, hoping his voice wouldn't shake. 'I no longer work for you. I will not kiss the ground you walk on: you have Knight Commander Peta for that, and the generals she deigns to promote. There are plenty of those you can fetch from Lesscia.'

Arren leaned back against the table. The room was warm, despite the breeze across the courtyard outside the window, too warm. Elo could feel heat creeping down the back of his neck, across the burn scars on his chest.

'You're still in communication with your rebel factions,' said Arren, looking casually over the remains of his map. 'I am aware your pacifist rebel, Naiala, remains in custody in Lesscia.'

Elo narrowed his eyes. 'Is that a threat?'

Arren frowned. 'No, Elo, of course not. I just know that the new Lord Yether has little loyalty amongst this guard. His sisters in Daesmouth have requisitioned most of them.'

'Is it any surprise they do not trust a son who killed his father at your instruction?'

Arren's mouth twitched, but then something in his face hardened.

'If you're expecting me to apologise, you will be waiting forever,' he said. 'I don't desire forgiveness. I desire victory. And victory we can claim with you at my side.' He offered his hand. 'The rebel and the king.'

Elo moved back, away from Arren. There was still a part of him that wanted to go to him, to hold him and tell him he would fix it all.

'I will fight for you,' he replied hoarsely, 'because I love this land, and the people in it. You can give me any title you want, but what I do is not for you any more.'

Arren withdrew his hand. He looked tired. The face he showed to the world, the lightness, the charm, was not the one he showed to Elo. They stood in silence for a long moment.

'Do you even think about it?' the king said quietly, not breaking their gaze. 'What I said to you in Lesscia?'

'You were never in Lesscia,' Elo reminded him.

Arren stepped towards him, lowering his voice. 'I told you I loved you,' he said. 'I meant it.'

Kissen's words echoed in his head. *Love and pain are not so different.*

No. Elo wouldn't go down that road and open the vault of his own heart. He had locked Arren's space in it away long ago. Instead, he remembered what Hseth the fire god had said, when she had tried to rip out his heart. For Arren. Because of Arren.

You are the last thing he loves, and he has chosen to lose you.

Elo shook his head. 'You chose to lose me, Sunbringer,' he said, flinging the name like the insult he intended and turning for the door. 'You cannot wish me back.'

CHAPTER FOUR
Skediceth

SKEDI FELT WEARY, WRUNG OUT FROM THE INSIDE.

And it was not just all the emotions singing around the city like a miasma of shining hues. Nor was it the ship. Aft to stern ran sharp and jagged with colour as the crew reckoned with the chaos that had befallen them, wrapping Tarin's lightless body up in sail-cloth and committing it into the hands of the useless Graiis guards.

No, this worn, weak feeling had plagued Skedi for weeks. In the desperate Lesscian rebellion, he had grown far beyond his size and strength, far beyond what he was supposed to be. He was not a big god; he was never meant to be great.

Inara said it had taken days for him to wake after finding themselves in Sakre. Skedi did not normally sleep. For him, there had been only darkness, the darkness he had once known before he had awoken for the first time in a child's arms. Memories gone. Shrines lost.

Memories he did have this time. Panic and anger in Lesscia, the cracking of thorns beneath his huge wings, the tang of blood in his mouth. The taste of pure power that came from sacrifice. Inara's sacrifice.

But in using that power, he had lost more than could be regained from the power of Inara's that kept him alive. The little independence he had built was gone, and the tether that bound them was as tight as it had been back in the Craier manor. He didn't know what to do about it. He had almost died, and it wasn't even dying. His lights wouldn't go out like Tarin's. He wouldn't have a body for Inara to weep over, nor shrines to shatter.

He would simply cease to exist, never to be born again, for there were so few people who really loved him.

Yet he wouldn't, couldn't, ask Inara for offerings to give him back his strength. Already, he hungered for the brightness he had tasted from her blood, her complete faith in him.

'What are you moping about, rabbit?'

Kissen's voice broke into his reverie, and he realised he had been crouching on the bowsprit, his ears drooping, wings down, staring at the ship's shrines.

'I'm not a rabbit,' said Skedi.

'I was trying to be nice.'

'Don't try to be nice. I can't stand a bad lie.'

Kissen smirked and folded her arms. She had put on a jacket and a fresh breastplate that cut her chest tattoo in half, showing only the top of the curl of the 'Fuck you' symbol. *Scal lufts* would be the Talician phrase, but she used the sign a human would make with thumb and forefinger, like the loose curl of an untied rope. Her northern looks, one leg, and aggressive bearing had earned her many angry stares in the city: one of the reasons she had moved to Lessa's ship long before it was ready to depart.

Skedi, too, had seen division in the way people looked at him. Lessa had told him not to hide, and he was certain he was a pawn in whatever long game she was playing with Arren and his reign. But the folk of Sakre were not so fond of gods as the pilgrims on the road, or the rebels in Lesscia. Most when they saw him touched briddite talismans worn around their necks, moulded in the shape of a man, a stag's head, or the pointed veiga symbol. Warding him away.

Unlike Lesscians, Sakreans still saw the king as their saviour, and Skedi was beginning to understand that there were as many moods in a single human as there were gods in the world. Let alone cities full of them.

Sitting by Kissen, her colours hidden, her manner familiar, was peaceful. A point of stillness in the rattle of activity across the deck and below. The ship was all music, and the sailors worked in rhythm with it. The draw of the ropes, the creak of the hull, the flap of the flags and the calls of the crew who knew their work as they knew the beating of their own hearts. They crawled up the mizzen and mainmast, unbinding the sails as the helm kept steady on the wheel, preparing to guide them out of harbour. All but three of the mooring lines had been freed from the quay, but a few others were looped around the posts on the harbour wall, ready to be released from the *Silverswift* itself, which already strained to be loosed from them, edging over each wave as the breeze caught it. Skedi had once ridden on ships like this, in the company of the great god of safe haven.

Lady Craier stood grimly behind the helm, Captain Lertes at her side, as Aleda bellowed orders.

'Heave!' She had lungs of brass and her voice cracked like a whip. 'Heave!' Her husband shone with pride.

The mainsail flapped, then distended, filling with an offshore wind.

'Tighten on the starboard! Helm, to port!'

'Port!' echoed the helm, turning the wheel so the ship moved away from the harbour wall.

'Draw in!'

The ropes whipped around the harbour posts with a sound like sawing, then splashed into the water before being reeled in, arm over arm, to be coiled neatly on the ship's deck as it slid away into the water.

All the blood had already been scrubbed clean.

'Inara has come a long way from not wanting to shoot rabbits,' said Kissen, as if sensing where his thoughts had turned.

Skedi ruffled his wings, catching them on the salty air. It was pleasant to feel the warmth of the new summer.

'Anger is a dangerous thing,' he said. 'And she is too young to hold all she has seen and not ache with it. All the injustice, all the sorrow.'

'I know anger,' said Kissen, leaning on her staff with her arms folded. 'I know every shape it takes. But . . . this was different.'

Skedi had seen it, the flame of fury burning up Inara all the way

39

down to her fingertips, her *need* to make use of it. 'Have you truly never killed a human?' he asked.

For a moment, Kissen's colours flickered, some buried emotion rising to the surface. Skedi hadn't seen enough of Kissen's colours to understand their shades and meanings, but he knew enough of her expression to understand guilt.

'I have killed,' she said. 'I did not rescue Maimee from the fires of Blenraden. I have failed to save people from their gods. But until Talicia, my blade had never taken a person's life. And he was just a boy, not much older than Inara.'

A truth, quietly spoken. Skedi was growing quite fond of truths, when they had a purpose.

'Ina frightens me,' he admitted in return. He had never said that before, even to himself. 'Sometimes. Her anger frightens me.'

Kissen nodded. Fear, she also knew in every shape. 'We need to help her control it,' she said. 'Help her understand it.'

We. So interesting to be 'we'. He and Inara were 'we'. But somewhere along the way, his and Kissen's hatred had faded to a kind of companionship. Inara had brought them together.

'I have so little power, veiga,' said Skedi quietly, now he was truth-telling. 'I fear losing Inara's faith. I fear fading. I fear death. What can I do?' He shrank a little, but Kissen did not gloat, or laugh, she frowned.

'She has lost a lot, our girl,' she said. 'But we're the few who still have her trust. I'll give her honesty; you give her love. She'll need both.'

Skedi nodded. As he did so, the great sails luffed for a moment, bubbling with wind, and then caught again, their streamers stretching southwards. The ship dipped on one side, turning about. Its prow now pointed to the pink and misted horizon. Open sea. They passed between the harbour walls of grey stone, and the breeze turned cooler, shedding the smoky haze of the city and its hills.

'On sea!' yelled Captain Lertes, and Lessa and the others raised a cry of ululation, strange and exuberant in the face of all the day had brought them.

Kissen did not cheer, her shoulders tensed as they moved away from the green hills and forests of Middren. The craft shuddered as the waves rose about them, higher outside the harbour, slamming against the side of the boat.

'Graemar!' cried Lertes. 'Slim! Rhiyande! Cages, barrels cups!'

If the ship had been active before, it now stirred like a hive of bees chasing a queen. Two of the crew swung down from the topsail they had been setting, landed on the deck and ran below, their colours bright with anticipation. Inara came out of her cabin beneath the aftcastle and helm, her face pale and her curly hair knotted back beneath a scarf. Her beautiful tunic had been bloodied, so now she wore a rougher jacket with wide sleeves and vines embroidered over the pockets. Her mother had been trying to buy back her affection with clothes, and it was working only a little.

Lessa called for Inara from behind the wheel, but she ignored her. Instead, she came up towards Skedi and Kissen.

'We're moving,' she said, holding on to the polished wooden railing and looking back towards Sakre, on the port side as the ship turned south. The hilled city was lit gold and peach by the light of the now-sinking sun. 'I almost thought we wouldn't today.'

'Take shelter with us,' said Kissen, putting a friendly arm around the girl's slim shoulders. Inara leaned in, and they stood in companionable silence. The look Lessa gave them across the deck could have stilled the heart of a god. Skedi hoped they wouldn't notice.

'Something else is happening,' he said, pointing his nose down at the main deck.

The two called Rhiyande and Slim had come piling up from belowdecks carrying a small barrel sealed with wax and wound with colourful ribbons. Three more folk followed, one bearing a wicker cage with a squawking rooster inside. Finally, Graemar the cook appeared with a half-open bag of greenlings, a sour citrus fruit, flung over his back.

'Of fucking course,' Kissen muttered, tightening one hand around her staff as if to hold herself back. 'Sailors are such superstitious bastards.'

'What are they doing?' said Inara as the crew on deck parted and the bag, barrel and cage made their way towards the aftcastle.

The shrines.

'A sacrifice,' said Kissen sourly.

Skedi sat back on his hind legs, spreading his wings with surprise. Sacrifices were illegal in Middren. But as the scent of the sea washed over him, clean and sharp as the edge of a knife, he realised they were no longer in Middren: they had passed Sakre's harbour into open water.

'Inara, Skediceth!' called Lessa as she descended the swooping stairs to the alcove shrines. 'Come!'

It was a command, not a question. Inara glanced up at Kissen, then at Skedi. His girl's colours were dark and muddy, like forest shadows, edged with orange anger. But, at the idea of an offering, a small thrill of violet fluttered over her shades. A colour that Skedi associated with Lessa.

'Go on then,' said Kissen, releasing Inara with only a hint of reluctance. 'I won't be stopping you. Or them.'

Skedi jumped down from the bowsprit and onto Inara's shoulder as, this time, she obeyed her mother's call and hurried down the steep steps to the midships. He kept himself small, his wings out to balance him as he thrilled with excitement. He had seen the prayers of pilgrims over stones, had seen blood given to a god, but never a formal offering, never a ritual.

The ship's bell rang, and the thirty-strong crew gathered around the shrines, whooping, clapping and dancing already as Lertes picked up the cockerel cage. The bird was a fine offering; its comb deep red, and brilliant green in its feathers.

'My lady,' the captain said, turning to Lessa, and the crew briefly quietened as he held out the cage to her. 'It has been my pride to captain this vessel since your business drew you to land, but the sea has missed you.' He smiled. 'We have missed you.'

Several of the crew cheered, and the rest joined in from where they had gathered. A faint flush rose to Lessa's cheeks, despite herself.

'The *Silverswift* was always yours,' said Lertes, 'and always will be.' He didn't lack sincerity, Skedi could see that, but there was a tug of reluctance in his colours, an undertow of foggy grey. After thirteen years, how could he not see the ship as his own? But this ritual was itself an offering, a truce. Captain to lady, equal to equal. 'Please, do us the honour of making our offerings.'

Lessa put her hand on the cage with a touch of shyness, strange for someone who could stare down a king. Skedi tipped his head; by human reckoning, she was quite young. Perhaps only a few years Kissen's senior. She must have been very young when she had borne Inara.

'The honour is mine, captain,' she said, then perhaps recognised the roughness of her voice, the sadness in her bearing, and stood straighter. She reached to the door of the cage, and in a swift movement, unhooked it and grabbed the rooster by the neck. It flapped and shrieked, but she held it at arm's length, unflustered. 'My blood still runs with salt.'

She lifted the bird to the crew of the *Silverswift*, then added loudly, 'And so does my daughter's!'

Inara tensed beneath Skedi's paws, her heartbeat quickening. The crew began to clap and hum again, then Aleda started singing:

> 'Good wind, good trade,
> Safe haven do we crave
> Strong sails, full hearth
> Our home 'cross the waves.'

The tune was surprisingly sweet, and the colours of the crew intensified with the music. Skedi watched their shades drift out of their bodies, prayers on gossamer threads. But, instead of floating towards whatever god they loved, the colours instead bound themselves to the cockerel: the offering itself.

A breath, a flash, and Lessa drew her knife and struck the blade across the bird's neck. Blood gushed out, warm and wet on the fresh-scrubbed decks, tainting the salt-air with copper scent. The bird's legs jerked and danced, and Inara reached a hand up to Skedi, digging her fingers into his fur. She would be trying not to see Tarin in the flash of knives, the rush of red that had stained Lessa's hands as the bird's did now.

But the rest of them had moved on. How much blood had they seen on this ship for one more death to mean nothing to them?

Looking satisfied, the captain took an offering cup from the first shrine with the bird totem of stone, then held it beneath the stream of blood.

And the colours of the crew poured with it into the vessel: hopes, wishes, faith. Skedi licked his lips, but it was not for him. Never for him. He had to control this longing, or it would consume him. Aleda's singing changed as the cup filled, and the others joined her.

> 'Give us blood in the cup
> Put feathers in our hair
> Fill the sails with fairest winds
> As we make your prayer.'

They repeated the ritual at the second shrine, Lertes with the cup, Lessa with bird, and the blood with the shining colours that only gods could see. Energy. Life. It was borne through the blood into the shrine, filling it with power.

> 'Good trade, open hands
> Friendly shores, wealth unplanned
> Give us barter, give us measure
> Bless our raft and give us treasure.'

Lessa paused as the final cup was held out. Yusef's cup. Safe Haven. Inara's mother looked over at her, her hands still wet with blood, the bird held just so, so the last of it wouldn't tip out.

'Daughter,' she said. 'Come.'

The crew all turned, their humming continuing, the song in pause, to look at Inara and Skedi.

Go on, said Skedi and she stepped forward, going to her mother, to the bleeding bird, to the shrine of her father.

'Left pocket,' said Lessa, nodding down at her jacket.

Skedi felt the lady's eyes on him, bright and dark, much darker than the soft amber-brown of her daughter's. Inara reached her hand into her mother's pocket, stilled, and pulled out a small object.

'What is it?' said Skedi out loud, his wings aching with curiosity.

Inara opened her hands, and within them lay a small soapstone statue, carved and polished in the shape of a hare. A hare with a deer's antlers, and an owl's wings.

Engraved on its base was his name: *Skediceth*.

It was him. A totem . . . for him. Skedi's fur stood on end.

'It belongs with Yusef,' said Lessa. 'Tarin . . . had it made for you.'

Inara looked up at her, perhaps seeking to identify some emotion, but Lessa had already looked away towards the shrine.

Still, despite the uncertainties, despite everything she had lost, a brightness broke through Inara's colours, vivid green and peach, then perfect citrine. Joy. Joy for him. She looked up at Skedi and smiled, then went to the central shrine, and carefully placed his totem at the feet of the great god.

Skedi couldn't speak . . . he opened his wings, lifted his ears and stood, looking to Lessa as she once again tipped the bird, and filled the last vessel with its blood offering for their voyage.

'For wind, for fortune, for haven,' she said. 'And for the promises and the precious white lies we will tell to get us there.'

> '*To safest haven*
> *Through heartfelt lies,*
> *To brighten hopes,*
> *And bless our skies.*'

Lertes placed the cup in the shrine, and the colours of the crew filled it, filled Skedi, brightening him with new life, new energy. He grew to his true size, the size of a hare, leaping up to put his paws on Inara's head and look to the people who prayed to him, their hands beating, their colours shining.

'To a god in our midst!' cried Aleda, and the crew cheered from mid decks to crow's nest. Skedi lifted his head, trying not to look towards Kissen, who was not cheering, not speaking, only watching.

The ritual was not over. The cook whipped the cockerel out of Lessa's hands and Lertes slammed his own knife into a beribboned barrel, cracking it open. Out washed a bitter, herby scent. Crew pulled cups and bowls from pockets, binders, belts and bustiers, driving them into the barrel and bringing them back brimfull. Each poured a tot onto the deck to mingle with the blood as a second offering, then took a half of greenling distributed by Rhiyande.

Inara wrinkled her nose as she was offered the sour fruit, but followed in squeezing the greenling into the hipgin and taking a raw sip as the songs turned more celebratory. Between sky and sails, crew and cloud, the colours astounded even Skedi's eyes.

> *'Libations libations, for the gods and me*
> *Greenlings, greenlings, to keep us hale and free*
> *Hipgin for our bellies and some warming just for me*
> *Blessings for our voyage on the sea, the sea, the sea.'*

CHAPTER FIVE

Hestra

SHE HAD TO LOOK. HAD TO SEE. IT WAS AS IF THE BURNING homes were calling her, her shrines crying out under cracking roofs and falling stone.

Daesmouth.

She found one. A forgotten shrine where three hundred years before, a wealthy merchant had sacrificed a goat and buried it with a moss-and-twig figurine. For her.

It gave her leave to appear into life in a burst of ash and twigs.

Someone cried out. She saw frightened faces. People huddled together in a room that had once been grand, but now had been emptied of valuables and provided shelter to what looked like seven families.

A great boom shook the windows from outside, followed by a cacophony of screams. One brave woman picked up a poker and waved it threateningly at the fire. Tears were leaking from her eyes.

'Leave!' she said. 'Leave here, fire god.'

Hestra recoiled. But she was here now, she would not run yet. Instead she threw herself up the chimney in a shoot of sprigs and embers. When she burst into the air, she realised why they were afraid of fire.

Hseth.

The god had manifested again. She stood towering over the city like a behemoth, smashing stones beneath her feet like a child who loved to crush insects and watch them die.

Behind her, the Talicians had raised their flags around the port. Amongst the wreckage of Middrenite ships, there were northern raiding boats and Restish battleships, only prevented from sailing upriver by a blockade that still held between two of the Daesmouth bridges.

But in the wake of the god there came soldiers in red, marching steadily. Between them, they dragged a burning, bloody brass statue on wheels.

A portable shrine. Hseth's shrine. A priest walked behind it, ringing a bell, while still tangled about its feet was a matt of burned hair from someone whose head must have been pressed there, their throat likely slit. By it, was a lone finger, curled like a question.

They had killed people to summon her. Had drawn her to their battlefront with death and pain. And now she was the worst kind of weapon of war: a being of horror and ultimate power. Her fire-flesh hardened into shifting armour, her red locks twisted between flame and hair. In her chest was a tangled weight of dull metal, a strange mirror to Arren's own wound, where Hestra usually resided. The ore clung to the great god like a spider, tendrils wrapped over her ribs. Briddite.

A cry came from below. A Middrenite brigade was charging through the city on horseback, light flashing on their armour as they went to confront Hseth. On the folds of their blue cloaks, Hestra could see the circle and rune symbol of the veiga. Godkillers. Ones that belonged to Arren's army.

But leading the charge was a woman in a cape of Yether-yellow. This was not the Lord Yether Hestra had watched murder his father, her will hot and fierce upon him. It must be one of his daughters.

This Yether gathered her forces in line with the fire god's passage, shouting orders that Hestra could not hear from her rooftop vantage. They took up their bows, dull grey, briddite-tipped, and took aim.

Hestra knew the pain of briddite; every god who had lived long felt its burning at some point, the curse of the metal that ate their flesh and burned their being. So, when the arrows flew upwards, she flinched.

But when the metal struck her fire-flesh, Hseth did not. The arrows clung to her, little needles, but did not make her scream.

Because briddite was in her making.

The great god's attention turned as the priest in white screamed instructions, their mouth a round black hole. She had already diminished in size, using her power too exuberantly. Soon she would have to disappear, wait for the prayers to build again. Or the sacrifices.

The yellow-cloaked captain held her ground, still bellowing out orders though her horse had its ears back in panic.

The godkillers nocked their arrows, tightened, and loosed. More of them stuck, but still Hseth came. She reached for them with her hands, smashing them through chimneys, through walls. She ripped blazing curtains out of windows. A woman screamed from a room now open to the flame, her children's beds half tipped from the shattered wall, the young ones missing in the rubble.

Hseth did not care. She was growing bright, bigger, twisting into a pillar of flame as she dove towards her aggressors. Hestra wanted to howl at the veiga who hadn't moved, at the woman in yellow whose skin must be burning in her proximity to the god.

The next wave of arrows burst into flame before they struck. Hseth was too close to them now, too close to run.

The god crashed down upon them in pain and light, eviscerating the defenders in an instant of fury; a terrible, brutal show of power.

And the Talicians cheered.

Hestra found herself screaming. All those brave lives, all those colours of feeling, ripped into darkness in a single instant. It wasn't even a sacrifice, it did not build her power. She had killed them for the sake of killing, when she could have left them alone and lost nothing.

Hseth rose from the wreckage she had made. Broken horses, flaming bodies, charred bones. She was smaller now, human size, her power used up in burning them.

Hestra ran. She let herself disappear in a burst of embers and smoke, and fled back to the dark safety of the king's chest, where a small spark of her power kept him breathing, his blood flowing, his mind alight.

'Hestra, what is it?' he said to her as she settled, silent in her nest of twigs, barely bigger than a shrew. 'Where did you go?'

She didn't answer. She didn't know what to say.

CHAPTER SIX

Arren

'ARE YOU CERTAIN THIS IS WISE, SUNBRINGER?'

Arren didn't answer his guard, as she trailed him down to the Reach gaols. He didn't need to. The long halls, barely lit by the dawn light, were filled with the clatter of preparation as Arren's cobbled-together army made ready to leave. Half of Daesmouth was all but rubble, the harbour fully taken, and Vittosk spies in the Bennites said the Talician army was moving west at speed.

If they did not race to meet them, they would be pincered between two claws. They could tarry no longer waiting for weapons and plans and people. Those they did have were disorganised, chaotic, loyal only to their Houses. Or, they were mercenaries, glory-seekers, thieves and cut-throats dragged from the gaols in return for offers of reprieve or pardon. He was a half-beggared king, and he couldn't be choosy.

But there was more to war than bodies. An army that did not trust its leadership would tear itself apart, and if Elo wouldn't give him his counsel, then Arren needed to seek power elsewhere. The power that moved nations. Faith.

He needed it now more than ever. Hseth was a deadly weapon of war because each victory made her followers believe in her more. All their sacrifices, all their pain, they could see it rise before them in fire and death. His own victories were few now, and tainted. He needed his people to believe in him. In his alliance with the Craiers and the rebels, in his ragged army that barely knew the back end of a horse from its front. Faith was what fired an army to face death on a field of war. He had seen it in Blenraden: lost, regained, remade, till the city of gods was won, then his country, his throne.

Even if it had turned to blood and ruin, treachery and rebellion. *You leave only blood and chaos in your wake.*

Elo had meant it to hurt, and it did. And for the first time in a long while, Arren remembered the voice of his mother. *You're born from nothing and will amount to nothing. Everything you touch is tainted with failure.*

Queen Aletta's loathing had been cold, disinterested. He embarrassed her as the unwelcome result of a dalliance with some House's lowly cousin, long banished now, and long dead.

Arren almost missed the days when his god's jibes had drowned out his mother's memory, like spirit on an open sore, cleaning putrefaction from a wound. Now the god was silent, and his mother's memory was not. Did Hestra intend to stay neutral in this fight forever?

Arren continued down a spiral stair, past the receiving hall where the winter tapestries had been brought down in favour of summer banners. His guards hurried behind him, holding the flaming torches he had bade them bring. They were not ready to leave, but Arren was. He had barely slept. He spent most of his nights awake, thinking, planning, waiting for footsteps at the door, daggers in the dark. He knew what it was like for death to come for him, but it was not death he truly feared: it was losing. Losing everything he had built.

They reached the gaols in the bowels of the palace, and all was quiet. Even as the summer warmed, the air remained cold and damp, and the rising sun did little to lift its chill weight.

Arren took one of the torches. 'Wait outside,' he said, but his guard looked troubled.

'Sunbringer . . . it is not safe.'

'The prisoners are in chains,' said Arren drily.

'No, my king, I mean the roof.'

Arren lifted his torch to brighten the vaults before them, and saw the sag in the ceiling, the cracks in the arches. Craier's blackfire had caused damage in unexpected places. The once-beautiful gardens had been shored up, stitched over with wooden planks and salvaged stone, but in the Reach some floors still sank, beams groaned, and walls crumbled after weeks of seeming stability.

The ancestral home of the House Regna, the House of the monarchs who had united Middren, was falling apart. If he wasn't careful, Arren would fall with it.

He hesitated. To die crushed by the falling stones of his own palace felt too bardic to bear. But that reminded him why he was here: to tap into the kind of faith that drove people to throw themselves at danger, murdering in his name.

And not just Sunbringer. Another name he had not chosen: *Fireheart*. He touched his chest, felt the heat of it.

'If it is safe enough for our prisoners it will have to be safe enough for me,' he said, stepping into the dark.

As he approached the occupied cell, he could hear ragged breathing. The flicker of flame from the torch and his dimmed chest landed on white dresses browned by dirt and dried blood. One of the women had struck her head falling into the harbour water, and was in a bad way. Her eyelids fluttered but did not open. The other winced and raised her hand against the light, then gasped and fell to her knees on seeing who had brought it.

'Sunbringer,' she breathed, the chains at her ankles clinking as they settled. 'You have banished my darkness with your fire.'

Arren hesitated, not sure what to feel. Elo had been right: this *was* what he had desired. The love given to gods. Still, it made him feel . . . discomfort. Wrongness. When faced with devotion, he still doubted that he had earned it.

He banished the thought. These were his mother's thoughts, that he was not deserving, that love was something he could never have. He tried not to think of the anger in Elogast's eyes.

'Why did you attack the Craier ship?' he demanded.

'They turned against you, my king, and all you have done for us,' whispered the prostrate woman, her words kissing the stones beneath her lips. 'Now they flee to foreign shores and false gods, leaving behind a mess of their making.'

Arren relaxed a mote.

'I am allied with Lady Craier,' he said, not hiding his bitterness very well. Bitterness he had nursed, locked in his own palace until the godkiller's report was confirmed. Then he had been forced to *negotiate* for his own throne, his leadership. Craier had only capitulated when the Vittosk strongholds fell, and Knight Commander Peta threatened to kill prisoners. 'She goes to summon armies to my aid, to Middren's aid.'

He would have killed them, Craier and her troublesome daughter. He would have found a way. But the Irisian council had refused to treat with him since he had banned the gods, and yet had signed Lessa's petition demanding he reinstate them. No wonder the rebels followed her. She made a good leader, with connections across the Trade Sea and beyond it, and a reputation for ruthlessness. She had returned as if from the dead to House Craier and its lands, pulling them out from financial ruin into wealth and success.

How he hated her. And her little brat with strange powers. But he knew in his soul that if he touched a hair on the little one's head, Elo would never forgive him.

'You do not need her,' hissed the woman, her hands balling into fists in the ground's muck. The antlers she had worn were gone, her braids falling apart into woebegone snatches of gold-blonde hair, reddened by the firelight. 'Traitor. Rabble-rouser. Doubter of your magnificence. You need only the fire of your heart, the light of your eyes, the power of your mind. Middren has long stood on its own.'

She looked up at him with a shining gaze, and Arren felt Hestra warm slightly in his chest.

'A small army that believes in you could lay thousands low,' she said. 'Your flame could overwhelm the Talician terror, if we let it burn as brightly.'

Arren swallowed. This is what he needed. More than anything. This passion, this certainty, Arren had seen it before. People willing to do anything for their gods, to sing, to kill, to die. Faith.

'What is your name?' he asked.

'Methsme,' she breathed. 'My companion is Hariet. The one who died was Yeomi.'

'I do not appreciate sacrifices without my consent, Methsme.'

The woman lowered her head again. 'My apologies. Our intention was pure, but we did not see the wider art at play.'

We?

'How many are you?' he asked. He could put her to the rack: he knew his staff still remaining used fire, metal, wires and tools to extract the freshest knowledge from any prisoner. But he did not have time for torture.

'A growing number,' said Methsme. 'The rebels have their connections, and so do we; in each and every land we have clerics who love you, Sunbringer. Without question, without hope of return. Because you can save us. Only you.'

Arren narrowed his eyes. The woman had perfectly balanced her breathy devotion with vulnerability and anger. He was no fool, and he could see when he was being manipulated. 'What do you want in return?' he asked.

The woman shook her head, looking again to the floor. 'Only your safety,' she said. 'You as our only king. Our only god.'

Arren tutted, pulling back the torch to cast her in darkness. 'Try harder.'

'Then . . .' she floundered. 'Your protection. Legitimacy, for us speaking your word. So we can go on loving you.'

A flicker in his body, a tongue of flame running along his human ribs where they were bound with Hestra's nest of moss and twigs. His god was listening.

Arren thought fast: Elogast had used archivists against him in Lesscia, holding hands and singing. Why shouldn't he also use his faithful?

'Then,' he said, 'perhaps there are songs you can sing for me, cleric, on our way to war.'

CHAPTER SEVEN

Kissen

THREE DAYS UNDERWAY, AND THE SUN WAS GETTING hotter. The early summer rains of western Middren had not prepared Kissen for the heat of the Trade Sea, the perpetual blue of sky and water. So, she had made a habit of enjoying the chill as the sun rose, the softness of the breeze when all was quiet.

The sea Kissen knew was storm-lashed waves, foam and cloud and rain. That, or distant blue, white-flecked, seen from shore. She was used to the green stillness of the forest and the silent breathing of leaves and moss, to the ache of her body moving her over hillock and mountaintop.

She was not used to stumbling over a tipping deck where she had no use, and no one wanted her.

She was born on the love of the sea, but a very different sea.

She watched the sun rise to the east, spinning Osidisen's dagger in her hand. The stone of it was still whole and shining, telling her he lived, though his waves were now laced through with Talician briddite. Every day she checked, though she did not fully understand why. What could she ask him, with no one to tell? What good did it do her?

A step fell on the boards behind her, and she tightened her grip on the pommel then glanced back to see which of the crew had decided to try their hand at pushing her overboard. They had made no secret of their dislike; she received the worst scum of the biscuit barrel, the meatless, fattiest slop of the stew. She ate alone on deck, her back to the sea. The only thing worse than crew would be . . .

'Ho, Lady Craier,' she said, not losing her guarded stance. Kissen had watched the lady work the deck from spit to storage, galley to gunwale, as if she knew it better than her own self. Lessa was barely in her third decade. How long had she been captain before she had handed the *Silverswift* to Lertes? How many of her secrets were etched into the wood?

'I got close enough to strike,' said Lessa, her hand on her sword. 'You should be more careful.'

She looked tired, weariness darkening the corners of her eyes, her mouth pinched. She was still vivid with a sharp-edged beauty, her nose crooked, her brows heavy and serious. Wearing an open shirt, with a slight curve to her chapped lips, she was breathtaking.

'Do you intend to?' asked Kissen.

Lessa's mouth twitched, but she released her blade. 'How's Inara?' she said at last.

'Better,' said Kissen. She didn't add that perhaps Lessa should go and see her daughter herself. The first two days of their voyage the girl had reeled with seasickness, spewing buckets. Chewing ginger root between sips of water had barely held it at bay.

Lessa glanced down at Kissen's knife. The air between them was tense, tightening like the string of a bow.

'Still carrying that Talician god's totem?' she said, and Kissen shrugged. 'You summoned his power to overturn my rebellion. What is he to you?'

Kissen sheathed the dagger. 'Are you here to pick a fight?' she asked. She owed her no answer.

Lessa scowled. 'I don't take fighting on my ship.'

'It's Lertes's ship, or is he not captain?'

'It's mine by right, and he knows it. So should you.'

That was clearly a sore spot. Kissen tried to relax her stance, elbows back on the bulwark, leaning into the dawn. She had left her staff in her cabin, wanting to practise her sea legs, but felt unsure without it. Still, she gave Lessa a crooked smile. 'Understood.'

They stared at each other, the silence stretching. Lessa's animosity was palpable, sharpened by losing Tarin, being forced onside with a king she had wanted to dethrone, and being in the position of a guest on her own ship.

'You know I mean you no harm, Craier,' said Kissen at last. 'We should make peace between us. For Inara's sake.'

That was not the right thing to say.

'Peace?' Lessa's eyes flashed with anger. 'You stole my daughter, veiga.'

There it was. Kissen winced. A burned manor, a broken coup, and at the end of it all, Inara had turned to Kissen. Not her mother. To Lessa, Kissen was a usurper, a challenger. A thief.

'I saved your daughter,' Kissen pointed out.

'You revealed to the world what she was when I had spent her whole life trying to ensure no one would try to use her, hurt her, take her.'

The wind blew between them, tugging at the loose hair around Lessa's face and neck, raising gooseflesh on Kissen's forearms. Well, if that was the card Lessa wanted to play, Kissen had a hand of her own.

'You hid, isolated and lied to her,' said Kissen. 'She's an angry kid with power that costs her dearly. I took her in.'

'Where did that lead her?' said Lessa. 'She gave her blood, her hair, pieces of herself to the gods she summoned. She put herself in danger, over and over. For you.'

'It wasn't only for me,' snapped Kissen. 'She wanted to be her mother's daughter. And, if not that, then her father's child.'

Lessa's jaw set, her shoulders stiffened with fury. She stepped closer and lowered her voice. 'When we get to Irisia, I want you gone. I don't care where you go, I don't care how much I have to pay you to find your family. I don't want to see your smirking face again.'

Kissen raised an eyebrow, and stroked the scars on her left cheek, the god's curse that left a white mark like a shattering. 'You wouldn't miss it?' she said.

Lessa scoffed and turned on her heel.

'I promised Tarin,' Kissen called after her.

Lessa paused.

'She told me to guard you.'

The lady whirled around. 'Tarin was loyal, skilled, and patient. She was my cousin, my captain, and I'd known her since we were girls. You are none of these things. I have no use for you.'

'Perhaps not loyal or patient,' said Kissen, 'but I am skilled.'

Lessa scoffed. 'I bested you easily.'

'Bah, I was half dead.' Kissen remembered well their brief spat that had ended with Lessa's knee on her chest. Less of this sparring with words and guilt: if it was a fight she wanted . . . 'Try me again. You might not find me so easy.'

Lessa had drawn her sword before Kissen finished speaking. The lady had been aching for an excuse to take out her frustration. Her curved sabre gleamed pale blue in the dawn light, a blade made for slashing and slitting rather than a knight's duel.

Two could play at that. Kissen drew her own cutlass, slowly, as Lessa turned into a side stance and held her sword point down. An odd move. Either for someone very stupid or very skilled.

Perhaps this wasn't Kissen's best idea.

'First blood?' said Lessa with a wicked lift of her brow.

Kissen stepped along the deck, testing her balance and settling between the capstan and the galley's chimney, which was already breathing out the first scents of charcoal. That reminded Kissen of Elo, and she wondered how he might square off against Lessa. Her weapon was lighter, sharper than a longsword, so he would use his weight and height, try to end it quickly. Kissen was broader than Lessa: she had the height and weight advantage. But she did not know the ship, and without Telle's prosthesis she was at a disadvantage.

First blood could be Kissen's last, if she wasn't careful. Accidents happened at sea.

Lessa did not wait for Kissen to move into a fighter's pose. She charged – light-footed – jumping up towards the chimney and kicking off it to give her height over Kissen, her sword slicing through the air, a hiss in the brightness.

Kissen brought her cutlass up to deflect Lessa's strike and used the force of her parry to shove the lady before she landed and found her feet.

Lessa stumbled, her cool, stern expression cracking to show

something fiercer, wilder. More like Inara when she was angry. She came back with darting cuts, aiming for Kissen's abdomen, her good leg, her eye, pushing her towards the aftcastle and the neat coils of rope that would tangle her feet.

'You don't fight like a lady,' said Kissen, her breath already quick. 'You fight like a thief.'

Lessa's long braid swung out behind her. 'I fight,' she snapped, 'like a pirate.'

Kissen sidestepped the ropes and brought her cutlass up and across in a swift movement. She leaned too heavily on her right leg, and grunted as her knee twinged, but Lessa was forced to step back with the speed and strength of the blow, use both of her hands on her sword to block it.

'A water thief then,' Kissen growled. 'That explains the blackfire that broke the city.'

'I knew what I was doing.'

They tested their strength against each other, leaning in, pressing hard enough that the edges of their blades squealed, sending a shiver up Kissen's spine.

Lessa adjusted her grip and ripped her sabre around, almost tearing the sword out of Kissen's grip. Still, Kissen managed to keep it, and backed away again, clipping the edge of the stairs to the aftcastle.

'Get her, cap'n!' came a cheer. It was Slim on the helm, and Kissen glanced up to see another ragged gadgie with him called Sallath. A couple of others who were on sail watch had started making bets over a scattering of pipeweed and glass beads. An audience.

'Piss and salt,' Kissen growled.

Lessa did not look up. She advanced, blade swinging.

Kissen wasn't about to be put back on the defensive. She judged Lessa's first feint and swung her shoulder back at her strike so the lady would overreach. Then, Kissen grabbed her wrist, twisting it, pushing her towards the chimney just as a breath of wind blew the smoke their way.

Kissen was prepared and took a breath, but Lessa was not, and inhaled a mouthful of the thick black. She spluttered, eyes streaming, surprised.

'Dirty trick!' cried an older deck hand called Arlo. 'Captain, stick her—'

They cut themselves quickly short, and Kissen realised that Lertes had come out on deck.

Lessa gritted her teeth and hooked her foot into Kissen's right leg. She would have sent her prosthesis skidding across the deck if Kissen hadn't leapt back. The lady's lungs were still straining as she held back her cough, but she regained her footing.

'Must sting you that they call someone else captain, eh?' said Kissen, goading her.

'Captain or not,' said Lessa, gasping, 'the *Silverswift* is mine.'

'Bah, the rest of the world is handed nothing and told to make do.'

Lessa bared her teeth. 'I was not *handed* the *Silverswift*,' she snarled. 'I *earned* it.'

'And who are the crew loyal to?' Kissen cut back. 'Lertes, or you? The sea, or Middren? Because I'm fair certain they give not a shit what happens to anyone but themselves.'

Their two blades rattled once again as they charged and clashed, over and over in the rhythm of their hearts as they moved around the deck. It was all Kissen could do to keep up with the shift of Lessa's sabre, the speed of her feet.

'You know nothing of loyalty,' Lessa growled. 'You who are faithless, godless. You're not on this ship for Middren. You've turned tail and ran.'

'Hah,' said Kissen, though she could not deny it. Should she not have stayed with Elo? Fought alongside him? 'You know nothing about me, my lady.'

They were getting into a rhythm, a clatter of steel, a break; they circled. Was this a spar or a dance, a practice or a duel?

'You call me thief,' continued Lessa, increasing the pressure, 'but it is *you* who stole Inara away and dragged her into danger.'

Kissen was getting truly angry now. 'Is that what you really think?' she said. 'Is that why you're ingratiating yourself with Skediceth, so you can maintain your sweet lies and not face the truth of it?'

Lessa drove forward, feinting left, right, then flipping her sword around so she could slide it up from beneath between Kissen's arms. Kissen stepped back, back, tipping up her chin before the point scraped it; then locked Lessa's blade and bore down on her, pushing her across the deck. She was sorely tempted to strike her dirty: a headbutt, a knee to the stomach. But she didn't want to give the crew another reason to spit in her eye. Or her food.

'You were so busy fighting for Ina that you never let yourself know her,' Kissen snarled, pressing forward. '*You* didn't notice that she harboured a god for fear of hurting you. *You* left her in danger in the dead of night without even taking a moment to say goodbye.'

Should she pour salt on this wound? Likely Lessa thought about it in her every waking moment. Perhaps if she had gone to check on her daughter that night rather than run off to Sakre, she would have seen that Inara was gone. Perhaps the manor would have been awake to face the soldiers that came for them.

The same 'perhaps' that had spun around Kissen's mind after her family had died. Perhaps if she had woken sooner. Perhaps if she had fought a bit harder, faster. Perhaps she could have saved them. Saved one of them.

'Everything I have done was for Inara!' snapped Lessa, holding well against Kissen's strength, not easily overwhelmed. 'I gave up everything I had for her.'

'What did you sacrifice, my *lady*?' said Kissen. 'A few warm nights by the fire? A cup of hot honey and oil before you slept?'

'This!' Lessa found her feet and bent a knee, pressing down on Kissen's blade before ripping herself free. Kissen let her, even as she whirled her sword around and stabbed forward.

Kissen didn't parry, and Lessa caught herself. Stopping with the sharp of her blade just short of piercing Kissen's neck. 'The *Silverswift*. My crew. My freedom. All for her. Do not tell me I have done nothing.'

Kissen reached up and grabbed the sword before Lessa chose to drive it further in. 'Then do not tell me I stole her from you. You want to protect her. So do I.'

The lady's cheeks were flushed with exertion, her skin glowing with a sheen of sweat. Some loose strands of her hair stuck to her forehead, her lips. She sliced the sword out of Kissen's hand, drawing blood, bright and red, but Kissen did not flinch.

'But I don't want *you*,' said Lessa. 'I don't need you. And neither does Inara.'

'You also thought you had no use for me.'

'And I was right,' said Lessa, showing the red on her sword. 'I beat you to first blood.'

'Did you?'

Lessa was breathing quickly, the fire of the fight still burning through her, and Kissen looked deliberately down towards her right hand. Blood was dropping from her wrist, pat, pat onto the boards. In their last break, Kissen had used the moment to nick the back of it.

Lessa stared at the blood for a moment, dripping down her fingers, then back at Kissen, her gaze appraising. After a moment, her mouth twitched in a strange, slight smile.

Then, her eyes focussed behind Kissen, and the smile fell.

Kissen turned, and there was Inara, standing at the door to her cabin. Beneath the pallor of sickness was a broken expression, somewhere between pain and anger.

Something more like betrayal.

CHAPTER EIGHT

Elogast

ELO BREATHED IN THE SCENTS OF WAR.

They had been a week marching through the greening boughs and soft mud of early summer. Across the fields, bright with crops, the aroma of bodies, animals, leather, oil, incense, meat, and bread followed them like a shroud. They moved at pace, travelling as light as they dared, resting in great encampments through the night in whichever noble's lands they passed through.

Elo had only Legs for companionship, steady and sure beneath him, amongst the whispers, the curious glances, some foul, some fair. Everywhere he went, soldiers seemed desperate to get a look at him, to prove to themselves that he was here.

'Good lad,' he whispered to Legs. Kissen was right, the horse was steady, carefully negotiating the press of numbers he must be unused to as a mercenary's steed. 'Fine hay for you tonight.' The horse whinnied in response, as if to say he had withstood gods and a thousand leagues, this was nothing to him.

Even this small army Arren had mustered was a beast with many mouths, shifting and swelling as it gained hangers-on, bloating the mass beyond structure and discipline into contingents based on fealty or locality. The king gathered banners from the great and lower Houses they passed, each adding a few to the melting pot.

The mood was tense, uncertain. The bursts of bravado and singing were short-lived, and quickly disintegrated into trudging

64

chatter. With summer came big winds and heavy rainstorms, soaking them through before brightening suddenly with a sun that seared them all raw.

They were going to Gefyrton. That at least was common knowledge, now they had passed the southern canals and the river Arrenon and turned north. The king's greater army remained south, defending Daesmouth. Though the news from there was grim. Arren was putting his faith in the leadership of the Yethers and Knight Commander Peta, that they would hold long enough for them to stop the invasion from the cold and treacherous peaks of the Bennites.

If they could keep the Talicians on the east side of the river Daes, they might survive this war long enough to work out how to beat their god.

Gefyrton was key. It was the largest crossing point over the river, connecting the rugged crofting slopes of the western Bennites to the rich farmlands in the central basin, where the Talicians would no longer need whatever supplies they had managed to maintain. Whoever controlled the belly of Middren would control the war.

They could not lose this fight.

'Lion of Lesscia—'

'—joined the rebels.'

'He killed Lord Yether.'

Elo turned to stare at a cluster nearby who had their heads bent together in gossip. His look silenced them, and they scattered, muttering about grinding their wheat for the evening's bread. This night, the eighth since leaving Sakre, the army's encampment had sprawled into the shadows beneath one of the fortresses Arren had renovated to protect the merchants on the trade roads. Most of the nobility stayed within the stone walls, while the army set up tents in whichever fallow fields were outside. Wheat, milk and broths were supplied from makeshift tents raised around the carrying ponies, to supplement what the soldiers carried, foraged and made themselves. No one went hungry, yet, but fights often broke out amongst the common recruits as they squabbled for the largest bags.

Only hope and fear held this rabble together. Elo could feel it.

When recruiting for Blenraden he had bards and brazen promises, as well as powerful gods and foreign allies on their side. No god would help them now, not if they sacrificed a thousand horses. Even if they might be bought, there were no great gods in Middren any more.

So, Elo stayed on watch, wearing the general's sash delivered to him by one of Arren's runners. They had come also with invitations, to join the war council, to sleep in the fortresses rather than on the ground. By the fifth day they had ceased coming.

'Ser Elogast?'

Elo turned in the saddle, and Legs let out a small huff of complaint. He was ready to be de-clad of his gear and brushed free of the road's muck. Generals' horses received good treatment, and Legs was among the best-liked in the stable, if not the most impressive.

'Sorry, friend, soon,' said Elo, patting the horse's neck and looking for who had spoken. So few addressed him directly; Elo made his own meals, slept alone in a narrow tent Legs carried and he erected himself. It felt strange, amid the familiarity of an army, the creeping nostalgia of a Middrenite war, to be in such solitude of his own making.

And the person who had spoken was the last man Elo would have expected to break it.

'Ben,' said Elo, surprised, then remembered himself. 'Captain Benjen.'

His old squire was holding a bowl of yellowy dough, and was leaning towards one leg. The one Elo had not injured when they fought in Blenraden. The relief Elo felt at seeing him well was quickly dampened. Like Elo, he had Irisian and Usican heritage, and no blood ties to Middrenite nobility. They had been close, once. He had shown enough promise for Elo to squire him rather than keep him a common soldier, and in return Benjen had loyally watched his back throughout the worst terrors of the gods.

But last they had met they had tried to kill each other.

'I heard you were back,' said Benjen stiffly. He stood in captain's colours as if he had been born in them. Despite the coldness of his greeting, and the pain of their last parting, Elo couldn't help a little burst of pride.

'I have no love of the Talician fire god,' said Elo.

Benjen glanced towards Elo's chest, but the lapis-studded lion of his breastplate hid the hand-shaped scar that had been fresh burned when they fought. The captain's jaw worked, and Elo waited for an insult, a curse, a challenge.

But then Benjen sighed. 'That's a rangy looking horse for a general,' he commented.

Elo raised his eyebrows and rubbed Legs's nose, and received a cross nudge in return. The horse was as impatient as Kissen. 'His name is Legs,' said Elo.

'"Legs"?'

'It's a long story.'

Silence stretched between them, heavy with things unsaid. Then, at last, 'You look hungry. Have you eaten?'

Elo felt his throat tighten. That was something their Irisian mothers would say. Something they would greet each other with when they survived a battle. A glimmer of an old life where they had shared heritage, shared food, shared beliefs.

'Not yet,' he admitted.

'You can join us.'

The camp was a constellation of cooking fires, flickering as the sky grew dark and groups clustered around them in the orange light, chattering over simmering pots. A hazy veil of smoke hung low against the slopes, cast into the air by too-damp wood.

Singing bubbled out of the dark, soft and unsure of itself, but growing louder as they reached areas where folk had already eaten and begun to drink, or were wandering from fire to fire looking for people to gossip or bed with. One song, Elo recognised as popular from Blenraden, sung by an older group of veterans who lounged beneath a bower of trees.

> 'I love the tips of the tits
> of the Usic god of wine
> And I'd make grog of all her grapes
> If she'd offer to be mine

And I love the balls of the god of squalls
With his asses to the wind
And should he fall into my stall
I'd quiver to kiss his rim.'

Elo followed Benjen, having left Legs with a girl to feed, brush and stable him. Someone spotted the two of them passing by, a general and a captain, and punched one of the singers. They all fell quiet, though not quiet enough to suppress their giggles and the splutter of one woman who had choked on her pipe. Elo smiled. Gods were not so serious once, beings of foolishness and vanity, as well as gifts and divine rage.

'Don't encourage them,' said Benjen quietly. He walked with a significant limp, though he mentioned nothing about it, and refused Elo's help with the things he was carrying. 'If a different general caught them they'd be shovelling shit.'

He wasn't wrong. And there was something in his tone, a heavy weight of meaning that he had yet to speak.

This, Elo thought, was probably a mistake.

Benjen's camp was up a slope. As they arrived, the scent of groundnuts was an earthy welcome, that and some kind of lean, smoky meat stew.

'Where the fuck have you been, Benj?' said a tall woman with short-cropped blonde hair, seeing them first.

'A fine welcome, Elseber,' said Benjen wryly. 'I lent Commander Safidah the oil we needed for the mtabga.'

Mtabga. That explained the interesting consistency of Benjen's prepared flour: a west Irisian bread stuffed with meats and spices, even older in style than Elo's favoured nameen.

'Has old Safi moved to Fellic-Farne?' said Elseber. 'Who's your friend . . .' She tapered off, either recognising Elo, his blue-lion armour, or his general's sash. With her silence, the others around the fire turned to see what had quieted her.

'This is General Elogast,' said Benjen.

'Don't! Per—' At Elo's name, a man sitting between the legs of another at the fire, having his hair braided, whipped around. He was now wincing, his braid kinked.

68

'Lotta, Perin, you remember Elo,' said Benjen, sitting down with a half-apologetic nod.

Elo swallowed. He had been at Lotta and Perin's wedding. Others in the group, Elo realised, he had known from the God War.

Definitely a mistake.

'Ah, piss and fire,' Lotta grumbled. He had been doing the delicate work of keeping Perin's braid in perfect line with the other rows as he worked the plait around the curve of his skull to the nape. The style was Usican, warlike, and with Perin's high cheekbones and proud nose, it made him look like ancient nobility. 'I'll have to start that one again.'

Perin waved his fussing away, glaring now at Benjen. 'Why the fuck did you bring the leg-stabbing traitor?'

Despite being born in Usic, Perin had the strongest northern-Middrenite accent Elo had ever heard, but it had softened over the years. Some of these people had been Elo's friends. A few faces he recognised, but they had all since fallen away when he hung up his sword and left the army. Lotta had visited him, once or twice, without his husband. But the third time, Elo had pretended not to be home. The memory shamed him still. At the time he had felt too broken, too lost, to be at ease with the people from the life he had abandoned. Except for Arren.

At least Lotta seemed only mildly annoyed to see him, compared to Elseber's horror and Perin's open disgust. He was Irisian and Talician, with freckled golden-brown skin and coiled hair that he usually wore in thin, tight twists. He had been born to a wealthy family of seasilk weavers under the protection of House Benin, and been squired to their guard at the age of six, but he wore the king's colours now.

Benjen shrugged at Perin's anger. 'We have more stew than we know what to do with,' he said. 'And none of you can bake for shit.' There were in fact two pots of bubbling broth on the fire, the smaller one filled with mutton and green peppers. Benjen patted the ground beside him. 'Sit here, general,' he said.

The scent of the food reminded Elo so intensely of his mothers' home that he almost gasped with the pain of it. He wondered if his mother-still-living, Bahba, had written to him while he was away. Whether she had received his letter about Yatho and Telle. If she hated him now he had left her alone for so long.

'Don't worry, general,' said Lotta, unwinding Perin's braid and beginning again. 'I have my husband by the strings. He can't stomp off.'

Perin scowled.

Elo steeled himself and sat down carefully by Benjen, who held out a bottle of oil.

'You remember how to make mtabga?' he asked.

What a question. 'Of course.' Elo held out his hand and cupped his palm so Benjen could pour a small pool into it, which he rubbed into the pads of his fingers and the lines of his palms, into the sword callouses that had grown fresh again with new use.

Benjen separated the dough into six balls, the size of apples, and between them they began to stretch them out, quick and sure, before their skin drank in the oil. Elo didn't need a wood roller when he had the spin and flex of his own hands, carefully not breaking the piece until it was large enough to be a plate. As they worked, the rest of the group settled back into chatter; whose feet hurt, whose sword-work was shoddy, who was hungry, how many days they thought they had left before they reached the highlands. The peace was shallow, but deepening.

When the first two pieces of dough were ready, Benjen flattened the coals at their side of the fire and they threw on the oiled and flattened bread. As it crisped and sizzled, Benjen ladled out some of the lamb stew, placing it in the centre of the dough and spreading it with the base of the spoon before Elo could pick up the edges with quick, hot fingers, folding the round into a semicircle that completely covered the meat. Each crescent rose and ballooned slightly, but Elo pulled out his dagger to press down the edges of the bread and seal it as the undersides cooked. Then, Benjen set to flipping the stuffed breads as Elo prepared the next ones to go on the coals.

He looked up, realising that the chatter had stopped.

'You didn't jest that he could cook,' said Elseber. The crowd of twenty or so were all staring at them both.

'That's all he's good for,' said Perin sourly. 'Cooking and causing trouble.'

'Is it true you killed Lord Yether?' said someone whose name Elo had forgotten.

'No,' said Elo.

'The pamphlets say you did.'

'Don't believe everything you read,' said Benjen.

'Aye,' Elseber added. 'Those fools waste a fortune turning good paper into shitcloth.'

'But you did fight in the Lesscian rebellion, general?' said another called Ainne.

'I did.'

'Why?'

'Bread's done,' said Benjen loudly, sliding the first mtabga off the coals and onto the top of a shield, where he cut it into fragrant pieces. The others crowded around to take their slices and fill their bowls, the hunger in their bellies rising to silence them. Elo continued baking, enjoying the simplicity of bread while hoping the distraction would last.

It didn't.

'If you fought against the king, why are you a general with us now?' This was a man called Cilean speaking between bites of steaming bread. In Blenraden he had been a young squire, but now he was broad and bearded. 'No offence.'

Without Skedi, Elo didn't have the skill for white lies.

'We called a truce,' said Elo, placing the last bread onto the fire for Benjen to fill and turn. 'The king and I disagree on how people should be ruled, but in the face of invasion we set our differences aside.'

'How should we be ruled, then?' said Perin, who was holding up a slice of mtabga to Lotta so he could eat without getting ash on his hands and into the braids. 'You still banging the drum of the gods?'

Elo felt, rather than saw, a warning glance from Benjen. 'I still hold that gods have a place in Middren,' he said anyway. 'People should be free in their faith.'

'Even faith for Hseth?'

Elo swallowed. The atmosphere grew dark, tense. Dangerous.

'Perin, love . . .' Lotta warned, but his husband pressed on.

'They say her priests round up our people if they're caught. Burn them or kill them as sacrifices. If they can't find Middrenites, they use their own foot soldiers. And what do you think they summon her for?'

Elo held his tongue. He had read many treatises on war. He knew all of the crimes a person could commit against the world, and each other.

'They summon her,' Perin continued, 'to burn good land, and claim the ashes for their victory. Is that the kind of worship that should be free?'

Elo felt all eyes on him, and sensed the fear in them, the rage. He thought of Kissen; her pain, her scars and fury. Her hatred of the gods. A hatred that, despite it all, he could not hold.

'Fire has many forms,' he said at last. 'The fire before us brings comfort and warmth. Not pain.' Perin scowled. 'Our own king, your king, has fire in his heart.'

A few of them settled at that. Did they comprehend what Arren had done? That he had made deals with gods despite his own laws? Or did they pretend to themselves that his flame was simply his own godhood, acquired out of some strange magic. Elo sucked his teeth. 'All power is dangerous,' he said. 'All power should be held in check. Hseth must be stopped.'

That set them all to whispering. Perhaps they even warmed to him. Without a god's sight, it was difficult to tell.

'This is nonsense,' snarled Perin. He leapt to his feet, and Lotta threw up his hands in frustration: another braid ruined. 'This bastard can't just turn his coat whenever he feels like it. He can't slice through Benjen's leg and have him dismissed from Blenraden after all we did to win it. The god-loving rebel should be in stocks, not a general!'

Elo stood too, slowly, but raised his hands, floury palms forward. If Perin's anger didn't pain him, he might have chuckled. To himself, he had been unrelentingly stoic in his pride, certain in his honour, but to all others he was as fickle as the sunshine on an autumn day.

'You're not wrong, Sergeant Perin,' said Elo. 'But I am here on the king's orders.'

'Yet all the army says you turn away the king's messengers if they come to your door.'

Elo hadn't realised that his wrestle of pride with Arren had caused gossip. He tried to fish for the right thing to say, but then the sound of singing stirred them. It was gentle, this tune, accompanied by harp strings, and the melody of it softened the crackle of the air, and the way Perin's fingers had twitched closer to his blade.

'Come. Sit,' said Lotta to his husband, tugging on his hand. 'You look ridiculous, your hair half done.' When Perin didn't move, he insisted. 'Please, Per. Between us and Elogast we have shared bread and a shared enemy, that has to be enough.'

'And shared wine,' said Elseber, snatching up a skin from the ground beside her and brandishing it out to them. Cilean eyed her with such affront that Elo suspected it was his. 'Let's drink!'

The others cheered, the tension broken. For now. Perin made a disgruntled noise in his throat and sat down. Lotta put a hand on the nape of his neck and murmured something soothing.

Elo breathed out, sitting back beside Benjen, who was splitting the last mtabga into two for the both of them. Elseber was being generous with Cilean's stash, much to his dismay, but it did the job of keeping people's hands occupied and away from their blades. Further away the singers' tune was being picked up by a few more voices. Elo caught some of the words: *Sacrifice. Breaker. Victory.*

'I shouldn't have come,' said Elo. 'I'm sorry, Benjen.'

Benjen scoffed, and Elo looked at him with surprise.

'Why do you think I brought you here, Ser Elogast?' he said. The firelight painted his old squire's face golden; his jaw was strong, with a ruff of dark beard growing beneath his chin, and he had arched eyebrows that made him look constantly on the edge of reprimand or surprise.

'May I speak freely?' he added. 'General?'

Elo held the warm food in his hands. 'There's been too much bread and blood between us for anything else,' he said.

Benjen nodded. 'You are no fool,' he said. 'You must have already noticed that this army is barely held together with prayers and fear.' When Elo's expression gave his agreement away, Benjen nodded at the others. 'Even here, we have seen war before, but still we bicker and fight. They are all still deciding who to believe, who to follow, whether it will be worth it. And you . . . in your pride and your silence, you put it all at risk.'

'Risk?' repeated Elo. Gods knew he meant them no harm. He had fought with these knights. He had chosen to fight with them now.

'People look up to you,' said Benjen. He rubbed his leg. 'So did I. I was a scared farmboy and you made me a knight, you told me what glory could look like, what songs are written for. I knew I could follow you and the king anywhere, into the darkest storm, because my faith in you was greater than my fear of anything.'

Elo didn't know what to say. Benjen had lowered his voice to a whisper, and against the crackle of flames, the sizzle of the stewpot that had been upended onto the coals to clean, no one could hear them.

'And now people are more afraid than they have ever been,' said Benjen. 'They look to people like you, like the king, trying to decide where to put their faith. If you, the Lion of Lesscia, the hero of Blenraden, does not show he believes that the Sunbringer can win, then no one will believe it.'

He didn't mean Lotta, Perin, Elseber, Ainne, Cilean. He meant all the gathered armies, angry and afraid.

'My life, my blood, my heart,' Elo murmured, bitterly. That was the belief he had drummed into everyone he commanded, everyone he had trained. After the main armies had fled with the death of Arren's sister, Elo had known that if he did not build hope in Arren, they would run, and Middren would fall. They had to be fierce, united, certain, to have any hope at all.

How far Elogast had fallen from that faith. How much remained of the man he had been? He had given it all to Arren, and been betrayed.

'If people do not believe we can win another God War,' said Benjen, 'then they will fall apart at the first breath of Hseth's flame. And if you don't help them believe, the king will find someone else. And I trust your leadership more than any stranger who has never seen a battlefield.'

It sounded as if he was speaking about something specific. The singing had come closer now. A group of folk in beribboned white were leading the music, similar to the palest greys and whites of Lesscian archivists, but these people wore ribbons of blue and yellow, and they had leaves in their hair.

'Oh, trust those pious performers to spoil the wine,' muttered Elseber. 'I think they're coming closer.'

'They're not performers,' said Cilean, snatching back the skin that had made the round back into Elseber's hands. 'They're clerics.'

'Same difference.'

Clerics? Elo looked towards the singers.

'Clear the way!' came a call.

Benjen's little gathering stood up, laughing and shifting aside so that a drummer in white and a harpist could walk through them.

Behind them came a woman. Her feet were bare, her dirty blonde hair wrapped neatly around her head, pinning in gaudy stag's antlers.

Her eyes met Elo's, and he recognised her, even as her mouth twisted in a righteous smirk.

One of Tarin's murderers. She was free. Elo drew his breath, ready to call for arrest, but then he saw the gold stag-and-sun emblem pinned at her throat.

Something of that grandeur could only have come from the king.

Not only was Benjen right, but perhaps Elo was too late.

CHAPTER NINE

Inara

INARA BARELY NOTICED THE ISLAND TILL IT HAD RISEN like a fin from the steel-blue of the deep sea. The wind was easterly, blustering and warm, soaked through with the sun.

At last, the tipping and turning of her stomach had eased, though she still dreamed strange, hot dreams of gods and death and fire and disappointed mothers. It had been three days since she had learned what Lessa had sacrificed for her.

'You should sort through your feelings,' said Skedi, sitting by her, preening his feathers. He had stayed hare-sized, but seemed brighter, more solid, than he had for a long while. 'Give them names.'

'I don't want to name them,' said Inara. 'I don't know how I feel.'

'Your colours are so dense and tangled. Maybe it will help pick them apart. Then you will know.'

When she passed by the part of the deck where Tarin had died, that 'tangle' tightened. Every time she met her mother's eyes and saw a stranger. Every time she got in the way of the crew, or heard them insult Kissen behind her back and to her face, Inara felt how useless she was with all these things she didn't know how to mend.

So, she found distractions. One of them, she held in her hands, careful not to let the wind tug it out of her fingers.

'Read it to me again,' said Skedi at last, when he decided that she was not going to speak about her mother.

Inara sighed and uncurled the long parchment. It was a song, transcribed and translated, it said on the note, from Old Usican. Telle, Kissen's archivist sister, had thought it important enough to give to Inara from the archives they had rescued from Lesscia.

> 'He called rain upon the Steppe, the child of the storm god
> Soft his tread, deep nights slept, the child of the god of storm.
> He sang to the gods of wind and rain
> Played with the gods of grass and thorn
> Till the invaders came, the invaders came . . .
> As they beheld a child so strong, so bold
> 'Neath open sky, their hearts grew cold.
> Hunt! They chased him, fleetest feet,
> Across the steppe, through long grass sweet.
> And across the steppe the stormchild fled
> Far from his mother's shrine he sped
> Away, away, till his soft feet bled.
> Cry! His mama watched his flight,
> Come back to me, where I can fight.
> Too far he had gone, too scared, too small,
> Then into the river, the child did fall.'

'It goes on and on about his death, her vengeance,' said Inara, rolling the parchment back up.

'It sounds like a lying song,' said Skedi.

'A lying song?'

'Stories, kernels of truths wrapped in lies. Parents make them up to warn their children of danger.'

He was approaching the subject of her mother again. Sideways. He was still devious when he wanted to be.

'Why would Telle want to warn me?' said Inara.

'Perhaps she wanted to tell you that all power has limits.'

Inara clicked her tongue, annoyed. 'You sound like Kissen.'

He huffed, his whiskers standing out straight with annoyance, and Inara couldn't help a smile; Skedi liked Kissen, she could tell. And, despite everything she said about gods, Kissen had warmed to him. The two of them had chattered Inara through her seasickness, dragged her up on deck, helped her wash the nausea away.

All while her own mother didn't seem to know how to talk to her. Of course she had tried, but Inara didn't know either, what to say, how to be. How to love her.

Before, love had been just basking in the light of Lessa's rare attention. It had been limited to toasted bread and stolen moments, never complaining, and always pretending that she didn't want more. What should her love be now, when Inara knew how tarnished her mother's was with regret?

'Ina . . .' said Skedi softly. 'It needs to untangle, or it will bind you forever.'

Inara took in a breath, then let it out. 'I feel like a burden.' She felt her throat tighten and swallowed back tears. What a silly thing to be sad for when there was war, when people were dying. 'Mama didn't choose me. Didn't want me. That's why she never was home. That's why she never looked for me and went to fight instead. That's why even Tarin dying didn't hurt her. Why only Kissen came to help with the seasickness. She wants her old life back. This.' She looked down at the wooden railing of the midship beneath her hands, so lovingly carved.

Skedi was silent for a moment. 'You didn't choose me,' he said. 'Do you regret it?'

'No.' How could she regret Skedi now, when they had been through so much? Done so much? When they had almost lost each other and come back to each other, time and time again?

'Then be careful of the lies you tell yourself,' he said, fluttering his wings. 'They're not always kind.'

'Stand by!' came a cry over the breeze. Sallath was sitting up in the crow's nest, his wind-whipped cheeks as red as the sky at dawn. 'Tip eighth to starboard!'

'Back the jib!' bellowed Lertes.

The wind was strong this close to the island, the sails flapped and luffed, the spinnaker billowing out before being dragged back, taut and heaving them forward. The helm, Aleda today, turned to the right. The sea changed in colour beneath them, from steel to gemstone, blue to brilliant aqua.

The deck was rushing with activity as Lertes bellowed, 'Ready about!'

'Ready!'

Inara shrank back against the rails as the ship tipped across the wind, holding on to the wooden banister and her scroll.

'Furl the topsails! Let the mains fly!'

Ten crew shimmied up the straining mast and others ran to the fore and tightened the ropes, others loosening as they bound the sails up and up, slowing the ship. She saw her mother too, up with the others, swinging from the topsail of the mainmast as they bound the cloth tight.

'Fourth to port!' came the cry, and the ship groaned as Aleda repeated the charge and changed direction.

'What are they avoiding?' said Inara to Skedi.

In answer, he leapt over the water and, in a clap of wings, took to the sky. High, higher than the mainsail. Her heart lifted. Her mother's totem, Skedi's totem, had given him more of his own power.

Rocks in the water, he called to her mind.

Inara put her feet on the ship's rail and pushed herself up to see the great sweeps of black beneath the pristine blue, like snowdrifts of ash. Between them was a narrow channel that the crew must know by heart. Each jibe and tack of the vessel came with a flurry of activity and calls Inara didn't understand. The *Silverswift* was now slowing.

Kissen, who had been stretching out her legs on the foredeck, evaded the sudden activity and came down to Inara's side, limping slightly. 'Are we stopping?' she asked.

'Guess so,' said Inara.

Skedi landed further back, the ship moving faster than he could fly, and came running back up towards them, jumping up to avoid the lashing of ropes.

'There are people on the island,' said Skedi, breathless. 'And in the water!'

'Aren't we in a pissing hurry?'

'We always stop for the waters of Iska,' said a passing crewmate, Rhiyande, who extended them all a snag-toothed grin. Even Kissen.

Lessa leapt down from the mast with a thud, her eyes bright and her dark brown arms bared. She kept balanced on her feet as, with a call and a shout, the ship lurched around further to port, then followed in a slow curve again towards starboard.

'I thought we were going to Wsirin,' said Kissen.

'We go there next,' said Lessa, contemplating her for a moment. 'Bring briddite,' she said at last. 'Time to earn your keep.'

Kissen's expression hardened with annoyance, and Inara understood what Lessa meant. 'We're meeting a god?' she said.

Skedi's ears pricked up, and Lessa turned to her, her brow raised in slight surprise at being addressed. 'If he is present, or allows us to summon him, yes,' she said. 'Satuan is not known to be fond of people, but, as your veiga says, we need allies.'

'Satuan?' said Kissen. 'The briddite-maker?'

The creaking of the ship grew louder as it slowed, remaining sails flapping, drifting towards a cluster of other boats all flying white flags of truce.

'Aye,' said Lessa. 'If your reports from Talicia have any weight, we must find out how a god with a briddite heart can be killed.'

Skedi sat up on his hind legs. 'Why would a god make briddite?' he asked. Inara, too, was surprised. A god making the very ore that could be used to kill them? So strange.

'There are tens of tales, and all say it different,' said Kissen.

Lessa shrugged. 'Why doesn't matter. What matters is whether he will help us now. Can you swim in . . .?' She gestured at Kissen's right leg, and the godkiller scoffed.

'Can? Yes. Will? No. It's wood and leather, and it won't like the water.' She clicked her tongue. 'And "prosthesis" is not a dirty word.'

'We'll take a skiff then,' said Lessa. 'But we should all bathe before presenting ourselves. No god likes filth in their shrine.'

'Gods should take what they can get,' Kissen muttered.

'I thought the king wasn't going to let gods help,' Inara put in.

'Few in Middren have enough power,' said Lessa, 'but the great gods of other shores . . . well, we would be fools to waste the opportunity.' She nodded at Inara. 'Irisia may not offer the help we need. We must explore every avenue before leaving the fate of our lands up to chance. That is what we owe our people as heads of our Houses.'

She's happy you're talking to her, said Skedi.

Don't lie to me.

I wouldn't.

Hah.

The island loomed closer, and the last of their sails were furled. The capstan was loosed and, rattling, the anchor plunged into the water beneath the boat, dragging along the seabed, seeking purchase.

'Brake the capstan!' Lertes cried.

The crew stopped its rattling spin, the anchor caught, and the *Silverswift* came to a halt beside the other ships.

'Arlo!' called Lessa to the older man with two wooden fingers. 'Prepare us a skiff.'

He nodded. 'Two shakes cap'n,' he said, then glanced towards Aleda. 'I mean m'lady. I'll finish making fast.'

He ran off, and the first mate watched him go, her shades bristling with yellow annoyance. Inara drew her eyes away, back to Lessa. Now they had stilled, the wind had softened, and the near-midday heat came down on them heavy and pressing.

'Can I come?'

Lessa looked at her, surprised. 'Of course,' she said, smiling tentatively. 'The seawater here is supposed to be healing: it will wash away the last of your seasickness.'

'No . . .' Inara frowned. 'I mean to see the god.'

Lessa hesitated.

'She could be useful,' Kissen offered. 'I've seen her fight before—'

'We won't be fighting him,' Lessa said sharply, irked by Kissen offering her opinion. She brushed stray ends of her fine black hair out of her face. 'Inara, I know you have great strength, but I worry that gods when they see you, know exactly what you are. Half theirs. Some will take that as affinity, but others will take it as a challenge.'

'A challenge?' said Inara.

'When I was pregnant with you, I tried to find records of other half-gods. I wanted to understand what it might mean.' She shook her head slowly. 'The few I could . . . spoke of fear.'

The manuscript, the warning song. The child of the god of storm had been hounded to his death. The gods who he had played with had not helped him. His own mother could not.

'On this ship,' said Lessa, 'you are with people I trust . . . but with strange gods? I fear for you.'

Inara and Skedi shared a look. *She's not wrong,* he said.

Aan didn't hate me. Scian didn't.

Hestra did.

That's because I tried to kill her.

Still . . . She'll have Kissen with her, and we can sneak behind, keep out of sight. He was trying to find a meeting place between her and her mother. *It takes two to make peace, little one.*

Inara looked over at Kissen, who looked as if she knew every little thought that was going through Inara's mind. Every piece of anger, every flicker of rebellion.

Inara sighed. 'All right,' she said.

When they were on the skiff that Arlo had prepared, lowering it down to the water, Lessa took the oars without question while Kissen sat loosening the straps of her leather girdle for her leg. The veiga's freckles had multiplied in the sun, and her burn scars and the white god's mark that had crossed her cheek shone starkly against her sun-reddened skin, like ripples in water.

Lessa looked different to every memory Inara had of her. As a courtier, Lessa had been so neat, restrained, but on the sea she had a freeness about her. The sunlight that had burned Kissen raw had nipped the top of her cheeks and nose to a perfect blush of brown.

The silence between them prickled with unease, but soon the noise of the shore bubbled towards them. There were so many bathers, some covered and some straight naked, sliding into the water or sitting on its edges, and a number of small skiffs just like theirs were tied to ramshackle piers. Clifftops rose about them, a high shelter from the wind, and Skedi chose to shrink to the size of a sparrow and fly up to wheel and dive with the birds, once more able to enjoy the sky.

They aimed for a long and empty makeshift jetty of barrels and threadbare rugs sticking out from the dark rocks of the shore.

'Take the rope, Inara,' said Lessa as they neared. 'Tie us on.'

Inara did as she was told, jumping off the boat and onto the barrels, and looping the thick hemp in a figure of eight around one of the bollards set into the stones.

Lessa looked across the sparkling waters, smiling to herself.

'When did you last come here?' asked Inara.

'Perhaps six months after you were born,' said her mother, then pulled off her tunic. 'There's nowhere like it.'

They undressed, though Kissen lagged as she looked at the cliffs, the sea, the boat, anything but at Lessa. Inara wondered if she was trying to give them privacy, or if she was annoyed.

Lessa slid into the sea, and Inara followed her, climbing down the hammered wooden slats of the jetty.

It was warm. More than warm. It steamed like a fresh-poured bath. Lessa showed her the way between the gaps in the stones to a place close to the shore, where it became hotter still. Green-and-yellow striped fish scattered around their feet where they scraped along the sand, and steely-shelled crabs that looked more bony than full of flesh. They passed over a deeper patch of water, and Inara clung to the rocks.

'Careful,' said Lessa. 'They're sharp. Best to swim.'

'I can't swim,' said Inara, though she could feel the bite of the rocks beneath her hands.

Her mother looked at her. 'Of course you can swim. Erman taught you.'

Inara hadn't heard her tutor's name in a while. 'Erman was afraid of water,' she said. 'A flood killed his sisters, remember? Kissen taught me to float, but I can't swim.'

Lessa's mouth tightened, and for a moment she looked lost, almost pitiful. But then they both were startled, as with a yelp and a splash, Kissen made her entrance.

'Are you all right?' Inara called back.

'Fine, yes, just let the one-legged woman throw herself into the water.' Kissen dragged herself onto the rocks before Inara could warn her, and hissed in pain as they sliced easily through her skin, drawing a bright red ribbon of red from her forearm. 'Fuck,' she muttered.

'Sorry,' said Inara, and Lessa muttered something that could have been an apology if she tried harder.

Kissen made her way to them, swimming mainly with her arms between the rocks. They mingled with the other bathers, and Inara caught snippets of different languages, and even saw a trio signing to each other in a kind of handspeak, their gestures too unfamiliar to Inara to understand what they were saying. The water washed through them in waves, sometimes too hot, so people would hop, wincing, away from the scalding heat until a cooler wave came in from offshore to soothe them.

Kissen pulled a face, one hand going defensively to the burns along her chest and neck that mingled like water-ripples with her skin and freckles. Over her heart, the circle of sea-script from Osidisen's promise had turned white. Above it, still black, her tattoo curled like an untied rope.

'My lady!' cried the first mate, Aleda, swimming past with a few others of the crew, including Captain Lertes. His glass-green eyes were even brighter than the water, and he had undone his plaits so that his hair washed about his shoulders. 'Enjoying your hot bath?'

Lessa laughed. 'Mock me all you want, Leda,' she said. 'You always feel and smell better after a swim in these waters.'

'I know some of your enemies that felt a lot worse,' said Lertes. 'They said it took weeks for all the blood to wash away from old Lughorn's crew.'

He spat in the water, and Inara looked at her mother in surprise.

'Another pirate ship,' Lessa explained, trying to be reassuring. 'They were already planning a double-cross.'

'So you double-crossed them first?' said Kissen, though she usually kept quiet when crew were nearby.

'Yes.'

'And you knew about it how?'

'Your father,' said Lessa to Inara, ignoring Kissen though she answered her question. Ina felt her heart beat harder, strumming against her ribs. Yusef, god of safe haven. 'We caught a tailwind, got here early, and hoisted them, their captain, half the crew. We needed to prove we were strong.'

'Murdering innocent people isn't strength,' said Kissen. The crew had already passed, but it seemed Sallath heard them, because he spat in the water and made a rude gesture.

'You murder innocent gods, don't you?' he said. Kissen declined to answer, but it was Lessa who spoke instead.

'Innocence is a luxury,' she said. 'One we do not all share.'

Kissen's jaw clenched. Even naked, up to her neck in warm water, her curly auburn hair plastered around her ears, she looked intimidating. She and Lessa regarded each other, and Inara saw for a moment the slightest shine of both of their colours, vivid sea-greens from Kissen, and rich purple and blue from Lessa, both sharp, domineering, aggressive. They both quickly withdrew, clamping down again on their emotions and drawing them inwards, but for a moment it was as if their brightness was drawn to each other.

'Is fighting back really the worst thing?' said Inara, surprising herself by coming to her mother's defence.

Kissen dragged her grey gaze away from Lessa and looked back at Inara. 'Violence breeds violence, *liln*. I've never known a cruel act that did not seed three more. That's how gods turn bad, and people too.'

'Are you calling me bad, *veiga*?' said Lessa, settling further into the water and unwinding her hair from its tie. Kissen frowned.

'Why did you leave Middren?' Inara cut in, heading off whatever insult Kissen might concoct. Lessa blinked with surprise; she looked hopeful.

'We were journeying,' she said, 'your grandmother and I, to her parents' lands in Lakaii.' In the Craier manor, there had hung great painted banners from that land to the far east, ancestral memories of a place she had only seen in maps. 'It was an ambassadorial ship, carrying many dignitaries. Pirates took their chance, and took hostages in a night raid.'

'You were a hostage?' This from Kissen.

'Yes. They kept me for ransom, but my parents were in debt, and Queen Aletta kept all her wealth for the gods.' Lessa sighed 'My parents tried. I know that. But I also knew that if I didn't make myself useful I would be sold or slaughtered. I was literate, trained in sword and bowcraft, strategic. Captain Samin recognised talent and worked me from ship's rag to crew.'

Inara could no longer see her mother's colours, but she could see the shine of her eyes.

'You loved it,' said Inara. 'Didn't you?'

Lessa put her head into the water, then wrung out her long hair, twisting it thoroughly. The gossip of the folk around them twittered like birds in spring bushes, gentle and overlapping. Kissen stretched out. There were some old rugs and thick pieces of hemp thrown over and tied on the sharper rocks, and she leaned back against them. Without her prosthesis, she looked comfortable, relaxed. Her sparring with Lessa, physical and verbal, dissolved in this moment of light and warm water.

'I did love it,' said Lessa at last. 'I learned I preferred the taste of salt to the taste of honey, and I let them think I was dead. I felt . . . free.'

Discomfort brewed in Inara's gut, sharp and aching. The tangle tightened, ready to choke her.

'You left it all for me,' she whispered.

Her mother leaned over and touched her head. 'I left for you,' she conceded. 'I feared my pregnancy, and our family deserved to know you. But in truth I meant to bring you back to the seas.'

'Make her a little pirate scrap like you?' said Kissen.

'Give her the freedom I had found,' corrected Lessa. 'But when I returned, our House was in chaos, worse than when I left. Your aunt Miria had taken ill, and the strain of holding the title was burning her from the inside out. My brother Larihan had taken up a life of study and faith in Lakaii. When they found I had survived, all their hopes took root in me. In us. Not just our family, but the other lower Houses, our tenants, our people. I . . .' She sighed. 'On the sea loyalty is what binds us, keeps us safe. I couldn't abandon them.'

A flutter of dark green colour drifted over Lessa's shoulders, betraying some depth of feeling. Despite how well she hid her shades, they were there, contained within her. 'Tarin was the only one who knew how much I wanted to go back to the sea,' she said softly. 'In another world I would have. I'd have left her as our cousin-steward, given you the choice of the life you wanted.' Her eyes were drawn inexorably back to the *Silverswift*, the home she had hoped for both of them.

'I'm sorry those choices were taken from us, Inara,' she said at last. 'I'm sorry I was so busy fighting for you that I never got to know you. I hope that can change.'

Inara looked at her mother with new eyes. She saw both the

holy of holies she once had been: the lady, the archer, the politician who could do no wrong. Then, the pirate youth, lost at sea and finding herself there, wild and free and vicious. And the commander, the rebel, the avenger for a daughter she didn't really know. There was so much pain between them, so many hidden hurts. She looked to Kissen, who, despite her dislike of Lessa, gave her a faint, encouraging smile. Inara remembered what she had said when she taught her to hunt: *Pain is part of life.*

She swallowed and reached out to take her mother's hand.

Lessa was surprised, but she returned the gesture, closing her fingers around Inara's. Their hands were nearly the same size now, and in the water looked so similar. The tangle loosened a little further, and light broke through, soft and sweet.

'I hope so too, Mama.'

CHAPTER TEN

Elogast

ELO STOOD BEFORE THE KING'S TENT.

For two days, he had eaten with Benjen and his fellows, who had, with varying levels of enthusiasm, accepted Elo as one of their own. Benjen and Lotta had braided his hair into thick rows, and Elo's scalp and heart still ached from it. He realised how much he had missed his people. How he wanted to do right by them. By himself.

It was time to stop wallowing in his losses and seething in his anger. If he wanted to protect Middren, he had to do it with his whole heart, or he would be leaving it to assassins posing as clerics, and kings posing as gods.

'What do you want, general?' said one of the guards who stood at the side of the door to Arren's holding. Elo recognised her as one of the runners he had turned away. The war tent was huge, erected with the flags of all Middren's Houses, and the king's silk banner ribboning out on the warm evening breeze. 'The war council is in session.'

They were not the only guards. Two more stood by a cart that was drawn up at the side of the encampment, presumably one of the many that carried the king's necessaries. There were barrels packed among the standards and colours. Oddly, they bore the Craier sigil: three trees and a bird.

They had passed the gutted Craier manor that day, where the

army might have chosen to bed had it not been a ruin. The steadings they passed were struggling to maintain the fields, and many were overgrown since the house had been burned. It hurt Elo's heart to see Inara's home, which once must have been so beautiful, but was now a broken shell of blackened walls and pulped earth. The dead had been buried, it seemed, in a line along what might once have been an orchard, their mounds brightening with green grass. All save one, fresh with turned earth and a wreath of ivy: Tarin's.

'I am here to apologise to the king for my absence,' Elo said. 'And to provide my counsel.'

He had dressed in a new shirt, a fine dark blue with green cording down the chest. This, he had tucked into leather breeches and covered with an ochre wool cloak. He would wear his armour later, but for now . . . he was a courtier.

'Send him in,' someone said.

It was not Arren who had spoken, but the guard relented, holding open the tent door.

First, was only smoke. A brazier of woven metals stood inside the doorway, filled with pine-scented charcoal that held off the sweat-stink from the masses outside. As the tent door closed, it muffled the army's noise beyond the cloth, and trapped the heat within.

The tent had three rooms. To the left, a space for the king's armour, weapons, cloaks. Different pieces, all grandly etched. To the right, half lit, Arren's bed, heavily draped, a washstand and chamber pot, for no king would shit in the latrine pits with the other folk. Behind the brazier was the largest room. It boasted a table built from barrels and wood panels that must have broken the back of the ponies that dragged them.

Elo had to remember, this wasn't the Arren he grew up with, the squire and the soldier. This was a king's war room. His king, for better or worse.

The man himself stood over sections of his great map, adjusting some details while a woman in the red of House Yesef read the enemy's movements to the east from a piece of parchment. Kyaum Yesef, sister of Lord Yesef, her curling black hair plaited in a long

89

tail. Elo remembered her from the last weeks of the God War. Arren did not look up, but she and the others did, their expressions ranging from curiosity to blatant aggression.

Elo recognised many others: Iuri of Movenna, whose hair had gone full silver since Elo had seen them last, and they had glasses clipped to their nose. Beside them was Elemni, who had been on the *Silverswift* when it had been mobbed. Lord Siridean Tiamh, husband to the current Lady Tiamh, was muttering something to her, standing with his legs apart and chest out, a show of self-importance; Elo was certain that it was he who had called him in. Siridean's wife had been aunt to the previous Commander General Antoc, killed by Arren in Lesscia. Elo wondered whether they knew the nature of his death.

But he knew by experience, Siridean saw himself as closest in kin to the king, himself the late Queen Aleda's cousin. But Tiamh was not the only House that bore connection to the Regna line. Blood did not claim as much power in Middren as choice: adoption could make monarchs, and banishment could break a noble's claim for generations. Even Arren had to be confirmed by a gathering of his Houses.

The others Elo knew only by the colours they wore: a general from House Crolle, and Commander Tulenne, representing the western nobles and raised to command through noble connection rather than any particular skill. None of these people were military leaders; they came to represent the interests of their own land and keep Arren onside. Gannets, vultures, and opportunists who would flee at first trouble, covering their own arses.

And behind them was the worst of the lot: the woman. The so-called cleric. Still in her musty white, her golden brooch pinned above her breastbone, and her hair neatly beribboned. The antlers were gone, but her harp was in her hands so she could strum and murmur lyrics while pretending not to listen in on the tactics of war. She glared at Elo as he came in. He ignored her.

Iuri of Movenna cleared their throat, drawing attention to whatever they had been discussing before Elo disturbed them. 'However the Talicians arrange their forces,' they said, 'Gefyrton should still be our goal.'

'Come now,' said Yesef. 'They'll be bottlenecked there by the Geralfis. South is where we can counter the raids along the coastline. Daesmouth will not hold much longer, and Lord Yether has already begged for aid.'

'They're a raiding people,' agreed Crolle. 'They're not experienced at land warfare, more effective on sea. That is where we should meet them. Send some supportive troops to Geralfi and take the rest to the coast.'

'I have no intention of splitting our force further,' said Arren. The others fell silent, and after a moment Crolle bowed his head.

'I quite agree, Sunbringer,' he said with an obsequiousness that made Elo's skin itch.

Elo cleared his throat. 'Should the invasion come west of the Daes,' he put in, 'splitting our force may be the wiser move. We have the defensive fortresses as bases from which we can harry their troops and wear them thin. It is a proven strategy from the Curlish wars.'

Crolle and Tiamh gave Elo a look so cutting that he almost checked himself for blood.

'What are you doing here, "Lion of Lesscia"?' said Tiamh. 'Or is it "Elogast of Sakre"? Or the "King's Lion"?'

'I was invited,' said Elogast. 'As commander general.' He looked to Arren, who finally met his eyes. The air in the room pulled tight, like dough breaking apart in the centre, cracking at the edges. He had put him on the spot, to deny him, or accept. Commander general was the second highest rank in the army, in control of the land army, or in Knight Commander Peta's absence, everyone under Arren's command.

Crolle began muttering fiercely to Tulenne, while Movenna chuckled. The cleric, however, went pale with anger, stilling her harp strings.

'Fireheart,' she said. 'You cannot have a non-believer at your side.'

'Who are you to command a king, and tell him who believes?' said Elogast, not breaking eye contact with Arren. That silenced her, and she bit her lip. 'Not all belief is shouting, singing and wounding. My belief is my life, my blood, and my heart.'

Arren pressed his lips together. He knew the phrases Elo had used to gain hearts to his cause in Blenraden, he understood what Elo was telling him: that he would do what was needed. It was all a white lie, a hope made from hopes, but if Arren still wanted his help, he was here.

And after the bickering and grovelling Elo had walked into, Arren did still need him.

If the king was surprised, he didn't show it. He gave a tiny, barely visible nod.

'My thanks for joining us, Commander General Elogast,' he said, tilting his voice to the room at large. 'Distraction has driven rumours of your disloyalty beyond the realms of truth. Our differences of politics are long settled, and your leadership is invaluable.' The cleric bit her lip, hard enough to draw blood, but bowed her head. A small victory.

'Then you agree with General Crolle?' said Tulenne, who wore the sash of a commander and looked faintly disappointed. 'We guard the south? I must say, I was hoping to see some ground action.'

'Not at all,' said Elogast, rather than tell him that he didn't give two figs for what he wanted. 'The king is right: a loss at Gefyrton will decide this war. We must continue hard till we reach the highlands. I only wanted to clarify that in war we must be prepared to adapt to survive.'

'Gefyrton was built by the gods to be a fortress,' said Crolle, pointing at the map. 'We need to focus on the areas that are vulnerable.'

Marked in ink were the points of Talician and Restish incursion. Daesmouth was black as a bruise, only the west side remaining in Middren's hands. Blenraden was fallen, the Vittosk lands to the north and most of the southeast coast. From here, Hseth's forces looked unstoppable. If Craier did not return from Irisia with a fleet of warships, no matter what they did, they might have already lost eastern Middren.

'Their sea raids are creeping west, Commander Elogast,' Kyaum Yesef agreed. Perhaps because her House had sided with Craier, but she had accepted his new title without a squeak, though she did the standard shortening from 'commander general' to just 'commander'. 'They do not care that they leave ruin, only that the ruin is theirs.'

'I read the summaries of the reports from the veiga who saved the king,' continued Crolle. 'And from Yether to the south who begs, *begs* us to come and help. You may not know this, as you have been absent so long, but Talicia have no qualms over who they kill, and what they burn with their god. They can and will wreak havoc on our ships and harbours and destroy our power as a trading nation.'

There were nods around the room. He wasn't wrong. Elo wanted to return to Lesscia, run to Daesmouth, face the Talicians and chase them away. Power on the Trade Sea was in filled ships, deep ports and fresh water. Middren had the last safe docking points on the long journey west, but if they were lost, other nations would not blink before turning to Irisian alternatives or claiming the wreckage and rebuilding the ports in their own image.

But these were Yesef harbours, Crolle harbours. Were they truly making decisions based on the tactics of war, or the fear for their own wealth?

'What else do they say?' he asked.

Crolle frowned.

'The reports you say I have not read, what do they say about the Talician forces?'

No one answered, all looking to each other, to Arren, who was keeping his expression carefully controlled, watching this play out and waiting for Elo to answer his own question. If Elo was the belligerent one, the dissenter, then it left room for Arren to be the calm voice, the ruler.

Elo answered his own question. 'Talicia have sent a huge part of their force over the Bennites,' he said, refocussing their attention on the tiny red flags that marked the long journey over the high peaks. 'Many are young, undertrained, underslept and, considering how difficult it is to maintain supply over this terrain, hungry.' He put his hand on the map, where Gefyrton spanned the river Daes, marking the turn from rocky terrain to arable land. 'But their rulers, the Three, chose this route on purpose. If the army crosses at Gefyrton, they will access Middren's heartlands, its food, its largest trading river. If they are truly using our people for blood and offerings, do you wish to give them access to busy farming towns? River traders? Cities? If they gain the crossing of Gefyrton, they will be able to crush our harbours from north *and* south. We hold the bridge city, or we lose. It's that simple.'

Silence fell, as they all looked at the Bennite force, inching closer, a blade waiting to drop.

'Lord Geralfi is certain the Gefyri fortifications will hold,' said General Elemni.

'They have barely been used in decades,' said Elo. 'Most are houses now. Furthermore, they are directed towards the eastern bank, not upriver. The docks themselves are poorly protected.'

Tiamh grunted. 'How do you know this, commander?'

'I passed through there recently,' said Elogast. On an illegal pilgrimage for his king, but he would not mention that. 'Our enemy use terror, gods and numbers, but they are inexperienced in war and have not won a brawl with us in over a century. We can stop them if we hold our mettle.' Arren said nothing, but he was smiling slightly, and Elo knew, with a complicated twist of his heart, that they still understood each other. After all this time.

The others, even Crolle, appraised him in silence. Listening. This, Elo had not expected. How many times had he been forced to shout for a room's attention in the God War, when they had all been disparaging of a knight commander so young? How often had his orders been evaded, or outright ignored? To accept him so quickly, they must be very afraid.

Though Kissen had too much of an impact on Elo's life not to press a nerve if he could.

'Perhaps,' he added, 'we could have a better chance if we recruited gods once more to our side,' he said. 'There are some still worshipped in Middren, in the shadows. Sali, for instance, one of Gefyrton's great founders.'

The cleric rose to her feet, incensed, and the other House emissaries dropped their eyes, cleared their throats. The alliances here were thinly wrought. How many would turn on Arren, if another way was offered?

Arren's smile didn't drop, but it tightened. 'These gods are as like to join Hseth as to defend Middren,' he said calmly, and nodded to Crolle, who looked about to burst a vein. 'And all of them lack the power to defeat her.'

Would he not consider it, even as the map turned red and black with defeats? But Elo inclined his head.

'At least, it seems,' Arren continued, 'the commander general has convinced you all of my plan. To Gefyrton, yes?'

No one protested.

'Then we should send a vanguard ahead,' said Elo, seizing advantage while he still had it. 'Support Geralfi, clear the trees upriver, and destroy Talician cover.' He had spoken of this with Benjen and the others who had been to Gefyrton or Blenraden. Failing to clear the Godsway of cover had allowed them to be ambushed once, and they had destroyed every shrine along it so it would not happen again.

'We're moving as fast as we can,' said Elemni. 'Our guards are exhausted. They want early summer feasts, not hard tack and broken horses. Twelve of my fighters grew sick five days last, I worry about it spreading.'

'Your fighters drank from a stagnant pond,' muttered Tiamh. 'You're lucky they didn't shit themselves to death.'

'You—'

'An advance of five riders will travel at twice our speed,' interrupted Kyaum Yesef, always pragmatic. She looked at Tiamh. 'You have been boasting about your fast horses, General Tiamh.'

Tiamh's chest expanded, ignoring the slight. 'Curlish-bred, Middren trained,' he said. 'Travelling light, they'd make double speed.'

'But what of the south?' protested Crolle. He turned to the king directly. 'Sunbringer, if Lady Craier forsakes us for Irisia and Restish, if the Talicians turn their god on harbour after harbour, we will be like trapped rats with nowhere to run. Is it not better to relinquish the east and hold the west?'

Arren hesitated. Though his expression barely changed, Elo saw his vulnerability, his fear. Recently, the House Crolle had been one of his most powerful and wealthy allies after rallying against one of their heirs who had tried to have Arren poisoned. If they broke from him, the others would follow in a heartbeat.

'Hold your faith instead,' said the cleric, breaking her silence. The others turned to her. 'Things may seem dire in Daesmouth, but the storm is darkest before it breaks. Trust your king. He has seen us through a war of many gods and destroyed them all. Hseth is only one.'

Ah, so this was why Arren had chosen her. The zeal poured off her like a light, a beacon, showing them the way to true faith. Arren lifted his chin expectantly, and the other nobles, captains, commanders, generals, put their hands on their chests, splaying out their fingers in the Sunbringer salute. Elo swallowed his pride and did the same. The fire in Arren's chest flared, but quickly dimmed again.

'General Crolle is right,' the cleric continued. 'It is high time for a summer feast when our Sunbringer must gather his power. We will make offerings, make prayers for Lessa Craier's safe return and for our Fireheart to defeat Hseth's fire of death.'

Offerings? Fireheart? Could they truly feast while they were on the edge of ruin? Then Elo understood: they would make use of the old traditions, allow the praying and dancing and hoping to chase away the fears of fire with the hope of warmth.

'This council is adjourned,' said Arren. 'Go to your preparations. Methsme, I hope your new songs do well.'

'I will have them crowing of your glory, Sunbringer,' said the cleric with a bow, 'before night is full dark.'

Elo turned with the others to depart, wishing heartily he'd never heard a note from the cleric's poisonous mouth. Even if Arren could overlook the fact that she had killed a fellow Middrenite, a captain no less, he could not. He had done what Benjen wanted, now he wished for a warm meal and nameen to chase the bitterness of it away.

'Not you, Commander Elogast,' said Arren. 'I would speak with you alone.'

'Sunbringer?' said Methsme quickly, turning back from the door before she followed Iuri outside. 'Is that wise?' The outside air was coming in, warm and muddy, clashing with the scents of the brazier.

Arren raised a brow at her, and she shut her mouth quickly. Elo begrudgingly let a certain kind of respect bloom in him. As a youth, his friend had been hot-headed, impulsive, and angry. Now, he had the confidence to command obedience without a word.

When the door fell closed the soft colours of Arren's tent fell back in place, enclosing them in the dim light. The king's circlet was half hidden by his curling hair, and he was wearing less stylised armour than he did on the move, just a leather cuirass with antlers and rays stitched in gold across the front over the more protective plates. He folded his arms, gazing at Elo with an inscrutable expression. Man to man, they beheld each other.

Elo broke the silence first. 'Entertaining assassins in your close court now?' he said.

'Ah,' said Arren, 'I wondered how long it would take.'

'For what?'

'For you to unsheathe your sharp tongue at me.'

Elo sucked his teeth, coming closer to Arren's map. It was a work of meticulous genius, using knights to collate information; Middren had never been recorded with such accuracy. Though Elo was pretty certain the northern part of their lands had been oriented further east.

'She has her uses,' said Arren after a moment. 'You yourself used bards in the God War for recruitment and spirit.'

'Bards, not murderers.'

'Well . . . that depends on what you thought of their singing.'

He was making a joke. Not even a good one. Elo bit his cheek. Methsme might play in Arren's favour, but Arren should know more than anyone how sour faith could turn.

'Why are you here, Elo?' said Arren when he didn't answer, dropping formalities entirely. 'I had given up on sending you invitations.'

'I was made to realise that my silence was worse than my anger,' said Elo. 'Other people would fill it with sound.'

Arren huffed. 'Your old squire Benjen is quite forgiving. Did you not stab him?'

Elo sucked his teeth, annoyed. 'Are you having me followed, Arren?'

'Yes.'

It wasn't as if Elo could blame him. They had no reason to trust each other.

'So,' Arren's mouth lifted in a half smile, 'I can entreat you for weeks and Benjen can convince you in an evening? You have a vice in you, Elo. You would choose stick over sweetness. You'd rather be injured than cajoled.'

'You should know,' said Elo coldly. 'You have tried both.'

Arren's smile faltered. 'Yet still you came.'

'I have allied to you,' said Elo, 'but I will not grovel to you. I will call you king, but I will not pretend you are a god.'

Arren stepped away from the map and closer to Elo. 'Don't you know?' Incense wafted between them, soft and sweet through the sour mud and warmth of the evening outside. 'It's all pretend, power. It's make-believe and storytelling. Some people just make better stories.'

'And the cleric will cloak the real you in the lies you desire,' said Elo. Arren was too close. Dangerously close. But Elo didn't step away.

Arren shook his head. 'You knew me best, Elo,' he said. 'But even I don't know how much was real. You never knew how much I loathed you, how much I loved you.'

Elo felt hot, discomfited. Was it fear or wanting? Even he didn't know. *Love and pain are not so different.*

He stepped back. He didn't want to talk about this, he didn't want to crack open the vaults of their past, and the desires buried there. Arren smiled once more, but it didn't reach his eyes.

'I have many regrets, Elo,' said Arren. 'But we are at war, and I must use every weapon we have to win it. Like the cleric. And like you.'

CHAPTER ELEVEN

Kissen

KISSEN HAD REALLY HOPED THE NEXT TIME SHE MET A god she would be paid to kill it.

Not this time. They were here for Satuan, and despite her better judgement, she could not deny that Lessa was right. How could they fight a god like Hseth without a greater power at their backs? Without Osidisen, Kissen would only have hurt Hseth by dragging her into the sea, not killed her.

But what kind of offering would it take, to bring a god with enough power back to Middren? Even Inara had to make an offering to draw a divinity away from its shrine. True, Satuan could not love the gods, to have found a way to sink bridhid ore into the earth and tell humans how to make briddite.

But caution had saved Kissen before. She hoped Lessa knew what she was doing.

They left Inara in the pools with some crew watching over her, and Kissen followed Lessa back to the boat and jetty to dress. There, she carefully adjusted her new prosthesis while doing her best to look anywhere except the shape of Lessa's back, the clinging of her dark hair to the smooth brown of her neck, the strength and grace of her hands.

Her infatuation with Inara's bloodthirsty pirate mother had to stop. It made Kissen more aware of her own body. Too aware. She felt, despite the years and self-love that she had put between herself and her pain, the pang of her childhood fears: that she was too ungainly, large, loud and scarred to be looked at with anything other than pity.

She didn't mind the doubt. It reminded her that she was still human, still alive. And, from the way Lessa also carefully averted her gaze, Kissen suspected that pity was the last thing on her mind as well. She had her own scars, a long, jagged line up her left thigh, a few more cut across her ribs, a knot in her shoulder that must have been from an arrow.

No. Not looking.

Kissen belted on her cutlass and her only briddite throwing knife, then followed the lady's sure stride along the jetty to the bank. There, the vicious rock of the ground was pitted and overhung with ragged stone that looked about to fall from the cliff above. Uncaring folks were squatted in the shade, boiling eggs in the steaming rockpools, fishing them out with grass baskets. A lean old woman was stuffing thick leaves with red berries and bits of meat seared on a nearby fire, tying them with a deft knot of coarse hemp and lowering them into the pool by the thread. She had a coin bag at her side and gave them a large gap-toothed grin as they came up.

Two copper for egg, she said in sign, *five for meat. Or equivalent.*

Lessa pulled Middrenite coin from her belt, notably not the new ones printed with Arren's face.

Two eggs, she signed, and Kissen remembered that Inara had learned her language from her mother, just as Kissen had learned it from Telle. She gave one bright brass coin with a hole in it, which Kissen didn't recognise, and the old woman plucked two eggs out of the steaming water and threw them. Lessa caught both, passed Kissen one without comment, then stepped deeper into the rock cave.

'What's this for?' said Kissen, as the other woman started peeling her egg.

'Snack. Keep the shell.'

Kissen decided not to question this small kindness and followed Lessa deeper into the shadows. Beneath the rock, the air grew hotter, sultry, and the cave beneath the overhang narrowed like a wedge. Here, there were hints that a great shrine was near: some untouched silver cups filled with what smelled like rancid palm wine; metal hands on leather thongs hanging from spikes in the rock, some holding hammers, some pointing; an arrangement of piled stones around a pit where a ritual fire might have burned the flesh of animal sacrifices. Then, on the ceiling, jagged script carved into the rock in a language Kissen was pretty sure wasn't Irisian or Middric.

'What does it say?' she asked Lessa, but the lady didn't laugh or chide her, and instead read out loud:

> 'Bone of earth, blood of hand
> Fire with blacken, quench in sand
> Join with iron, grind with sea
> 'ware the god, and leave him be.'

Kissen rolled her eyes. What theatrics.

'So,' she said drily, 'the briddite rhyme.'

Yatho had taught it to her, for one of the ways the people had fought back in Blenraden was by the smiths teaching each other how to forge briddite weapons. The rhyme held the skill within it: bridhid ore from old volcanic flows had to be mixed with iron and heated wildly hot with crumbled coal, called blacken, then cooled slowly, quenched in grey sand, and ground with seawater. It required the work of several hands.

Though the last line was the one Kissen usually preferred. In Middric it was "ware the gods, and leave them be'.

'Seems so,' said Lessa, and headed deeper in. The cave was quickly becoming a crevasse.

Kissen tongued her gold tooth as she assessed the shadows ahead. 'You've not been down here before?'

'I'm not you. I don't bother gods for entertainment.'

Kissen scowled. 'It was always your plan to bring gods into the war,' she said, 'wasn't it?'

'This is a gods' war,' said Lessa. 'It has always been my plan to win.'

'Does that mean you'll use Inara as well?'

Lessa stopped and glared back at her.

'You said you wanted to win,' said Kissen, cracking the egg with her thumb and peeling it one-handed. She was all for mother and daughter reconciling, but she had seen children used for less, and by people who were supposed to love them.

'I will not put the fate of our land on the shoulders of a little girl,' said Lessa coldly. '*My* little girl, who has already seen too much, given too much. I would rather die.'

Kissen was surprised by her certainty, but warmed too. 'It seems, Lady Craier,' she said, 'there are some things we can agree on.'

Lessa tutted. 'Tarin did not ask such stupid questions,' she muttered, then turned into the narrow passage to the smith god's shrine.

Here, as the bright sunlight eked away, the air grew hotter still, thick with salt and steam. Prongs of dribbling rock hung down from the ceiling, green and white and almost glowing in the darkness. The way narrowed, and the shadows crept in around them. Soon, scalding water ran past their feet, and they kept to the dry bank to its left, though sometimes they had to leap or climb around. Twice, instead of shuffling around a thin edge, Kissen just stepped through on her prosthesis, mainly to annoy Lessa and prove that she could.

Eventually, the dark swallowed them whole. Then, Lessa began to drop the shell from her egg, piece by piece onto the floor. It formed a faint but clear line, reflecting the tiniest edge of light still threading in from behind them. A distinguishable trail.

Smart.

Lessa soon ran out, and Kissen took over. More than once, she felt the scrape of rock like a blade along her scalp, her shoulders, her fingers. A claw that scratched, a tooth that bit. And every time her flesh touched stone, it seemed to thrum, beating in a rhythm she half recognised.

Then, between one step and the next, the sea scents of salt and stone disappeared, replaced instead by hot metal and earth. They had crossed a threshold, and now the beat was not only in the rock, it was in her ears, in her very bones. The air reverberated with the sound of metal striking metal, over and over, hard and strong. It reminded her of Yatho, a smith at work.

A god was near, already manifest. And they had crossed the border into his shrine.

Lessa continued, and heat washed over them, sizzling on their skin. Kissen's shirt dried on her back, stiffening with crystals as the path brightened again with an orange glow that made her burn scars prickle. The stone teeth from ceiling and floor looked about to snap closed and swallow them whole. They were beaded, too, with shining globules. Ore, spat out from some furnace, glinting like jewels.

Kissen felt instinctively for her chest, where the vial of Aan's water used to hang as a protection against burning. Of course, nothing was there except the white mark of Osidisen's fulfilled promise. She had no defences. Her flesh felt delicate, her breaths too quick, burning with the memory of flame and terror, the screams of her loved ones, the last kiss of her father.

That was long ago. Flame was flame, and burning was its nature. It was in her nature to feel fear, and let it go.

They passed through the teeth into a cavern, and light drenched them. Hot rock glowed a vivid, molten orange, brightening the cavern that opened around them. Rivers of hot water flowed across the ground beneath a cloud of fog, circling a vat of stone and an anvil ten times the size of Telle's largest.

Above it, stood a titan.

There was no other word for the being who was hammering at an ore-stone the size of Kissen's torso. It looked as if he was holding a blasted piece of burned bone, but as he hammered it, sparks of impure metal flew out onto the anvil and into the vat of lava he used for a firing oven.

His back was half turned away from his shrine's entrance, but Kissen could see the god had a human shape; that of a broad man with a tremendous belly and legs rippling with muscle. His hands, however, were made of blackened metal, glowing with heat, cracking red across the knuckles and fists.

This was the heat that steamed the seas. Molten stone from the depths of the earth, and a smith god at his forge.

Lessa went down onto her knees and put her hands forward, bowing low. Kissen stayed standing. She didn't bow to gods unless she wanted something from them. All she wanted now was to get Inara's mother out of this with all her limbs.

'Humans know better than to come here,' said the god before Lessa spoke, not sparing her a glance. His voice rumbled over the sound of his hammer, and he plunged the metal he was striking back into the magma vat in a spray of hot rock. Droplets of melted stone flew out, sticking to the ceiling or dropping to the floor. The god's hair hung long and knotted down his back, black, brown and russet, and through it Kissen could only see the curve of his ear, the array of steel earrings he had plugged it with. In the wavering stone-light, his skin looked golden brown, though blasted with charcoal and dusted with white ash, he did not look as if he belonged to any land or state that she knew. The origins of Satuan were indeterminate, and this god was older than most borders that had been drawn through mud, rivers and hills by the strikes of bloodied swords.

'Our apologies for intruding on your solitude, Satuan,' said Lessa. 'We come with tidings, and to hear your wisdom.'

'I want none and offer none. Leave.'

With his final word, the furnace blasted out a wave of searing heat. Kissen looked around and noted no offerings within the cavern. No baubles, totems, food or drink. Curious. Then she noted the basket. It hung above the furnace vat, not unlike the one in which the woman had been bathing her wares. As she watched, Satuan plunged in his hand and pulled out some trinkets; metal hands by the dozen, rocks with eyes carved in the stone, embroidered pieces of art and prayer.

He tossed them into the lava. He did not need to burn them, the offerings that Skedi would give a wing for, his size was already indicative of his incredible strength.

He just had no desire for them.

'A fire god has been reborn with war in her making,' said Lessa, lifting up her head. 'She now leads an army into our lands killing gods and humans alike.'

'What's that to do with me?' said Satuan. At last, he turned to them, showing not two eyes, but three, one in the centre of his forehead. One for the forge, one for the hammer, one for his hands, so the saying went. 'The flame god tried to entice me too, appearing in my fires, spinning threads of blood and war, crowing over a king she had won to her side. I sent her away with a sting in her tongue, and I will do the same to you.'

It took rare power for gods to speak to one another in their shrines. There was little point; gods scrapped for prayers and had no interest in each other's woes. But water could speak to water, flame to flame, and Hestra's double had travelled great distances as long as Arren sat in her hearth.

Hseth had clearly come recruiting before Kissen killed her.

'Great Satuan,' said Lessa, 'the god has brought war and ruin. She was killed then resurrected with Bridhid ore in her making, and now your briddite blades cannot hurt her.'

The god threw down his hammer, shattering the stalagmites it hit, then heaved the metal he was working back into the boiling vat. Hot spits of it spattered his chest, and Kissen flinched as some came close to her and Lessa.

'You taught us the ways of briddite,' the lady pressed, playing on his pride, 'gave us the means to defend ourselves. Aid us now before the fire god destroys us all, mortal and immortal. I can bring you offerings, if you would extend your power to help our people.'

Kissen held her breath. Lessa spoke so passionately, a plea such as hers might tempt any god. But Satuan was not acting like the gods Kissen knew.

'Ware the god. That is what Lessa translated. God. Not Gods. Satuan.

'Offer me?' said Satuan. A bubble of magma filled and burst next to him, brightening his face and, for a terrifying moment, turning his glower into a mask of pure rage. 'I want nothing of your offerings.' He raised his fingers to his face, staring at their metal. Even as Kissen watched, they began to cool, stiffening away from the heat of the fire. 'I plunged my own hands into the molten bowels of the earth and gave them so I could write my boon into the lava flow, where no other god could touch it. An offering that hardens in bridhid, so humans and gods could turn each other back to ashes and dreams. So I might rest.' His three eyes narrowed. 'More fool I.'

Kissen took a breath of hot air, steadying herself. This was a mistake. She knew nothing of this god except the gift he gave veiga, and even that he saw as a failure. Satuan was almost as powerful as Hseth had been, and Kissen had barely scraped by with her life using every trick in her cloak. She had now two weapons, and neither of them much use against a god so strong.

'So what if a fire god has taken briddite into her bosom?' said Satuan, putting his hands again near the lava and flexing them in the heat. 'She will be naught but power and blood, a mindless rage that her coddling priests will make her, my curse eating at her reason, her will, the things that make a god a god.' He cracked a smile, and sparks flew out of his teeth. 'A pity about the green things of your land, but green grows again from ashes.'

Lessa glanced at Kissen, uncertain, and Kissen carefully crossed the fingers of her left hand and shook them.

Ready? She meant in sign. Are you ready to go? To run?

Kissen had met many gods who had sneered at humans. They found them pathetic, manipulable, but necessary. Some few seemed to actually like them. Aan, perhaps, Skedi . . . though Kissen was still not sure what he would do when he did have a sniff at power to call his own.

But she'd never met a god who hated humans.

Lessa shook her head slightly. *Not yet. Not ready yet.*

Fool. But they were in the god's domain, and Kissen wouldn't leave her here.

'She has taken over forges, Satuan,' Lessa tried. 'She was a god of flame in the wild slopes, but has enriched her lands through brass and smithwork. She steals your worship.'

Satuan barked out a laugh. He leaned down and picked up his hammer by the base with his left hand and whirled it around so its head slammed into his right, bending the metal there.

'I care not,' he said. 'Humans desired me into being, bound to the working of fires, the forging of metal. I had no choice but to be what I am, caged by your imagining.' He scowled, another flare of heat singeing the lashes of Kissen's eyes. 'You mortal creatures grow and fade like fungus, daring to imagine gods from your desire for power, for purpose. One day, I will burn this whole island to dust and see what purpose you can scrape off it then.'

'Please, Satuan,' said Lessa, her voice cracking, to Kissen's surprise. 'I cannot let our people be murdered for a god who does not feel their pain.' She was normally so cool, so controlled, but there was more feeling in her than she dared to reveal. 'I have seen it before, in the God War, and read of worse; ages when gods take dominion of the lands they live in, and shatter them when they do not fit their image. We need your help.'

It was then that Kissen realised that Lessa truly wanted to save Middren.

This was what had driven her to sacrifice her rebellion and ally with a king who had tried to kill her, who *had* killed her own people, and burned her house to the ground. Kissen saw beneath her armour, into her heart of hearts: Lessa held to her duties, her home, because they were hers. She would fight for Middren, the home she had already given up so much for, no matter what it would cost.

What would Kissen do?

Satuan scoffed. He reached back into the vat of magma and pulled out another molten piece of metal with his bare hand, its ore-flesh re-forming from the damage he had given it. He slapped it down on his anvil, dripping and thick with clinging heat, like a fish he was about to gut.

Lessa looked down at the ground, clearly thinking fast and coming up short. Kissen choked back some doubts. She wanted to help Lessa, Elo, Inara. She was here to help.

'You are right, Satuan,' Kissen said. 'It is my life's work to sepa-rate gods and people.' She drew her cutlass, though Lessa looked up sharply in warning. Normally, baring briddite in a shrine would anger a god, but Satuan was already angry. 'I am a briddite wielder, forge-god, I hold the line you drove between people and the divine. I tried to hold it against Hseth and failed.'

The smith god regarded her, his hot orange eyes raking over the broken curse on her face, the burns at her neck. Kissen lifted her chin proudly.

'The fire god rides to war like a king on the shoulders of her followers,' she said. 'Adored, not feared. Humans mark themselves with patterns of her favour, give their children to her purpose and her worship, and each land she crosses, she and her priests try to turn to their desire. One god, loved and feared by all.'

He paused, lifting his hammer again and giving the metal an experimental tap. Kissen noted that she saw none of his creations around the cavern. He did not keep what he forged . . . he must toss it back into the fires, making and unmaking everything he created.

'And what should I do about it?' he whispered, running his hands over the metal.

'Fight her with us,' said Lessa. 'Help us to defeat her.'

Not the right thing to say.

Satuan turned on them. 'I gave you a gift!' he roared. 'A gift for defeating gods! And you *wasted it*.'

The room was getting hotter, Kissen felt the trickle of sweat down her neck. She tightened her grip on her sword.

'You have had enough of my magic,' the god growled. 'Make your own. Your human magic. Only faith can break her now.'

'Give us better shit than that,' Kissen spat back. 'She has faith. Faith is what *makes* her.'

'Then unmake it and leave me the fuck alone. Faith cannot be forged in fire. Break their belief, or steal it away. Now get OUT.'

He moved to swing his hammer towards them, and Kissen grabbed Lessa by the arm, dragging her to her feet and out of the way as he struck it deep into the stone where they had just been standing, shattering the rock like ice.

Satuan froze there, breathing hard, as if his arm had been caught in a trap. Sparks flew out of his eyes as he looked up, panicked, glaring, and Kissen whirled.

Inara was standing a few steps behind them, her hair curled stiffly out from around her head. Her gold-brown eyes were wide and fearful, and Skedi was sitting on her shoulder, small, his ears flat.

'Go back, Inara,' said Lessa, her voice shaking as she backed away with Kissen.

'The water outside is getting too hot,' Inara said. 'It burned Aleda. They're scared.'

Satuan's rage must be boiling the hot springs, turning them hotter than the sea could quench. Kissen winced to think of hot-headed Aleda given another reason to dislike her. Or Lessa.

'What thing are you?' murmured Satuan, looking towards Inara.

Kissen gritted her teeth. He wanted gods and humans to be separate.

Inara was both.

Shit.

The magma flared thick and hot from Satuan's forge, and with a wrench of power he stood, snapping Inara's hold on him. Will against will, Satuan was the more powerful: he was an ancient god, and Inara was just a girl.

'Halfling,' he hissed. Lava frothed and grew from his vat, the furnace, cracking the floor. The base of the hammer began to glow, and his hands burned hot with rage. 'Monstrosity.'

Lessa widened her stance defensively, her muscles taut with anger.

Inara frowned at him as if he were not three times her size. 'We come in peace,' she said, 'to bring you offerings . . .'

'I want nothing from *you*, bastard of two bloods. Abomination!'

He lifted his hammer, but Inara steeled her jaw, and Kissen's practised senses stirred as she felt the girl summoning her will once more. If she focussed, Kissen could hear her intent like a whisper.

Stop. Stay back. Leave us be!

Satuan roared, caught with his hammer still up in the air. Kissen took the moment to grab Lessa, dragging her away from the god and towards the tunnel.

'Run!' she yelled at Lessa. 'Take Inara. Run fast!'

With another roar that shook searing stone down from the ceiling, Satuan broke Inara's will again and slammed his hammer down on the edge of his furnace, shattering its side. Molten rock and metal flew out, sizzling where it landed. Kissen saw it strike her prosthesis, catching light in a guff of smoke. With a swipe of her cutlass, she scraped it off before the flame caught.

Inara turned and sprinted ahead, Skedi gliding, and Lessa coming up behind. Lava flowed thickly into the cave-river, bursting up clouds of steam that scalded Kissen's throat. She held her breath as the god bellowed, reaching into the tunnel for Inara, his hot hands smashing through the pointed rocks as if they were made of frost.

Kissen turned and brought her briddite cutlass down across his forefingers, slicing through the two of them. Satuan howled and wrenched them back.

'You call yourself godkiller, and you protect this creature? Traitor to your kind! Traitor to all!'

'Kissen!' cried Inara, but Lessa grabbed her daughter's wrist and dragged her into the misted shadows.

Kissen backed away, keeping the god's attention, giving them time as the magma seeped out of his furnace.

'Fucking kill *me* then!' she snarled at him.

'You'd give your life for a runt of no litter?'

'I'd rather die for something than waste immortality in a cave of my own madness.'

The lava was getting too close. If it got any nearer it would kill her without even touching her. She could already feel it searing her skin, setting fire to her lungs.

The god bellowed out words in a language Kissen didn't know and threw himself at her.

She had been waiting for this. She drew her dagger and flung it hard.

It struck Satuan in the third eye, and he stumbled and fell under the weight of his own body, splashing into the lava and roaring as it set his hair alight.

Kissen turned and pelted after Lessa and Inara. Her breath was hot, burning, and her vision blurred. She clamped her lips shut, trying not to breathe. She knew this feeling, the scalding of her inner flesh. She stumbled, vision wavering, after the shining path of broken eggshells.

'GODKILLER!'

Satuan could not be kept distracted for long.

The water along the tunnel ground was flowing black as ash and ink, boiling and bubbling. Kissen charged through it, smashing her head and limbs more than once on rogue teeth of the cave. She blinked blood out of her eyes, close behind the others.

'Go left!' she bellowed, hoping they would hear and Satuan

wouldn't over his own raging. She threw down all her emotional guards, hurling her thoughts and voice towards them all. *Left and climb.* 'Left and climb!'

I hear you. Skedi's fierce thought came back to her, and she gasped with relief. She shouldn't have; steam tore into her lungs and she hacked and coughed before breaking out into the light.

The sea was simmering with heat. A black cloud had spread out into the water, like ink poured into a well. All the bathers were gone, save for one human body floating in the water, and a few dead fish.

Kissen sprinted right, away from Inara, Lessa, and Skedi, running for the jetty. She stumbled twice, mistiming her right leg's rhythm and slamming her knees into the ground, steam and smoke flying from her back, her hair, her burned skin. She picked herself up and flew towards their boat, slicing through the rope that held it with her cutlass and throwing herself in with enough force to push it into the water.

She still couldn't breathe, away from the steam. The pain of her lungs was dizzying, and she barely held on to consciousness as she paddled out and out. Looking back, she could see people clinging to the cliff face, having climbed to escape from the deathly water. Staring, watching.

Good.

The sound of splitting stone snapped out over the harbour. Dust rose as the cliff hanging over the tunnel cracked outwards, flinging three people down to a bloody death on the sharp rocks.

Better than boiling, Kissen hoped. No time for guilt, no time for shame.

She kept paddling out in the black, a lone figure in the dark of the sea. The water wasn't boiling here; the tide from beyond the island rushed in to cool it, beating back the magma-fuelled rage of the god.

Satuan burst out of the tunnel, taking half the cliff with him. He did not care for the screams of the bathers, instead slamming his hammer into them for good measure. Kissen saw Arlo from the *Silverswift*, his eyes widening as the god's weapon crushed the rocks below him and shook him loose. He wailed as he fell.

The other crew of the *Silverswift* were close, too close to the god's fury.

'Satuan!' Kissen cried, trying to distract him. As petty and irritating as Lessa's crew was, they didn't deserve so brutal a death. 'Here I am!'

Satuan saw her. His remaining eyes widened, and he strode towards her through the water, lava oozing slowly out after him. Anger made fools of both humans and gods.

'You think you can escape me?' the god bellowed. Kissen paddled further out, trying to keep ahead of the heat. But he was gaining, so she stood, brandishing her cutlass.

'You think I give a fuck?' she cried from her aching lungs. Was this far enough? She wasn't even being paid for this.

He dived for her, his metal hands reaching down to tear her apart, still hot and smoking. Kissen braced herself, holding out her cutlass, wheezing with pain, then, just as he was about to strike, she leapt into the sea.

No Osidisen to save her this time. No father's promise. She had no gods on her side. Only hope. And brains.

Satuan's hammer and hands smashed straight through the boat, breaking it to pieces and plunging into the cold waves from the deep sea. As his hot-metal hands struck, they stiffened. Froze. The god cried out in pain, his wail reverberating through the cliffs.

Kissen grabbed onto a piece of driftwood, trying to push herself further from the god as he drew out his hands, his hammer dropping. He shrank from titan, to giant, to man, and the briddite knife fell from his eye.

Satuan looked up, his hands in front of him, and at last saw the cliffs of the cove, the people clinging to them, staring at him. A god, in the world, powerful, terrifying. She wondered if he could see their awe, their fear. Their belief.

Hundreds of people who might beg forgiveness, give him offerings, who would pray. Love would come from fear, love from the humans he detested. And it would keep him alive.

Kissen, barely able to keep her chin above water, was choking on salt and damaged lungs.

Satuan bared his teeth. 'Curses on your war,' he hissed. 'Curses on your half-god. She will be used by you humans and tormented to her death. And I hope that day you are made to watch.'

With that, he disappeared in a breath of wind and ash. Back to his shrine, back to solitude.

Kissen coughed, tasting blood. Lava was still pouring from the cliffs, filling the water. She would boil soon like a frog in a bath, and she hadn't the strength to save herself. She had no more tricks in her arsenal, she had no more promises to call upon.

Kissenna.

She heard a voice in her weakening mind, familiar. A flap of wings, the flash of a button, and a string of green beads.

CHAPTER TWELVE

Hestra

HESTRA COULD HEAR THE PLOTTING OF THE KING AND his council. When she peeked, she could see their fears flaming from them in every jagged colour, burning like evil lanterns in endless battle with their faith and terror. They would all burn each other, perhaps, if they did not control the fires.

Did she want to help them? Their hopes bound her closer to Arren, entwining them together in the body that had become her home: Fireheart. Sunbringer. Saviour. God.

No. She had her own shrines. She could feel them still, far from the warmth of the king's chest, in the highlands where the families still held to the old ways. Many of them were cold, now their people had fled from the burning.

Then, she felt one warm again, not far to the northeast of Gefyrton. A flame. A hope, if not an offering. Perhaps it was not so bad. Life came back. Her life could come back.

Hestra went to find it. She manifested smaller this time, a spark, a twist of smoke, a floating crumb of heat, in the hearth that had been her shrine.

She knew this home. She had been here more than once, on cold nights where the winter drew in. A small farmstead had stood here for over a hundred years, its family and its children tending the ancient olive trees that grew silver and half-wild on the long slopes.

The trees were gone.

From the hearth, Hestra could float far enough to see a broken window, its shutters blackened with fire, and beyond them rising smoke against a haze of blue sky. The other shutters were broken too, charred from the outside by some great blast. Within, much had burned. The roof had half given way at the left side. The other shrines the family had kept above the mantle, for health and clean water, were torn apart and ransacked, emptied of all offerings.

But a fire had been lit. Hestra was here. The home was not empty.

Three boys and two girls sat in the part of the building that had not fallen. They looked young, but they had swords on their belts, rusted, bent things yes, but swords nonetheless.

Their jackets were red. Talicians. A roving party most like, looking for food or weapons to forage and bring back to the main army.

Two of the youths, a girl and boy, had salvaged a chessboard from the wreckage, burned beneath but mostly whole. They had swapped some of the lost pieces for bits of rock and stone, and a whittled doll. A child's toy.

'Male kwes,' said the girl to the older lad she played with, smiling as she took one of his pieces. *Bad play.* Hestra found herself flaring. This was not their home. This was a place they had burned. But they were barely more than children. Children played. Their faces were mucky with dust, and wan with lack of food. One had lost a finger, it looked like, to frostbite. There was no pot on the fire they had lit in the hearth, only some bones from what looked like a rat. None of them, it seemed, had been supplied with a bow and arrows.

She became aware of quiet sobbing. There was a boy in the corner where a table once had been, sitting with his back to the wall and his head on his knees, his emotion radiating white flames of grief and heartbreak. Another lad sat next to him, rubbing his back wearily as he wept and wept and wept. The comforter spoke softly in Talic:

'Haare, Tomek.' *Be well, Tomek.* Hestra, of course, understood the languages of all peoples who had made prayers to her. Talicia once had many. '*Don't hurt yourself so.*'

'*They didn't have to take my brother,*' said the one called Tomek, voice hoarse and grating. How long had he been sobbing? Or was this the harshness of lungs that had too long been inhaling smoke? '*They didn't have to. I cannot even mourn in the way of our family.*'

'*They wanted Hseth,*' said the boy comforting him. '*He gave his life happily for her when all the fool Middrenites ran away.*' He spat as he said 'Middren', as if it were a poison on his tongue, but the action appeared to be more habit than spite. '*They needed someone to sacrifice.*'

'*Is it truly all for Hseth?*' said the last of them, another girl sitting with her feet up on the sill of another shattered window, looking at the smoking fields and the green mountains. She looked older than the others, but not by much. '*It is her priests who do the taking. They take and take and leave the rest of us with hungry bellies and black lungs.*'

The weeping boy sniffed. '*My aunt said the kerl families cared more for us than the priests do. They killed her for the cause as well.*'

'*Silence,*' said the boy who played chess, glaring up from his pieces. '*Or I will tell Krka Estefin, and you'll be next.*'

'*Even the krkas say such things,*' snapped the girl. '*Most of them are from the old families. Estefin as well.*'

'*Then he chose his loyalty to Hseth wisely. Every sacrifice brings us closer to victory.*'

'*Is this victory?*' She gestured out at the smoke. '*Is this worth it? Are we to burn everything that we claim? The Three who lead this war sit pretty in Talicia, while they send their maddest to do their bidding.*'

The Three. Hestra had heard this term rarely from Hseth. She called her people 'mine' and 'my priests' and 'my loves' before she was killed, not the names they gave themselves. But The Three were the first who pledged loyalty to Hseth over the broken Raider clans, the ones who led her down from the mountains. They were long dead now, replaced by others who took their titles.

'*I just want to go home,*' Tomek whispered, his colours dim and thick with doubt, but soft at the edges with longing.

Then at last the girl at the board spoke. '*I'm so hungry.*'

This made the angry boy snap. He threw the chessboard at the wall, scattering the pieces, and slapped the other player, hard. Hestra flinched.

'This is our home now!' he said as she fell to the side, gasping. 'This is ours. That is what they said when they came for us.'

Came for us? Were they not volunteers? Did they not come on faith alone? Their shining told her no. Their faith was there, bright and vivid, part fear, part fervour, but there were so many shades, so many conflicts, so many terrors for the children at war.

'The old ways are dead. While Hseth is our god, and the priests our leaders, there is no going back.'

Hestra could watch no more of this. There was no hope here to be found. There was nowhere safe, nowhere where love had not turned to fear of fire.

Nowhere but Arren.

CHAPTER THIRTEEN

Elogast

GIVE ARREN HIS CORRUPTED LITTLE DUE, METHSME'S songs were silly things, but people loved them. Elo could go nowhere without hearing her tunes, and her last named all the gods he had killed and called him Sunbringer, Fireheart, Shrinebreaker, God-king.

They could not remove the space in people's hearts where their gods were born, Arren was simply taking up residence there. And, looking for hope and simplicity, the army swallowed it whole. If some thought on it, they didn't care. And to Elogast's chagrin, he did care, but he couldn't think on it.

Instead, he rode with Arren, his days on full display, his nights making and breaking bread with his old companions. Things became easier between them, and the roads were gentler than the rambling pilgrimage trails he had followed with Kissen and Inara last time he had ascended the Bennites.

He loved it. He could not deny that he loved it; the beat of structured days, the chatter of friends over crust and stew, some flirtations, some stories, some flavours of a world he had long departed. Being with Kissen, Skedi and Inara had given him a taste of it. His interactions with the Yether captain, Faroch, Naiala had the strains of camaraderie and a common cause.

But they had not been trained as knights, guards and warriors. They did not fall into rhythm like Benjen and Lotta, and their moody Commander Safidah, who was among those of high rank who weren't noble enough for the council. This was the life Elo had worked for. Had wanted for all his childhood when he had worked so hard to catch up with the youths who had trained almost since they could stand. With Arren at his side, sometimes it felt as if nothing had changed. Elo hated how much he felt at home.

However, despite being offered larger, grander horses, he had refused to give up Legs. A reminder of Kissen, her irreverence, her distrust of power and her faith in herself. The arrow scars in the horse's flanks too, meant Elo kept his head, didn't grow too comfortable. A few months before, most of these knights he rode with would have happily spat in his eye. If Elo ever met Knight Commander Peta coming back from Lesscia, he had no doubt she would stab him through the back for betraying her god-king.

They were close to Gefyrton now, the air dense and warm with summer. Insects and birds rattled out their song from the trees, only just audible over the shifting, stamping, chatting, and laughing of the host of fighters sore on their feet. It was going to be a mast season for the beeches, and Elo could see seed pods growing in great clusters. Legs was enjoying the green leaves that Elo caught for him from the lower branches, when they heard a cry from above, a bird's sound, and looked up. A hawk. Flying low.

No, swooping down.

Then, up ahead, the hammering of hooves.

'Protect the king!' cried General Elemni.

Arren reined in his horse. Tulenne drew his sword, as did Elemni, determined to rectify her failure from the *Silverswift*, but Elo held up his hand.

'It's two horses,' he said calmly. 'Not an army.'

He was right. Two high stallions and riders charged through the Middrenite host ahead, one in colours of indigo and green, another in blue and red: Geralfi and Tiamh.

A whistle came from the captains behind them and the hawk that had been circling dived down onto the arm of its gloved woman handler in Arren's colours and snatched a dead mouse from her hands.

The riders made it through. Elo recognised one of the vanguard who should have arrived at Gefyrton only a few days before. 'W-we didn't dare hope you had followed so quickly. We sent the bird ahead.'

Something was wrong.

'What's happened?' he said. 'Make it quick.'

'The Talicians have breached the eastern gate,' said the Geralfi guard. 'We're holding them, but—'

The generals and commanders were silent for a moment. Their worst fears realised: they were too late.

'King Arren, you should retreat to safety,' said Crolle first. 'If the bridge is breached—'

'They have taken only the eastern gate,' said Arren. 'We can fight back.' He looked at Elo. The great train of warriors was slowing up behind them, and those closest were whispering back, knight to knight to soldier to straggler. What would they do if they panicked? Turn and run? Their cohesion was skin deep at best, and the slightest breath of loss down their necks might rupture it.

What Elo did now would change the momentum of the war. He had been gifted the highest rank in the army besides Knight Commander Peta and the king himself. Handed it on a silver platter.

Now he must earn it.

'Steel yourselves,' he said, lifting his voice. 'Send the runners through the ranks, tell the commands to form and prepare for battle. I want every general at the front lines, ready to be briefed, on the bridge by sundown. We move at pace.'

'Commander general,' Crolle said. 'If the gate is breached, the bridge will not be long to fall as well.'

'The bridge will not fall,' said Elo turning on him. 'Stay with the king.'

'But Ser—'

'I am your commander on the field of battle, Crolle,' said Elo. 'And I do not take insubordination lightly.'

The general bit his tongue. A guard he was, a knight, and no matter which House he represented, he had been trained to obey orders. In council, they might be equals. Here, Elo was in charge.

Elo turned and raised his voice again, projecting certainty, speed.

'Commander Safidah.' She was close by, with her captains: Benjen and Lotta. They all stood as one unit, well organised knights. Even Perin stood tall beside his husband, waiting for Elo's word. 'I need your command at the front immediately. Organise yourselves for defence and battle, the rest will follow.'

Commander Safidah, all dark curling hair and proud bearing, nodded, mounting her horse and barking orders.

'General Tiamh,' Elo said, 'Commanders Yesef and Tulenne.' They sat up straight, knowing what was coming. 'With me.'

He spurred Legs on, not looking back to see if they would follow. They would, because they had to. He was rewarded by the sound of horns, shouting, and shifting hooves. The messengers pulled alongside him on the cart road, their relief palpable as they matched Legs's sure stride.

'Tell me everything,' said Elo, patting Kissen's horse on the neck. Elo would not take him on the bridge, he was not a warhorse, but at least he was keeping his own amongst the rest of them. Elo hoped he was doing the same.

'They reached the east bank a week ago,' said the Geralfi messenger. 'Our fortress towards Arga fell and the surrounding steadings, the olive groves. They burned most of them, and we saw the smoke, but by the time we sent boats upriver to take down the trees, the banks were already occupied. And . . .'

His voice faltered over something he didn't want to say.

'This morning they launched an assault with a battering ram,' said his companion, taking over. 'The east gate was in poor repair, and their advance got one street in before we managed to blockade them.' She paused and glanced at the Geralfi messenger, but did not stop. 'Commander, the Geralfis are preparing to run.'

Elo tried not to curse. He had been relying on the Geralfis holding the bridge till their arrival, and now the nobles were ready to flee after one setback.

He thought fast, moving the Houses and their units in his mind like pieces on a board of chess. Tulenne and Yesef had brought a good number of fighters between them, and other than Crolle they had the most to gain by supporting a retreat west, to their own lands. He would bring their soldiers to the very front and mix them with Safidah's experienced command. That would be enough for a first defensive line without the numbers getting in their own way. The blockade may have felt right to the Geralfi guard, but they should have pushed the Talicians back harder before they let them gain a foothold in the narrow Gefyrton streets. Now both sides would be limited in combat.

A second blockade, Elo would have raised at the bridge's centre point, leaving enough space for the first line to fight, but also a place to plan a fallback should the Talicians break through. Tiamh would command it. He took every opportunity to lick Arren's boots, but Elo suspected he'd turn in an instant if someone offered him better leather. Bringing him close to the fray would elevate his standing, but also put his skin in the game. Stick and sweetness.

During the God War, one of his and Arren's first mistakes had been to keep naysayers and postulators far from the front lines. They had sped from hard battle as fast as their little legs could carry them, pissing themselves along the way. Let them lead from the front and know that there was the rest of the army and the king behind them to stop them running.

Finally, at the west gate, would be the weaponry, the food supplies, reinforcements and a final defensive line before the army, which would camp in the woods beyond the falls.

Three stages of defence. Elo hoped only the first would be used, but the easiest way to lose a war was through a chaotic retreat, and the best way to prevent that was to have a plan.

The roar and mist of the falls rose about them before they reached the gate. It was a cool welcome after the heat of the day. They were not stopped as they hurried along the main road to the western gatehouse. In fact, Elo and the war leaders were paid barely any mind. Folk were instead distracted by their own hurried activities: packing, gearing, trading, shoeing horses and sharpening weapons. Legs let out a friendly whinny, clearly recognising where they were, unaware of the situation they were coming to.

The gates stood shadowed within a cloud of bright, glittering spray, and around it an encampment of hunters' lean-tos had been built out of forest branches, evergreens and moss. Last Elo had seen this side of Gefyrton, the gates had been wide open, bedecked in budding branches and flags. Now, there were no banners, neither Geralfi's nor the king's, and the gates were shut. Instead of music and excitement, there were harried faces and a hum of fearful chatter. Many folk looked like they had their whole lives gathered about them, likely boar and deer hunters or farmers from the other side of the river, where the slopes of the Bennites rose beyond the city like a gathered storm.

Land they had already lost to Hseth's armies.

'Lord Geralfi!' Elo called as Legs charged through the camp. Finally, people started paying them heed. Two or three people cheered by the gate as they saw them riding, shining and sure. Elo was glad he wore his armour. Though, when he reined in as he reached the gate, he had to use all the strength in his legs and back not to let the weight of it tip him forward over Legs's mane. Luckily, his body still remembered how to charge in plates.

As he came to a halt, a pale-faced man Elo vaguely recognised poked his head out of a grand tent: Lord Geralfi of Gefyrton and its surrounding lands was in damaged leather armour, his hair falling wildly out of its tail. Quick behind him were two women, the lady and a wet-nurse with a babe in arms, another young lad old enough to walk, and an older girl. Inara's age. These were in travelling clothes and hunting boots, and Elo glanced around to see horses bridled to packed carriages.

'You're here!' said Geralfi. 'We're saved!'

'Are you going somewhere, my lord?' asked Elo.

The man's face fell and he glanced quickly to the women and children.

'To safety,' said the lady. She wore a sabre and had a crossbow on her back.

'They've broken the eastern gate,' Geralfi agreed. 'I will hand over my guard to you, aside from those we need, but I will take my family west. My wife's House has a fortress still—'

'You will stay where you are needed,' Elogast interrupted, dismounting. He tried not to look at the little girl or the wet-nurse, whose face had crumpled from hope to fear. Geralfi spluttered, but Elo would give no room for contradiction, instead turning to Tiamh.

'Order your guard to have the king's flag raised over the gate. And I want it open. His portrait should be in the gatehouse. Hang it where people can see.'

Tiamh obeyed. The refugees and guards from the camp were standing outside their tents, watching them take control. Unsure who to follow, they would listen to the loudest.

'Commander general?' Geralfi was still reeling. Elo had always seen him as a powerful man with good sense. Only in peacetime, it seemed. 'You cannot . . . just . . .' He looked to Tulenne and Yesef for support.

'Lord Geralfi,' said Elo, 'you are now a general in the king's army. Congratulations on your promotion. This bridge is under my command, and so are you.'

Geralfi looked to his wife, who put her hand on the shoulder of the young girl. Elo was forcing a child's father to stay and face battle or death.

'Lady-heir,' he said, trying for a softer tone, like the tone he used for Inara. 'What's your name?'

'Freia,' she told him nervously.

'I am sorry for the change of plans. Are you good with horses?' The girl nodded, her face pale.

'Then take mine.' He took his helmet from the saddle and held out Legs's reins. 'He is not for the fight, so he is yours to look after well until we win the bridge.'

She looked at him sceptically. 'What's his name?' she asked.

'He's called Legs.'

She smiled. 'That's a funny name,' she said.

'I'm sure he thinks so too.'

She looked to her father. Geralfi nodded, and she took the reins from Elo and Legs followed her obediently to the ostlers with the local horses, cart beasts and farm ponies, corralled by the gate. Safe, as Elo promised.

With her gone, Elo stepped towards Geralfi and lowered his voice. 'Either you rise to your own defence, or you will be remembered as a coward who abandoned his city. The punishment for desertion is a loss of a hand and a week in the stocks. Is that how you want Freia to remember you?'

Geralfi bristled, but after a breath he looked away. 'Aye, commander general,' he said.

'Then come with us into the city. The king is not far behind, and I would have him see you encouraging your guards.'

The gates were already opening. Tiamh's fighters were working with Geralfi's indigo-clad court of lesser nobles, merchants and guards into raising the banners. Commander Safidah's units were arriving as asked, and Elo saw Benjen, stern and hiding his limp. He met Elo's gaze and nodded.

'Dismount!' Elo ordered. 'Follow me in lines of four. Flags high. Yesef, we need drums.'

The city, as they entered in hastily aligned phalanxes, was more alive than Elo had expected. The square that had teemed with festivity and flowers in the spring now hosted a roughly made barricade of barrels and pieces of boat. Arrows were being cut and flighted, helmets repadded, or the dents hammered out. Several injured lay on rush mats being tended to by healers. At least whoever Geralfi had left in command was doing something right.

As they entered the bridge town in their armoured certainty, a true cheer followed them, passing down the main avenue, spinning off into the side streets. Yesef had found the one drummer, who rattled out an old marching tune.

So recently, Elo had watched a march like this from a tangle of roses in Lesscia, planning his vengeance against the Sunbringer. Now he had joined them.

As they passed the first square, Elo didn't pause, but turned to Safidah. 'Commander, stay here, gather what information you can, and prepare for the king's arrival. Report back to me by sundown.'

'Aye, commander.' She peeled away.

The central avenue of Gefyrton was a long straight road, overhung on both sides by wood-and-wash buildings. Most were rammed up side by side, but ginnels and alleys separated others. The occasional cross-streets made clear paths either north to the docks and the rapids, or south to the falls. Even under attack, these were heaving with noise and clamour, people going about their businesses. This city was four centuries old, older than the ruling

Regna line; older than a united Middren. It took more than a siege to stop it moving.

'Last I was here,' said Elo quietly to Geralfi, who walked peach-pale beside him, 'there were rumours that your line still spoke to the gods of the forest. Is that true?'

Geralfi swallowed. 'It was,' he said quietly, pitching his voice so the others could not hear above the noise and clamour.

'Have you tried for their favour?'

He looked at Elo askance, but after a few moments, he nodded.

'And?' pressed Elo, and the lord sighed.

'What can wood gods do against flame?' he said. 'They have not spoken since the northern olive groves burned.'

'And the gods of the bridge and falls?' It was the truce between Gefyr and Sali that had built the city. Their headless statues still held up the foundations.

'Gefyr was killed after the God War by the king's veiga. Sali faded.' Geralfi frowned. 'Does the king allow—'

'No,' said Elo quickly. It seemed Arren was right. The big gods were too great a target after Blenraden. There were none left. If they had shrines enough, they would already have sought refuge in foreign lands.

Tulenne came striding up to Elo from behind, joining in their whispered conversation. 'People are still trading,' he said, brushing down his favoured golden yellow cloak. 'Should we stop them?'

Elo wasn't surprised. The main street was full of energy. Even now, market stalls were operating out of the lower houses, selling spring greens and live chickens, baskets of eggs and smoked fish. Children ran between them, pushing barrels or swiping at rats with switches. Most people appeared to be wearing half of their clothes, ready to run, and sweating in their layers, but one old man was even hawking a cart of ice that must have either come from upriver or down from the mountains not long before the Talicians had.

'You never made it to Blenraden, did you?' said Elo.

'We were tasked with—'

'I remember what you were tasked with, commander,' said Elogast. 'You ran the protection of the west coast.'

Tulenne nodded. 'It was a dull war,' he admitted, though scowled at a snigger from Lord Tiamh.

'The city never died,' said Elo. 'Even in the depths of war, the people of Blenraden still worked, married, traded, lived and prayed.'

'Well it's dead now,' said Commander Yesef. 'And these trading stalls might hinder our retreat.'

'We will plan for that,' agreed Elo. He was already taking note of likely choke points.

As they passed the city's halfway point, Elo felt its rhythm change. The stalls thinned to nothing, and the commonfolk were replaced by guards in Geralfi colours or with ibexes on their jackets, pushing carts of arrows and weapons, or bags of river sand. The buildings clustered closer, lower as they neared the eastern edge, and Elo could smell smoke over the cool water of the falls: pitch and stone, ash and blood.

Soon after, they came to the first real barricade. It was made from heavy crates, furniture, tables, someone's bed, anything heavy. There were barrels of water everywhere, along the edges of the street, high on the shingles of the houses, ready to be tipped over to quench the beginning of a burn. It seemed the Talicians were already using fire on the wooden bridge-city. They must have a death wish.

That would make them harder to fight well.

Beyond the barricades, Elo could see the heights of the gate. Just. The doors had shattered off their hinges, and the gate itself hung in red banners, daubed in darker red with the shape of the bell. Hseth's symbol. Elo hoped it wasn't blood that had marked them, but he suspected it was.

They reached Geralfi guards, many of whom were sitting with their back to their barricades, sharing cups of tea or a pipe. There was a long empty stretch between the makeshift defences and the Talician force, about the length of a good crossbow bolt, and the Talicians had many of those at their disposal, brought to pierce knights' armour.

The two armies were at an impasse. Elo had no doubt that anyone stepping beyond the barricades would be met with a bloody end, stuck with shafts and feathers.

'Lord Geralfi!'

A Geralfi guard was coming forward to meet them, hastily straightening the indigo surcoat that covered his mail and trying to hide his surprise at seeing his lord back on his own bridge. His chin was scratched and bloody, as if it had hit the ground and been dragged several feet, but it was his palms that were bandaged. Raw, Elo suspected, from swinging a sword. His red hair, brighter than Kissen's, was braided back from his face and down his neck, and he wore a cloth cap to protect it from his helm. He stopped in front of Elo and did the Sunbringer salute, fingers splayed across his breast.

'You must be Commander General Elogast,' he said, bowing also to Tulenne, Yesef and Tiamh, who had followed in line. 'Word precedes you. Thank you for those the king sent ahead, I can only apologise that they were too late, and we too ill prepared.'

'This is Captain Larsen Maura,' said Geralfi. 'My wife's cousin of the House Maura. Cousin, tell the commander general about our defences.'

'We are holding strong, and pushing back where we can,' said the captain. 'The ranks of our guard have been bolstered with the help of a hundred from Craier and some local veterans.'

Larsen nodded in the direction of mid-aged folk, some of whom Elo vaguely recognised from the Fisher's Stay. They looked different in their dented armour, and stared at him hard. Likely having difficulty placing the man who had sung a ribald song in their tavern as this knight in blue and steel.

'Craier sent fighters?' said Tiamh, genuinely surprised. 'She's not even here.'

'The lady is honourable,' said Geralfi, putting up a fight for the first time. 'Her lands neighbour ours, and she knows the importance of this crossing. We have fifty from Benin too, though I understand that line is fallen?'

Elo felt his chest stiffen. They had word, also, from Peta, that the House Benin had retreated to Lesscia, their lands overrun; their lord's head, its hair burned away, had been raised on a pike above the wall of his fortress. Benin's lands had been the last of the eastern Houses before Yether. Once more, Peta and Yether had petitioned for the king's aid, but Elo was now glad that he had advised against turning south.

'Good,' said Elo, ignoring Geralfi's question. It was not for Elo to confirm or deny a House's survival, not when the situation was so precarious. 'This is a war we fight together. What weapons have you?'

'Some pikes and spears,' said Larsen, taking the interrogation in his stride, 'but mainly swords, axes, bows.' He touched his own battleaxe. An antique; it looked like it had seen many fights. 'Gefyris are archers, but the Talicians are fearless. They send boats from upriver, burning, sometimes with . . .' his voice faltered. 'With people on them. Sometimes ours, and sometimes their own. But the Talicians . . .' He was competent, but his voice shook, 'they set themselves alight and run into the city, taking people with them as they die.'

Elo put his hand onto Larsen's arm. 'You've done well,' he said. 'We're here now.' Larsen nodded, and Elo turned to Commander Tulenne.

'Take forty fighters to the north docks,' he said. 'Support the command there and see what we can do about the runners.'

Tulenne looked about to protest, glancing at the front gate, his hand flexing on his sword, but he decided against.

'Yes commander general,' he said.

'General Tiamh,' said Elo, and he stood to attention. 'Have your people bringing food and weapons to the front, and help where you can to shore up the blockades. Captain Benjen will assist with choke points going back through the city. Give the Gefyris a rest where you can. Commander Yesef.' Kyaum was staring ahead at the Talician banners on Middrenite land. Though they could not actually see Talicians, they were so close. So very close. 'I want yours at the front,' said Elo, and she nodded. 'Shields up. And relieve the current watch. Captain Geralfi, go with her and encourage your fighters.' Geralfi made a bow to Elo. Only time would tell if he would respect him or hate him, but at least he followed Yesef.

'Larsen,' Elo turned to the captain, who was swaying on his feet. He looked as if he hadn't slept in three days. 'Get some rest,' said Elo. 'We have more troops not far behind.'

'I . . .' Larsen began, then nodded. 'Thank you, but first I need to show you something.'

'Of course.'

Elo left the others to their orders and followed Larsen through the buildings south of the main street, downriver, where they stretched over the thundering waters of the great falls. Here, at the edge, the mist was thick, clinging to skin and sword.

They reached the walkway over the falls. To the west was the forest Elo had come through. He could see the shining battalions of the army, making it at last to the city they had come to defend, but this was not what Larsen wanted to show him.

The captain instead pointed east. On the other side of the waterfall was sheer rockface, as if the mountain had been sheared away by an axe. There, the tanneries and slaughterhouses should have been working, releasing gusts of stink and smoke into the air. Instead, the sky was woven through with thin trails of campfires, hundreds of them down and up the river, back into the distance. The Talicians had brought a great host to this crossing, determined to destroy them all.

And on that bare stretch of the cliff face were bodies.

They had been stripped naked, some hung by the feet, others by the neck or arms; all of them bloody, their skin flayed in places, blackened with flame and terrible burns. The ropes had been carefully aligned so that the bodies hung in the shape of Hseth's bell.

What terrible offering was this?

'Some of them were still alive,' whispered Larsen. 'We've tried to shoot them down, but the fletching gets damp, and the Talicians return fire. Now, they are occupying the part of the bridge where we might have . . . might have reached them.'

He stopped, his eyes etched with exhaustion and horror. How many had he been forced to watch, writhing and twitching, gasping out their last? Most would have been tanners, known to the city, or guards from the eastern fortresses, captured before they could be killed.

Elo knew that look. He had felt it. That heart-crushed deadness that could become a beast of fury and eat him from the inside out.

That was what the Talicians wanted. An act of such cruelty had one purpose: to break their spirit. That was truly the test of an army's mettle, one against the other. Not which was biggest, or strongest. The truth that finished a war was that of faith. Whose would break first? Middren's? Or Talicia's?

Elo understood a little more why Arren had turned to clerics and song, sacrifices and godhead. Why he gave them something to hold on to, in the face of a god whose priests did . . . this.

Elo wished he could be like a god, and impart some strength to Larsen. He thought of Skedi and came up with a lie. Not a lie, a story. A hope.

'I swear to you, captain,' Elo said, hoping the lie would take, that he would believe him. That he would believe himself. 'We will stop Talicia crossing the river. We will win.'

CHAPTER FOURTEEN

Skediceth

THE COLOURS ON THE *SILVERSWIFT* WERE TENSE, THE shades of distant storms, purple and bruising.

Inara's weren't hard to read: her fear was black and hung like smoke. Arlo was dead, and another crewmate whose name Skedi could not recall had been so badly burned they had left her with a medic from another ship. Three more crew were injured, and Aleda would not stop nursing the blistering on her arm and muttering about getting involved with foolish wars of gods.

'Kissen will be all right, Inara,' said Skedi for the hundredth time, sitting in the porthole in the warmth of the sun setting over the water. 'She's indestructible.'

'She's not.'

Inara had been trying to mend the chipped bits of Kissen's leg, filing them down and rubbing the bubbles out of the boiled leather. Skedi was fairly certain that Kissen didn't care what her leg looked like, as long as it worked, but doing something made Inara feel better.

The veiga had woken twice but had muttered in Talic and Middric. Sometimes names that neither of them knew, sometimes names they did. Tidean, Mell, Lunsen, Inara, Osidisen, Yatho, Telle, Pato.

'It's my fault,' said Inara. 'We should have listened to Mama.'

Skedi shook his head, shivering at the thought of that great god.

'I've never imagined a god who hated humans,' he said. Was that true? Skedi himself had once seen humans as weak, manipulable. Could he have become like Satuan?

'Or hated things like me,' said Inara quietly.

Skedi sat up. 'You're not a thing.'

'He said I was a monster.' She sighed and put Kissen's leg down. 'Maybe he's right. I've killed gods and people. Hurt them. Let them die.'

Skedi thought back to what Kissen had said to him. *I'll give her honesty; you give her love.* And if Kissen wasn't around? Who would give her honesty? Could he change his own nature to be what she needed? He was just a god.

At least he could try.

'You're still human, Inara,' said Skedi. 'With room to change and grow. That's what humans do.'

It wasn't a lie; it wasn't a truth either. It was something different. She looked at him with troubled eyes, and what little of his heart there was broke for her.

There was a knock at the door, and Inara tensed. 'Come in,' she said.

It was Lertes.

'Captain,' said Inara, then remembered herself and stood respectfully. Lertes nodded at her.

'Is the godkiller awake?' he asked.

Inara frowned, moving defensively in front of Kissen.

'She'll wake soon,' lied Skedi, but the captain's colours didn't look aggressive, instead they were soft carnelian, like a polished gem.

'Well,' he said, 'when she does.' He held out a cloth-wrapped bundle, and Skedi recognised Kissen's cutlass. 'Rhiyande found it,' he said, unwrapping the pommel, which had been bound in green. 'Had it ground back and reshaped. And I've asked Graemar to make her some more of that cool broth.'

'I thought you all hated her,' said Inara.

Lertes scratched his scruffy chin. The lines of his eyes were deep cut, like cracks in the surface of the earth. 'I do not hold with killing gods,' he said. 'But no sailor forgets a debt. It isn't our way.'

Kissen had drawn Satuan away from the crew on the cliffs.

Whether she had intended it or not, that act of courage might just have won them to her. At least a little.

'Lertes?' came Lessa's voice from the doorway. She was stood there holding a bowl, her brows raised in surprise at seeing him. The captain frowned at her, his colours darkening with anger.

So Kissen had won some respect, but Lessa had won the captain's ire. Skedi understood that he blamed her for putting his crew in danger. Worse: putting his beloved wife at risk.

'You best still refer to me as captain, my lady,' he said. 'In case we forget who makes decisions for the safety of this ship.'

Lessa narrowed her eyes, just slightly. 'Yes,' she said. 'We best not forget the order of command.'

Before, only Aleda had truly grated at Lessa's hold over the *Silverswift*. Now, his body stiffened at her comment, the reminder that the ship was still hers. But then he softened, and stood aside to let her pass.

'I appreciate what you're trying to do, captain,' he said quietly, calling her such for the first time in Skedi's hearing. His words were barely audible over the creak of the ship as it dipped and shifted on the waves, sending the light from the porthole dancing over the walls. 'I backed you when Commander Samin gave you this ship for saving her life. You were but a child, rash sometimes, but decisive. Different. I gave my word to serve you, and I will keep it, as long as you keep yours to us.'

Lessa passed the bowl to Inara, who was keeping quiet, her eyes darting between her mother and her captain, the one who owned the ship and the one who ran it. The lady turned back to Lertes, hands on her hips, chin high.

'I have kept my word,' she said. 'I have protected you from attack, from treachery, from poverty, and from gods. I turned you honest traders, rich ones, while keeping you your freedom. You can remind Aleda of that. I assume she is the source of these mutterings?'

Lertes swallowed, but made no denial. 'Then how is it that two are lost in one day at Iska?' he said. 'Our place of safety? Of rest? You have entangled us in the business of gods and kings when we are but commonfolk and cut-throats. I warn you now that they do not think it right.'

Skedi shrank, sharing a glance with Inara. She caught her breath.

'We are fighting a war,' said Lessa.

'It's not our war, lady.'

'It will be if we lose.' Lertes swallowed at the certainty in her tone. 'I told you of Blenraden, I have seen what less powerful gods can do when they have blood in their teeth. I am loyal to my crew, those on this ship, and those on my land. You agreed that you would all be one and the same.'

Skedi stretched his wings, trying to think of a way to ease the tension, but he did not know enough about Lessa's and Lertes's lives before Inara to come up with the right lie.

'It is as you say,' said Lertes at last. 'Just be careful, captain, that you do not forsake this crew for loyalty to another.'

He glanced towards Inara, briefly, but then nodded to Lessa and ducked out through the door. Lessa watched him go for a moment, her brow troubled, but then consciously tried to smooth it, to cover her feeling. Another little white lie. Skedi felt it in his heart.

'I never expected to be reprimanded by the captain I employ,' she said wryly, turning back inside and putting a touch of humour carefully into her tone.

She's hiding something, said Inara, straight into Skedi's mind. He pricked up his ears.

Not exactly, Ina, he said. *She's pretending she's not afraid so you won't be.*

Inara sighed.

'Any change?' her mother asked, nodding towards Kissen.

'Not yet,' said Inara. The wounds of Kissen's flesh were healing, but they did not know how far injury had spread inside her. The veiga looked more vulnerable than Skedi could ever have imagined. When the light moved through the porthole, he could see the skin peeling around her neck and face, and her head and arms were covered in scratches. It was too hot in the cabin, too pressing, but all the seawater in the world was not enough to keep it cool. Occasionally, he fanned her with his wings, which seemed to ease her breathing. He was starting to think that he quite liked her alive.

Lessa sighed. 'I'm so sorry. I should have been better prepared.'

'I was the one who angered him,' said Inara. 'You said to stay away.' She put the cool broth on the floor. Seaweed floated in it, along with some lumps of softened grain. Its spoon was an oyster shell, and Skedi had heard the crew talk of how drinking from it was good for healing, as it was the symbol of the Curlish god of medicine.

'I still thought he would help us.' Lessa sat down on the edge of Kissen's bed as she spoke. 'I was wrong.' She frowned at the veiga as though she was a riddle she couldn't solve.

'I underestimated her,' the lady added at last. 'She could have saved herself, but she saved us. Me. I owe her my life now, as well as yours.'

'She helped me,' said Inara, sitting back on the stool she had brought in, beside the bucket of boiled salt water she had been using to bathe Kissen's burns. 'Before she even knew me. Her sisters too.' She hugged her knees.

'Oddly generous for a woman who kills other people's gods.'

Inara frowned and looked somewhat like her mother in doing so. The ship creaked again, Skedi could hear the straining of the sails to catch wind enough to keep them going south. Irisia was not far away now.

'Her family was killed by Hseth,' said Inara. 'When she was small. A sacrifice. No one else survived.'

Lessa was silent, then managed a very quiet, 'Oh.'

'Do you know what he meant,' Inara said, changing the subject, 'by breaking the faith in Hseth?'

Lessa paused, then hummed under her breath. 'Something King Arren does understand is that nations are built on faith. If not in a god, then in whoever is in control. Armies are much the same. But it takes more than one action, one moment. Breaking faith in Hseth will take more than a single battle, and even then it may not be enough.' She shook her head. 'Without gods on our side, without being able to use briddite to fight Hseth herself, I don't know what we can do against the faith of thousands.'

'Last time . . .' said Skedi, 'Kissen dragged Hseth into the sea. Like Satuan.'

Lessa nodded. 'Elemental gods dislike their opposite. She's clever.'

'But she used briddite on her hands,' said Inara. 'Had blessed water from the river god to stop her getting burned and used a promise from a sea god to kill her.' She bit her lip. 'What about Yusef?' she asked. 'Gods can hurt gods.'

Lessa smoothed her hair back from her face. For a moment, Skedi saw a flurry of her colours, whites and blues, spikes and swirls. Complications.

'I hope to ask his help,' she said. 'But . . . he will be a different god now. A Restish god, and most of his priests are from that land. If I cannot convince Restish to turn against their allies in Talicia, and Irisia to declare for us, then I do not think he will be minded to support us.' She gazed towards Skedi. 'Particularly as last time I called for his aid to Middren, it got him killed.'

Skedi shivered. His memory of his history was as broken as Yusef's shrines. He remembered fragments of wild gods, storms, and churning water. 'You asked him to fight in Blenraden?' he said. He wondered if he should feel angry, that it was this that had got him killed, but he didn't; it was a different life.

'Not to fight,' said Lessa. 'To help people escape. He owed me, and he came.'

Inara chewed her lip. 'Did you love him?' she asked. In her childhood, she had not been deeply curious about the other parent who had made her, only since she had begun to discover her power, her godhead.

Lessa looked towards Skedi.

'I do not remember him, my lady,' he said, wondering what that look was for, what she wanted him to say, or what lie she wanted him to tell.

'I adored him,' said Lessa softly. 'He took an interest in me. I helped negotiate the treaty between Commander Samin's ships and Restish. To him, I had left safe haven for a harsher life, and as with all gods, he found a contradiction to his nature . . . curious. I was,' she crossed her hands on her lap, purposefully keeping her posture calm, open, 'I was a curiosity.'

Skedi shrank a little in the porthole. This was perhaps not a happy story. What had he imagined? Some secret romance? The idea had seemed so strange, even when he understood what Inara was.

Humans and gods were different. Humans were made from blood and dust, gods from love and faith . . . were they meant to meet?

'He would come to the ship's shrine at night,' said Lessa. 'We would speak over games of tactics, talk of the history he had seen. He taught me how to hide my emotions from gods, how to navigate by starlight, how to give hope through lies and tales.' Skedi ruffled his feathers. 'I was enthralled, and perhaps so was he.'

'You don't sound too happy about it, Mama,' said Inara.

'I wasn't many years older than you, Ina,' said Lessa. 'Just nineteen. It's easy to charm a child who knows little of the world's ways. The more I saw you grow, the more I questioned whether a centuries-old god had a right to lie with a woman so young, whether he intended to get me with child. If I was just . . . another game. Despite how much I wanted it, desired it even . . . over time I wondered . . .' She cleared her throat, and smoothed her trews over her legs, her hand resting over where the scar cut through her thigh.

The boat sang its song of the sea; dipping and dancing, it reached a trio of waves. Light slipped through the porthole, then away again into shadow.

'I saw him die,' Lessa continued. 'Even a great god can be overwhelmed by smaller divinities. And it took away the conversation I wanted to have. The questions I needed to ask.' Lessa frowned at the bowl of briny soup on the floor.

'I'm sorry, Inara,' she said. 'I spent years trying to think of a better story than a childish infatuation, and growing regret.' Then she winced. 'Not you, Inara. I don't regret you. I chose you. You were so good and so smart, so kind. I—'

'It's all right to regret,' said Inara, and her mother quietened. 'I know that feeling. I regret never telling you about Skedi. I thought I was protecting you both, but I know now you would have helped me. I regret some things I did. People I hurt.' Her mouth tugged down at the corners. She didn't feel like the girl Lessa spoke of. The good girl. The smart girl. The innocent. Skedi knew this.

'I regret not revealing myself,' he added lightly. 'I could have taught you both some nicer lies than the ones you had to keep.'

He was trying to lighten the weight on Inara's colours, make her laugh, and she did, just a little. Lessa, too, managed a smile.

'Mama,' said Inara. 'Do you . . . still love me?' Her voice became small as she spoke, and she quailed into herself, her knees tightening up to her chin. 'Even though . . . even though I'm not good any more?'

Lessa stared at her in surprise, and Skedi shrank himself down to the size of a mouse, staying very still. He shouldn't be there. This was not for him.

The lady moved towards Inara, putting a hand on her knee, squeezing, reassuring. 'Ina, you are, and always will be, my greatest love.'

Inara looked at her mother, and Skedi knew what she was thinking: the colours. The truth of Lessa that she kept tucked away, hidden from gods. Hidden from her.

Don't lie to her, said Skedi, gently, to Inara. *Tell her what you need. Give it a name.*

Inara swallowed. 'I need to see it,' she said.

'See what?'

'The feelings . . . that you hide from gods. Mama, I need to *see* that you love me.'

Lessa did not understand at first, but slowly her face changed. 'You have a god's sight,' she said, and Inara nodded, her chin and brow creased.

If Kissen had shown her colours when she needed to, in the king's palace, so could Lessa.

Lessa took Inara's hand, as she had done in the waters of Iska, and held it. Then she closed her eyes, breathing in, and finally breathed out.

Slowly, like the breaking of the day, beams of colour burst from her. A ripple of aquatic blue, perfect, salted, bright. A proud and certain edge of green hope and steely anger, the Craier colours. Her home on the sea, and her choice of home on land.

Then, russet browns, with reddish-gold tints like light through a spring river, like the turning dark of leaves, like polished wood, or the brown of jasper stones and amber set in gold.

Like the colour of Inara's hair, and her eyes in sunlight.

The brightness of Lessa's feeling filled the little cabin, shining over the walls, bathing her daughter in it. And Inara's eyes filled with tears, seeing for the first time what her mother felt for her. All the colours of her love were her daughter, her home, and the sea.

A cough came from the bed, and a turn, then a hiss of swearing. Kissen cracked open her eyes.

'Why,' she muttered, her voice hoarse, 'does everything *fucking* hurt again?'

Her gaze landed on Skedi, tiny and unobtrusive in his porthole seat, then she glanced over at Lessa and Inara.

'Oh shit,' she said, seeing their clasped hands. 'Did I ruin a moment?'

Lessa's colours flashed a strange bluish grey, and then disappeared again before Skedi could read the emotion. Irritation? Attraction? Sometimes it was hard to tell with humans.

The colour was, however, not far from the shade of Kissen's eyes.

'You're awake,' said Inara, jumping to her feet and letting go of Lessa's hand.

'You're all alive,' said Kissen, her head sliding back on the pillow. Through split lips, she smiled. 'Next time you try to fight fire with fire, Lady Craier, plan it better.'

CHAPTER FIFTEEN

Inara

FIGHT FIRE WITH FIRE.

Skedi had offered to keep vigil beside Kissen so that Inara could sleep. Despite her grumblings, the veiga had been too tired to protest too hard. Her breathing sounded painful.

She had been right. By going to Satuan, Lessa had been trying to find a god powerful enough to challenge Hseth. Fire with fire.

But Inara didn't need to go to find them. She could call them to her.

She pulled a piece of cloth out of her pocket and unwrapped it carefully. She could not see anything in the dark, but as the cloth finished unfolding, she could discern the faintest glow around a long, dark hair.

Aan.

She had taken the piece of hair back from Kissen, and washed it of the godkiller's blood. It had been enough to summon Aan's power to show the invasion of Talicia, but with Inara's strength, perhaps it would be enough to hear her speak.

Aan, she spoke in her mind, curled on her little cot. *Great goddess of the river.*

The hair in her hand cooled, she felt it like a wire in her palm, then it frosted over.

Ah, child, she heard the god's gentle voice. *Only you could call me from so far without a shrine.*

So quickly she had come. Inara gripped the hair, her heart pounding with excitement.

Kissen passed on your message, said Inara. *The king marches.*

Even now, I fear it is too late, my unraveller. The Talicians break shrines wherever they go, and replace them with their god's bell. Middren's forces are outnumbered, and already far behind the play.

Inara swallowed. It was one thing to hear it supposed, another to hear it from a god. Aan was an ancient god, and powerful. Water, Hseth's opposite. Surely . . .

We need the gods, Aan, said Inara. *We need you.* She imagined her surrounded by water, black hair spilling out across the depths, her round and supple body soft as snow-covered hills. Aan had one of Inara's hairs too, surely she would be willing to help.

Aan chuckled bitterly, her voice like the sound of bubbles rising through meltwater.

I know, my dear, but the king will not summon us. Will not build our shrines, will not bend his pride. And it would take the combined strength of every puny god left in Middren to make even a dent on Hseth's flame. Even then, without a great offering, it would not be enough. No god wishes to die fighting beyond their strength.

Inara's heart sank. She had thought she was so clever, so powerful. She thought she could come to her mother, answers in hand.

I am sorry, halfling, said Aan. *Only one god has the potential now to gain enough power to fight her.*

Inara swallowed. *Who? Me?* She had barely been able to hold Satuan.

You? The amusement in Aan's voice was humiliating.

Yusef?

No, child.

Fire with fire. Hestra. The king. Inara clenched her fist, her heart hammering. No, not the king. That cruel, burning bastard was as bad as Hseth. *He is not a god.*

Not yet. Aan's voice was fading, Inara's will not enough to hold her so far away from her shrine. *Not yet.*

The hair turned warm again, the ice melting into Inara's palm. It retained its shine of the goddess, but the voice was gone.

Inara threw herself back on her sweaty sheets, nursing wounded pride and fierce anger. 'He is not a god,' she whispered. 'He can't be.'

But Hestra was.

She would not be defeated. She slipped out of her own cabin onto the darkened deck, the only light a lantern that hung from the aft above the helm. The breath of the salted air was warm, as if from the lungs of an ancient god, and all around, the sky and sea were a cavern of darkness. It felt as if the ship was a lone thing in the world, and all the rest was night. She shivered.

At least the crew didn't seem to mind. Because it was cooler and fresher than belowdecks, most slept on deck as they moved further south, ready to take up their posts should they be attacked or hit a sudden squall.

Inara glanced up past the lantern to the ship's wheel. The helm for the night was holding it in place with a stick, a scarf over his left eye to keep his night vision keen. She recognised Glib: a quiet fellow who talked about sweets from all the different lands he had been.

'Evening little captain,' he said.

'Just going to the latrines,' said Inara quickly.

'Your bowels are your business, kid.' His uncovered eye slid back up to the horizon. 'And we call 'em "heads".'

Inara stole a peek at the shrine to Yusef, but after speaking with her mother she wasn't sure how to feel about the great god. And did not want to try calling where anyone could see her.

She went down the ladders to belowdecks, listening carefully and hearing just the snuffling of sleep, farts, or some nasty grunting, as well as the mournful bleating of the animals further below. She put her hands over her ears and crept through the hammocks and pallets, creeping around the colours till she found the ladder to the storage, brig and galley, then followed it down.

She never came down here. Graemar kept a tight kitchen and disliked anyone nosing at his work. The door slid open to tidy counters, and the scent of oats, pickles, salted and smoked fish, as well as the sweet warmth of the oven's raked-over coals. The smell of manure was stronger, too, though the animals were another deck down. Inara was glad Kissen had not brought Legs. She could not have imagined him trapped in the stinking dark below the waves.

No one was sleeping in the galley, not even Graemar. Too hot outside of the winter season. No colours of dreaming shone in the dark.

It was strange to be sneaking around without Skedi. He could be so reliable when he wanted to be, but he would not approve of this, and she didn't want to frighten him.

She felt her way towards the oven door. It had two handles on a board of fitted wood, its inner edge was covered with a blackened and hammered sheet of metal. She heaved it out, and pushed it to the side. The faintest of embers greeted her, carefully buried in a grave of ash so the heat would be preserved but the sparks kept dormant. She had read more than one little tale as a child of a galley cook annoying a divinity who burned their ship to dust.

There were no gods here that Inara could see, but there were symbols carved inside the oven. Superstitious folk hoping for the luck of gods, creating little shrines, the tiniest thread that connected them to the god themselves.

Should she? Hestra was her enemy. They had fought each other already.

But Kissen had nearly died. Elo was fighting a war that even Aan thought they would lose, and they still weren't in Irisia. She could not be so useless, she could swallow her pride, just a little.

She clambered up to kneel in the oven's mouth and picked up one of the cooler bits of charcoal to make her own drawing inside its walls. Two lines down, one line across. A hearth.

Inara uncovered a glowing ember from the ashen pile. Hestra would take more enticing than Aan, so she pulled a hair from her head, and fed it to the flame. It curled and fizzled with a twist of acrid smoke; a paltry offering, but it was something.

Hestra, she called with her will, her intent, her need.

She wouldn't come, Inara was almost sure of it. But she was also sure the god could not resist the lure of a new half-shrine.

Hestra, please.

The oven's scent changed to pine sap and burning straw. Inara's skin prickled.

You dare *to summon me?*

Hestra's voice was like the sizzle of steam off hot coals, her greeting less pleasant than Aan's. But she had still come. What had brought her? Gods did not appear with every offering. Hestra could have felt the slight tug of her prayer and ignored it. There was something, too, in her voice. Something tender, something vulnerable.

We spoke with Satuan, the smith god, said Inara.

Did that grumbling piece of rot have anything useful to say?

He tried to kill us, said Inara.

A small laugh echoed around the oven, smoke roiling out from the coals. *Good.*

Inara had a vision of Hestra sending an inferno smashing into the sides of the galley. Bursts of flour, hipgin, sailcloth, rope, and blackfire, and the ship would be shattered from the inside out. No one would survive. Inara held her breath until the laughter stopped. Eventually, it did.

What do you want from me? said Hestra, when Inara gave her nothing else to gloat over. *I am small and old, watching shrine after shrine, home after home, disappear into nothing. Hseth's fires burn even me. Do you know what gods are like without worship, girl? Do you know what it is like to fall?*

I do, said Inara. *I have seen them. Shadows of nothing. Dangerous nothing. Some power, no will, clinging to life till someone ends them.*

Hestra fell silent, perhaps detecting the threat in Inara's tone.

Hestra, you can be more than that. Inara breathed out. She loathed the king with every part of her being. He had taken so much from her and regretted none of it. But her mother had chosen him, Elo had chosen him; Kissen had saved him.

Was she going to be a monster, or a fighter?

Her faith can break too, Hestra, said Inara. *This is what Satuan told us. To break their faith. And Aan said we need a god to defeat her . . . you—*

For a moment, the fire sparked upwards, and Inara saw Hestra in the flames. A twig-like being, built from branches, but she looked different. She had flesh like a film, floating over her bones, her hair had curled slightly. And her eyes . . . her eyes were paler than they had been.

I am not a candle to be held to Hseth, she said. *You are a meddler, a thing that doesn't belong. Do not try and entice me with your offerings. Hseth has a thousand deaths to give her strength, I have stolen wishes from a half-dead king. Only death can match Hseth's strength.* She smiled, white bones and sparks for teeth. *Perhaps yours would do. Would you offer me that?*

Inara swallowed, and the smile dropped.

See? You want to die as little as I do. At least I have accepted my fate.

Grey smoke blew out of her mouth in a sigh, her hair curling in orange embers. *It is a shame, but the king is one battle away from defeat. Even if he wins this, then it will be the next and the next and the next until all has gone to ruin.*

This was useless. The gods had nothing for her but riddles and bitterness. Inara had to cover up the embers or the smoke would wake the crew.

Inara clenched her fists. *We will beat her. You can watch.*

The god laughed, diminishing into a flicker of sparks, a flame, an ember. But she gave one last whisper as she departed. *Despite it all, you are not the best liar, beast.*

CHAPTER SIXTEEN

Elogast

ELOGAST WAS RESTING IN HIS ARMOUR, LEANING AGAINST a wall in one of the houses they had cleared and moved into; a safe place to sleep. It had been two weeks since they had arrived in Gefyrton. With appalling regularity, flaming boats arrived from upriver with cargos of screaming, burning bodies. But Tulenne had succeeded in his task of holding them off, sinking them from afar. Very few made it to the docks, lucking into the right streams that allowed the vessels to be carried forward without shattering on the rapids.

Elo didn't know which he hated more, the smell of burning flesh, or the sight of the rotting corpses on the southern cliff face. Even hardened fighters couldn't bear to keep the south watch where the bodies fell, piece by piece, to be set upon by river rats where they landed.

Still, Arren had tried calling him back to the west gate, to rest in safety, but Elo had refused. Politely this time. He would not abandon his post.

And they had reached a rhythm, beating the Talicians back with planned assaults, step by step, pushing them towards the gate.

But when he heard the first horn – three sharp blasts – Elogast knew he had grown too confident in that rhythm: a Talician attack had broken through.

He opened his eyes. The darkness around him flickered with

lamplight, and so did the sky beyond the windows. Night had fallen, and the city was on fire.

He leapt to his feet, not even pausing to shed his dreams. 'Up! Up!' he cried.

Everyone camped near him rattled to their feet, already clad in whatever armour they had. Benjen's weary eyes met Elo's, and he drew his sword.

'With me!' ordered Elo.

He led them out of their shelter and back onto the main street, where they entered chaos.

The south side of the town was aflame over the falls.

'Commander!' Perin was running up to him through the dark, blood on his chest and a horn around his neck. He must have sounded the alarm. 'They climbed down the southern face and up onto the bridge,' he said. 'Six buildings are burning. We've sent fire crews . . .'

The side with the bodies, where the soldiers hated watching, where no other attacks had come. Where they had expected the raging of the water and the slick great beams of the undercity to deter any foolish climber. How many Talicians had died falling before they made it high enough to set the buildings aflame?

'Leave the fire,' said Elo, though he could feel its heat. 'Gather to the centre.'

'Elo, we can't let the bridge burn,' said Benjen urgently.

Elo pulled on his helmet where it sat snug on his braids. He could see now how it would play out. While they were distracted between dousing the flames and finding who had lit them, the Talicians would charge in and split their force, breaking them at the centre and routing them in panic. Panic would end them.

'They mean to scare us,' he said, striding not south to the water, but east towards the gate. 'Few of them could have climbed up without being spotted. Sound the gather for the centre and let the water deal with the fire. We have barrels of it on the roof, on the bridge supports, and a waterfall around us.' He put his hand on Benjen's shoulder. 'You asked me to lead you,' he said. 'Trust me then. My life, my blood, my heart.'

Benjen swallowed, and nodded. 'Sound the gather, Sergeant Perin,' he said. 'That's an order from our commander.'

Perin hesitated a moment longer, but lifted his horn and sounded a long blast, then a second rising at the end.

'To me!' Elo cried, starting to run now as the others gathered. Middrenite fighters were gathering from all sides, from the buildings, from the alleys, from the inns and wherever they had slept for the night. 'To the gate! Form a battalion, leave the fire!'

Yesef, Safidah, and a riot of House guards, knights and common soldiers spilled into the centre, shifting aside the barricade and forming lines of four, quickly becoming a fighting unit still protected by the blockade on either side. Somehow, Elogast had managed to cobble together some coherence from Arren's patchwork army, but how long would it last? The flames were roaring from the south, and he flinched as a building collapsed, fire chewing through the beams. What if he was wrong? What if the fire took hold? What if his instinct led the city to burn?

No. He was right. To his relief and terror: he was right. Through the red flags of the eastern gate, charged the Talicians in wild force, blood and charcoal smearing their faces, bells shining in their hair. They carried torches that seared an orange glow out of the night of mist and smoke, as if they came shrouded and veiled. Most held shortswords, but many had axes, picks, clubs and makeshift weapons. They ran without formation, without sense. Was that a child? An old woman? It did not matter, it only mattered that they were enemies.

'Lock in line!' Elo screamed. 'Shoulder to shoulder. Hold!'

Somehow, those that heard him carried forward the command. 'Hold!'

The Talicians faltered, seeing through the barricades not chaos but an organised defence.

'For Sunbringer!' Elo yelled, locking himself into the centre of the battalion as rows formed up behind him.

'Sunbringer!' called Benjen to his right, Elseber to his left, and another whom Elo did not know. 'Fireheart!'

Elo could feel the terror of the fighters around him. It clung to him like sweat, prickling across his skin. Cilean, Lotta, Perin, Larsen, Ainne, – he could see them in the phalanx. Elo had made combined units, teaching them common practices, common goals.

Together, they were stronger.

'Brace!'

The Talicians broke around them, howling as they tried and failed to smash through their wall of defence. The fighters at the edge held up shields and planks and whatever they found, and the second one in thrust their swords through the gaps, lacking as they were in pikes and spears. Like sparks spat from an errant fire, the Talicians were extinguished against the wall of iron.

Elo couldn't think of the enemy as people. Not the girl whose face he tore open with a strike from his longsword, not the old man with a splintered spear and the hungry eyes who was still writhing over the stomach wound Elo had left him. He wished he was fighting gods. It was easy to see the wolf that tore through their ranks in Blenraden as a nightmare, a dream. The skeletal horse, the stag-headed god of war, the god of the hunt with his screaming mouth and endless arrows.

At least each one didn't remind him of Kissen, of Ina, of Benjen, of Arren.

Elo's arms grew weary with the strike of sword in flesh, his ears filled with guttural cries as humans found their death upon a blade.

The flames on the southern roofs were fading. Wet wood didn't burn well. Not without Hseth. And they hadn't summoned her yet.

They had a chance here. And Elo would take it. 'Forward!' he yelled, and he heard Perin's horn behind him picking up the order with a sharp blast then a long.

The night grew hot and thick with screams as they pushed into the Talician onslaught, heading back towards the gate. All was panic and shadow. Arrows flew down from either side as the attack intensified. Ringing bells from beyond the gates, and indiscernible howled orders drove the Talicians onwards, stumbling onto the boards to meet their end.

A sparse few made it past. They sprinted into the shadows of the alleys to the north and south, where they would soon be picked up by the archers on the roofs: Tiamh's second line of defence. Tulenne's contingent guarding the north docks would protect against further surprises.

'Forward!' Elo cried again. As one force, they moved. Elo felt the shivering of the bridge's timbers as a hundred feet shifted. *Forward.* A step. Another, another. How many more till the gate? If they took advantage of the Talician fear and confusion, could they take the city? Take back their land? Push the enemy back to the Bennites to starve?

'Forward!'

A cheer went up from the Middrenites as they realised they were moving further and further beyond their forward barricade. Let them cheer. Soon they would feel what Elo felt: the bodies beneath his feet, the bones of fallen friends and enemies. With luck, they were dead already.

No stopping. Forward: towards the gate, towards reclamation. Whenever a gap formed, a Middrenite filled it, so that the Talicians would never know how many they had killed, how many remained. They pressed further onto the occupied bridge, and Elo could hear the panicked cries of Talician krkas, possibly even their priests.

Forward.

Slow step by slow step, strike by strike Every minute felt like aeons as they took on the fight. Elo was rooted in the storm, people he trusted at his side. His people.

Hope, he felt it. They were going to take the gate. Gefyrton was theirs.

But something was wrong. It shouldn't be this easy. He saw no priests, no kerls, no statues of Hseth that Kissen and the reports from the south and east had described.

This couldn't be all of their main force.

'Benjen,' Elo hissed to his companion, spitting sweat and blood from his mouth. 'Take ten to the docks. Make sure Tulenne is maintaining their defence.' What if their northern defence had heard the horns and come to the centre? What if there was no one watching the banks?

'Aye commander,' said Benjen, understanding. He turned to Lotta, Ainne and Perin behind them, whispering the need for a swift exit from the formation.

Elo glanced behind him, trusting Elseber to his left to defend his side while the gaps left by Benjen and the others were filled.

She had a slash across her face, but grinned as she stabbed a Talician in the armpit.

Elo could see Kyaum Yesef fighting alongside the others as if she had been born with a sword in her hand. Good! Geralfi was not far from her, several rows back in a short tabard of green, scared but there. Elo was relieved, his doubts lifting. Tulenne had stayed in post.

No, there! Twenty rows back: a cloak in shining white and yellow. Too fine for a common soldier. Elo didn't need to see the face beneath the helm to understand that the lord had decided he'd had enough of missing wars.

Fool! Why would the Talicians attack on two sides, when they could attack on three? So far, the fireships they had been sending downriver had been small, but under the cover of the trees of the east bank, who knows what kind of rafts they might have built?

'Captain Benjen!' Elo cried out. He had to tell Benjen and the others they might be running into a fight. 'Benjen!'

But Benjen was too far away to hear him over the noise of the battle. His group broke out of the protection of their formation, heading for a side alley towards the docks.

A hail of crossbow bolts flew from the black.

Cilean died instantly. Benjen threw himself to the ground, but Lotta saw what was coming and did not duck, or hide, but moved in front of Perin. As Arren had done for Elo when they faced the god of war.

A bolt took him in the throat, the chest, the hand, piercing through his armour and slamming him into his husband.

Perin caught him, falling back.

'Lotta?' Elo saw, rather than heard, the question. Only then did Perin understand what had happened. Only then, with his husband already dead in his arms, did he realise that Lotta had used his last breath to protect him. Perin screamed, but Benjen and Ainne were already back on their feet, dragging him back, back to safety.

'No!' Perin cried. 'No, Lotta! I can't leave him!'

More arrows came. Benjen pushed Perin down as a second wave slammed into the Middrenite force. Elo threw an arm around Elseber and dragged her head down, but the arrow meant for her struck the man behind through the cheek. Blood-splatter hot on his neck where the helm and his armour met.

'Split up!' cried Elo. 'Left flanks, defend the docks!'

It was too complex an order to understand: a bare few obeyed before a charge from the north took their advance in the side, and tore a hole in them.

Elo could hear screaming all around him as the Talicians split their phalanx into front and back, exactly what he had hoped to avoid. He had lost sight of Benjen, of Elseber, of anything except sweat and bodies, blood and death. Their front had been crushed into a melee.

A sword glanced off his chestplate, tearing away some of the lapis of his lion. An axe slid, sparking down the side of his helm, while a fist or a hammer – he couldn't tell – slammed into the underside of his chin, where it was unguarded. But he fought back, sword stabbing anyone, anything in red cloth, with bells in their hair and murder in their intent. He could see hands and bodies, wide eyes and Talicians howling, screaming.

The Middrenites around Elo fought back, rallying after their surprise and pushing out of the crush. Unlike the Talicians, many were veterans of the God War, no strangers to terror or clever strategy. But they couldn't hold for long against such a hammer blow. How many more of the enemy would be coming from the river?

'Get back to the docks!' Elo yelled, hoping someone in the severed back half of the formation heard him as the pressure at his sides lessened and his force scattered into individual fights. He glanced towards the gate. All around them was littered with bodies. They had been so close. They were still so close.

But beyond the gates, Elo saw that perhaps they had never had a chance.

The gathered force of Talicians on the other side was larger than anything Elo had imagined. Row upon row of fighters in red, all moving forward. Not sparks from a fire this time but a wave of flame. What had Hseth and her priests promised them, that they did not fear death? Elo had heard of such cults in the long-ago past, in which some perfect afterlife was given to warriors of renown, where they would feast with their favoured gods. But he had heard of no such thing from Talicia. Were they now so in thrall to the god, so embedded in the life lived for her, that they saw no other way?

A large bell rang twice, and those nearest the gate stepped aside to reveal a large bronze statue borne on the shoulders of white-robed folk in plated chest armour. A shrine. The sculpture was hollow, its eyes burning, mouth smoking through a grille set where its teeth should be. Reports could not describe the horror of the glow of hot coal filling it up, turning its brass and briddite chest incandescent: enough to strike terror into the heart of any knight who had seen a god.

Hseth.

A set of soldiers in red jackets with white sashes were gathering the injured, the felled and still breathing. From reports, these were not krka, the army leaders beneath the priests, but hvars, the rank below. The priests' assistants. They dragged those they captured towards the feet of the statue, not caring if they were Talician or Middrenite, struggling or barely moving. All of them were brought to the feet of the bronze statue, and their cries cut short as their throats were slit. Blood gushed over the statue's feet, hissing where it stained.

'Take down the statue!' cried someone behind Elo, and a number of arrows flew past from the Middrenite roofs. There were still some archers holding position. One priest fell, buckling as an arrow found their throat, but a soldier immediately stepped in to lift the shrine before the fallen one was replaced by another in white.

'No! Leave it!' cried Elogast. He could see the Talicians raising their crossbows. Even as he watched, two of his own soldiers were cut down by the bolts. They needed to re-form some kind of defence, or they would be picked off, or overwhelmed by an attack. 'Back to me! Protect each other. Lift any shield you can find.'

Arrows flew from the front now as well as the side, and now they had little to shield themselves against them, Elo ducked down, hunching into his armour. Two arrows glanced off him, and he whispered thanks to Naia, who had gifted him her plates.

His fighters were coming back, forming a protective unit as Elo dragged himself to his feet, holding up his sword. He flinched as he heard a woman scream before her throat was opened on Hseth's shrine.

How much would it take for them to summon her?

'Commander!'

He turned. It was Safidah, blood pouring from her nose, her head, her chin, spattered across her helm. She had a shield on her arm, somehow she had kept it despite the crush. 'We must fall back!' She grabbed him by the shoulder, dragging him away from the gate, back to the rest of their battered force. But they both stopped.

There were Talicians on all sides, from the docks, from the gates, from the alleys. And Elo could see the rear half of the army retreating, running for the second barricade.

Leaving them to die.

CHAPTER SEVENTEEN

Arren

ARREN HEARD THE HORNS FROM WHERE HE SLEPT IN THE western gatehouse.

He knew the signals that Elogast used, and this one told him that the Talicians had attacked.

No, that they had broken through the first barricade . . .

'Rouse yourselves!' he yelled, throwing himself out of bed. 'Prepare for battle!' He had requisitioned Geralfi's ancestral house and slept with open windows to the square below, where his main guard had set up barracks. Anyone who did not know what the horns meant would have to hear him.

No time to think, or wait for a dresser. Elo was on the front lines. Elo, whom he had put there once more. Whom he had dragged out of his peaceful bakery and into his own battles.

Arren had tried to call him back to the west gate, to stay with Crolle and Elemni and just send orders to the front. But, of course, Elo would not leave the fight behind.

That was why Arren hated him.

That was why he loved him.

His padded gambeson was by the bed, and he dragged it on over his shirt, tying it with fumbling hands, pausing as he reached the chasm where his ribs parted, where his heart should be. There, the flesh seemed to have changed, becoming softer-edged where it turned into branches and twigs. Within, Hestra's flame still flickered.

Hestra? He tried reaching for her.

They are coming, came Hestra's mournful whisper. *She is coming. It is time for this to end.*

Arren scowled. She had finally answered and had nothing good to say.

'Not tonight,' he muttered putting his hand to his chest. Her flame felt softer, quieter, it licked around his fingers, but didn't hurt. Like a goodbye. 'Hestra, you want to be loved, but who will believe in you if you do not believe in yourself?'

Who will mourn for a fire god, she returned, *when flame has brought them only destruction?*

'Then bring them something else,' said Arren. His chest flickered, brightening. 'Bring them hope.'

Silence. Then, *I don't know how.*

The door to his room slammed open and Arren leapt to draw his sword, but it was Commander Movenna, and Methsme quick on their heels.

'Attack,' Iuri said, breathless. 'They've broken through.'

'I know,' said Arren. 'Help me arm.'

The commander paused, and Arren saw a faint glow around them and the cleric as well. It could not have come from the lamplight, there was some colour in the shades, spiking and fearful.

Arren blinked, and they were gone. Iuri started forward, grasping Arren's mail from its stand as Arren pulled on his padded hose. Methsme looked as if she was working on something to say, though her gaze was fixed on the chasm in Arren's chest with something like hunger.

Iuri found the mail, and Arren knelt so it could be lowered over his head. This was too slow. With each moment, each breath, he could imagine Elo fighting. Could see him falling, on spear, sword or arrow.

Why had he tried to kill him? To close the book on the fantasy that Elo might one day come back to the palace and stand by him, love him, hold him? Because he wanted power more than he wanted to pine?

Movenna was fixing Arren's chestplates when two squires arrived. These plates Arren had stylised in a burning circle with rays of flaming sun leafed in gold to his shoulders and chest in a twist of antlers. The squires stared, stilled with awe, but then more horns sounded, and one of them flinched at their cry.

'The horns are messages,' said Arren, to soothe him. 'It is our commander telling our force to unite.'

Elo must be forming a battalion, which meant that a large force was coming in. This was no test of their defences: the Talicians intended to claim the bridge that night.

'It's not the enemy?' said the squire.

'The enemy use bells.' He turned to Movenna. 'Thank you,' he said. 'Go shore up the second defensive line with Tiamh, we may need it.'

'Aye, Sunbringer.'

Arren nodded to the squires. 'Come, help me with the greaves.'

'No, stop,' said Methsme, and the squires paused. 'Sunbringer, Fireheart, are you planning on going to the front?'

Arren frowned. 'I have never backed down from a fight,' he said. Though that wasn't entirely true; he had tricked his way out of several.

'You are king. You are our leader. Send a body of flame instead, as you described your feats in Lesscia.'

As if Hestra would have the power these days. Or the will.

Arren pulled on his gloves. 'Who are you to command a king?' he snapped. Then realised as her expression closed that he had used the same phrase as Elo.

The squires hadn't moved. They were hanging back, staring between him and Methsme.

'Do you intend to disobey me, squire?' Arren asked softly. He had noted that shouting and bellowing moved fewer hearts than a cutting word. As long as the world could go silent for him, he would command it. The two younglings leapt into action. 'What are your names?'

'Marion,' said one. 'Of Weild.'

The other swallowed. 'Nattino,' he said. 'Barkson.'

'You're Gefyri?' said Arren, and the boy nodded.

'Y-yes. I joined the guard three weeks ago.' He went for the greaves, and he and the other squire bound them with quick, sure hands.

'Do not be afraid, Nattino. The fire god will not take Gefyrton while my own heart still burns, and while my subjects remain loyal.' He looked up at Methsme, who drew in her breath through her teeth.

'Gods do not go running into battle for their lovers,' she hissed, her voice low, as if that would stop the squires hearing. He saw the light again: a golden glow shone and rippled around her. 'Men do. Fools do.'

'Call me a fool again, cleric, and I shall have your feet whipped,' said Arren. 'Ser Elogast is no lover of mine, he is a commander.'

'My king . . .' she said, desperately. 'He will ruin you. That lion of yours is a heart-thief, and he will bring you only pain.'

Arren paused. Was she right? Was he being a lovelorn fool?

'You must cut away the pity that dims your heart, Sunbringer,' Methsme pressed. 'Act as a god. Not a man. A god's death must be sacred, important, for it to have power. Do not risk yourself for nothing.' The faint halo around her brightened and she put a hand to her heart, her fingers splayed.

Hestra brightened in his chest. Arren felt his blood warm, and the colours around her brightened.

Faith, this shining must be faith.

What light would Elo have? If he saw him again?

'If I have your faith, Methsme, go sing of it,' said Arren. 'Let the Talicians hear that we are not afraid. *I* am not afraid to face their god.'

'If I have your love, Sunbringer,' said Methsme, 'you will keep safe your holy fire. Not waste it on false betrayers.'

Arren stared at her. He had seen such devotion before, in people who had killed for it. Powerful, all-consuming. Vicious. It wasn't love of his flesh that she desired. It was shining, divine love. Big enough to lift her, to add wind to her lungs, purpose to her days.

'You have my love, cleric,' lied Arren, shaking the fears of his past away. 'But I will not leave my other loves to burn.'

His armour was bound. He had waited long enough. He grabbed

his helmet from young Nattino and strode out of his chambers. Down the spiral stairs of the Geralfi household, he passed the daughter of the House who spent all her time with the ostlers and layhorses by the gate. She had taken a shine to Elo, refusing to leave, and she carried a hunting knife and a crossbow. With her were two servants, who whispered prayers as he passed.

He burst out into the gatehouse square, already hot and sweating in the sultry night. There, he found to his relief a flurry of activity. Knights, guards, conscripts wakened from sleep, armoured and ready to fight, their squires or apprentices following them with arrows, or blades, or shields. There was also a steady stream of working folk leaving the city, great baskets on their back. Those who could lift a blade, Elo had already instructed to gather on the bank. A last defence.

A defence Arren did not plan to use.

'I want ten horses with me,' he said, striding into the fearful shadows and shifting bodies.

General Elemni turned, about to give him a telling off, then blanched as she realised who it was. 'Sunbringer,' she said. 'We can't use cavalry in Gefyrton.'

'The front is half a city away,' said Arren, 'and ten will not topple the bridge.'

'You're going to the . . .' The general caught herself, then saluted. 'Yes, Sunbringer,' she said. 'I will ride with you.'

That took him by surprise. Lord Elemni had held back many of his forces, professing that he intended to protect Sakre should the army make it that far. Arren suspected that 'protection' would turn into a land grab should they lose hope in him.

But Elemni was willing to ride into battle with him? Perhaps trust in him was growing.

Watch closely, my fireheart, Arren thought to Hestra. *We will keep their faith.*

You have not felt Hseth in fury yet, little king. I have seen what she wreaks.

Elemni left and returned with the horses quickly, as well as willing riders. They were in mixed colours: Regna, Elemni, Tiamh and Geralfi. As they mounted, folk stopped to stare. Though they were little more than shades in the night, when Arren squinted he could see the shine around them, blue and gold. His colours.

He patted the horse he mounted, urging her into a proud, quick step. 'For Gefyrton!' He roared, and the other riders followed, even Elemni. 'For Middren!'

'For Sunbringer!' someone else took up the cry, and then the whole square was cheering. It was not unlike the chaotic parade through Sakre, but warmer, surer.

'Fireheart!'

'Sunbringer!'

He turned the horse around and directed her east as the west of the city took up shouting the names Methsme painted for him.

The people parted, and Arren set off at a trot till the way was clear enough to gallop.

The others kept pace, and he could hear the huffing of their war steeds, the sound of hooves on pounded earth. Around him in the night he could catch only the gleam of a bridle, the flash of a gauntlet, orange light on a helm from fires that must be burning at the eastern gate.

They heard the central defensive barricade, Tiamh's, before they saw it. People were everywhere, knights, fighters, soldiers, many of them still panting, still running. A retreat.

Arren reined in his mount. 'Elogast!' he called. 'Commander general!' He could hear distant cries over the constant crashing of the falls, and the sound of metal clashing. A battle ahead still. A few red bodies of Talicians were broken on this second blockade, but it seemed the fire worshippers were still focussed on the front line.

He heard another blast from the front, two long blows on the horn, then one short.

A request for aid.

Arren recognised Tiamh, staring ahead, unmoving, and beside him a runner, blood on her face and over her hands, a deep gash in her shoulder. Then there was Tulenne in his yellow cloak, panting with his back against the blockade. Geralfi, Yesef. They had all made it.

Apart from Elo.

'Tiamh!' barked Arren. 'What's happening?'

The general looked up, blanching at the sight of Arren. 'Your majest— I mean, Sunbringer! You should be back at the west gate.'

'I would look our enemy in the eyes, Tiamh. Report!'

'They came from three sides,' said the runner, taking over despite the wound in their arm. 'The south first, then a charge from the gate, then three boatloads from upriver broke straight through the defence. They flanked the front and cut us off from them. The rest retreated.' They glanced at Tulenne, who was swallowing.

'We were c-called to the centre,' he said. 'We came to help!'

'You had orders to stay at the docks,' snapped Yesef, who had an arrow sticking out of her back, buried in the muscle. A healer was trying to take it out, digging around the barbs with a knife. She swallowed a scream. 'Of all the fuckery, I did not imagine you would abandon your *gods damned* post.'

'You cannot speak to me that way, commander,' snapped Tulenne.

Arren cut through them. He would deal with Tulenne later. But now, there was only the fight. 'Where is the commander general?'

Yesef looked up, her expression apologetic. 'He was at the front,' she said.

Cut off. Surrounded. Arren needed to hear no more. 'Fifty fighters!' he shouted. 'Spears and shortswords, come to me and prepare for close combat. I want Gefyris, front and centre. You know your city better than anyone.'

'Sunbringer, the front is lost,' said Tiamh. 'The commander general fought well, but it was not enough. They are bringing the Hseth statue forward, Geralfi saw it. They mean to summon her.'

'I will come.' This was Lord Geralfi, blood staining his legs and greaves; not his own, judging by how easily he still stood. Whatever Elo had said to the older lord, it had scared him somehow more than the Talicians.

'You lead them, commander,' ordered Arren. 'Head for the docks and take them by surprise. Clear the way as far forward as you can, then shatter any pathways they might use to advance. Go sly, go quiet, and unless you can hold them, retreat when I give the clear.'

'Yes, Sunbringer.'

'Go.'

Geralfi turned, his voice robust as he barked out orders. Indigo fighters leapt up at his commands, lifting their weapons.

'I need archers,' said Arren, turning to the rest of his war council.

'I have twelve,' said Yesef, indicating a group crouched by the blockades, organising arrows. 'Captain!'

One of the archers looked up.

'To the king!'

The archers leapt to their feet, and Yesef yowled as the healer finally wrenched the arrow out of her muscle, immediately applying a herbal pouch to the freshly bleeding wound.

They had to move quickly. A few archers, his own mounted riders, and the element of surprise would have to do.

'Prepare to follow and save our people!' cried Arren. 'Open the barricade!' He already knew that Elo would have created a route through with just a few shifts of barriers on wheels.

The archers lined up with the horses without argument, and Elemni neither dismounted nor faltered. She was ready too. Arren hoped Tulenne was watching.

His command was echoed with a blast of a horn. One long call of sound.

Prepare.

All the Middrenites prepared for him to ride, readying the barriers, watching for his order.

What is the point of resisting? Hestra spoke to him. *What is the point of all this?*

'Now!' Arren cried to the soldiers of the second blockade.

The barriers shifted, and Arren spurred on the horse. Ten cavalry, at pace with an array of other fighters. It would have to be enough. At the same time, Geralfi would be moving towards the northern docks.

They broke into a controlled run as they passed the last of the blockers which were pulled shut behind them. Here, there was an open stretch of road, dusty and empty, bereft of its people.

'Spread out!' Arren called. 'Create a line! Keep pace with each other!' He would remind them that before he was a king he had been a commander, and before he had been a commander he had been a knight.

Why do you do this? said Hestra. *Why do you throw yourself into the fire over and over, King Arren?*

We have to save our people, Hestra, he said into his heart. *Ours. Fire and sun, hearth and hope. We make the future, we tell our own story, or we die trying.*

She warmed in him, soothing his aching bones as he led the charge over the eastern bridge between the narrow buildings. There were bodies here, red and blue, steel and leather. Blood stained the ground.

None of them were Elo.

Arren looked ahead. From the back of the horse, he could see over the red of the Talicians that were converging on a last battalion that had somehow managed to gather itself together into a protective knot. They were all but surrounded, and beyond them, there was a statue, borne by priests. Bronze. Burning. Hseth.

Her feet were painted with blood. Even as he watched, the injured were dragged to her, their faces pressed to her hot metal flesh, their lives ended upon her body.

Sacrifices.

CHAPTER EIGHTEEN

Elogast

THE STATUE WAS APPROACHING, AND ELO COULD HEAR each scream as their numbers dwindled.

The shrine-bearers had run out of victims, and Hseth had not yet come, but the statue was getting hotter, red with heat.

Elo's defence was holding, but barely. They were holding broken blockade boards up to shield themselves now, but were slowly being crushed behind them. Larsen was at his left shoulder, breathing harshly, struggling to lift a heavy plank. Elo grabbed it and heaved it with him, just in time as two stray bolts slammed into the wood. The scars on Elo's chest stretched and burned as his arm vibrated with the force, and the sweat on his neck ran cold. He grunted, shifted his legs, and managed to hoist it higher, feeling his muscles burning. No skill with a blade would help them now.

'Hold till reinforcements come!' cried Elo. 'Do not be afraid of the fire! Flame is ours too! Our fire-hearted king! Sunbringer!'

'Sunbringer!'

'Fireheart!'

'Do not be afraid!'

'The sun is coming!'

They were all going to die. There was no way out of this, and they knew it, but they held to the hope that they would live. Or, if they did not, that it would be worth it. Better a fool's hope than no hope at all.

Then, hoofbeats. A hiss in the air, the sound of singing wood, followed by screams in Talic. Elo risked a glance back, and what he saw made his heart rise and twist: Arren, aback a horse, riding with knights at his side. Was it another of his tricks? No: his helmet was open, and Elo could see his eyes, the curl of his hair. He could smell hot metal, hot blood, coal smoke and woodsmoke. In his ears the sound of gasping, grunting, shouting. Assurances to themselves and to others. They were alive, still alive.

The press on their left side diminished in intensity. The arrows were fewer, the shove of bodies stopped.

'What's happening?' gasped Elseber.

Elo could hear cries of pain, the strike of steel through flesh and bone. Not close this time, from the docks. He lowered the board and peered over it. Lord Geralfi was advancing through a ginnel with his own contingent, chest bloody, sword in hand, where the Talicians had been.

A moment. A breath. They had it.

Elo breathed in. 'Retreat!' he yelled. 'Retreat!'

CHAPTER NINETEEN

Kissen

THE PORT OF WSIRIN BEGAN LONG BEFORE THE LAND DID. The Long Harbour, they said it was called.

Anchored ships were tied together with bouncing gangways, and smaller ferries, skiffs, rafts, set up shop around them, forming floating markets that appeared to sell everything from snack food to pre-made shrines.

They passed flags of a thousand colours, decorating mast to prow, and several ships so barnacled that Kissen knew they would never be seaworthy again, instead becoming another part of the port. Birds floated in great clouds over fleets of fishing boats, and the fresh land-breeze carried with it scents of spices and mountains, forest and lakes.

Kissen breathed it in, feeling her lungs ache but not catch. Her burns now felt more like the red she got from sitting out in the sun. Her other wounds were shallow, and her head had stopped splitting. She could walk around with her staff tucked firmly under her arm, and suddenly was given first pick of biscuits and the least rotten greenling with her hipgin.

It seemed she had got lucky. Again.

She smiled and touched the white mark on her chest where her father's gift had been, sitting beneath the strings that laced her shirt together. She'd had nothing but her wits and water, and it had worked.

Gods were made to fit the world: the world didn't change to fit them. For all their power, all their strength, fire and water still made steam, and metal still cracked when cooled too quickly. Satuan, a god of smiths, should have known that.

But it was his hatred, too, that had saved her, realising that everyone who watched him attack would pray to him after, strengthening and building him over and over into a being that could not die.

She tapped her tattoo. 'Fuck you, smith god,' she whispered under her breath, and wished her lungs hurt just a tiny bit less.

'There it is!' said Skedi from where he crouched beside her. Wsirin rose like palaces of air over a haze of smoke with a reddish tinge, domed citadels not unlike the Lesscian cloche.

At his cry, Inara came running across the deck from the forecastle, having just helped Lessa raise their own flags of peace and trade, Middren and mourning, along with a circle struck through to indicate they carried weapons and livestock. Perhaps a deterrent to pirates, though Kissen noted they also had the black flag of piracy tucked in the storage case with their other colours.

They had even raised Arren's banner of the sun and stag.

Inara clattered to a halt beside Kissen and Skedi, beneath the rigging on the starboard side. Her palms were chapped from the ropes, but she didn't seem to mind. Young Craier had gone quite brown between the sun and water, her dark curls burnishing as if the sun had been caught in their strands. She suited the sea, but there was something forced about her smiles and lightness, as if she was play-acting the child she thought she should be while hiding some fear, some disappointment. Demigod or not, trying too hard or not, she was still just a little girl at heart.

'Look, shrines!' she said, pointing down at the teeming waters as they passed flotillas of floating statues surrounded by tiny coracles that boasted offerings of fishbones or incense, sweets or tiny bottles of wine that must have been made for the purpose.

Skedi flapped his wings, and Kissen wondered if he was looking for a shrine to Yusef, or maybe even a totem of his own. 'Irisians only have one god though,' he said. 'Why all the shrines?'

'It's a harbour on the Trade Sea, isn't it?' said Kissen, her voice crackling. Still hoarse. 'People must bring their gods with them when they come.'

'And Irisians say all gods are just parts of their god of change,' said Inara. 'So, they're welcome.'

'Even scrappy little demigods?' said Kissen.

Inara bit her lip and gave her a shy smile while swinging back on the ship's railings.

'When did you know what I was?' she asked at last.

Kissen shrugged, then winced as her shoulders hurt. 'I knew there was something odd about you,' she said. 'Of course, your little rat notwithstanding—'

'I thought we were past "rat",' said Skedi, who had grown to the size of a fox.

'But you looked at people as if you looked into them,' said Kissen, ignoring him. 'Like a god does. So, when you broke a god's power . . .' she nodded at Skedi, who flattened his ears slightly. Good, he was still ashamed. 'It fell into place that you were more than human.'

'A beast,' muttered Inara.

Satuan hadn't called her that, but it didn't matter where it came from, only that it had hurt her.

'Humans are beasts too,' said Kissen. 'Evil isn't something that belongs to shadows. It's in all of us, with our cruelty, our envy. Our fear.'

'You're not afraid.'

'I'm always afraid,' laughed Kissen. 'As is wise for a person who has pissed off a few gods. But I know myself. Better, maybe, than people who have never been through loss, or pain.' She rubbed the burns of her hands, holding them to the light. The old scars, and the new. 'I have frailty in me, and cruelty too. I live in pain because pain is what the world gave me, and I am powerful with it.'

Inara was listening, silent and thoughtful. She was getting taller, older. When was the right time to say such things to a young girl? Telle would know, Kissen was sure. But Telle wasn't here.

'What I'm trying to say, Ina,' said Kissen, 'is that there's no perfect evil or perfect good. There's no easy answer to a question of right or wrong: they're not two sides of a coin you toss. What's important is the question.'

'Well,' Captain Lertes had wandered over with his hands behind his back, 'the question right now is whether you're going to get changed or not, young Craier.' He smiled, his eyes reflecting the aqua light of the Irisian coastline. His clothes were formal, a tunic of green and charcoal grey rather unlike his usual bright colours and jewels. Whatever tension she had sensed between the captain and the lady, he had still decided to dress in the colours of the House Craier.

'Change?' said Kissen.

'Well, the little captain is on a mission of diplomacy, and she looks like she's ready to scrape the bilges.' He looked at Inara and smiled lightly. 'Half the battle is the right equipment, girl, I believe your mother has selected some items for you.'

'Are we expecting a fight?' said Kissen.

'Only of wits,' said Lessa, coming out of her cabin.

Kissen drew in her breath and held it. Lessa's hair was loose for the first time, and brushed so well that it cascaded down her back like a fall of silk, oiled to its ends. She wore a dress: a fine sweep of pale linen, embroidered at the open neck, and over it a long sleeveless tabard in pale green, trimmed and detailed with gold.

'I have something for you, Kissenna,' she said, holding out a bundle. 'Folk will help you find your sisters if you also look less like a bilge rat.' She looked pointedly at Inara, who sniggered and stepped away from the railing, heading towards her cabin. Not without a knowing look at Kissen, who decided that it was a good moment to shut her mouth.

'Though if you would like to rest some more,' Lessa added, 'the ship is yours.'

'I'm done resting,' said Kissen, glancing back towards the shore. There was music, pipes, drums and strings straining out over the wavelets. 'I thought you wanted me gone?'

'The Irisian philosophy is one of change.'

Lessa moved to stand next to her, looking at the shore. The *Silverswift* had moved closer to the waterfront, deftly guided by Aleda again, who was steering with one hand, her other burned arm still raw, protected by bandages and poultice.

Now, Kissen could see the harbour more clearly. It was lined with rows of limestone houses draped with flowers of vivid red and purple. Many of them were brightly tiled, not just the window ledges as in Lesscia, but more like the painted houses of the pleasure district in Blenraden; carved, inked, fired, glossed and gleaming, as if the land itself was raising banners.

Somewhere there she hoped to find her sisters. Did Elo's letters get through? Did they know now she was still alive, and coming for them?

But . . . why was she torn? Why did part of her want to stay on this ship, with Lessa, to return to bloody Middren and fight for it tooth and nail? The home she had chosen, and that had chosen her?

'I'm going to see if my wife needs help,' said Lertes, turning towards the aftcastle steps so he could head up to the helm. The *Silverswift* had passed through most of the Long Harbour, and its prow was pointed towards another one, with high sandstone walls and watchtowers beneath what looked like a grand fortress.

'I'll – ah – take a look from the nest,' said Skedi. As he took off, Kissen realised that everyone wanted to leave her and Lessa alone. She didn't want to be alone with Lessa, she didn't know what to say to her.

At least that made two of them. Lessa put the bundle which appeared to be a shirt and cloak down on the railing, tapped it once with her finger, then slid it along towards Kissen, who took it.

'What makes you think I don't want a dress?' she said, trying to ease the atmosphere. Lessa smiled. Gods, she had even painted her lips a pleasing rose. She didn't say that Kissen looked as if she hadn't even glanced at a dress in her entire life, which would be close to true. Skirts got in the way of her leg, useful only for the larger pockets she could sew into them.

Well, so she often thought, until she saw a beautiful woman like Lessa wearing one. But then, it wasn't the wearing it she wanted, it was the woman inside it.

Bad thought.

'I understand the cloth can get in the way of a crutch,' said Lessa. 'And I saw you had your trews adjusted to accommodate your prosthesis. But I can prepare one if you prefer? I'm not bad with a needle . . .' She put a palm up to Kissen as if to measure her, and Kissen snorted.

'No, thank you,' she said, pulling the bundle apart. The shirt was pale blue and printed with tessellating patterns in curls and flourishes. The cloak was even more rich, a brighter green than Lessa's dress, lined with yellow, and embroidered with silver birds.

'This . . .' Kissen said. 'My lady, this is too much.'

'It's a loan,' said the lady. 'You'll be hard pressed to find much of mine from the last few years not covered in the symbols of our House. When we greet the Irisian council, the Mithrik, we will ask for their aid in finding your family. As a Craier representative, they will be bound to give it to you.'

'I don't belong to your House.'

'It owes you a debt.'

The lady's long hair was fluttering at her waistline. She didn't move as the crew of her ship sprinted past, calling and waving. Small boats had come out to greet them, flying Irisian wave-and-claw flags of white and blue dyed fabric. They must have come from the country's council. The *Silverswift* was expected.

'You saved our lives,' said Lessa.

Kissen tongued her gold tooth. 'I would have tried for anyone,' she said.

The lady shook her head. 'That's beside the point.' She sighed. 'More than that . . .' Her mouth twisted, and Kissen waited, quite enjoying Lessa's squirming.

'You saved my daughter,' the lady said at last. 'In so many ways. I am,' she twisted her nose, '. . . grateful for it.'

Gratitude? From Lady Craier? She really had warmed to her. 'I don't know,' Kissen said, smiling crookedly. 'She's a feisty little thing. She'd have thought of something.'

Lessa laughed, and lifted her hand to touch her ears, as if unused to the weight of the gold earrings that now adorned them. 'I should have been there for her more,' she said. 'I'm glad you were. Are.'

Kissen bit her tongue to stop saying something stupid. Like declare undying loyalty or swear fealty to the beautiful lady and her terrifying daughter. That was what fools did in stories. Kissen was no fool. Their paths would not stay together forever, one day the two of them would go where Kissen did not, could not belong.

But she could put on the nice shirt, the pretty cloak, and decide later whether she would beg a ride with them to join a fight she was no longer sure Elo could win.

'Do you need help?' asked Lessa. 'Your wounds are . . .'

Kissen paused. Lifting her arms in and out of a shirt made her wince to think about it. She could do with the assistance. 'Yes,' she said. 'Please.'

Lessa put her hands to the ties that went down Kissen's chest, unthreading them one after the other till Kissen's belly was exposed. She wasn't shy; on open water like this a bare chest was a common offer to the cooling wind, where shirts could be expensive and quick to wear. Lessa helped pull her sleeves down over her shoulders then folded the shirt onto the deck, glancing up at Kissen as she did. Her eyes raked the wounds that had stopped bleeding, the red stain where steam had peeled her skin raw, the scars beneath it.

'They look worse than they are,' said Kissen.

Lessa took the new shirt from Kissen's hands and lifted it over her head. Not a tied one this, it came in one piece, billowing out at the bottom like a dancing skirt. There was no pity in Lessa's eyes, only acknowledgement, interest, warmth. Their eyes met, and Kissen felt her own breath quicken, a rush of heat in her belly, descending. Those dark eyes, that crooked nose. Did the lady know how captivating she was?

'Inara told me,' said Lessa softly, 'what happened to your birth family.'

Kissen blinked in surprise.

'They're not the first,' she said looking down and tucking the shirt into her girdle and sword belt. She had only her cutlass and Osidisen's dagger again. She needed more weapons. But she gave the shirt credit; its cloth felt kind on her brutalised skin. 'Nor will be the last.'

'I had heard of such things,' said Lessa, 'but had never known it to happen outside of Blenraden. I did think Satuan would help us.'

'Gods only help when it serves them,' said Kissen, then hesitated, thinking of Skedi, and of Osidisen, who needed to show no affection to his lover's children, but did. 'Most of them.'

'I've only ever known goodness in gods,' said Lessa, helping her on with the cloak now. This was a fine piece of work. Its silver birds flashed brightly, as if flying through a leafy forest, caught in beams of sunlight.

'Even gods who take advantage of young women?' Kissen asked.

Lessa paused, her hands around the clasp of the cloak, her warm hands tenderly close to Kissen's throat. Kissen didn't dare to breathe.

'You heard that?' said the lady, and Kissen regretted the coolness that crept into her voice.

'Heard what?' Kissen asked. It seemed she had missed something, some revelation. She shook her head, then dared raise her hand to touch Lessa's elbow. 'I heard nothing,' she said. 'I only . . . I have my own history with gods taking humans as lovers.'

Lessa bit her lip and tugged Kissen's cloak better around her shoulders, sweeping it so it rested over one side, then fastened the clasp. 'I don't need you to be angry for me,' she said. 'I made my choices. I loved a god, and he loved me.'

'He should have loved you enough to leave you alone,' said Kissen.

'Perhaps. But no matter how Inara came to me, I chose her. She is a gift.'

Kissen didn't have a response to that. Instead she sighed and ran her fingers through her salt-tangled hair.

'Oh don't do that,' said Lessa catching her hand. 'Let it be.'

'It's a mess.'

'You'll make it messier. Just don't touch it. Or let me fix it.'

'You want to fix my hair?' said Kissen incredulously.

'No. Well . . .' It was Lessa who was blushing now.

A horn sounded, and they both turned to the shore. The crew were tossing ropes to the flotilla of small boats that caught them and began to tug them towards the high-walled fortress harbour.

The fort itself was like nothing Kissen had seen: red stone sloped up from brilliant blue water in high, angled walls that surrounded imposing round towers studded with beams. Across the stone hung great, bold banners in reds, yellows and blues. Kissen swore she could smell Elo's bread, the nameen and the herb and oil mix he insisted on carrying with him, and wished he had come.

'Is there some sort of festival?' she asked, as Lessa's gaze went up toward the watchtowers for the smaller harbour they were approaching. There were patrols armed with Irisian longbows on top of the harbour walls, and in the towers that guarded the entrance. Was it to stop folk getting in, or getting out?

'There's always something,' said Lessa, answering her question. 'Do you see the braided grass in the eaves?' She pointed up towards the fort. In the sloping walls were small windows of dark wood, the same as the roofs that topped them. There, dangled long trains of braided grass that must have taken some daring to hang. 'They're for the spring change,' said Lessa, 'or the dry season in southern Irisia. At midsummer replace them with palm leaves.'

The *Silverswift* slid into the closed harbour, and as they passed the watchtowers, the music and noise of outside was cut off. Now, instead of the chatter of fishing boats and the heavy swaying of scruffy merchant vessels, they were surrounded by fine ships, clean scrubbed and carefully kept. Kissen felt as if a prison door was closing behind them. Despite the cheer and welcome of hazy Wsirin, Irisia had once been a nation of war, and now she was reminded of that.

'I'll stay,' Kissen offered, 'and guard you. In case something goes wrong.' She caught sight of a prow shape she had last seen in the light of Hseth's flames: Restish. Moored in the harbour, no one visible aboard. Lessa had seen it too; she frowned.

'It's not violence I fear,' she said. 'It is inaction. Irisia, Middren and Restish signed the treaty of Belhaven, promising not to arm our enemies or each other, and keep the balance of peace between us. The only times this was broken before was the war on the Talician kerls with Pinet, and the God War. Both agreed by all three states, the latter regretted by our allies.'

'Restish has been supplying Talicia with ships,' Kissen protested. 'Is that peace?'

'We have no proof,' said Lessa calmly and surely. 'And if Restish say they are neutral, then Irisia may remain so as well.'

'Sounds like fucking nonsense,' said Kissen. 'If people ask for help, you give it.'

'The Trade Sea has long put profit over people,' said Lessa. 'They turned from their gods of safety and love to gods of fortune and trade. Many will not reach out a hand unless you put a coin in it first. Like people, like gods.'

'On that we agree,' said Kissen. She longed to explore this woman's mind, her knowledge of the seas and their history, her view of the gods neither clouded by hatred, nor choked with devotion.

But they were reaching the dock. The ropes from the small boats had been passed to folk on a long wooden jetty, who were pulling the ship in closer. Sallath and Slim had swung themselves down to the boards and were helping make fast the ship, while several others were preparing the gangplank for their descent.

'Yameti'i melikami yataghayar!' shouted one of the people down below in shining saffron robes who had just finished tying off one of the ropes. 'The god of change brings good tidings!'

'Kama alaik yatagha,' responded Lessa confidently. 'As tidings change with the god!'

'Ah, you speak Irisian, Lady Craier!' said the caller. 'I expected nothing less.'

'A little,' she said. 'And you are . . .?'

The speaker was tall and dark, with hair cropped short and ears layered with precious gems and hoops. Everything about them spoke of wealth, despite the fact that they had been hauling ropes moments earlier. Kissen could not place their gender.

'Welcome to Wsirin,' said the councillor, keeping to Middric, 'our beauteous capital, jewel of the south Trade Sea, and home to you for as long as you wish.'

'Thank you for your kind welcome,' said Lessa as Inara came running over, her hair tamped down beneath a green scarf and her sailing clothes exchanged for bright skirts threaded through with purple and red, and a formal tunic split at the hips and capped at the sleeves for ease of movement. With her were Rhiyande and Shah – a broad, tall Irisian whose loosely coiled hair was bound at his nape. Shah was short for Shahirazen, which he apparently hated. They too were dressed formally, even wearing rough cuirasses with the Craier symbol.

Rhiyande winked at Kissen. 'Clean nicely up, don't we?' she said.

'A bit of shine doesn't hide all the scuffing,' said Kissen, waving a hand at her scratched-up body, and Rhiyande laughed. Shah even gave her a small nod and a smile.

Inara was looking Kissen up and down with a mildly bewildered expression, as Skedi swooped down from the crow's nest and landed on the girl's shoulder.

'Never seen you look so bright,' he said.

'Quiet, you.'

'It looks nice,' said Inara.

'Hm. You, too.'

Lessa was headed for the gangplank, she looked back and moved her hand in a decisive call for attention, signing to Inara, *Give greeting*.

'*Yameti'i melikami yataghayar*,' said Inara, her accent almost as perfect as the Irisian's as she hurried after her mother down onto the jetty.

Kissen moved more carefully, using her staff to help her down the steep slope to the bouncing planks. There were guards posted along the way towards the harbour walls in leather and scale-like plating that covered their chest and belly. Lighter than a Middrenite knight's armour, and likely better in the heat.

'*Kama alaik yatagha*,' replied the Irisian to Inara. 'I am Mitha Aslani of Tioron and Nala, one of the Mithrik, great council of Irisia.' They bowed towards Lessa. 'And you are Lady Craier, representative of Middren and . . . ally of King Arren? Or enemy?'

Lessa smiled tightly. 'Ally against invaders, Mitha Aslani,' she said, and received a sparkling grin in response. 'I bear his signet.' She lifted her hand, showing the ring Arren had given her. 'A sign of our unity, and his hopes for an alliance with Irisia.'

Aslani smiled noncommittally. 'And who is this?' they said, turning to Skedi. 'A *quya*?'

That was a word Kissen understood from her youth in Blenraden. *Quya*. Irisian for 'god', though it meant something like 'fragment' or 'vestige'. Lessa had advised that Skedi stay in sight, but small and unobtrusive, and he was about the size of a kitten.

'This is Skediceth, a god of white lies,' said Inara. 'A travelling god from Lakaii. He can go far from his shrines.'

Kissen felt the tickle of Skedi's will as he pressed it towards Aslani.

Shrines, lots of shrines, a travelling god from Lakaii.

It was not a powerful lie, it didn't have to be. 'And this is Kissenna,' said Lessa, 'a veiga of Middren, Captain Lertes of the *Silverswift*, and his crew Rhiyande and Shah.'

The Mitha's eyes passed over them, lingering briefly on the scar of a god's curse on Kissen's face, then on the crew that had joined them on the harbour deck.

'We are happy to converse in Irisian, Mitha Aslani,' said Lessa. 'I have been practising, though my daughter is the superior linguist.'

'Oh no, please,' said the Mitha, to Kissen's relief. 'I haven't had a chance to speak Middric in a year. Your favour to us, I swear. Though I understand in Middric you have no word for a third gender, *asha, ashi'i, ashil*? You instead speak man, woman, plural?'

'You're right,' said Lessa. 'Middric has some . . . rigid qualities. Though, as we may discuss, there is always space for change.'

Aslani laughed. 'Then I am plural,' they said, giving nothing away of where they stood on Lessa's hints at alliance. Kissen hated politics, all this polite dancing of tongues instead of blades, no one saying what they meant, only for them to depart dissatisfied? She had nothing to bring to the table apart from bravery and tricks. For fuck's sake, she couldn't even read Middric, let alone speak in Irisian.

'Come,' said the Mitha. 'Your crew can trade in Middren should they wish, but we have been waiting for you, Lady Craier.'

The Mitha went ahead, leading them up the dock, and Lertes looked up to Aleda where she still stood at the helm, signing to her in handspeak, *Be ready. Keep watch.* Then he turned to Kissen, saw her looking, and smiled. *Trust no one*, he signed to her. *The only language of trade is profit.*

That, at least, Kissen understood. As Mitha Aslani led them down the bouncing planks towards the fortress, she glanced once more towards the Restish ship. It seemed innocuous enough, but she could not help her fingers aching for her blade as they moved along the harbour towards an open door, set deep into the wall of Wsirin's great fortress.

As they stepped into its shadow, the air cooled like a hand on the brow. Stairs led up from the postern, spiralling and lit by small windows cut into the outer wall.

It felt like an age to the top, the heat in Kissen's body rising again despite the blessedly chill air and her right leg shooting with pain that felt like long needles being slowly pressed through the shin-that-was. But, once there, the Mitha opened a door and led them into the shelter of a long hall, ribbed with dark wood that had been inlaid with cloud and wave patterns, picked out in pristinely polished gold. The red stone floor shone in the light from clear, diamond windows set high in the sloping roof. All were open to the east, allowing a gentle breeze to drift down through the shadows and play across them, as well as pools of sunbeams and brightness, like the moonlight in Osidisen's cave.

'Kissen.'

Kissen looked to see who had spoken. Inara wasn't looking at her, but Skedi was. They had moved ahead and were standing at the far end of the hall. There, rippling silks hung long from the rafters, and there were several long, comfortable chaises set before low tables, creaking with plates of delicacies. Kissen could smell roses and honey, toasted nuts and alcohol. There were also eight people standing, waiting, and one sitting, staring at her.

'Yatho,' she whispered, then seeing the woman at her side, her heart all but cracked through her ribs. 'Telle!'

CHAPTER TWENTY

Arren

'why did you come?'

Elo was furious, but alive.

They had made it back to the second blockade, sprinting behind them in the brief reprieve that Geralfi managed by surprising the Talicians at the docks. His team had also returned, and the Middrenites were safe behind their own lines.

The enemy did not yet give them chase, instead regrouping themselves around the statue of Hseth. They were in arrow's reach, but how many did they have to waste on mad firing into the dark?

Elo's armour was bloody and dented. He stank of pitch and smoke, but he was alive, still alive. And angry. But it was not Arren he was angry with. Not this time.

'I swore we would hold this bridge,' said Elo more to himself than to the king. 'I swore!' He turned, wrenched off his helm and threw it at the closing barricades. 'Where is Tulenne? I am going to *drag* him back to the front.'

Tulenne was nowhere to be seen. Tiamh was giving orders for shoring up the blockade, Elemni was taking count of their remaining forces, and Yesef was overseeing the replacement of blades that had been dropped or broken.

'Elo,' said Arren, holding his arms and trying to calm him. Elo did not look too injured, only half wild, ferocious with the fight and the failure. 'Commander general, calm yourself. I need to speak with you.'

'We could have claimed it,' Elo hissed, his voice hoarse. 'We were so close.'

'I know,' said Arren. He looked up. There were no stars above them through the mist and smoke, but he could see the slight hardening of the sky, from deep velvet to stone-grey. Dawn was coming.

'They're going to summon their god.' Elo was still looking towards the east gate where the Talicians were regrouping, clearing the buildings, getting ready to march. 'If we can't retake the bridge before that then we're lost. They don't care how many die as they have more than enough to overrun us.' He tried to step back, but Arren held on to him. 'Release me! We must send in a charge!'

'Elo!' Arren shook him. 'Listen to me!'

Elo looked at him as if seeing him for the first time, his breathing slowing as the war-rage faded.

'I have another plan,'

If they lost Gefyrton, even if Irisia came to their aid, it would be too late. Bloody Craier would come back to a wasted land and a dead king. If she came back at all. Talicia had moved fast, hard and brutally. If the veiga hadn't warned them of the invasion, hadn't stopped the coup, they would have been decimated before they'd even known what was happening.

Arren glanced around. 'Come,' he said, and pulled Elo away from the barricade, towards the broken door of some kind of dresser's shop. Inside, all the tables, mirrors, furniture was gone, taken for the blockades, and only a few spools of fabric remained, trodden into the floor. There were two people in there already, one weeping while the other held them, but as Arren entered they gathered themselves and left the two of them alone.

'What?' said Elo, as impatient as he had ever been. Arren turned to face him. He had hoped it wouldn't come to this.

'The barrels,' he said. 'I had them strapped to the beams of the lower bridge.'

'Water barrels?' said Elo.

Arren pinched his nose. 'Not water, Elo. Blackfire.'

Elo understood. His face changed, and his temper cooled to icy. 'No.'

'If we destroy the bridge, the Talicians cannot cross into Middren,' said Arren.

In the weeks after the coup, Arren's guard had found a cache of Craier's blackfire beneath the Sakrean palace that hadn't caught with the others.

He had known it would come in useful.

'What is it with you and breaking your own cities?' said Elo, incredulous. 'Don't they matter to you? You scuppered Blenraden, marched on Lesscia, now you intend to burn Gefyrton . . .?'

'You said it yourself. If we lose the bridge, we lose the war. They already control the eastern gate, half the dock, and they'll soon be coming this way. With Hseth or no, this way our people will survive.'

Elo would survive.

They could hear the bells and drums, quaking the darkness of the pre-dawn. They could smell flesh burning as the Talicians kept calling for their god to come and tear them all away.

'If you burn your own kingdom,' hissed Elo, 'you will lose it.'

'Give me another way, Elo,' said Arren. He clasped his friend's shoulder, urging him, hoping that he was smarter, wiser, that he had another choice. 'Any other way that will save us, and I will try. I will call the gods, I will slaughter our horses, I will throw myself on their blades, but tell me it would work.'

Elo shut his mouth. He was running through possibilities, options, hopes, and coming up short.

What if it isn't the king who burns the bridge?

Hestra's voice cut through both of them, Elo wincing as she came into his mind. Arren felt his chest warm. Light crept up from beneath his plates, flames brightening the room.

What if Talicians bring their army onto the bridge, the god at their front, and it is she who sends them burning to their deaths?

'Hestra?' said Arren, releasing Elo. She sounded shy, uncertain, but was this her offering help?

The only way to defeat Hseth is to break the Talician faith in her.

Elo shook his head. 'Even if we throw her into the falls she wouldn't die, not with the power she holds.'

It would begin it. An army ready to win, then destroyed by their own god. The story would spread from soldier to soldier, all the way to the coast. They are already so tired, already starving, this is why Hseth has not yet come. Give them hope enough that she will hear them, then break it. Nothing shatters love more than failure.

Arren put his hand to his chest, feeling the warm metal.

You are willing to hope? he said to her, mind to mind.

Hestra was quiet for a moment, then, *Perhaps I still have some story to tell.*

Arren and Elo met eyes. Could they do it? Elo looked sceptical.

'Gefyris know how bridges work,' said Elo. 'They saw you setting the barrels. They will not be fooled.'

'Then call it a sacrifice,' said Arren, 'but call it a success. I will take responsibility for my actions, but the Talicians would have no knowledge of them.' He paused, then began to pace. 'My fear is that by clearing the bridge of people they will realise they are entering a trap. It won't work.'

'Unless,' said Elo, a shade glimmering around him, a colour. A deep flurry of blue, edged with gold and silver. Then it faded. 'Unless we fool them,' he said. 'Keep a skeleton of fighters maintaining the defence, have the Talicians push far enough that they can't run back.'

'Slow their advance,' mused Arren, 'but not stop it.' He hadn't spoken to Elo like this in an age. No barbs, no points to score, just a battle, and a plan. This was what had made them, and broken them too.

Elo put his gauntleted hand on his head, thinking. He looked so tired. Would he agree to this? Or would he once more lay down his sword and walk away?

'It could work,' he said at last. 'I will lead the defence.'

'Elo, no.'

'If I plan it well enough, we can keep casualties low. I will not ask of anyone what I would not ask of myself.'

Arren shook his head. He had just ridden into a battle to rescue Elo, he would not lose him again. 'I won't allow it.'

'I won't give you a choice,' Elo declared, their brief moment of cohesion breaking. 'Isn't that what you wanted? To make a martyr of me?'

Arren flinched. 'Elo,' he said, 'why do you think I came for you? I *need* you.'

'Ask someone else!' snapped Elo. The weight of all he had seen that night, in Lesscia, in previous wars, looked as if it were coming down upon him to crush his struggling heart. 'You ask too much of me. You *always* asked too much of me.'

They could hear the bells ringing. Each moment was tipping by, but no one had sounded that the Talicians were advancing yet.

Elo pressed his gauntlets to his face. 'Ask someone else,' he said again.

Arren put his own gloved hands on Elo's, holding them. Hestra kept quiet in his chest, out of respect? Or pity?

'I know,' Arren said, and his voice cracked. 'I'm so sorry Elo. I know. But I'm asking you now. Do not sacrifice yourself. Elogast, my still-beating heart. Please live.'

How many moments had they shared like this together? So close, so tender, when all Arren could think was how little it would take to lean in and kiss him, to tell him, to hold him.

But then Elo would back away, the wall would go up between them. Prince and knight, king and commander, noble and merchant's child. Friends. Arren never tried. Elo had never let him.

And, as if he heard Arren's thoughts, Elo stiffened and stepped back, breaking their hold. His eyes were dark in the gloom, his bearing proud.

'You ask me to die, then ask me to live,' he said. 'No. No more. You made me your commander, King Arren, now let me take command. I will force the fire god to come, and I will have her kill them.'

CHAPTER TWENTY-ONE

Inara

COLOUR. EVEN KISSEN COULDN'T CONTAIN IT. LOVE BURST from her in shades of the sea, glittering as if with salt or frost. For Telle her love was greens on greens, cut through with sweeping gusts of yellow like sunlight. Yatho's love was the red glow of heated metal, sparks and fires, joyous and blooming with perfect violet.

Love in all its colours. Inara caught back a sob as the three of them fell into each other's arms and held each other as the waves of light around them softened, gentled.

She felt a hand on her own shoulder. Lessa, frowning askance. *Sisters*, Inara signed.

What were they doing here?

Lertes had half drawn his sword but slid it back into its sheath with a sigh.

'You absolute fucking bastards,' said Kissen, more to herself than to them, for she then signed. *Are you safe?*

We were invited when your ship was sighted, said Telle. She looked well, her dark hair recently cut, her tan brightening her scars. *They have been helping us.*

She looked towards Inara and held out her arms. Skedi almost fell off as she dived into the archivist's embrace and held on tightly. Telle put her palm to her back, gentle but firm.

'I am glad I was able to reunite you,' came a voice from the front, and Inara pulled reluctantly away to see who had spoken.

A woman had come forward. Her tightly coiled hair was shot through with silver, worn free and out around her head like a halo. She looked familiar, less by her shape, which was small, with slender shoulders and round hips, than by her bearing. Straight backed and sure, chin tilted up, proud.

'I am Mitha Bahba, of Antioc and Ellim. I believe you know my son.'

Telle stood back and signed to Inara. *She saved us. Elogast saved us. He wrote to her.*

Inara looked towards Bahba as Skedi settled back on her shoulder. 'You're Elo's mother?'

'One of them,' she said, inclining her head. 'Ellac, my heart's love, died the winter before last.' She had a deep, strong voice. A voice that could fell trees or raise a storm from the ground.

'I didn't know Ser Elogast's mother was one of the Mithrik,' said Lessa carefully, with a sharp glance at Kissen, who shrugged and shook her head.

'I was selected and elected eight months ago,' said Bahba. 'Unlike Middren, Irisian governance is through choice, not birth.'

Lessa raised a brow. 'More often than not, a blood relative of the predecessor gains the seat, do they not?'

To Inara's surprise, Bahba smiled, though there was a flutter of chatter in Irisian from the others. There surely weren't enough councillors here to represent the whole of Irisia? And two stood slightly apart, dressed in matching robes of purple. One had hidden their colours; the other shone in pretty coral hues of satisfaction.

Yatho was signing quickly to Kissen and Telle, and Kissen looked back.

They are Restish, she told them.

Inara felt her chest tighten, but Lessa was still speaking. 'I am glad the godscripts made it safely here to Irisia.'

'The wealth of Lesscia comes running into our arms,' said one of the Mitha gathered by the feast arranged on the tables. 'Your king appears to be haemorrhaging more and more each year.' The air around them was thick with the scent of sugar and nuts.

'And yet still there is much to lose,' said Lessa calmly. 'And much to gain. The Talician invasion is set to cause irreparable damage to our deep-water harbours, which we all know are valuable for our merchants travelling west.'

'Invasion?' said one of the purple-robed ones, the one with the pretty colours. 'If your king can't handle a few summer raids what is that to do with us?'

Lessa levelled her gaze at the speaker, and Inara held tightly to Telle's dress, leaving her hands free in case she wanted to speak.

'I may be misunderstanding something,' said Lessa softly. 'I came to treat with Irisia, not yet with the Restish. You are?'

'I am Advisor Efana,' he said, then nodded to his companion who wore a string of red beads. 'And this is Advisor Mirim. We came to ensure you did not have to journey further to Restish before you return to Middren. Travelling all this way on the back of your king's fearmongering is not what I expected of you, Lady Craier.'

Liar, said Skedi. *They came to plead their own case.*

Kissen straightened up, frowning. 'Fearmongering?' she said. 'I've seen the work of the Talicians first hand, *and* the Restish ships they are using for their invasion, just like that one outside. Do you know they burn little children for their god?'

'Kissenna,' warned Lessa, as Aslani cleared their throat loudly, but it was another of the Mithrik council, a man with bone earrings slotted through his ears, who spoke up.

'And we should believe the word of a *godkiller*, why?' he said. 'I am Mitha Chalada, elected of Wsirin, I don't like the idea of a *harasa* in my city.' That must be the Irisian term for a veiga. Something Inara's tutor hadn't included in her vocabulary lessons.

'Oh pipe down, Chalada,' said Bahba. 'Kissenna is under my protection, a friend of my son. And just because you find a job distasteful doesn't make it worthy of your derision.' She looked at Lessa. 'But perhaps we should let her return to her family?'

Kissen shook her head. 'I said I would stay with the Craiers.' Yatho looked at her with surprise, and Lessa smiled, but shook her head with only a touch of reluctance.

'Please,' she said to Kissen. 'Reunite with your family. It is, after all, why you came.'

They held each other's gaze for a moment, but Kissen at last muttered an assent as Telle turned to Inara. *Join us?* she asked.

After, signed Inara, and stepped back towards her mother. *This is where I belong.*

Telle nodded. She and Yatho drew Kissen through a door to the right of the chaises, and Inara, her mother and the crew of the *Silverswift* were left with the Mithrik and the Restish. Skedi tightened his claw on Inara's shoulder.

There is danger here, he said into her mind. *Conflict. Even in Bahba I see little lies.*

Bahba was Elo's mother, and Inara was inclined to like her, but Skedi was right, she had little currents of deception in her colours, carnelian and silver-sly. Strange.

Lessa stood calmly, waiting for the others to make a move. She kept her hands loose, her shoulders back, and Inara remembered something she used to say to her: *a quick tongue's edge dulls faster than a cautious one.*

Eventually, an older man broke the silence, sitting down on one of the loungers with the aid of a cane.

'P-please, come sit,' he said. His robes were pale, soft rose, and light, though he had a wool jacket loosely draped around him. 'We are leaders of our nations, n-not children.'

Inara glanced at her mother, who nodded, and she came forward to the chaises. Aslani sat beside her, and, stiffly, the others followed.

'My name is Sosul,' said the older Mitha, 'I see we hav-v-e a *quya* in our p-p-presence.' He nodded respectfully to Skedi.

'Skediceth represents the gods who still have shrines in Middren,' lied Lessa, and Inara resisted putting her hand up to stroke him as he instinctively lent some of his will to the untruth.

'And he is a god of . . .?' asked Mirim.

'Travellers,' said Aslani lightly. 'There are few *quya* that can travel so far from their shrine. He is half-wild, and clearly ancient. And as such welcome to our discussions.'

A white lie. Skedi grew slightly on Inara's shoulder with excitement. *Are they an ally?*

What if they just didn't understand?

I don't think so, look at their colours.

Aslani's colours shone the colours of burnished metal, curling, playful. They knew they were pushing truths. Skedi was right; an ally, perhaps, or at least not an enemy.

'I will continue with introductions,' they continued. 'I am Mitha Aslani, elected of Traada.'

They nodded at the next councillor, a woman. 'Mitha Imani, elected of Sicara.'

They went round in forced politeness, but Sosul gave Inara a small smile and nodded down at a black lacquered box on the laden table between some of the pastries that were drizzled in honey and greened with pistachio.

She opened it, and inside were mirrors, shining and smooth, and between large blocks of ice, barely melted, was a bowl of crushed snow, pomegranate seeds and zither herbs. Inara heard Rhiyande's intake of breath.

'There are a good thirty Mithrik not in attendance,' said Lessa, as the introductions were finished. Skedi crept down to sit in Inara's lap, small and unobtrusive. 'Many I would consider friends. Am I to understand I will address them at a later point?'

The silence was uncomfortable, palpable, like a surrounding of moss and shadow, full of unseen dangers. Lessa leaned forward into it, picking out a date from the offering set before them. Inara cast her eyes over the colours of the council, but nothing in them changed, and two others reached for the same. No poison then. She took Sosul up on his offer and put a spoonful of white ice into a bowl. She offered it to him first. His hands trembled and moved, as if he struggled with control of them, but he chuckled and shook his head.

'Bikul, bikul.' Eat, Eat.

Inara took a mouthful. She hadn't had ice since the Craier manor burned. They used to bring it down with the snows. It crunched delightfully, the pomegranate seeds popping in sweet, acidic bursts. She blinked, and grinned, turning around to Rhiyande. 'You have to try it,' she said, offering the bowl, and the spoon.

Rhiyande balked, looking at Lertes, who shrugged. The three crew were still standing while everyone else sat. Perhaps to act more like guards than councillors. But still, Rhiyande took the bowl and the silver spoon and took a bite, her eyes lighting up before passing it to Shah. The tension eased.

We'll ask for some after, said Skedi. *I'm sure I could wish it out of them.*

Inara bit back a smile. *Enough for the crew?*

Let me flex my wings.

'Those you see here represent most of our country's interests,' said Bahba, as the one called Imani poured some cups of tea, offering them around. 'We decided it would be enough to understand your king's message, and what he asks of us.'

'We understand,' said Chalada, 'you are in some border dispute with Talicia?'

'Talicia has invaded Middren,' said Lessa. Efana scoffed.

'I told you they were sea raids—'

'Daesmouth is half burned,' Lessa continued as if he had not spoken, not missing a beat. 'The Vittosk lands have been overrun, Benin is like to fall, and my own lands to the east of the Daes have been forcefully evacuated.' She turned her gaze to Efana. 'If you consulted a map, advisor, you might note those lands border the Bennites, not the sea.'

She turned towards the Mitha and held out Arren's signet ring, marked with his sigil. 'I have come on the king's behalf, for aid in weapons, arms and soldiers, to fight back against the Talicians and their god.'

'We have a l-long held agreement . . . hmm . . . to remain neutral,' said Sosul. 'Providing arms violates that t-treaty.'

'We have received reports, too, of civil strife within Middren,' said Bahba. 'After we lent weight to your petition, there have been mass arrests, protests, dead gods, and spilled blood. Unhappy stories of a kingdom at war with itself.'

'Your son may exaggerate,' said Lessa curtly. Was she annoyed at being blindsided? Or that Bahba's intervention had lost them Kissen?

'My son has told me nothing,' said Bahba calmly. 'Irisia is not blind any more than it is dumb. You yourself led a coup against your king, and now expect us to supply you both with arms to use against each other.'

Lessa picked up the tea she had been given, turning the cup in her hands. 'And yet I come bearing the king's sigil,' she said. 'At his request. Does that sound like civil strife to you?'

'We hear he burned your manor to the ground,' said Mirim quietly.

Inara saw the flash of Lessa's colours, bright white with anger, before they were hidden again. Inara swallowed, remembering the blackened bodies, the sound of the king's knights, laughing.

'Our dispute has been settled,' said Lessa quietly. 'Which shows how seriously we are taking this threat from the north.'

Settled, dispute is settled. Inara felt Skedi's power working, but the Restish who had hidden colours was not looking at Lessa; he was looking at them. Inara held his gaze, trying to blink innocently. If she could hide her colours, perhaps she had been trained also to hear the whispers of gods, like Kissen.

'You have thrown your lot in with a king who had chased Irisians *and* Restish from your land with their gods,' said Imani. 'Last time we provided aid, we reaped no reward, and great gods of the world were killed.'

Mirim nodded coldly.

'You cannot have us believe you would join arms with the king out of honour and duty,' said Chalada. 'You wish to benefit.'

Inara was about to protest, but a warning glance from her mother stilled her. She wished Kissen was here. Her anger would have been so vivid they would all have been forced to have a taste of it.

'Of course I wish to benefit,' said Lessa, picking up her tea and taking a sip. 'Do you think I desire for my daughter an inheritance of ashes? You think this is a squabble of swords? No, this is a fight for the heart of the Trade Sea, a battle against a god who desires to dominate them. A god of flame and war, greater than anything I have ever known.'

'You speak of Hseth,' said a councillor who had introduced herself as Narikast. Lessa nodded.

'Nonsense,' said Mirim. 'Hseth was killed only months ago. Even great Yusef took three years to return to life.'

'And we d-do not meddle in the w-w-w-ays of-f *quya*,' said Sosul, his left hand trembling in agitation, like a bird unready to alight on a bough. 'If you h-had done the s-s-s-ame, your gods would not have t-t-urned mad.'

The others did not interrupt Sosul, nor express any impatience. They leaned on his words as they came, respectful and quiet.

'Hseth is no normal god,' said Lessa gently. 'Her madness started long before the God War. You must have heard stories? They paint their own faces as if they have been burned. If that is the pastime of the lucky ones, what do you think they do to those less fortunate?'

Bahba looked to Sosul, who appeared perturbed.

'And Mirim, it is strange that you do not know,' said Lessa. 'The Three great priests of Talicia ordered living beings to be sacrificed for her resurrection. Hseth is reborn as a god of war, and she comes for all of us.'

Inara found herself brimming with admiration. Her mother would neither be silenced nor spoken over; she was greater than all of their prevarication.

'I am not here to ask for pity,' Lessa added. 'I am here to advise you all to fight for your future.'

The Mithrik were silent, looking at each other. Their colours had been so certain, already set when they entered, and now they danced, unsure.

'What, then, of your king?' said Imani.

'What of him?' said Lessa. 'I speak for him.'

'He did not tolerate our Irisian faiths,' said Chalada. 'Our people. Even Mitha Bahba here lived in Middren over twenty years, but was forced to leave because of his intolerance.'

'I didn't realise our personal lives were on the bargaining table,' muttered Bahba.

'Our king is a man still,' said Lessa. 'Mortal, and fallible. Unlike Hseth, his strength will wax and wane like the moon on water, and so will his conviction. Tell me what reassurances you need in return for your aid, and I will make them certainties. Above all, the king desires peace.'

'Is it true . . .' said Efana, 'that King Arren fashions himself *Sunbringer*?' He smiled. 'I heard despite all that he professes to believe, he has a god's fire in his heart.'

Can we lie? Inara threw to Skedi.

Not with my power, said Skedi. *It is too great a lie.*

'Are we to help such a man as that cling on to a throne that has almost been wrested from him?' laughed Imani without humour. 'Are we to sacrifice our own people, our lives, for his cause?'

'It isn't just his cause,' Inara blurted out. 'People are dying. People who need your help.'

Imani shook her head. 'Countries are not built on pity, child.'

'Maybe they should be,' said Inara. 'Maybe it would make them better.'

Lessa smiled softly, and Inara wondered if she had made her proud.

'Hseth is a threat to all of our world,' said Lessa. 'Ask the archivists you now harbour, what other gods have done when they turned to tyranny. Save Middren, save Talicia, save the Trade Sea. That is what I ask.'

'To us, *you* are the foreign threat, Lessa Craier,' said Efana. 'You and your pirate captain there.' He nodded up at Lertes, who smiled brightly. 'They masquerade as merchants and gentry as if that dispels what they once were.'

'Y-yes,' said Sosul thoughtfully. 'You rebelled ag-g-ainst your own king, Lady Craier, and now expect us to join-n you against another nation that has already made treaties of its own.'

'Mitha Sosul,' came a sharp reprimand from Chalada, as Efana's shades turned a sudden murky pink. Ah – a secret.

'Oh,' said Bahba. 'Is it not true that some of our own Mithrik have entered trade agreements with the Restish and Talicia? Or is that your personal life, Chalada?' Bahba maintained a look of innocence, but Chalada scowled, his colours turning bleached aquamarine.

Ah, agreements had been reached before they had even seen the Long Harbour, before they had set sail perhaps. Inara could feel her mother's fury like a cold breath of air. Inara's face flushed, but Skedi grew slightly larger, pricking up his ears.

'May I speak?' he said out loud.

Skedi?

Skedi had no love of Middren, nor of the king. He had spent

the past years of his life bound to her, in hiding, afraid of being hunted and killed. He had hated being trapped, hated the world for forgetting him. Inara knew that it was not so long since Skedi had pushed his power on her to try to free himself. Even before that, he would have flown away from her in a heartbeat at the slightest taste of freedom. Perhaps he still would, if he gained enough shrines. He had no reason to speak for them.

Trust me, Skedi murmured to her. *Gods can change too.*

He had proven himself to her over and over since his first cruel betrayal. Though their trust had been broken, it had been remade stronger, like wood that had knotted over a wound.

I trust you.

'You m-m-may,' said Sosul.

Skedi hopped down to the table, landing delicately between plates of food, and sat back on his haunches.

'I wish to ask whether you were there?' He looked at Imani first but turned then to Efana. 'In the God War. Did you come with the ships, into the harbour? Did you try to save people, Irisians, Middrenites, Restish, from the fury of the wild gods?' The gathering was silent. 'Do you remember what made them angry?'

Efana didn't answer, none of them did.

Skedi tipped his head. 'I was there,' he continued. 'Lady Craier too. The fury of the gods was not just at Middren, it was anger that their worship was fading, changing, dying in favour of the new gods of the Trade Sea. The ancient versus the new, the wild versus the profitable. They did not care whom they hurt or why, be it *quya* or commoner, knight, lady or king.'

It was half a lie, a remembered history that he had barely survived. His power covered it though, his will soothing the shades of the others, drawing them to believe him. Gently, gently.

'I myself fought,' he said. A truth. 'Alongside the great god of safe haven.' Mirim frowned. She put her cup down. 'He died begging for mercy, not for himself, but for his charges.' A lie? Even Inara wasn't sure any more, so drawn she was to this tale he was weaving. 'For his people.'

Skedi had them, they were listening, even the Restish.

'Hseth is not like Yusef,' he said. 'I have seen her try to drag

Lessa Craier's daughter into flame for daring to stand before her.'
Inara blushed. 'I have seen her kill indiscriminately, cruelly, painfully.
Her priests sacrifice humans, and destroy any gods that dare defy
her. Is that the work of a *quya*? Of your god of change?'

No one answered. Mirim looked slightly ashamed, but Efana's
colours had gone puce with anger.

'The tale of Blenraden is one of bravery,' said Skedi, growing
slightly larger so they would not interrupt him. 'One of human
strength, and gods' compassion against madness and fury, but it is
not a finished tale yet. The battle for the heart of the Trade Sea
goes on, between peace and trade, fear and faith, tyranny and
oppression. This is the next part of that story.'

Inara held her breath, trying not to burst with pride. Skedi's
will lent power to his storytelling. He used no threats, no great
falsehoods, nothing outside his nature, he simply told what he
knew, and pretended what he didn't. They knew he was a god and
could exert that influence, and perhaps they could resist it, but
they could not resist the sound of his voice, the certainty in his
proud stance.

'I am a god of people,' said Skedi. 'Of little lies, little hopes, little
stories. Middren has not been kind to me, but its people have. A
godkiller has helped me, a child has saved me, a knight has cared
for me.' He looked at Bahba. Her expression was unmoved, but
she knew of whom he spoke. 'There is hope still in the land and
hope still for its king. But if you avert your eyes from Middren
now, the story told of Irisia, and Restish, will be of cowardice.'

Aslani swallowed, looked hopeful, glancing sideways at Sosul,
then Narikast and Chalada. The latter, at least, seemed moved, his
cheeks flushing, his colours soothed from aggressive stabs to a
softer, deep violet.

At last, Efana moved, sitting up, making them all aware of his
presence. Then he smiled. 'A wonderful yarn that is,' he said, picking
up a small pastry. 'But treaties are treaties. And if Irisia moves in
favour of Middren, their part in it will be broken.'

He stood, popping the sweet in his mouth, and Mirim stood
with him, then Imani and Chalada reluctantly got to their feet. No
one protested, no one denied them. Efana's colours spiked around

him bright and glistening, oddly playful, victorious. The meeting was over, the unspoken threat of Irisian enmity hanging over them.

Inara dragged her eyes away, breathed in a shaking breath and shared a look with her mother. Skediceth's wings dipped in disappointment. The Mitha would not help them. Their work had been for nothing.

It was only then that Inara deciphered what the colours might mean. So insistent, almost like burning.

Like violence.

CHAPTER TWENTY-TWO

Kissen

GUILT. KISSEN FELT IT HEAVY IN HER GUT. SHE WAS ON A horse-drawn litter, waiting to be borne into a great city with her sisters, while Elo fought alone in Middren. Gods, she hoped not alone. She hoped he'd found someone interesting to spend his time with. But his mother had helped her, helped her sisters, on his word, and she had done nothing to help him. Even Skedi and Inara were being more useful than her.

She, Yatho and Telle spoke a little in sign as they descended into the noise of the port city, and Kissen was grateful for their language of gesture and movement. The air was thick and hazy, and she could barely feel her own thoughts as the cart moved into a crush of bodies, through the sprawling markets, the driven livestock, the smells of spice and charcoal, sweet wine and manure.

Are you brooding? Yatho signed to her.

Kissen forced a smile. Telle sat beside her, one hand tight on Kissen's elbow, as if to reassure herself that she was here and real. Yatho suited heat, in her open shirt and loose trews, but she was less soot-stained and singed than Kissen was used to. *I was thinking you both look well*, signed Kissen.

Liar.

Telle signed that, lightly, gently.

Kissen found tears building up in her throat and eyes. There were no words, she didn't know how to speak this . . . this relief. This joy. This fear. This remorse.

Soon their cart slowed to trundling, and beggars and scammers ran up to them, palms upturned, jostling for space. It was a fine cart, after all, and had come from the fortress.

Reminds me of us, signed Kissen, wishing she'd brought some coppers with her. Yatho grinned, reached down for a secret pocket she had fashioned into the seat, and pulled out a roll of copper coins on a long string, which she unclipped and began unloading onto outstretched palms.

You do realise if they were like us, they likely don't keep their coin, signed Telle. Though her gestures were small, and sad, she smiled as Yatho was buffeted with thanks and cries and requests for more. Maimee, who had made them beg, had taken all of their earnings as pay for 'debt, room and board', as she put it. Yatho soon ran out and held up her empty hands to a few cries of protest and regret. They quickly dispersed, and the wagon continued.

If they're anything like us, they'll find a way, said Kissen. *Speaking of, is it true you risked your life for a few books?*

Yatho frowned a warning at her. *Is it true you risked your life for a king we hate?*

Kissen chuckled. *He seemed the lesser of two enemies*, she said.

'He's an arrogant arsehole,' said Yatho out loud, and signed, *He's a coward.*

Telle, knowing exactly what Yatho had said both times, huffed out a laugh of agreement. *And what about the lady?* she asked.

She agreed to unite to help Middren, said Kissen.

Telle raised an eyebrow, a knowing look in her eye.

What? said Kissen.

She dressed you up like this?

She wanted me to look dignified.

'Hah,' said Yatho, then signed, *Sounds like she staked her claim.* She shared a glance with Telle, who bit the inside of her cheek. *And that you want her to.*

Kissen reddened, then laughed, running her hands through her hair before signing, *Am I so obvious?*

She's just your type, said Telle.

I don't have a type.

Yes you do. You're attracted to power.

'What?' Kissen protested, too shocked to sign and her sisters both roared with laughter. *No,* she signed at them, but she made certain her expression read *Fuck off.*

They were descending again now, towards large warehouses and a number of other carts and wagons going back and forth with produce. The streets here were cobbled with round stones, to Kissen's annoyance, and the kerbs were high. When they stopped, she balanced herself carefully, leaning her staff against the cart, and helped the driver and Telle bring down Yatho's chair and move it to where Telle indicated. A doorway arched with bright tiles, like the walls of the harbour front, the door wide and painted green, with a knocker in the shape of a jackal's head.

Telle lifted the knocker and rapped it while Kissen went to pick up her staff.

'A bit grand, this?' she remarked.

'It's one of Mitha Bahba's warehouses,' said Yatho, taking the brakes off her chair as the cart went up again, back to the city. 'She said it would be safe for us and the scripts. And there's a home attached.'

The door opened, and a young man standing behind it glanced across the three of them, then stood aside.

That was a quick visit, he said to Telle in sign, and looked at Kissen with mild disgust. 'I suppose you're the veiga,' he added out loud, disdain dripping from his high-class Blenraden accent. The kind of accent that Kissen would once have followed to pick their pocket.

'Be nice, Cal,' said Yatho, as Kissen took the back of her chair, pushed her up the ramp to the door and into the building after Telle. 'You too, Kissen.'

'I'm always nice,' they both said, and then threw each other irritated looks. Kissen resisted sticking out her tongue.

Beyond the door there was quiet, focussed activity. A series of open crates and boxes were marked with Yatho's worksmith crest of a hammer and wheel, but in them were manuscripts rather than metals, stuffed tightly and carefully tucked in with straw and the occasional bag of grain. The walls rose high around them, pink-painted and with small windows open to the sky, fixed with glass to keep the rain out and let the light in.

And within the pillars of light that fell, there were two people working, taking careful notes on paper scrolls: an old man with gold front teeth, and a tall woman with thick dark hair that she had netted with silver. She was as pale as the man was dark and, though neither wore grey, Kissen could tell by the way they looked at her and Yatho, as if they were only half there, that they were archivists. However, they both smiled to Telle and signed a respectful greeting.

The back of the warehouse offered a half-open gate to a pulley system that seemed to go all the way down to the Long Harbour, and from their height, Kissen could see its mass of movement and colour. Telle turned left before they reached it, past the pulley and through a trellis door in the side of the warehouse.

Beyond, they entered a grand room which held several chairs woven with grassy fibres in pretty repeating patterns. The floor was tiled in copper-coloured stone, and the pink walls continued, but the ceiling was lower than that of the warehouse, softer lit, and dimmed further by a sky darkening with the threat of imminent rain.

There sat an old man by an indoor fountain, surrounded by greenery. His silver hair was grown out, and his beard too, and he looked pale and unwell. His right arm had recently been removed, Kissen could tell by the smell coming from his thickly poulticed bandages, and he was practising writing with a brush in his left hand. Even to Kissen his letters looked wobbly and unkempt. But beside him was Bea, Yatho's furnace boy, also writing with brush and ink on paper, frowning in concentration.

The man looked up and scowled. 'Oh gods, you've brought a veiga.'

'Oh great,' said Kissen, 'another one.'

Yatho laughed, and Bea looked up, spotting Kissen. 'Kissen,' he said. 'Master Yatho's sister.'

Kissen was faintly surprised to be recognised; she had only met the boy once and had exchanged few words with him, as he had no fondness of speaking.

'Good to see you, *liln*,' she said.

'I'm Bea,' he said, frowning.

'Sorry, Bea. It's good to see you.'

He nodded, hummed under his breath, and returned to his letters. He was making good work of it. When something interested him, Yatho said he had more patience and focus in his littlest finger than Kissen had in her whole body. Well, she hadn't said that last part out loud, but Kissen knew.

'His brother has found work,' said Yatho, 'but Bea misses the forge.' She sighed. 'So do I.'

Sit, I'll make tea, signed Telle, went up a set of stairs into the higher parts of the building, presumably the living quarters.

'Ah,' said Cal, following her. *I'll help. Solom will need lanterns.*

'Bahba owns this?' said Kissen to Yatho, as they both went to the fountain. Kissen took a seat with relief. Her chest hurt even from that short walk. She wondered what Lessa and Inara were speaking of now? How many soldiers Irisia would send? Would it be enough?

'Mitha Bahba,' corrected Solom. Kissen scowled. 'She cleared it for us. We had been kept in harbour for *weeks* awaiting permits before she saved us.'

Forgive him, signed Yatho to Kissen. *His wound sickened him on the voyage, we had to remove it.*

He's not the only one here who has lost a limb. And I manage not to be a dick.

Yatho gave her one of her Looks.

Well, sometimes, Kissen added.

'Speaking of limbs,' said Yatho, wheeling herself opposite Kissen and looking down at the chipped, burned and boiled end of Kissen's prosthesis, where it stuck out of her trews. 'What the fuck is that?'

Kissen laughed and scratched her right knee where her burns were itching. 'Your last leg met a slow and sorry end,' she said. 'But it lasted all right after that bastard fire god melted it.'

'I'm impressed with myself that it managed to withstand Hseth,' said Yatho with a smile. Then, it faltered, dropped. She swallowed.

'Yath . . .' said Kissen, leaning forward, concerned. As she did, the heavens above them opened, and rain began to hammer against the windows.

'Sorry,' Yatho said, and her next breath shuddered. 'It's . . . it's been hard. Thinking you were gone. Leaving Middren. And now you're here, with Ina too, the wee fiend.' She laughed and palmed a tear from her eye. 'You taught her some bad habits.'

'Don't blame me,' said Kissen. 'I left her with a knight with a stick up his arse.'

'You knew he'd be just as bad.'

'I did hope.'

Yatho managed another smile, but it was tight, uncertain. 'You forgive him? Even after he called Hseth . . . almost got you killed?'

'We've all done mad things for love, been hurt by people we trusted,' said Kissen. She shrugged. 'Anyway, he's a good lay.'

'Ugh. I've never understood you and men,' said Yatho. 'There are plenty of nice women around. You just love mess.'

'I do not.'

The lady? Yatho signed, so Solom and Bea wouldn't see, bent as they were over their practice. *You nearly purred when you showed off your cloak.*

Nothing is going to happen.

I see spending time with a god of lies hasn't made you a better liar.

Solom looked up at the flicker of their hands and they both stopped. He tutted. 'If you're going to sign your secrets, go somewhere else,' he said. The sky darkened a shade further and rain rattled down outside, and a flash of lightning followed. Bea jumped.

'Soft, now, Bea,' said Solom, his voice gentling as he spoke to the boy. 'It's all right.'

'You're very lucky,' said Yatho to Kissen, while keeping a watchful eye on Bea. 'I didn't throw out the spare I was making.'

Kissen sat up. 'Spare? You have a spare?'

Yatho grinned. 'Aye, it's in parts, but we used it to cover the paper we stole. Won't be able to measure you though.'

'Thank salt for that.'

Just then, Telle and Cal reappeared, Telle bearing a large copper teapot that steamed with the scent of sage, and Cal with two lanterns hanging from his arms that brought some brightness back into the room.

'Ah you blessed boy,' said Solom, truly smiling for the first time. 'You do too much for me you know.'

They were all drinking and swapping stories, Cal even telling them about Inara and Skedi helping him sneak into the archives, when a flurry of noise from the warehouse stirred Kissen. She stood with her staff, her hand going to her cutlass, but it was Bahba who hurried through, followed by Lessa and Inara, and then Skedi, who popped out of the sleeve of Inara's dress.

None of them looked happy.

'Shit,' said Kissen. 'Irisia won't help?'

'Worse,' said Inara glumly. 'We think Restish is planning to attack.'

CHAPTER TWENTY-THREE

Elogast

ELO HAD A PLAN. HE BEGAN WITH THOSE HE TRUSTED: Benjen, Larsen, Ainne, Safidah, Elseber. Perin, who was grey and shattered with his loss. Knowing, too, that they would never recover Lotta's body. Not if all went well.

They all chose to stay.

They went about recruiting and setting orders, as the enemy, still in disarray, fought and clustered amongst themselves. More Talicians were coming from upstream, landing at part of the docks they had occupied, and joining them on the bridge.

The nobles were told to evacuate, Geralfi weeping as he was led away. Tiamh clapped Elo once on the back, but didn't look back as he retreated. Many of the guards of the western Houses also left. But before they went, shields, arrows, bigger weapons, were brought to the front, sawhands from the bridge set to make sabotages and boobytraps. Moving quickly, quietly, the Gefyris dismantled their own docks, breaking down struts and supports so the Talicians would fall or be forced to the central street.

A skeleton force of soldiers remained. Many of those who had chosen to stay wore the king's colours, and they stood there grimly. But some of them . . .

'I recognise you,' said a man with a yellowed beard, as Elo passed, instructing an Elemni soldier on the barriers they must raise at the final gate. Elo stopped, and frowned.

'You're Leir,' he said. 'From the Fisher's Stay.'

'And you're the singer who almost brought the house down.' Elo wasn't sure if it was a joke till Leir smiled. 'Come back to finish the job, eh?'

Despite himself, Elo felt his lips twitch. It was laugh or cry, and weeping would ruin his vision. 'You don't have to stay,' he said.

'Most of us grew up on these boards,' said Leir, looking around him. Elo recognised the others, including the owner of the Fisher's Stay, Tip. It seemed the old veterans had not lost the will to fight. 'Others found peace here, and work, after the war. We've put our lives on the line for Middren before, and we'll do it again. For the Sunbringer, and his Fireheart.'

'And I thank you for it,' said another voice.

Leir blinked rapidly, backing away. 'My king,' he said, bowing.

Elo turned to see Arren behind him, his helmet under his arm. He was beautiful in the firelight, and sad. To anyone else, he would have looked serene, but Elo could see the dint above his right brow, in the corner of his mouth. The tension there. There had been a moment, a soft, fragile, moment, when Elo had wanted to spill himself into Arren's arms. He had wanted to unravel it all and begin again. And then he had remembered himself.

Arren was with someone. A man Elo recognised by his yellow-and-white cloak, even before he lifted his helm.

'Tulenne,' Elo growled, his stomach clenching in a fist of fury.

Perin, who was near him stacking flour bags, spat down at the lord's feet, and he winced. They all knew who had been guarding the docks, who was supposed to protect them from surprise. Elo remembered Cilean, flung back, studded with arrows. He remembered Lotta, stepping in front of his husband. He remembered the moment he had known they had failed.

'I wish to offer my blade,' said Tulenne, his voice low.

'I have no need of the blade of a fool,' said Elo to Tulenne, but looking at Arren. Was this his doing? The king shook his head, slightly. No. This idea was all Tulenne's own. 'You are a lord,' Elo went on. 'Go back with the nobility.'

Tulenne swallowed, his face flushing beneath his thick brown beard. 'I thought about it,' he admitted. 'I watched them go. But I owe it to Sunbringer, to Gefyrton, to myself.'

'You owe it to all of us,' said Elo. 'You owe it to the dead.'

'Then let me pay my debt.'

Elo wanted to tear off the man's cloak, his armour, his head. He would still have him stockaded if they survived this.

But he would be a fool twice over if he refused an extra hand.

'Then you are not a commander here,' said Elo. 'Not a noble. You are a knight and nothing more. Captain Benjen will be your superior officer. If you flee I will cut you down as fast as any Talician, and I will be thanked for it.'

Tulenne's chin trembled, but he nodded.

'Go.'

Benjen was limping badly, his injured leg clearly aching, but he took Tulenne in his stride, immediately advising him of the plan, the traps, the approach. The lord, to his credit, did not protest.

Elo looked back to Arren, who had not moved. Eye to eye again.

Elogast knew what Arren wanted. He wanted to ask Elo again to come with him. To run.

He stood up straight, and then, slowly, bowed his head.

No.

Arren nodded, almost to himself, then turned to the assembly of fighters. Hestra was burning brighter now than she had for a long time, and the glow in his chest shone through the underside of his armour.

He really did look like a god.

'Fight well, my Middrenites,' he said. 'Stay alive, and I will see you at the west gate.' He looked at Elo. 'I will stop at nothing to get you out before the bridge falls.'

He turned, mounted his horse, and rode back west. The bridge felt empty as he left, the rest of the army gone. They had built the walls of the blockade high, so that the Talicians wouldn't see the space they were running into.

Nor what awaited them when they made their final attack.

The sky was still brightening. They were ready, and the Talicians still hadn't advanced. Perhaps they were uncertain; they had given so much blood to Hseth and yet she had not bothered to come.

Perhaps the god was wondering what more they would offer her to burn the Middrenites into ash.

Well, if the enemy refused to move, then Elo would begin. He stood behind the second line of the blockade with the few fighters remaining. He lifted a war horn to his own lips and blew. Once.

There was only one signal now.

The archers they had mounted on the taller buildings loosed flaming arrows, doused in grain spirit and lit on blacked-out lanterns. The streaks of flame made golden beacons in the lightening sky, like rays of the rising sun.

Many of the arrows went out before they fell, too dampened by the air, but some flamed, and found their targets in the Talician front, catching on their soft jackets, setting them alight Some screamed *Hseth Bleannat*, Hseth Blessed, but others just screamed.

As expected, the Talicians retaliated. No more waiting. Their bells rang, the priests in white once more picking up their travelling shrine, calling for attack.

And attack they did.

The first Talician foray hit the pikes of the front wall that they had buried between the gaps and topped with helms to make it look as if their force was larger than it was. They attacked wildly, confused, before they realised they had been fooled. They began breaking down the barriers, climbing over them and into the routes through, shoving them aside, taking their time to form enough space for Hseth's shrine to enter.

It was not long before they reached the next defence.

Elo and his team of fighters released props that were holding up a series of broken-open barrels. Those bastards were big, heavy, and full to brimming with fish and gizzards. At least five Talicians were crushed immediately beneath them, what little life they had between charging and meeting blade slammed into nothing by wood and stinking weight.

But the true intent was the contents themselves. Guts and blood slid everywhere, sending the enemy tumbling, slamming into each other, yelling to each other in Talic.

An easy target. Elo blew his horn again.

Around him, a second set of archers – brave souls all – stood on their barrels and loosed their arrows into the confused Talicians. They didn't need the fancy crossbows; they were Gefyris, hunting people, and they were deadly accurate. Captain Larsen, and Tip the innkeep took down enemies in the throat, the eye, while Tulenne, Ainne and Leir lit flagons of spirit, throwing them down to smash, burning into the invaders, ruining their night vision and destroying their sense of control.

'Fireheart!' bellowed Benjen. 'Sunbringer!'

'Sunbringer!' their coterie picked up the cry, and Elo too, screaming into the night, with all the rage of *Fuck you.*

Better to believe in something.

The Talicians committed a further force, picking up the faltering attack of the first wave and coming down the bridge.

Elo watched through the finest gaps in the boards. The night was brightening as the sun crept over the Bennites, and Elo could see wave upon wave of the enemy clambering through the slick guts and bodies, hammering their way through buildings, climbing to rooftops for better vantage points. They were scrambling over, following the heat of their own fervour, the ringing of the bells, the certainty now that Middren was on the run. That they were winning. Between the bodies, Elo could see the shining glow of the statue, refilled with coal, her legs blackened with spilled blood. The smoke of it filled his every breath.

Several Talicians found their way to the front. They climbed up the barricade, diving down on the knights below who were nocking their next arrows.

Elseber and Larsen charged them, Elseber swinging her shortsword with a deft hand, Larsen his battleaxe. The Talicians were too blood-hot to hesitate at the sight of their straggled unit, and rushed straight for them, stabbing wild and furious. Elseber killed two, then leapt to the top of the barricade to stop more spilling over. She thrust her sword down, down as she fought back the Talicians, trusting Larsen to guard her back.

'Fuck you!' she snarled. 'Fuck you for Lotta! Fuck you for Cilean! Fuck—'

'Elseber! Get down!' cried Elo.

A spear flew through the night from the Talician side, striking her through the hip and sending her sprawling down to the ground. Some crossbow bolts followed as Talicians found position, one striking Safidah across the helmet before Perin pulled her down. Two more struck, one slamming into Benjen's shoulder as he threw a flaming gourd. Tulenne caught him as he fell back, but he shoved him off, taking aim again and managing to hit a Talician square in the face as blood flowed down over his chestplate.

More would soon follow, and they would see how few they were.

Elo blew his horn. The next stage.

Retreat.

Larsen picked up Elseber. The spear had already fallen out, blood spilling thick over her armour, but she was alive. He lifted her, mail, plates and all, and ran with Elo, with all the others, away from the wall, leaving it to the Talicians to scale and break.

It felt like a long way to the gates. Every moment, Elo expected the slam of an arrow into his back, the strike of a spear through his thigh. Tulenne was carrying Benjen's swords as the captain limped and ran, blood spattering his lip. Perin was breathing heavily, but he was still uninjured, while Tip and Leir were together, their straggle of gnarled veterans running with them. The others were all safe. All alive.

They made it. They slipped through the bottleneck of the final blockade and closed it behind them, pulling carts and crates across to shore up the gaps, leaving only a narrow corridor within that no one could get through more than two-abreast. The throughways at the watersides had been shattered, broken, sawn to nothing, so now there was only one route through to where they would make their final stand: the plaza where he had first entered Gefyrton with Kissen, Skedi and Inara.

The rest of the Middrenites had followed his orders well: the courtyard was clear. In the pale dawn light, Elo could only see a few pieces of blanket, a half-drunk bottle of wine, and a little belt someone had been weaving from coloured thread.

He blew his horn again. This time, it meant *Hold. Spread out. Spread thin.*

On came the Talician army. Elo could see the smoke from their glowing statue now, a black streak against the sky. Their belief must have reached fever-pitch, with almost all of the bridge in their hands. Would Hseth be drawn by the strength of their certainty as the battle turned in their favour?

Come on, Elo thought towards her. She'd had enough sacrifices, surely? Gods were drawn not just by prayers, but people's intent, their will. The Talicians had to be wishing for her now.

If Hseth didn't come, they would lose the bridge and gain nothing except a dent in the Talician forces. No devastated morale, no broken faith. The enemy front would be suspicious now that the second barricade had fallen so quickly, but those behind would have no idea why they were winning, only that victory was near.

All they needed was faith in their own god to destroy them.

And Elo needed to hold on just a bit longer.

Benjen and Larsen were dusting the bottleneck with the barrels that had been set there for them. The last of the blackfire Arren had stolen. Perin was dragging a barely conscious Elseber back towards the gate as she groaned. 'No . . . no, take mmmme back.'

Perin looked Elo in the eyes, and understanding flickered between them. Elo was not going to stop them. They were down to less than a hundred now, but anyone injured couldn't keep fighting, and there was no point to letting them die lying down.

Besides, the man had already lost enough.

Elo tightened his grip on his sword, staring at the narrow passage between the blockade, feeling the shaking of the bridge through the soles of his boots as the Talicians approached.

And then he heard it. The singing. Not the Talicians; the singing of the Middrenites, the Gefyris, the lords, the children, guarding the banks behind them.

> *'Fireheart, lightbringer*
> *Bravest king of kings*
> *Sacrificer, god breaker*
> *Victory he brings'*

The Talicians reached the narrow passage. They sprinted along it, yelling for Hseth, for victory! For the west gate! They had crawled through a night of horrors, and they had made it to the other side.

They did not stop screaming as they reached the wall of Middrenites.

Leir cut the first one down, Tulenne the next. Elo felt his breath come quick, his heart pounding inside his chest. But this was what he knew, this was the fight in his bones. A Talician ran at him, breathing heavily, and Elo could see it in his face that he knew he was about to die. He stabbed him through the chest, the red coat not thick enough to provide protection from his blade. Beside him, Benjen was fighting too, grunting with pain.

'You should go,' hissed Elo. 'You're injured.'

'Not yet,' Benjen grunted, and jutted his chin ahead. 'Look ahead, commander.'

The statue had been raised over the third blockade where the Middrenites could see, its bearers struggling to fit within the narrow passage.

'Hseth! Hseth! Hseth!' they called, willing her forward, celebrating their triumph. One in white grabbed another, stabbing them through the neck so their blood sprayed upwards. Priests killing priests.

At last, a seam of flame ran along the arm of the statue, then another from the split and twisted skirts. She was catching. Finally, their faith had been enough to call her here. In a roar, flame licked up the statue, bursting upwards in a torrent, and Hseth came tearing out of the shrine like a storm summoned from the dark.

Heat. Terrible heat. It seared the hairs on Elo's skin, and his braids grew hot beneath his helm. He felt as if her hand was back in his chest, reaching for his heart.

But that was where any familiarity with the old god stopped.

This Hseth, this new incarnation, screamed at the sky, a dark weight of metal hung where the ribs of a human might be, her body around them twisting and writhing with flames. Dripping. Hot.

This was not the Hseth he had encountered before. That god had been beautiful, controlled, clever, fearsome. This was a behemoth, bigger than a fortress, an abomination of a god. Still beautiful, but born out of only suffering. Even as she rose, she split into pieces, and remade herself, in slightly different shapes, as if cracks were running through her.

To Elo's pride, the soldiers alongside him did not yet run. Did not falter. They stared down the god who would kill them. And some of them smiled, even as they pissed themselves, even as tears shone down their faces, falling steaming to the floor. And they held.

This was it, exactly what Arren wanted. An army, a people, that believed in him enough to die for him. Elo blew his horn one final time.

Retreat.

Hseth's flame caught on the blackfire of the narrow passage, setting it and the Talicians inside alight.

Retreat.

They ran for the gate, Elo picking up anyone stumbling, anyone falling, and shoving them towards safety.

Hseth howled, echoing the screams of her people. No sweet chiming, no blessed call, but a gong that shook Elo to his very bones, to the core of his self. Her shriek was manic, deathly; wild.

A spear appeared in her hand, and she threw it, shrieking past them and slamming into the gate beyond.

Elo stumbled back as the west gate caught fire, blazing up in a hideous inferno. Their exit, destroyed. They were trapped.

Then, Hseth launched herself forward like a wave, slamming into the Middrenites' left flank, killing two instantly.

'Return fire!' Elo yelled. What else could he do?

Their archers grabbed their briddite arrows and fired with shaking hands, Ainne, Leir, Larsen. They stuck like needles in her fire flesh, but did not hurt her, they barely distracted her. She turned to them, eyes burning coals, and reached for them with white-hot hands.

Elo sprinted for them, but Tulenne made it first. Determined to redeem himself, he drew his sword and slammed it into the god's leg. Its briddite edge, like most knightly swords, plunged deep into her flesh.

It made no difference. Hseth's attention landed on him.

Die.

Her voice cut through all of them.

'Tulenne!' Elo bellowed, but it was too late. Hseth dived towards the lord, tearing through him like parchment, like silk set alight. His armour melted, his body gone.

Elo stumbled. There was nothing for it. Fire or no, they had to go through the gate or they would face certain death. He could hear the shouts of those on the other side, straining to douse the blaze and open a way, save them. They needed a distraction for the god, but they had none. She delighted in picking off their fighters, one by shrieking one. The Talicians, too, were finding a passage through the burning blockade as its fires dimmed, risking the wounds for Hseth's blessing.

'Run!' cried Elo. 'Run for the gate! Break it down.'

Some grabbed barrels, risking themselves in the flames to smash at the inferno. But not Benjen. He was running towards Hseth. His helm was gone, leaving him only his cap and a spear in his hand that he had picked up. He sprinted at her feet, darting closer, striking her, then away.

'Benjen!' Elo yelled.

Benjen had survived the God War, had convinced Elo to take up the mantle of command. Benjen whom he had hurt, who had reached out to him, who had tried to kill him. Who was proud of him.

'Ben!' cried Elo, and ran after him, dodging spears of flame as they slammed into the ground. Hseth roared in annoyance and smashed through a building, sending it back across their blockade and striking some of her own army. Hot beams fell, bricks and ash, smoke and mist danced together, choking. The god was brighter than the sky, lit now to pink and red, like spilled blood and blush.

'Ben,' Elo reached him, grabbed him by the pauldron and began to drag him to the gate. 'Let's go!'

'I'll distract her!' Benjen said. He dug in his heels and tore himself loose. 'Get the others out!'

'Gods *damn* it Benjen!' Elo grabbed him by the wrist. Arren was supposed to have fired the barrels as soon as Hseth had risen, which meant he was holding off till they all escaped. Till Elo escaped. 'She will not care if you die. The king will not care! He has forgotten how!'

Benjen tore his arm from Elo's grip, turning to cut down a Talician who had come too close.

'It does not matter!' he shouted back. 'All that matters is that after all this, after every mistake, every god, every death – all that matters is that there is something left of us. Some song, some tale, some hope. My heart, my blood, my life for hope!'

They both flinched as an arrow flew past. Elo looked back at the god, whose flame-flesh was glowing with power. She grew larger still, towering over them, her light too blinding to look at directly.

Benjen smiled at him. 'Tell them to sing a song for me,' he said. 'Commander.' Then he ran, not for the gate, for the god.

Elo wouldn't leave him. He made chase.

But then, the gate doors burst open, charged by a run of horses, panicked and driven from the west bank. Four, five, ten, twenty. Elo couldn't count. They were not war horses: ponies, rangy mares, thickset geldings, screaming as they raced through the flames. With them they drew in the cold air from the forest which, as it pushed back the fire, allowed the Middrenites a moment to escape.

Hseth's attention was caught: horse, human, sword and noise. Benjen was still harassing her, the horses shrieking and stumbling. She hissed, reaching down to swat them away. Benjen dodged one strike of her fist, but the horse racing by him was not so lucky. Its mane and tail caught light, and it charged through their wrecked blockade, crushing Talicians as it fled.

But Benjen's plan was working, the distraction for Hseth had dimmed the fires of the gate, and their coterie was escaping through it, helped by knights wearing protective cloaks.

Then Elo recognised one of the horses in the plaza. Whinnying, terrified.

Legs.

'No!'

He could not take this. He could not handle one more death. Not Legs. He had promised Kissen. He ran for the gelding as Benjen howled out threats to Hseth, but then Elo felt hands on his armour, his arms, dragging him back, back towards the gate.

'Commander! You have to come now!'

'No! I have to go back! I have to get Legs! I won't leave them!'

He must have sounded incoherent as he was dragged underneath the arch of the gate, struggling and fighting.

The fire god burned white-hot, her flesh dripping, her eyes

burning brands. No more the red-haired woman of Talicia now, only of war and death.

I am god. Elo heard her voice scorch a path through his head. *I am rage. I am power.*

She spun up into the air, and crashed down upon those that remained, Benjen and the horses, the fallen and the dead, a show of blazing victory, utter destruction.

And her flame plummeted into the ground, beneath the god-made solidity of the bridge, into the struts, the homes, the arches, the pits, the waterfalls and the barrels of blackfire. There, her sparks ignited them.

Elo was barely through the gate when the barrels exploded. First, a shattering of splinters, a burst of rubble and fire, spraying outwards, smashing the cliff face, splintering the trees.

A moment of held breath, only the sound of the waterfall, relentless, endless, the crackling of Hseth as she looked at her own hands, as confused as a little girl at the explosions her power had wrought.

And the sounds of the horses screaming.

'Legs,' Elo whispered. 'Gods, Kissen. I'm so sorry.'

Legs dying in flame and terror. Legs dying at war. Another promise broken.

Then, the bridge groaned. The sound of cracking beams whipped through the air. The foundations of the bridge were shattering, weakened by fire, buckling under the force of the waterfall.

Then the great statue of Sali that held up the west of the city cracked, her arms and torso splitting. The west gate broke away from the bank, dust turned the waterfall spray grey. The bridge was full of Talicians, and they began to shriek.

A few ran for the gate, leaping to the bank where they were pinned and captured One or two horses managed to follow the way back, but none of them was the familiar brown steed with the white stripe on his nose.

None of them was Benjen.

The snapping bridge was peeling away from the rocky cliffs. Homes above and below the city, the tall inns, the markets, the docks, crumbled into the falls, borne down by the weight of the water. Down, down into the river's depths.

And with them, the weight of more than a thousand soldiers fell, tumbling, howling, little red drops in the flood.

Hseth did not move as the city fell. She gazed at it as if it had nothing to do with her, shattering to pieces at her feet. There were still Talicians on the opposite bank, seeing their victory turned to flame and dust.

Then, their god laughed. Delighted at what seemed to be her own trick, her cackle echoed over the roaring of the water, the cracking of the stone, the breaking of history.

And then, as the sun broke over the Bennites, she tipped her head upwards and twisted into nothing, to find another sacrifice, or another shrine that had not been swallowed by the water below.

CHAPTER TWENTY-FOUR

Skediceth

LESSA CRAIER HAD GLOWERED IN WELL-PRESERVED SILENCE on the way through the town, like a spirit in a jar, potent and ready to be released. Bahba and two other of the Mithrik, Chalada and Sosul, had joined them on the journey down into town in a fine gilt carriage with a canopy that protected them from the sudden downpour. The rain thundering into the streets, streaming into deep gutters, and washing filth, fallen fruit, dust and market leavings away towards the sea, leaving only the scent of warm stone and rising steam.

But when they reached the centre of the market, the others had alighted with polite goodbyes, and Lessa had managed to acknowledge them. Skedi could tell by their shades that they did not believe her one bit.

He was getting better at this human thing.

Inara's colours were seething like a simmering pot. Skedi was frustrated too, for his attempt to sway the council had been overridden by their own wills.

You're right, he said to Inara. *The Restish colours held violence after the council. We should tell your mother.*

But we do not know why, or what it means.

She might.

Bahba was watching. They didn't know if she could sign, but

Skedi could speak to Lessa without being seen, if she would let him in.

Lady Craier, he had pressed into her mind. Hard. Harder. Human colours were an entry point. When they were hidden, it was like looking for a crack of light while blindfolded. He pressed harder, lowering his antlers. *Lady Craier!*

The lady winced, flinched. Looked at him.

The Restish have some plan in motion. Something violent. Inara and I could see it.

She pressed her lips together and released just a touch of her emotions. He could see them, rich and stirring, threaded through with green and silver. She was thinking of her House. Of Middren.

She glanced at Bahba, then at Inara. And very slightly, she nodded.

It is likely they intend to launch an attack, she said, her voice cool and serious in his head.

On us?

On Middren. Sosul and Bahba all but told us they had made a trade deal with some of the Mithrik councillors. My bet is that it includes our ports.

By the time they reached the warehouse, the hush about them was so thick that Skedi felt even moving would shatter it into sharp and bloody pieces. Kissen, however, had no care for the delicacy of silence.

'What the fuck do you mean, Restish will attack?' she said, and then remembered to add sign for Telle's benefit.

'Indeed,' said Bahba, staring at Inara now. 'What makes you think so?'

Inara glared at her but said nothing.

'It is no secret that Restish have been building warships,' said Lessa. 'And no lie that they have sent some to support the Talician invasion. Why set so much store by a treaty, unless they are hiding more than just a few ships?'

'Well,' said Bahba, folding her hands over her chest and leaning back in surprise. 'You're even more astute than I took you for, Lady Craier.'

Lessa raised her eyebrows at Bahba. Elo's mother's colours were steady now. They had flickered briefly with surprise, but it didn't last.

She knew.

'I have prepared a meal,' she said, to Skedi's astonishment. 'In the night market. We will dine together. All of us.' She smiled at Kissen, who returned the expression a little nervously. 'Make it seem friendly-like.'

'I'm afraid we must be leaving, Mitha Bahba,' said Lessa, trying her best to hide the fury Skedi could see was filling up her insides. 'We must head for Restish and see if we can sway them from this course.' Or sway their gods at least, Skedi thought. 'Each hour is precious.'

'The tide is out,' said Bahba. 'Your crew is dispersed. Come, break bread with me, and we will discuss our options. You will not be departing tonight unless you wish your hull cracked on our harbour.'

Skedi, Inara said, her voice coming into his head clear as a song. *Her colours . . .*

Skedi had noticed it too. Bahba's colours in the fortress had been edged with thrills of strange amethyst and a dark stream of jade. Contrarian, contrasting. Deceptive. But now they were pure and shining gold. She had something for them, some generosity.

'Lady Craier,' she said, 'I wish to be better friends with you.'

'Mama, I think we should go with her,' said Inara.

Lessa frowned, Likely she had no intention of setting sail: she simply wanted to take her bad temper to her own cabin. But she looked at her daughter, then at Skedi. 'Very well,' she said.

'God Skediceth,' came a voice from near Yatho. Skedi turned, and his ears pricked with delight. Solom, the giver of his finest offering: the green-beaded bracelet on his antlers. The archivist was frailer than he had been, but his colours, oh his colours. They were azure and ruby, bright as fresh ink on pale parchment. Skedi knew that steady brightness: faith. But – he could feel it in his feathers, his antlers – this wasn't faith for another god. This was for him. 'I have something to show you.'

Inara didn't say a word as Skedi dug in his claws, excited, surprised, nervous, and walked straight towards the archivist. Skedi didn't even question that she should come with him as Solom led them around the fountain towards the back of the foyer. The sound of rain on the roof was gentle, like beads being poured from a basket into a bowl, and there was the faintest scent of incense in the air. Sandalwood.

At the back, beneath the stairs, a small house had been raised, painted bright, vivid red. It was a simple thing, two walls, a roof, but beautiful. A shrine.

And within it, was a statue of Skedi. He was made of polished wood, swirling and knotting with the grain of the original branch. The wings were tucked close to his back, but they were whittled in painstaking detail, while his antlers were made of carved white bone, brighter even than the shining amber eyes that had been inset delicately. The sound of the rain faded, the murmuring of folk, and all of Skedi's senses focussed on this vision, this totem: his fur, his wings, his self. Every shape and part of him.

'God of telling tales, and giving hope,' said Solom. 'You stood against a great old god of knowledge and protected us. It was the first thing I had made when we came.'

For him. Just for him. Skedi danced his paws on Inara's shoulder, unsure what to do, but she reached up with her palms to him, and held them out. He lifted his wings slightly and stepped into them, then she lifted him towards the shrine. He shrank enough to fit it, and stepped inside.

Colour. The statue, the totem, had colour. Light. Feeling. Faith. An offering of ink sat in a bowl before his statue, and sandalwood burned, held in a pincer of pewter in a slot at the edge of the shrine.

This was not sharing Yusef's shrine. This was not a tie on a little girl's heart. This was for him alone, built with love.

You deserve this Skedi, said Inara. *You deserve people to believe in you.* She paused. *Skediceth.*

'Thank you, Solom,' said Skedi.

He knew he had been feeling stronger, brighter, bigger, but he had thought that was all to do with the shrine Lessa had added him to on the ship, partaking of offerings to Yusef. But the old archivist, injured and worn as he was, had made good on his promise to make Skedi a home of his own.

He wondered if he had colour like a human, what it would look like now. If he could weep, whether he would. But he could see the emotion in Inara. It bloomed around her like the petals of roses, like the dead god Makioron, swirls of ink and paper like Scian – pale and red and peach shades flowing out and blossoming. Her memories and emotions flowed around her, around him. Love, and loss, the knowledge that one day they would be parted, and the joy that he had somewhere to be. Somewhere he belonged.

She cried for him, his human.

CHAPTER TWENTY-FIVE

Inara

BAHBA BROUGHT THEM BACK OUT TO THE CARRIAGE AND into the city, Yatho and Telle joining at her insistence. Though the rains had almost stopped, the sky was only getting darker, and the night market was a glow at the feet of the sharp slopes that descended towards the Long Harbour.

This is what we get for mixing with highborns, said Yatho, as she sat, looking less than comfortable on the brocaded seats, her wheelchair this time tied to the back of the cart along with the pieces of Kissen's new leg. Never one to do one thing at a time.

The highborns can understand you, said Kissen. Lessa gave her a distracted smile, but it fell quickly. Inara could practically feel the churning of her mother's mind as she tried to understand what Bahba was planning.

This isn't an easy place for you to use your chair, Kissen signed to Yatho, clearly trying to improve the mood. *It's steep.*

Yatho rolled her eyes and nodded. *I can't wait to come home,* she said, then hesitated. *If we can.*

You'll come back? signed Inara.

Telle bit her lip, then touched her wife's arm in a gentle, reassuring way, but the flush of her colours was closer to shyness. *Yes,* she signed. *Not to the archives. I want to make a school.*

Yatho smiled at her proudly. *For children like us, or Bea. Disabled, or in trouble. I could make useful things.* She nodded at Kissen. *You could teach green spaces, plantlore, fighting and rehabilitation.*

I haven't the patience for teaching, replied Kissen.

I thought that, before you met her, said Telle, nodding at Inara.

She's right, said Inara, smirking, *she doesn't.*

Yatho snorted, and Bahba looked towards them. 'Anything interesting?' she asked.

'Your guests want to go back home,' said Lessa to Bahba, pointedly.

'And I hope they shall,' said Bahba. 'Lady Craier, you seem to be under the illusion that I have the power to sway all the Mithrik to my favour?'

'You seem to be under the illusion that I care a whit for these niceties when my country is on the edge of ruin.'

This is going to be an interesting dinner, Inara thought to Skedi, who shook out his feathers. The night was growing hot and heavy after the rain, and he still didn't like being wet.

The carriage wobbled as it descended. They passed money changers, instruments from western lutes to southern kora with their multitude of strings, and into herb-smokers, salt-sellers, sweet-makers, bread-makers. The streets were wide enough that the stalls were in several layers, some permanent around the edges and some set up as temporary covered tables rippling out from the centre.

They came to a halt, mid-market, by a large, covered dining area between the stalls, lit by glass lamps hanging from poles. The scent of charcoal, zither and sweet thyme filled the air, along with crisping bread, herbs and steam. Several charms hung from the awning, in a number of different symbols for gods Inara didn't recognise.

'*Yameti'i melikami yataghayar!*' a woman called, coming out to greet them.

'*Kama alaik yatagha,*' responded Bahba, Lessa, Inara and Yatho following suit, as well as the drivers of their carriage, in an array of greeting cries.

'You bring friends from Middren, at last!' said the woman in accented Middric. 'You look hungry! Have you eaten?'

She added in Irisian to Bahba that they all looked as if they needed a proper meal. The colours were warm between them, bright and in rhythm. Affectionate. The host's colour of greeting was the beautiful, earth-and-ochre tones of Bahba's freckled skin.

'The lady speaks Irisian, Albia,' said Bahba, with a slight tone of warning.

'The famous pirate of Middren, I should expect no less,' said their host, unflustered. 'Come, come in. Take tea.'

There was a man standing to the side holding an ornate tray of etched silver, bearing steaming glasses of bitter tea. Inara took one, and they followed Albia and Bahba through brightly coloured awnings, painted silks and muslins decorated with images of changing seasons, crashing seas, skeletons and children dancing together.

The god of change is everywhere and nowhere, Telle said to Inara, Yatho having taken her tea so she could still sign easily. Such a small grace, a loving offering. *They have no totem, excluding their meaning: death, life, seasons, sky and sea, growth and decay. I understand that if they have manifested, it is not as something visible.*

Inara nodded, looking up at the vivid colours. *What is change but change?* she replied, and Telle put her hand approvingly on her head.

There were other patrons, in rooms that they passed behind thick curtains. Only when someone passed through did Inara see motley collections of folk from all over the world, sitting around low tables covered in plates of food from around the market. They were all indifferent to their passage, focussed on their own chatter and negotiations.

No threats, said Skedi, and Inara nodded. *No deception, no lies.*
But what does she want?
I don't know.

Albia lifted a curtain and revealed a small marquee lit by lamps and braziers, with one side open to the busy market to let in the air and show the sights, but the rest enclosed so that it was quiet and cloistered, private. The seats here were arranged differently too, all tipped in towards each other around a table that was heavy with steaming plates. Another woman in light, simple robes was uncovering them: yellow rice dotted with currants, green seedpods steamed by a thick, sweet-smelling stew of purple vegetables, walnuts, onions, and chicken legs, sprinkled with pomegranate seeds like little gems. Beside it was a baking pot of tiny birds surrounded by dark pink fruits and white butternut, while on a grill over a metal tray of coals was a whole fish, broiled in a reddish broth, still bubbling and further decorated with fermented crumble.

There were also stuffed gourds, red and round and filled with egg mixed with herbs and rice, as well as long yellow tubers sliced in half, their innards baked and dusted with spices. These were arrayed next to what looked like sticky dates stuffed with cheese and nuts and then fried with a strip of fatty meat around them, and finally, four or five dips of red, pink, beige, and white yoghurt.

There were several kinds of bread: small corn-yellow balls that looked more like cakes, the round flatbreads that Elo made, covered in the same mixture of seeds and herbs, and flat and plain disks dotted with heat where they had been cooked in the humped clay ovens that Skedi had seen across the market.

Everything was freshly prepared and hot. Lessa seemed lost for words, and Bahba took the host's hand in hers, and kissed the ends of her fingers, one by one.

'This is a mixture of foods from around Irisian lands,' she said when she released it, 'but also to the south, east and west. This market is a haven for weary travellers, and this is my favourite place to break bread and meet new people.' She smiled at Kissen. 'I brought Elogast here when he was just a boy, before he had decided to take up the sword.'

'Oh I remember that lad of yours,' said Albia. 'Couldn't stop eating!'

'Ellac did indulge him. If he didn't tend towards length in leg, he would have been wide as a ship, I swear!'

'Wives are meant for indulging, Bahba. Oh,' Albia turned to Yatho, 'my friend, I have chairs that should help support your back.' She gestured at a low chair with a shaped base and a back support, not unlike her wheelchair. 'And I arranged the seats to face inwards so your wife can better read faces and mouths.'

'Though please do tell me if I speak too fast,' Bahba put in, with a self-deprecating laugh.

Telle watched Yatho's translation, and then smiled. 'Thank you for this feast,' she said out loud.

They sat in their circle and put down their teas as Bahba picked up a glass bottle and poured them all a cup of a clear liqueur, then followed it with a spoonful of molasses, and another of honey which pooled in the bottom like old blood and fresh gold.

'Please, a toast,' she said, passing around the glasses to everyone. 'To friendship and good fare, and the god of change.' She poured a drop on the floor behind her, a gift to the god on the fresh reeds beyond the edge of the carpet.

'To the god of change,' Inara murmured, and after making her offer, took a sip. She spluttered, coughing at the strength of it, and Kissen laughed at her, took a sip after making no offering, then spluttered as well, tears coming to her eyes. Skedi stood up on his legs, likely afraid that the glasses were poisoned.

'I forgot to say,' said Bahba, 'it's quite strong.'

The people helped themselves to food, while Skedi watched on. To one who didn't eat, Inara knew he thought it an odd human custom. With so much terror happening in the world, at home, to their loved ones, how could they take pause? But Inara saw how peoples' colours changed as they filled their bellies, pleasure blooming and warmth piling up. Even her mother sat more at ease, her expression softer as she and Bahba kept suggesting different plates to the others, ordering in some more; fresh clams dipped in a spiced, clear sauce, a bowl of green vegetables with oils, vinegars and lemon zest.

'Why did Elo never come for this?' said Kissen at last. 'Living in a little village, all on his own? He could have been feasting.'

Bahba sighed. 'When he did not come with us from Middren we thought he might spend his time at court. But then he left that too, and we hoped it would not be long until he followed. We didn't understand how much he was hurting, and we let ourselves get busy. Busier. Then, Ellac died, and . . .' A rosette of grief in light blue blossomed around her colour. It was not a harsh pain, like the grief Inara had seen, but more of a deep ache through her colours, down to her soul. A yearning that shone with pain and warmth in shining currents.

'Tell me about him,' Bahba said to Kissen. 'He wrote like you knew each other well.'

The veiga looked at her, and lowered the piece of gourd and rice she was holding. 'Do you want softness or honesty, Mitha Bahba?' she said. 'We've a god here who doesn't like it when I speak plain, but I never learned any other way to be.'

'Speak plain to me,' Bahba assured her.

Kissen tongued her gold tooth, and sighed. 'Your son is heart-wounded,' she said, 'and tied to a king who has done little but hurt him. When some of us go through bad things, it haunts our body, our mind. Waking nightmares, shakes, pain, it feels like your enemy is your own self.'

Telle nodded slowly, and Inara remembered her own pain and panic when first hearing Hseth's bell in Blenraden. The terror that had frozen and trembled her all through.

'When I met him, I . . . pitied him. Proud bastard that he was. I could see he held that haunting.'

True pain crossed Bahba's colours, a tainted, coppery red. Her expression, guarded, did not change, but Skedi shrank a little. He was likely wishing, as Kissen had said, that she was better at telling gentle lies around her harder truths.

'I also saw that he had a kindness in him,' said Kissen. 'And strength. And he's a bit of a prissy fucker if I'm honest.' Telle widened her eyes with warning at Kissen, but Bahba chuckled. 'If he had children and gave them half the attention he gives his bread they'd lead very loved lives.' Inara, who had saddened at Kissen's first description of Elo, managed a laugh. 'He's also smart, most of the time. But he's gone far away from himself, and he can't find the way back.'

Bahba breathed out. 'His heart has always been the king's,' she said. 'Ever since we allowed him to go squire at the palace. He was a sad, lonely little boy, that Arren.'

'Now a sad, lonely little king,' said Kissen. Bahba huffed a small laugh.

'He would come around to our home,' she said. 'He was charming, but you could see it in his eyes. Half-starved for love, he hungered for it always. Our Elo wanted nothing more than to protect him.'

Inara considered that, looking at Bahba and seeing the shine of her care for her son. With two mothers who felt such a way, who poured it into him, Elo must have experienced so much love growing up that it had filled him, and he wanted to pour his cup into others.

How godlike humans could be, said Skedi, directly to her. *I will never understand why Hseth would take pain when she could have love.* Inara reached out to him, putting her hand on his back, but Lessa spoke next, thumbing her glass.

'I have little pity for the king,' she said. 'Yes, he was badly treated as a boy, but many have suffered pain and not burned others for their power.'

Bahba smirked over her cup. 'I thought you were here to plead for your king, my lady,' she said.

'Mitha, I came to plead for my country.' Lessa nodded at Kissen. 'The veiga told me the king could assure our survival. That uniting with him would renew the trust of our old allies.' She glanced up, pointedly. 'It seems the effort was wasted.'

Kissen clicked her tongue. 'I was advised by wiser folk,' she said.

'You were advised by gods,' said and signed Inara, taking no small pleasure in saying so, and making Yatho and Telle laugh enough for Kissen to glower at them as Skedi fluffed his fur.

A parade had started through the night market, following small palanquins and playing music, trailing flags. The noise was discordant and joyful, and loud despite the curtains that separated them.

'Your gods are also against Hseth?' said Bahba, looking askance at Kissen. 'So much that they sought help from a godkiller?'

'I was born in Talicia,' Kissen said, signing easily as she spoke. 'I saw it fall to riches and ruin, then lived in Blenraden with the worst of the gods' scraps—'

What a rude thing to call us, Yatho signed, and Telle snorted. Their colours were liquid and woozy now; perhaps they had also had too much of the strong liqueur.

'But when I saw what Hseth would become . . . the gods knew I'd believe them. Osidisen of the north sea, Aan of the river,' her scowl deepened, 'Faer of the north wind. They once were well loved in Talicia, but were forced out by Hseth. If the fire god takes on more power, more faith, more killings, she will eat everything in her path.'

'Elogast said that she also had gods on her side,' said Bahba, gazing over at the parade. The palanquins were covered, but Inara could see the glow of colour around them. Totems for gods were inside, and the parade was collecting coin as offerings from those they passed. This was an interesting turn to the conversation, from sons and childhoods to gods and the war.

'Used to,' said Inara, and Skedi looked at her in surprise. 'Hestra, god of hearths, was her ally, but now Hseth has left her behind.'

'Ah, harvest, haven and hearth. I have heard of Hestra. She was popular in Restish for a while, before trade and haven cults took precedence. Few care for their homes when they can have wealth and riches, and the Restish king saw the other gods as better for his coffers.'

Bahba looked across at Lessa. 'You have a fine daughter here,' she said. 'A god who has blessed you, smart women around you. A ship and connections, pirates and riches. Now Irisia has turned you down what will you do?'

Lessa lowered her glass and Inara watched her. In her heart, she knew what she thought was right, even here among all these beautiful things, she could feel the hot breath of the war in Middren. She wanted to go home. What did her mother want? Lessa breathed in, and then out.

'I will return to defend my country,' she said at last. 'I am loyal to my House, and my land, and I believe that between the intelligence of Elogast, and the ruthlessness of King Arren, they may yet win. I will be damned if I let them fight for my people without my help. I will do my daughter proud.'

I can see why you like her, said Yatho to Kissen, once again forgetting that Lessa and Inara could understand her. Kissen put her palm to her face for a moment, then signed back to her sister weakly.

I hate you.

Inara decided not to notice, and Lessa only had her dark gaze on Bahba. 'You do realise, Mitha,' Lessa added, 'that if Restish and Talicia take over Middren and build their alliance, Irisia will be next.'

Bahba sat back, her fingers on her chin, and considered her at length. Then, something in her colours turned steady, and her mouth lifted in a smile, and Inara understood why she had brought Lessa here, fed her alcohol and good food, loosening her defences. It was a test. This was where decisions were made, in private meetings, over wealth and dinners. A special, separate kind of lie.

'Yes,' said Bahba. 'I realise that. And so do others besides. A few of the Mithrik have made their own deals with the Restish in return for a blind eye, believing the end of this war is already certain. Others . . . well, we are prepared for another outcome.'

Lessa's face stilled. 'Prepared how?' she said, lowering her glass.

'The god of change is not passive,' said Bahba. 'There are those who see the future as inevitable, and others who see it as opportunity. *I* see it as an opportunity to save my son, my country, and our future. I have a few ships at my disposal, with arms and supplies. And Irisia has a well-trained army that you sorely need.'

'Your army will not move without your council's agreement. And they have already refused.'

Kissen and her sisters were silent, watching the exchange and signing to Telle what words were said.

'That would change if Restish were to commit an act of war,' said Bahba.

Lessa's barely controlled temper flared up. 'If you think we can wait to make a *pissing* painting of them landing on our coast, you are—'

'I do not mean an attack on the coast,' said Bahba calmly. 'I mean an attack on a king's ambassador, bearing his seal.'

Lessa paused, and Kissen sat up straighter. Yatho still signed to Telle, but her wife stopped her. The parade was coming past, louder now, covering their speech. If someone could read their handspeak, someone paying attention to them, the secrets of that table would be revealed. Had Bahba planned that too? Inara was starting to see where Elo got his strategic mind.

'She is not lying,' said Skedi, sitting back on his haunches.

'I have no lies to give you,' said Bahba, leaning in and lowering her voice. 'Only danger. My allies believe the Restish intend to capture or stop you from setting sail. Most likely, they intend to ambush you on your ship as you return.'

Lessa tensed, then stood. 'My crew,' she said. 'Are they in danger?'

'Do you trust them?' Bahba asked. 'Fully and completely?' Lessa didn't answer, and Inara knew why. They had been loyal, they had been true, but then thirteen years had passed without her as captain. After Satuan, they didn't trust her, not fully.

And so no, they could not trust them.

Bahba nodded. 'Listen a moment longer, then you may decide,' she said. 'My spies tell me the Restish intend to consolidate rule of Middren under a puppet monarch, once the current king is killed. I understand you have some relation to the Regna line.'

'Most Houses do,' said Lessa, sitting back down, slowly, her hand tight on her sabre.

'Most Houses didn't manage to rally half the country into a coup,' said Bahba. 'You are the only monarch the remaining Middrenites might be moved to accept. Hence, you are now in great danger.'

The lady's jaw clenched, and Skedi grew defensively. Inara knew he was trying to make her feel safe, but it wouldn't work. He should save his power. The parade was almost upon them, and several of the dancers eyed their little party, their colours showing not violence, but deception. Inara realised that the palanquins had been just large enough for two humans, and balled her fist in her skirts. Whatever Bahba wanted, she'd better make it clear, or they would have to run.

'My original plan was to keep you here and hide you,' said Bahba, 'even against your will.' She looked over at the parade. Inara was right. The palanquins would have been enough to fit her and her mother. And, when Bahba held up her hand, knuckles to the dancers, they spun away, colours softening and carrying the shrines into the market. 'But I believe you have some fight in you my lady.'

Lessa was neither flattered nor soothed. 'You have kept me here while you *knew* my crew was being either bought or killed.'

'It was them, or you, or both,' said Bahba. 'This is life or death, Lady Craier. I know the balance of battle better than you think.'

'The fuck . . .' hissed Kissen.

'If you return to your ship, you will be captured by the Restish,' said Bahba. 'On Irisian land. Most likely they will have your crew capture you first, and then transport you to their ship out beyond the Long Harbour, where there are fewer prying eyes.'

An act of war. Inara's heart was thudding against her ribs. Her mother on a throne? Restish planning an attack?

'No,' said Kissen. 'This is ridiculous. There are a hundred ways it could go wrong.'

'This will sway the Mithrik to help Middren?' asked Lessa. 'They will be able to use it a reason to override the others?'

'I swear it on my son's life,' said Bahba. 'I have not helped him as I should.' She looked at Kissen. 'This is the way I have found. More than weeks of council negotiation, a scouting mission, a petition, we will catch Restish in the act, and be able to move swiftly in retaliation to Middren's shores. Inara can come with me . . .'

'I'll go with Mama.'

'You will not,' said Lessa.

Inara had expected that. 'Then . . . I'll go with Yatho and Telle.' They knew what she was, what she could do, she wouldn't sit idly with Bahba eating sweets. Besides, Skedi's shrine was with them, he deserved to see it one more time. Telle reached over and squeezed her arm.

Kissen shook her head, but what she said wasn't what Inara expected. '*I'll* go with you.' Inara's heart stopped its thudding, and it swelled. Kissen wanted to help. Kissen would protect her mother.

'Don't be ridiculous, veiga,' said Lessa. 'You've found your family. Your part is more than done in this.'

'I . . .' Kissen looked at her sisters, and bit her lip. Her control slipped for a moment, and Inara saw the heady rush of her colours, the rage, the love, the gentleness, the violence. The fear. And Inara knew then, before she spoke, that Kissen would go back to Middren, that she would fight, because she would not forgive herself if she didn't.

It would be pointless to try to stop you, wouldn't it? said Yatho. *Like trying to stop the tide.*

I want to bring you home, signed Kissen. *I want to see your school. I want to save Elo, and stop Hseth.* She turned to Lessa.

'I'm your guard, aren't I?' she said. 'It would be strange if I didn't come with you.'

'I told you I wanted you to stay behind.'

'And I told you I could be of use. Your daughter needs her mother safe, Craier, and you need me.'

CHAPTER TWENTY-SIX

Kissen

KISSEN HAD WALKED THROUGH MOUNTAINS IN THE sprawling dark and seen them rise around her like ships against the sky, great bodies in the midnight shadows.

Now, the ships around her felt like mountains. Looming, drifting and creaking. Threatening. The bodies of beasts.

She and Lessa had returned to the enclosed harbour beneath the Wsirin fortress walls, walking down from the guarded entrance. Every ship in this harbour had been invited in. Whoever entered and left did so at the request of the Mithrik.

The Restish ship was still quiet. Kissen glanced at it warily. It was larger than the *Silverswift*, double the size. At least it wouldn't be hard to lose amidst the chaos of the Long Harbour. She walked behind Lessa, trying her best to keep her breath and not focus too much on how much her lungs still hurt, how her wounds itched.

'Why are you coming with me?' said Lessa, probably taking the shortness of Kissen's breathing for what it was: fear. 'You should have waited on the shore with Inara.'

They were walking the boards between the other vessels now, and Kissen could just make out the *Silverswift*'s prow. From this distance, nothing appeared amiss. There was a lantern lit on the topmast, and a few on board, but there was no movement in the dark. Most of the crew should have been spending the night ashore.

'I've never been much good at waiting,' said Kissen. 'Anyway, I can only look after one Craier at a time. At the moment you're doing the stupider thing.'

'Ah,' said Lessa. 'Then it's not because . . . how did your sister put it?' She repeated Yatho's phrase in sign, *You "like" me?*

Kissen gave her the curled finger into thumb sign that meant 'fuck you' in Talic, and Lessa laughed. If anyone had been watching, they might be put at ease.

'I'm with you for Inara,' said Kissen. That was starting to become a lie. Lessa was infuriating, even worse than Elo, and without the gentleness that softened his edge. 'Just because you're bonny doesn't mean I'll die on my blade for you.'

'You think I'm bonny then?' smiled Lessa, moving ahead.

Kissen frowned at her back. For a woman walking towards her potential death, she seemed rather light-hearted about it. 'You know I do,' she said quietly.

Lessa glanced back, her stride slowing. Kissen couldn't read her expression and decided not to try. She knew she shouldn't want her. It was too complicated, for Inara, for herself. This . . . attraction to Lessa filled her up with voiceless want, and baseless imaginings.

Yatho was right. She loved mess.

'Come,' said Kissen, nodding up at the ship now above them. The *Silverswift*'s sails were neatly furled, and all was silent other than the whistling of the breeze through the ropes. For a night in port, Kissen wouldn't have expected it teeming with the crew, but she would have expected some broken-barrelled carousing among those left on board, or at least some chatter over the sweets Inara said she had sent them.

Instead, there was silence broken only by the waves kissing at the poles of the jetty and the hull, and the sound of the ropes slapping against the mast.

Kissen wondered what Lessa hoped for; that her crew were dead, and had not betrayed her? Or that they had turned her in to her enemy and lived?

Lessa set a foot on the ramp chained in place to connect the ship to the shore. The wind coming off the harbour was soft and salt-laced, a refreshing relief after the heat of the city and its people. Kissen breathed it in, feeling it freshen her lungs, power her body.

She now wore Yatho's briddite-and-leather leg, a beauty that fitted her perfectly. Hers. Her self. She felt her power, despite her injuries, in the cutlass at her side, in the air in her lungs, her muscles and strength, her determination.

Through dalliances, families and wars, her strength was her greatest certainty.

Lessa reached the deck, with Kissen behind her.

'Ho, Captain Lertes?' called the lady, her hand, for show, going to her sword. 'What kind of boat do you keep, man, that there is no watch aboard? I could steal away the gold you've stashed a'neath your bunk.'

'Not today, my lady,' came a voice from aft, and with a sinking stomach, Kissen recognised it. Lertes had stepped out of his cabin, sword still sheathed. Aleda was with him, looking grim, her arm still bandaged from her burn. Whatever Lessa thought, she kept her face inscrutable.

'What's going on?' said Kissen, feigning innocence. She wasn't a good liar and was glad it was dark.

'Time for you to go, veiga,' said Aleda. 'This doesn't concern you. Consider it gratitude for saving us from the smith god.'

'What of my gratitude?' said Lessa, her hand tightening on her sword, and she gave a chill little smile. 'Is this mutiny I taste in the air?' She tutted. 'How pathetic, Lertes, I thought you were a clever bastard, not a weak one.'

Lertes drew his cutlass, and Kissen felt the boards shift beneath her left foot. There were others on deck, in the shadows, moving around them.

'Can't mutiny if you're not the captain,' said Lertes, his voice rough but sure, though his expression was tinged with the slightest shame. 'And you made me captain, my lady. As such, I will make decisions that best befit this crew.'

'This is my ship,' snarled Lessa, her mask slipping.

Lertes shook his head. 'I was given this ship by Lessa the pirate. Young scourge of the waters, demon with a blade, and friend to the gods. Now you're endangering your crew for a country we have no love for, intending to sail her back for a war that you will lose.'

He looked at Aleda, and she tipped her chin, affirming him.

Lertes turned back and firmed his stance. 'I am sorry,' he said, 'but I will not risk me and mine on a losing game.'

Lessa drew her sword, and Kissen followed suit. 'You think I won't fight for my own ship?' she growled.

'It doesn't matter,' said Lertes. He lifted his hands and clapped.

Into the pool of torchlight, four crew stepped forward. Kissen recognised Rhiyande, looking sorry, with Shah beside her, his hands trembling slightly. Sallath appeared positively gleeful, and Slim, his jaw tight and the glass beads around his neck rattling. Then out of the hatches came several more, people Lessa had sailed with, worked with, eaten with, commanded.

'The Restish want you dead or alive,' said Lertes. 'It can go either way, Lessa, but I would rather not dirty the boards again.'

'What the fuck?' snapped Kissen. It wasn't the fight that frightened Kissen. Dead or alive? Bahba had been certain the Restish wanted her living. They were counting on it.

And if they didn't mind her dead, it meant it wasn't Lessa they intended for the throne.

It was Inara.

CHAPTER TWENTY-SEVEN
Skediceth

SKEDI KNEW INARA WOULD DO WHAT SHE DID BEST: GET into trouble.

They went back in the cart with Telle and Yatho, while Bahba went to send messages to her allies on the Mithrik council. Elo's mother must trust Albia, considering how much effort she had put into their meeting, the sweet luxury of the meal, and the closeness of the danger.

She said she intended a rescue, but Skedi was sceptical. She had also thought she would be able to kidnap Inara and her mother and whisk them away in plain sight without bloodshed. He knew they would have brawled with every scrap of their beings rather than be taken prisoner, and so would the others.

And if Bahba could underestimate them, then they couldn't trust her fully. Kissen was right, a hundred things could go wrong.

But all Inara could think about was the Restish, and the shrine she had spotted in the harbour.

He won't know us, Skedi told her. *Gods do not remember, even if they become again.*

We will make him remember. Or make him an offering.

What can you offer, Ina? More hair? Your blood? How much is too much?

They passed other god-celebrations, lantern festivals, priests, hundreds of little altars that permeated every stone and brick and wall of the city. The city's language was movement, its lifeblood its ever-flowing tides of peoples, traders, pirates, dockers, lords and ruffians.

There were gods too. Some shrines had only incense inside them, but at others, a deity had manifested and come into the open. A jesting god danced on air before a gathering of people clapping to her rhythm, their colours bright with worship. She wore a painted mask of carved wood over her mouth, its lips turned upwards in a wide smile as she beat the air with her feet, power and energy in her step. Music rang out, and Skedi saw Inara's feet twitch with the call of the god's will, her fingers stretching for a coin to offer. The god's eyes were shimmering pools of gold, entrancing, and her hair hung in long braids to her ankles.

Thrum, thrum, a story comes, settle your seat and tap your thumbs . . .

Another god was in the shape of a small black cat on quiet white paws, but six of them. It sped behind some screaming, running children before disappearing in a gust of smoke.

'Are you two speaking?' said Yatho, and Inara jumped. Skedi looked up: the cart had come to a halt again, and Skedi realised they had let the city go by in silence and they were back at the warehouse. It was late, but the street was bustling. People who worked and lived there were drinking and carousing or playing games with their children on the cobbles.

Inara smiled apologetically. *I'm sorry,* she signed.

'She's worried,' said Skedi out loud to Yatho as Telle alighted with a swift leap, 'about her mother. And Kissen.'

Inara didn't glance at him, and he was pleased that his lie was so smooth. She *was* worried about Kissen and her mother. The two bickered like cats around a scrap of fish, but Skedi knew they would look out for each other. As a child, Inara had seen her mother as almost divine, while her first meeting with Kissen she'd been less than impressed, but now she saw them both as human. Skedi wondered how she saw him now. No longer a pet, nor a treacherous god. The two of them had enough failures and successes that they wove into one rich history.

Telle used a key to enter the warehouse this time. Inside, they walked into paper-and-vellum-scented silence. Strange and thick after the happy chatter of the evening. As they passed the crates of manuscripts Skedi felt a rush of amazement that so much had made it here to Irisia, so much had been saved.

And yet Telle had separated one, and given it to Inara.

Inara motioned to Telle, who tipped a quizzical brow. *The scroll you gave me*, Inara signed. *The song about the storm god's child.* Telle nodded. *What did you mean by it? It was sad.*

His girl was getting better at asking for what she needed, understanding her own frailties. Skedi was proud of her.

You wanted to find out what you were, replied Telle. *But you didn't need me for that. Instead, I wanted you to have something more precious.*

What?

To know that you are not alone.

To not be alone. What a precious thing. He thought of his shrine and took off from Inara's shoulder, gliding over the paper dust and ahead through the quiet foyer with its running fountain. He was like an owl in the dark, and landed softly beside his own statue, the last curls of sandalwood incense floating up around him. Fresh ink had been poured into his bowl, and he felt the warmth of it in him. Solom had added his own fancy to his creation, this 'god of tales', but Skedi didn't mind it. Solom was an archivist, he wanted a god that suited him.

There were five teacups still on the table by the fountain, two half-drunk. One of them lay on its side in a pool of water.

Yatho and the others came through, *We should sleep if we can*, the smith was saying with a sigh. Her colours were troubled by darker grey, not far off mourning-dark. Worried about Kissen, or Middren, or both. *It will be a long wait till morning . . .*

She frowned, looking at the fountain, and Skedi followed her gaze: the water was tinged a strange colour, even in the moonlight. Reddish.

Then beyond, half hidden between the chairs were two pairs of feet in soft shoes.

Inara stepped forward, her face stricken, and Skedi stood on his hind legs. Cal and Solom lay together, their faces frightened, their throats cut. Dead. Skedi had not noticed them, for all their colours were gone.

His first faithful, dead.

'*Run!*' Yatho signed and spoke, turning her chair towards Telle who had pressed her hands to her mouth in horror. But then there was a shift of feet in the dark, at the top of the stairs above Skedi, and Yatho grabbed Telle's hand and pointed. A glow of light, and someone stepped out of the door into the house.

'Do not move,' said a voice Skedi recognised. He shrank. 'We have crossbows.'

'Mitha Imani,' said Inara, determinedly not glancing at him. How could they? Solom was irascible perhaps, but in his heart he was a kind man. Even Cal disliked everyone but him. They didn't deserve to die, after making it so far, saving so much from Lesscia.

Survive first. Grieve later.

Skedi leaned forward, slowly, so he could peer out from under his shrine's roof. The Mitha had stepped out onto the stair with two men, promised bows in hand, drawn and ready to fire. They were not looking at him. They hadn't seen him.

'I understand you have been speaking with Mitha Bahba,' said Imani. Her colours were heavy, threatening, purple like the uniforms of her guards, flaring a bright, vivid turquoise with suspicion. 'What did you discuss?'

'Discuss?' said Inara, clearly thinking quickly. Telle and Yatho's colours were churning with fear. 'She took Mama and me out for dinner with our friends.'

Help me lie, Skedi, she said. She didn't need to ask. Skedi pressed his will with her words, using his strength to nudge Imani's colours, slightly, gently, softening them.

She knows nothing.

Telle was shifting closer to Yatho, slipping a hand into the bag at the back of her chair while Yatho did her best to look small.

'We know her son,' Inara added. 'A-are you here to see her? Are Cal and Solom all right? Can I—' She stepped towards them, and one of Imani's guards fired. The bolt struck the floor before Inara's feet and ricocheted, flying past Inara and leaving a cracked tile behind. She let out a squeak and it took all of Skedi's control to not cry out. Inara knew the lightlessness of death as well as Skedi did, but feigned naivety might play in her favour, perhaps even lower their guard. And it took her another step away from Yatho and Telle.

'Stay where you are,' said Imani. They were coming down the stairs now. The archers with their crossbows held steady and sure, but all three of them were looking at Inara. Skedi's will telling them, *Not a threat, not a threat at all. You have her cornered. Just a child . . .*

'Where is your *quya*?' said Imani. Skedi kept his wings and ears down. They had not detected his voice or his will.

'My "*quya*"?' said Inara. 'What is that?'

'I thought you knew Irisian?' Imani scowled. 'A god, child. Where is the god who was with you?'

'Skediceth w-went back to his shrine on the ship,' she lied. 'Where are the archivists, and Bea and his brother? Are they hurt?'

'Ah, good,' said Imani. All three of them relaxed. 'It is bad luck to harm a *quya*.'

'Please,' said Inara, her hands trembling; she looked at Imani, pleading, and Skedi wasn't sure how much of it was real and how much pretend. 'Tell me they're not hurt.'

'No one else will be hurt if you come peacefully,' said Imani, without remorse.

'Where? Why?'

There wasn't supposed to be anyone there for Inara. Why would they want her?

Imani straightened her shoulders, standing as if about to pronounce an execution. 'You, little girl, are to be the last surviving heir of House Craier,' she said, stopping between the stairs and the fountain, still flanked by the watchful guards. 'And we will assist you to the Middrenite throne.'

There was no twist of deceit in her colours, no lie.

They don't want Lessa on the throne, Skedi threw across into Inara's mind. *They want you.*

A child. Someone they could manipulate.

'My mother is dead?' Inara said, her voice hoarse. Skedi knew what she was thinking: what of Kissen? Would they kill them both? Were they walking into certain death?

Skedi, she thought to him. *Can you get to the ship's shrine?*

I . . . I don't know. I could try, but . . . He shrank, he couldn't help it. He could feel the ship's shrine, but like a whisper of wind in the trees, impossible to grasp. He wasn't tied enough to it. *I'm scared. What if I die?*

He would lose everything to a god's mortality: lack of faith. All his slowly growing hopes, torn to nothing.

He looked around them, trying to think like Kissen. They were underestimated, they had that on their side. They did not know he was still there, and Imani was unarmed. She must not have been expecting much of a fight with only two guards. The archivists must have let her in: Cal and Solom would have served the tea they didn't drink before they killed them.

'She will be,' said Imani, a tinge of regret in her voice. 'Tomorrow they will take the tide beyond Irisian waters. We thought to use her, but it became clear she wouldn't break faith with your king.' She smiled tightly, sadly, and her archers stepped closer. 'I told you, young Craier, countries are not built on pity. You will be good for us, won't you?'

Good? If Skedi could, he would have laughed. Imani didn't care about Middren, about Arren, about Hseth. She cared about maps traced in gold and gods, in a game of hidden pieces.

Fight with me, he heard Inara say.

You know I will, he told her.

But it was Telle who laughed. Skedi sat up. Had the archivist been reading Imani's lips? Why was she drawing attention to herself? These people, who Inara never should have met, never have dragged into rebellion and danger.

She doesn't know you at all, Telle signed to Inara, who could not help but smile. *Who you are. What you've done.*

'What did she say?' said Imani, narrowing her eyes at Telle.

'She says,' said Yatho, 'get your ignorant arse the fuck out of our house. And take your muscle with you.'

The Mitha bristled. Yatho's shades had turned bright and fierce as a new-set flame, orange and ready to roar. Telle's, too, were firm and vivid green.

'Now, Skedi!' Inara cried.

Skedi leapt out of his shrine and dived towards the back of one of the guards. He slammed into his head, and scratched at his neck with paws and teeth, growing heavy and hanging down as the guard screamed. Unlike the king's knights, these did not wield briddite and did not know gods to attack humans on a whim. He reached around, trying to rip Skedi off, dropping his bow.

Telle ran for the other guard, her fists balled, her eyes furious, as Inara looked for something, anything, to use as a weapon. The archivist released one hand, throwing a spray of seeds towards the guard, who flinched and misfired. Telle raised a half a greenling she must have lifted from the table, grabbed the guard's neck and slammed it into his eye, squeezing the fruit with enough acid to make him reel back, yelling.

Then, Telle turned towards the guard still struggling with Skedi, who had come around to his face now and was beating it with his wings. She grabbed the man by the hair and wrenched him down. Skedi tumbled off as she delivered a good strong knee to his nose.

Yatho, who had followed behind her, stood up from her chair, hammers in her hand, and drove one up into the chin of the first guard, who was still rubbing at his eye. Blood and teeth sprayed out and he fell back, unconscious.

'Stop!' cried Imani. 'I command you to—'

Skedi fell to the side, exhausted. The guard grabbed Telle's dress. Though his neck was matted with blood, he used a heave of strength to throw her to the ground. Telle crashed into one of the seats, but even as he threw her she dug her nails into his sword arm, leaving bloody trails in their wake. He bellowed out a curse and drew his sword.

Yatho roared. 'Get your fucking hands OFF MY WIFE!' she roared, stepping towards him, her colours a trail of blazing glory so bright it seemed like the afterglow of lightning. She swung with all the considerable force of her shoulder and upper body, crunching the head of the hammer into the side of the man's face, then with her other shattering his knee with a sickening crunch.

Inara used the distraction. She ran to the sword he had dropped and grabbed it. It looked heavy, but she didn't need to be good: she needed to be smart.

And the Mitha had no weapon.

Inara held her blade as Elo had shown her, one hand on the pommel, one on the hilt. She ran, blade pointed at the Mitha.

'Mercy!' she cried, backing away, her voice deepening with panic and confusion. 'Please!'

Skedi leapt up. Inara could do it, he knew. Barely more than a child, but she could run her through, for threatening her, her mother, her country. It would take more strength than she had, she knew that, Elo had made her stab the body of a dead goat to be sure. But she had momentum.

Kissen doesn't kill people, Skedi called to her.

Inara stopped, her captured blade just at the Mitha's belly.

I am not Kissen.

She had fired an arrow from a distance and killed a person. She had reached a hand out to a god and wrestled with it in the hope it would kill the man who bore it, but she had never felt her blade pierce flesh, muscle, bone.

You get to choose who to be, Inara.

Inara's blade was pressed against Imani's belly, but she drove it no further. The first guard who had been struck with the greenling and the hammer had picked himself up, drawn his sword, spitting blood. The second was still groaning on the floor.

'*Tell them to stop fighting*,' Inara snarled in Irisian, '*and kneel.*'

Imani clenched her jaw. 'I am one of the Mithrik, girl,' she snapped, though she was breathing fast and scared. 'You won't kill me.'

'I am Lady Craier's daughter,' Inara growled, pressing harder with her sword, and the woman's colour screeched black with her fear. 'And I'm not strong, so it will be a slow death.'

The woman's hands shook, and she spoke not in Middric, or Irisian, but Restish. '*Twfei.*' Kneel.

The standing guard looked towards her, then to Skedi. He paled, threw down his blade, then slowly dropped.

'You too,' said Inara to Imani.

The Mitha fixed her eyes on her, but slowly, carefully, went to her knees.

She had thought she was facing a quiet archivist, a wheelchair-using smith and a noble's girl, but she was wrong; she had chosen to come for two brawling survivors from the Blenraden gutter, a god, and his powerful protector.

CHAPTER TWENTY-EIGHT

Kissen

'AT LEAST YOU KEEP A FAIR BRIG,' SAID KISSEN.

The cell, it seemed, was rarely used for anything other than storage. Their hands and feet were manacled with hard iron, locks, and loose chains. Not, thankfully, tied to the walls.

'It stinks,' muttered Lessa.

'*You* can't smell anything,' said Kissen. Lessa had a bloodied nose from fighting back when they had dragged her down, and a purpling bruise on her jaw. Kissen herself had taken a pounding to the gut and thrown up most of the delicious food she had put in it. Her nice cloak had been ripped off her neck. That was the sorest loss.

The ship was unmoored: Kissen could tell by the way it rocked. It must be nearing dawn, which meant the tide would be high enough to cross the harbour sandbar. There were boots on the boards above, and chattering, whispering, shouting as the crew had returned, and, apparently, accepted the fresh change of control. The only person that had come down to them was Sallath, who was standing guard.

'I've smelled worse anyway,' Kissen added.

'You smelled worse when I first met you,' Lessa muttered.

'Aye, well, that wind's arsehole Faer thought it was funny to throw me in a pigsty.'

Sallath glowered at them, sliding a whetstone down his blade. 'You bicker like an old wed couple,' he said.

'I have a skill of bickering with anyone,' said Kissen. She was standing, leaning back against the cell wall by the bar, absently flexing her right leg.

'And I don't listen to mutinous traitors,' spat Lessa. She sat with her arms on her knees, her fine dress torn.

'Don't tell me you're surprised, highborn?' said Sallath. 'Those Restish bluffers offered more than a loser's fight. Free trade in the eastern seas, *and* through to the west when your Middren falls apart. Clemency, too, for being part of Commander Samin's fleet. Then a good box of gold to sweeten it.'

'All for sad little Sallath the Scrawny?' said Lessa, her mouth curved in a bitter smile.

Sallath scowled. 'Some of it. *Lady.*'

'How old were you,' said Lessa, 'when I lifted you from the gutters of Belhaven?' Sallath straightened, baring his teeth. 'Six? You didn't know for sure, since you'd been left to starve by your sisters.'

'I owe you nothing,' he snarled. 'You worked me to the bone. And your own precious daughter-child has soft hands and softer clothes. I wonder how soft they'll find her when they sit her as a prisoner on a throne.'

Lessa lunged for him, but her hands met air as the pirate stepped aside, laughing. 'You think I'm an idiot?' he said.

Lessa smiled. 'Yes.'

Sallath had stepped closer to Kissen, who reached out, grabbed him by the shirt and slammed his head once against the bars, then again, knocking him out cold.

CHAPTER TWENTY-NINE

Inara

INARA STOLE DOWN THE COBBLES OF WSIRIN, SKEDI FLYING at her side as small as he could be. Mouselike. He had used some extra energy in his fight with the guard, but he had not mentioned it. Instead, silent and certain as an owl, he joined her on the hunt.

Yatho and Telle she had left behind to rescue the archivists who had been locked in their rooms, and get a message to Bahba. But Inara had other plans, and they hadn't stopped her.

It wasn't hard to find the harbour. All roads led down to it like drains from roof to gutter. All she had to do was follow the waters rolling downhill. Soon she was in the night market again. It was quiet now, folk changing over for the coming morning.

She had seen a shrine for Yusef in the harbour, but it would take an age to find it again in the dark amongst the hundreds. Surely a god so great would have one on land too.

'*Where is the shrine of the god of safe haven?*' she said in Irisian.

The person she addressed had on long, colourful robes printed in vivid reds, yellows and strips of purple, an array of golden filigree around their neck and turban carefully arranged on her head. She was pushing a cart in the direction of the water and looked at her askance. She had not understood.

Inara raked her mind for the languages she had been taught as a child, the patterns in the different tongues, the structures that ran all the way through the families of meaning. But Skedi tightened

248

his claws in her, and the woman's eyes widened, hearing the god's voice in her head.

'*Go down three streets,*' she said, and to Inara's surprise, she recognised the tongue: Western Harisi, her tutor's father's language. '*Turn right and you will come into a square with red blooms.*'

'*Laquia,*' said Inara in return, dredging up a piece of the language she remembered. *Thank you.*

The woman was startled a second time, but her eyes lit up. '*How do you—*' Inara ran before she had finished speaking, though she quietly blessed the memory of her tutor, long-burned, and Erman's joy in teaching her. He would be appalled to see her now, sprinting through a foreign city with a god, her fine clothes ragged and damp, seeking out a shrine.

Check above for guards, said Inara.

Skedi tipped his wings and went up. At some point, one of the Restish allies would notice Imani had yet to return with her prey.

No guards, but I see the shrine. Keep going.

There. A narrow square lined with trees, blossoming their last red petals around greening globes of pomegranate fruit. Beneath them was a man in purple robes, sweeping fallen petals and leaves with a straw broom as he hummed a tune.

And beyond, at the end of the courtyard, was the shrine.

Pillars held up a portico of fine marble slabs, sheltering a dark doorway into the shrine itself. The pillars were delicately carved in Irisian style, the image of waves at their base, droplets of water rising like dimples to meet etchings of storm and cloud. A tribute to the god of change.

But the frieze above the door showed whose shrine this really was. This was carved in a relief of meeting peoples around a feasting table, wheat and grain carried in the arms of the other comers, a fire burning: haven.

Inara went into the square, breathing in the scent of trees and stone. Cicadas buzzed around them as if they were trying to shake off the humid night, and ivy grew up the courtyard, half covering a long crack that ran around it which had been plastered over and smoothed. These walls were also etched and painted with caravans of peoples, ships by the hundreds, travellers on foot, by horse, by cart, all moving towards the hope at the centre, the promise of the god.

The caretaker looked up, seeing her. Inara was sweating in her grandly layered clothes, her curls plastered to her head and neck. She was not used to this heat that filled her up, feet to crown, and she must look a sight.

'*No visitors till dawn, girl,*' he said in Irisian. '*The god cannot hear every prayer. It is not yet morning.*'

Inara levelled her gaze at him, biting down on what she wanted to say and instead saying it to Skedi.

I'm not going to let some pompous git stand between me and my family.

Duly noted, said Skedi drily as he swooped back down from the sky and alighted on her shoulder.

The caretaker cocked his head at him. He was an older man, white hair wisping around the long lobes of his ears, weighted down with rings of brass and heavy beads in shades of purple. '*You,*' he said. '*I know you.*'

'*I travelled often with the god of safe haven,*' said Skedi in Irisian. '*In his previous life.*' Inara looked through the arch into the shrine and saw carved feet in the dark, lit by a glow of lanterns. '*My name is Skediceth, and this is my Middrenite caretaker, an acolyte of my humble temple.*'

The lie was light and sweet, sharpened with Skedi's own longing. His will stretched out to Yusef's caretaker, surrounding him. The man's recognition stirred a perfect, cherry-blossom pink.

'Oh, yes,' he said softly. 'God of White Lies. There are records of you, but you were thought long gone, not like to return.'

'White lies are more powerful than you might think,' said Skedi, with enough affront that Inara knew he was less than half-lying now. 'A promise is just a lie unless it is fulfilled. And Yusef made promises to me that he kept.'

The man nodded, feeling the truth in that.

'We have no prayers and no requests,' added Skedi, 'only thanks.' *Only thanks. Just a little thing, a god to a god. A kindness to a kindness. Yusef would like it if you did not stand between us . . .*

The caretaker looked at the shrine, then at last nodded. 'The

other priests are not yet awake for morning song,' he said. 'Be quick
with your thanks.' He looked Inara over more closely, taking in the
fine cloth of her dress, but noting her bedraggled curls.

'I've counted everything in there,' he said. 'So, watch any sticky
fingers.'

Inara smiled and bowed to the caretaker, who nodded and went
back to sweeping the fallen leaves.

Then, through the pomegranate square, she stepped towards her
father's shrine. Her breath felt strangely shallow in her chest, as if
she couldn't quite catch it. She reached the steps and closed her
eyes for a moment to steady herself, and then went up all three,
and through the door.

Inside was cool and silent. It was also sweet with colour.

The shine of feeling, the energy and will that brought gods life
and power.

It came from six great bowls set on a low dais of stone by the
carved feet Inara had seen from outside. The first was filled with
ash and sticks of incense, burning thickly. With each one that had
been placed, someone had offered a love, a longing, a hope, a prayer,
and it lingered, bright and shining, giving Yusef their faith and
purpose.

The second was full of coin, bits of copper of a hundred different
mintings, and gold too. Bracelets, earrings, gems.

The third held fruit, split open and drying, but around this were
scattered hundreds of tiny cups filled with wine, adding a sickly,
too-sweet tinge to the rising smoke.

The fourth was spilling over with pieces of paper and vellum,
layers upon layers, tamped down so that more could be added.

The fifth was empty, but there were pieces of straw and some
droppings. Animal offerings – chickens, lambs and rabbits. It
seemed the Irisian government was not as squeamish as the Middric
about offerings of blood. She suspected the priests like the pirates
would bleed them then use the carcasses for their own supper.

The final, the sixth, held hand-made offerings. Small statues
carved from scented wood, strings of beads and notes of paper.
One small bowl that looked full of babies' teeth.

To Inara's eyes, the bowls were aglow with the fire of faith. Pain,

love, hope, longing, passed into gifts and laid at the feet of the god
of safe haven.

Inara looked up into her father's face.

The statue was of an oddly young man, carved in marble, but
with real ribbons woven in knots about his neck and head, which
reminded her of the safe haven tree in the Bennites, by the great
lake under the mountains. It was new, that much was clear; all that
remained of whatever statue had been here previously, when the
god had died and his shrines were shattered, were the feet and the
hands, which were greyer and darker than this freshly painted
figure.

Yusef was a stranger to her. His hair loose and coiled over his
shoulders and painted in shades of reddish brown. His eyes were
of inset ruby, but his nose, at least, was similar: sure, straight and
strong, while her mother's had a crooked hook to it that Inara had
always adored.

Inara.

Skedi fluttered down to the statue's left foot. There, half-hidden
in the robes that draped the older piece of stone, was a hare. With
a deer's antlers and a bird's wings.

There was no name on the carving, but Inara knew it. 'Skediceth,'
she whispered.

'Here I am,' he said, soft in his return. 'Here is how we started.'

Inara went up to the feet of the statue and touched the little
carving. The proof of what bound them. Her father's promise.

'It is not just his promise that kept me,' said Skedi, as if hearing
her thoughts. 'His will might have thrown me to you, but it was
your gift that kept me. Half-haven. A shrine beyond a shrine.'

'What if some gods don't deserve a shrine?' said Inara, looking
up at her father. An ancient god, who had got her on a young
woman. She thought of Satuan, condemning humans and gods
alike with his hatred. Of Canovan, his fealty to his mother, and
his wife who had died at the shrine of her ancestor. Scian, who
was built on a human's bones. Hestra, and her unstable ambivalence.
Hseth, and her human-stoked terrors. Kissen, and the things that
she had seen, the cruel gods she had been paid to destroy. At least,
the ones she had told Inara about. White lies, perhaps. Or just

brutal truths, aimed to challenge Inara's path, give her some taste of the grey waters of the world she lived in.

'Not all things are certain,' said Skedi. 'Not all things last forever.'

Inara sighed and nodded, then pulled a small knife out of her pocket and slid it along her palm. She grimaced as it bit – it did not get any easier. But then she let her blood drop, drop onto the slabs at the god's feet, hiding it so the caretaker didn't see what she was giving.

'God of safe haven,' she called.

Yusef.

'Father mine. Recognise your daughter.'

Recognise me. Rise for me.

Would the blood be enough, just a few drops? But poor Solom had seen signs that the god was risen, that he was back in the world, brought back into shape by faith and will and hope. A great god of this new age of trade and commerce, a bastion against the wild, till the wild had killed him.

Nothing happened, but Inara held her will, not allowing it to waver, reaching out to the statue, to the offerings, not to the place of the god but to the divine within it, *beyond* it. Skedi sat above her, watchful, careful.

Then, after a long, long moment, she sensed a change. A scent. Green earth and rain, a crackle of woodsmoke and charcoal, so intense she could almost feel the warmth of a homely fire, the feeling of coming in from the cold to bright comfort.

Then the scent changed again, to the smell of polished wood and well-thumbed coins, to pine-pressed silks, and sweet, rich pomegranate.

CHAPTER THIRTY

Kissen

'WHY DIDN'T YOU COME TO BLENRADEN WHEN YOU WERE offering out free piracy to gutter-waifs?' said Kissen to Lessa, dropping the unconscious Sallath to the floor. 'We could have met a lot sooner.'

'I was presumed dead in Middren, remember?' Lessa replied.

Kissen reached down and undid her trews at her knees. The pirates hadn't noticed that her leg had changed, the hard lump of wood and leather replaced by plates of briddite, finely wired together around the strong core to give it shape and protection. She unclipped the footpiece from the leg, and took both out of the manacle, freeing herself.

'I thought you had a lock pick,' said Lessa.

'This is easier,' said Kissen. 'And funnier.'

She then lifted her shin-plate and took out some of the spare items Yatho had brought with her to the dinner table and temporarily attached to the inside. Her sister always had something to fiddle with, and the long pieces of wire she'd had in her bag along with hammers, bolts, pliers and all the pieces of Kissen's leg, made passable lock picks. These, Kissen gave to Lessa, reattaching her foot with her right hand while Lessa came over to undo her left manacle. She made quick work of it, and the lock was soon free.

Sallath was already coming around, so Kissen reached through the bars and dragged him upright against them before he could put a hand on his sword. She wrapped her unchained arm around his neck and put her other hand on his mouth as he groaned back to awareness.

'Are you going to be quiet and tell us what the plan is?' said Kissen into his ear as Lessa worked on her own manacles, her feet first.

He struggled, and she squeezed his throat till he choked. His face went red, he stopped resisting. Kissen loosened her hand so he could speak.

'Meeting the Restish beyond the harbour,' he said hoarsely. 'Advisor Mirim and Efana wanted to kill her themselves so they could ensure it was done. It was Aleda, she convinced us. Please don't kill me.'

'I don't kill people,' Kissen muttered, knowing it was a lie.

'You should,' said Lessa, one foot free, working on the other. 'You will.'

Sallath's body tensed to yell, and Kissen put her hand back over his mouth, tightening her grip on his neck again. Tighter, tighter, Kissen squeezed, as his face went red, his lips blue. Then he went limp, his head flopping down, and she dropped him. They didn't have long. Kissen could hear the shouts from the harbour, but none of alarm. It was likely they had already passed the walls of the fortress, and other early risers were beginning their day, or ending their night.

'Where's the trigger for this escape?' said Kissen, grabbing Sallath's sword and pulling it through the bars. The man didn't move, and Kissen hoped she had not, in fact, killed him.

'Third board from the left wall,' said Lessa. With a click, her other foot was free. She held out her hand for the sword, and Kissen found herself hesitating for a moment. So demanding. Lessa was locked on her own ship, betrayed by her own crew, yet the woman still seemed to have no flicker of doubt in her. It was enthralling. It was frightening. What did she want with it? To stab Sallath and finish Kissen's job?

'Honestly, nobles are more cunning than thieves,' said Kissen, handing the blade over.

'I have been both,' said Lessa. With a stab and tug of the blade, she hacked through her skirts, tearing them from waist to hem so she would have freedom of movement when this inevitably came to a fight. She cast a crooked grin at Kissen, before putting the sword down and grabbing the pick once more. 'So, I am the worst of the lot of them.'

Noble, thief, rebel, commander. She had more titles than the baker-knight. Even more than the king. Kissen had only ever been two things: a girl who wanted to kill gods and a girl who did. She fingered her way along the boards by the left wall, high up in the dark. One was slightly lighter than the others, but with no other clear markings. Kissen pressed it upwards, as Lessa had told her in the night market. It moved, and she slid it to the right, revealing a code mechanism, a twisting spiral of symbols arranged in letters.

'The password is "Persevere",' said Lessa.

Kissen looked at the codex, then back down towards the lady. 'Did you think I was being cute when I said I can't read?'

'Can't or won't?'

'Both?'

Lessa scoffed, finishing her last chain and leaping to her feet, passing Kissen the lock pick so she could deal with her remaining manacles.

Granted, Kissen had used a pick more than once in her life, but dexterity wasn't her forte, given scar tissue and the occasional tremor. Luckily, these weren't the finest padlocks. Still, it was a dance with the dark, lifting bolts, as Lessa quickly turned the dials on the codex to match her word.

'You sure your captain doesn't know about this?' asked Kissen, tongue on her gold tooth.

'I never told him,' said Lessa. 'Commander Samin had it built and advised me to hold my tongue. I was a very young woman in a big sea, with a fine vessel. In honesty, I'm surprised he didn't try this over a decade ago.'

'Why didn't he?'

'Perhaps because I cut out the tongue of the first person who tried, and then had "traitor" tattooed across her throat.'

Kissen paused in her picking. She was no stranger to mutilation. But Lessa said it so matter-of-factly. Had she just pushed the horror of it so deep that she didn't see it any more?

'That's . . . fucked,' she said, and Lessa nodded.

'All things have a cost,' she said. 'No one lives long with faith alone to feed them.'

Kissen fiddled with the pick, wiggling the bolts up, gently, *tap*, *tap*. 'You're not wrong there.'

The lock clicked, and Kissen's left foot was free. Lessa stood back from the dials, as a catch in the wall shifted with a small clunk. No time to finish the last manacle on her wrist; she could hear more activity above them now, the stamping of feet. Instead, Kissen bundled it around her hand, covering her knuckles. Better a weapon than a problem.

Lessa was listening at the boards of the wall. She held out a hand to Kissen. *Wait.*

A shuffling of feet, the creak of a barrel, and chatter from the galley. Kissen realised they would be performing the ritual again, the hipgin, the citrus, the request of blessing for a new journey.

The footsteps passed, and Lessa put her fingers to the door and *heaved.* It didn't move easily. Kissen came to help her and they dragged it in one squeaking shift, before it stopped, just wide enough for Kissen to squeeze through.

There was someone there. Glib: the long-limbed, skinny galley assistant. He had a half-open wrap of cloth in his hand, and pink pastry carefully preserved inside it that he must have bought from the market. Expensive, precious. He would have smuggled it down here to eat it without being seen. So silently that Lessa hadn't heard him.

He blinked as he saw them, then his chest swelled as he took a deep breath.

'Don't—' Kissen tried, but Lessa darted through the gap with Sallath's sword in her hand. Her strike was sure and true and went straight through Glib's throat. She drew out the blade, and a rush of air came out with a spurt of blood that spattered her fine dress. Glib collapsed to the floor, crushing his sweet, blood still pumping.

'You didn't know—' Kissen began with a hiss, trying to squeeze her decidedly broader frame through the narrow gap.

'If he were to sing my praises, did he need so much breath?' Lessa looked back at her then, spattered, brutal and magnificent. 'I will not risk my life, my country and my daughter on mercy.'

Kissen made it through; a shelf and rack of heavy cooking implements had stopped the secret door opening fully. 'You could have knocked him cold.'

Lessa clicked her tongue. 'Honestly, if you'd rather let me die than get your hands dirty then you should have run when they gave you the chance.'

Kissen glowered. As a child, she had just tried to find someone in the world not to hate. Yatho, Telle, others who believed in gods of small things, hopeful things, like the gods of makers, gods of ovens, or even greater gods of safe haven and midwifing. She had hated gods, but wanted to love the people who loved them.

'I won't let you die, lady,' she said. 'I promised Inara.'

Lessa's mouth tightened, then she nodded. They took as many knives as they could find: shell shuckers, cleavers, small filleting blades. The chef, it seemed, collected them from trips around the Trade Sea. They would be shit for throwing, unbalanced, half-blunted, but enough to sting. Lessa kept the sword, and Kissen suspected she would need it most, so she grabbed a long bread shovel from the oven, a flat pan at the end of a long stave. It would do, for balance, if not to fend off a few strikes.

They ghosted up the ladders quietly, reaching the crew's quarters. All was quiet below, though the deck above them was heaving with sound. Drumming and dancing, but also ropes landing on deck, cries of orders, of urgency. Kissen realised she could no longer hear clearly the sounds of the Long Harbour.

A heavy thud and scraping shook the hull, and Lessa hissed through her teeth as if the sound of wood splintering caused her physical pain.

Another ship docking, she signed. *Badly. And early.*

They must have worried they would let you go.

Just then, someone stirred in the crew quarters. Kissen reached for her knife as Rhiyande sat up in one of the hammocks, disturbed either by the crack of wood or Lessa's noise. There were dark bruises under her eyes that were more than from lack of sleep. Like Lessa, she had blood crusting under her nose.

She turned, saw them. Her eyes widened. Lessa pulled a knife, flipping it around to throw, but—

Kissen grabbed Lessa's arm before she killed again. *Wait,* she signed with one hand, not daring to speak. Rhiyande was one of the few to show pity. And, unlike Glib, she had not drawn in a breath.

The three of them stared at each other, and after a long moment, Rhiyande lifted her hands and signed. *I'm sorry,* she said. *They're boarding already.*

There was no way out of this without blood. They could not wait for Bahba to come and rescue Lessa and cry war. She was not a hostage, she was being led to her death. If the Restish were aboard, it was coming sooner than they had hoped.

Maybe I can help, said Rhiyande. She touched her nose, wincing. *Aleda didn't like it when I said we should let you loose.*

Lessa relaxed slightly, and Kissen released her arm.

Why? said the lady. *Why aid us when you helped put me here?*

Rhiyande flushed, looking at Kissen beseechingly, then shrugged. *I'd never tasted ice before.*

If they're already here, we're fucked, signed Kissen, and Lessa bit her lip, looking up. It had taken so long for Sallath to get close enough for them to catch him. What if they had Inara already? Did they need to find another way? Hide, maybe, till dark. Pretend they had already fled?

The indecision held them just a moment too long. A shadow appeared above, a pair of feet.

'Well . . .' It was Aleda, 'I was just coming to fetch you, my lady.' Her voice dripped with sarcasm as she stood silhouetted against the dark stain of the sky. 'You must be blessed by six gods and fucked by seven.'

CHAPTER THIRTY-ONE

Inara

WHO CALLS FOR HAVEN?

The voice shook the flames of the shrine lanterns and set all the little cups of libations trembling. Inara heard the clatter of the broom, footsteps running over cobbles outside, but she ignored it.

Your daughter calls for you, said Inara.

Daughter? Incense whirled around them, then a strange, boyish laugh. *I have no daughter, but your offering . . . it tastes so sweet. Is there more?*

A wind rushed in through the trees, petals blew in through the door.

And then he was there.

The statue didn't move. It was only his totem; it was not the god. Yusef appeared as if he had stepped out of a dream, standing in the shadows of his shrine. He wore robes of purple silk, long and drifting along the floor like a fall of water. At his neck were chains of heavy gold and silver, inset with red, decorated with doves, seeds and pomegranates. His fingers were full of rings, thick with precious gems: tiger's-eye, sapphire, emerald. He dripped with wealth.

And he was young, with auburn hair and bright brown eyes, his skin unlined. Younger than Kissen. It seemed the people who prayed him back into being did not see him as he had been: a great and ancient god of the travelling peoples who had settled Restish. The god who had died had been created anew, and his new form was one of wealth and plenty.

'I am Yusef,' said the god, 'god of safe haven. What do you wish of me . . . child?'

Skedi, likely sensing Inara's confusion, grew to the size of a dog and swept down to stand on his hind legs beside her, tall enough that she could put her hand behind his ears.

'Great god of safe haven,' said Skedi. 'I am Skediceth—'

'Little god of white lies!' said Yusef. He grinned, and opened his arms. 'What a joy to see you!'

Skedi half raised his wings in surprise.

'They read me my scriptures about you,' said Yusef, beaming and exuberant.

'They did?'

'With so much danger on the roads, they said I sought something to keep people's faith strong.' The god leaned down to take Skedi's paws in his glittering hands, ignoring Inara completely. 'And I found a shrine to you. A children's story, a locals' tale.'

Skedi tried to hide it, Inara could see, but she also saw his whiskers twitch, excited.

'You made a promise to me,' her god said shyly. 'That I would journey with you, in your shrines, to keep spirits up, and hopes steady. You promised to keep me safe with all your power.'

'Quite right,' said Yusef, stepping back again, putting his hands behind his back. He looked up, admiring his shrine, then ran his eyes with interest over his offerings and their colours. 'A century we travelled together, little god, a boon binding us, a bond of divinities.' His face darkened. 'Until Blenraden, where the Middrenites allowed me to lose my life.' He looked down. 'And I had no more power to give. Were you not killed then too?'

'I was,' said Skedi, 'in a way. But your promise kept me living and bound me to a power that your death left behind.' He looked up at Inara. 'Her.'

Inara could feel her body trembling as Yusef gave her a mildly affronted glance, as if he had forgotten she was there. She had been hoping to find a father, a saviour, a sage. Not this . . . god-child.

She met his gaze, feeling his power, like a physical pressure on her skin, a squeezing of her neck.

Yusef crossed his arms and frowned. 'You do look . . . different to other humans. Brighter. Like an offering.'

That made Inara shiver. 'I am the daughter of Lessa Craier,' she said. 'And you in your previous incarnation. Gods call me halfling, demigod . . .'. Her chest tightened. *Abomination. Beast.* No, those words were not hers. 'I have some of your gifts, but you owe me more than that.'

'Owe?' Yusef blinked, his robes floated wide, drifting over his shrine as if to protect it.

'The Restish are trying to hurt my mother,' said Inara, steeling herself. 'Your lover.'

The god twisted his nose.

'The woman you left *with child*.'

Didn't he get it? Didn't he understand? 'Who protected you until you died and left her with me. I am your daughter.'

'Whatever my . . .'. the god shrugged. 'Whatever my past incarnation did, what has it to do with me now? The priests told me nothing of *you*.'

Inara narrowed her eyes. 'Perhaps your priests tell you what they want you to hear. Hseth's tell her the same.'

The god's expression changed at mention of Hseth. His mouth turned down, his brow creased. 'The fire god is beyond our ken,' he said coolly.

'The fire god has plans to invade every shrine, every home, every heart,' said Inara. 'To consume all hearths, to burn all ships unless they bear her plenty. Look at me and see if I lie.' He should be able to tell by the surety in her colours, the lack of twists and changes, of deception. Not all gods were good at telling lies, but certainty was easier.

'Craier,' Yusef repeated at last, as if testing the word, pacing now. There was a stirring of recognition. 'Craier!' He stopped in front of his own feet. 'The records do show that I met with a Craier. To broker a treaty, that her commander later broke by raiding a Restish ship.'

All he knew was his own scripture, the lines his priest thought it best to preserve and teach him.

'You spent many nights with her,' said Skediceth.

'You remember this?'

Skedi fluttered his wings. 'Yes,' he lied, and no white lie it was either, but he had worked out that Yusef's innocence might play in their favour. 'This girl has a god's power. It is a flattery to you, great lord, that she has such strength in her.'

Softly, softly, gentle lies and lovings. The god beamed, and in a glimmer of light and burst of smoke he ascended to the lap of his own statue and looked down at them. 'You say my priests lie to me?' he said, more curious than angry.

'No,' said Inara carefully. 'I tell you they do not speak the whole truth.'

'And what truth is that?'

'That Hseth is a threat, and you should help Middren. Help my mother. Help me.'

He did not seem moved. Inara swallowed. She could see daylight creeping in outside the shrine. What if even now her mother was being taken by the Restish? What if they were already about to kill her?

'If not for me,' said Inara, trying not to panic, trying not to cry, 'then . . . for an offering?'

At this, he perked up, tipping his handsome head on one side. He did have the look of a classic Restish man, in his human-like size. Other than his jewels, the only thing beyond human about him was the coldness in his eyes.

'What will you give me?' he asked. 'I get a lot.' He looked at Skedi. 'Will you give me back my helper?'

Inara's heart twisted. Slowly, carefully, she looked towards Skedi, who was still on his hind legs, standing enthralled by the god above him. His ears were up, his whiskers forward.

'Skediceth is a god,' she said at last. 'He isn't mine to give away.'

But Skedi turned to her. They both knew that was a lie. The love she held for him could be an offering. And Yusef could give Skedi everything he had wanted: powerful protector, freedom, purpose. Haven. The great god beamed down at her hare, and she tried to draw in her colours so that he wouldn't see her pain, her fear.

Inara, he said at last, the button she had given him gleaming on his antler. *If you ask me to go with him, to save Kissen and your mother, I will. But . . . you are my home. I belong now with you.*

Inara felt her chin tremble, her eyes burn. She looked at Yusef, who was staring at her and Skedi, unblinking. She had thought going to Yusef would solve all her problems, that finally there would be a god who would see that he should help them and have power enough to do it.

But the smallest god of roses in Lesscia had more generosity than this behemoth of faith would give to her. She needed to think of a better offering, an exchange. Something.

'I will raise a shrine to you,' said Inara.

Yusef did not look impressed.

'Greater than this one, a temple. In Middren.' She looked around this grand space. It was bigger than any shrine she had seen. 'There are so few gods left in Middren, you will be the greatest.'

That piqued his interest. He considered it.

Inara, no, said Skedi. *Don't make such a promise to a god. Choose me instead.*

I won't. I don't want to.

'A shrine in a land that has abandoned gods,' said Yusef. 'How will this happen?'

'I've changed my mind,' said Skedi out loud. 'I will . . . I will go with you.'

Yusef looked at him. 'It is not enough,' he said. 'It is her sacrifice, not yours, if she wants something from me.'

Inara ground her teeth. She thought about what Kissen had told her, that gods were greedy. All they wanted was more: more faith, more power. They did not care for bonds of family, or friendship.

'I will ensure it,' she growled. She was glad he had already lost his desire for Skedi, the fickle-hearted bastard. 'If I have to break the king myself, I will, and I can. I've done it before.'

'You will raise me a shrine in a godless country,' said Yusef. 'You will bind yourself to this promise? On your flesh? It will connect you to me, the link unyielding.' Now, he appeared more godlike, more serious. He drifted down from his throne, coming closer to Inara. 'I will curse you if you do not keep it, or find another god

264

to break it. My reach is far, and I will condemn you to have no home, no hearth that doesn't crack, no haven that doesn't flood.'

They would be bound, she and her father. Forever.

Kissen won't like this, said Skedi, for the second time calling on Kissen as the arbiter of sense.

Kissen doesn't have to.

Skedi put his ears down, flat on his back, but he nodded his support.

'I swear to it,' said Inara. 'By choice or by force, you will have a shrine in Middren again if you save my mother, save the veiga, and see us and our Irisian allies safe to our land.'

Yusef's eyes shone. 'Then a boon ties us,' he said, and grinned. 'My first, now that I have risen.'

Inara felt . . . empty. She had come to find a father, but instead she had found a god, venal and self-serving. But she lifted her arm.

The sound of several running feet came from the courtyard. The caretaker had brought the other priests. 'No, *great god!*' cried someone in Restish. '*Do not*—'

'Make me a boon, Father,' she said.

The god raised his hand, and light came off him, deep-blue and silver, like winter sun on a still sea. It threaded towards her, wrapping around her wrist as three priests threw themselves towards the shrine entrance.

Too late.

The bowls of offering flared and bubbled, and Inara could feel it: the bind of another god's will, Yusef's will, embedding itself in her skin, her flesh, her soul. A manacle, a chain, twisting in a script that was all shape and colour, like hills and waves, something between sea-script and stone-script, from a god of both land and sea.

It seemed that this would be the only thing she gained from all of her searching for her father.

Yusef shrank down, using too much power. In an impulsive swoop of greed, he had detangled himself from the desires of his priests and politics, and instead, forged a bond with a child he did not, would not recognise.

The priests had fallen to their knees just inside the shrine, gleaming with piety and awe, and bristling with anger that their god had done such a thing without them. Their records. Their say so.

Then, Yusef began to laugh.

He opened his arms and his flowing robes turned to streams as he dived forward. Skedi sprang up into Inara's arms and the god of safe haven caught them both up, sweeping them out into the vivid sky.

CHAPTER THIRTY-TWO

Kissen

THEY TRIED TO FIGHT, THEY DID. THEY ALMOST MADE IT to the ship's rail and the water, though there was nowhere to go save for the Restish ship. The flotillas of the Long Harbour were already far behind.

Lessa had run first, seizing those few moments between surprise and reaction and swiping her sword towards Aleda.

The first mate was quick. Sparks flew as her own blade met Lessa's.

Kissen had barrelled up behind the two of them before the rest of the crew could dive on the lady. She charged around the duel and headed straight for the next man, whose name she barely remembered. With the bread pan she met the swing he made for Lessa, shoving him backwards across the deck.

She glanced around, taking stock of their situation. Not good. The deck was lit only by a few lanterns as the sky lightened, and bound by mooring lines to the great hulk of the Restish ship, four-masted and blunt-prowed. Its deck was alive with folk running as they bound the two vessels together.

'Run, Lessa!' said Kissen, but each time Lessa tried to break out of the vicious dance she was in with the first mate, Aleda caught her, quick on her feet and quicker with her shortsword.

Kissen's opponent found his stance and came back with his cutlass, drawing another knife, and Kissen was forced on the retreat,

267

keeping him at bay with the bread pan, stabbing at his stomach, his legs. He sprang back, and she grinned.

'The fuck are you laughing at, *harasa?*' he spat.

'Thinking about a friend who would enjoy my choice of weapon,' she said.

He tried feinting, desperately obvious, then darted around to her left. She slammed his ribs with the hard edge of the pan, put her left foot down and swung her right leg with all the force she could manage as he bent double.

Of course, he put up his knives, but this was her new metal prosthesis: no blade could cut her. A leg's worth of finely tuned metal slammed into his ribs. Though Kissen winced as her ghost-shin stabbed with pain, the force of it sent the pirate skidding to the deck.

Kissen brought her leg back down and planted her foot, and looked back towards Wsirin. The city was all pre-dawn shadow, a grey ghost behind them. Act of war be damned, the chances of them being found were low, of making it to shore . . . impossible.

The crew of the *Silverswift* had been gathered at the forecastle, the deck already red with the blood of their animal offering. A goat this time. But they had heard the ruckus, and now were running.

Kissen backed away, moving towards Lessa, who was locked in a battle of darting blades with Aleda, spitting insults. Kissen grabbed the knives she had tucked in her colourful shirt and threw them. One, a curved bastard with a chipped handle, spun towards Shah and hit him pommel first. The other whirled off into the water, but the point of the third slammed into Graemar's leg. He howled.

Kissen felt Lessa's back touch hers, as if she already knew the shape it would make against her spine.

It was no mistake, she knew that too. She spun around with her long-reach weapon while Lessa ducked down to the side.

Aleda was caught by surprise. Lertes cried out a warning, and his wife reeled back in time to avoid the slam of the bread pan, and even managed to parry Lessa's feint with her sword.

But she did not block Lessa's second strike with the carving knife. That, she plunged into Aleda's chest.

The first mate grunted, her cough drawing the faintest pink spittle to her mouth.

'Aleda!' screamed Lertes.

Kissen took that moment to release the loose manacle from her hand, swinging its chain around her wrist in a whirl as she ran, bread shovel and all, towards the others, yelling and hollering with every ounce of threat she could muster.

'*Scal lufts!*' she cried in Talic. *Loose ends.* It was what she had always said to the world that had tried to kill her, a world that didn't want her. A world of greed and gods and monsters. *Fuck you.*

She'd made enough terror of noise that their witless defence all converged on her.

'Run!' Kissen yelled again to Lessa.

'No,' came Lessa's reply.

No what? Kissen swung her manacle into the face of a pirate, slammed her capped knee into the someone's groin. Shit, she even slammed the staff towards Lertes's ankles as he ran, sword drawn, towards Lessa, howling his rage.

'I will die on my feet with a sword in my hand!' cried Lessa. 'Not in the water with an arrow in my back.'

Fucking nobles. *Now* she decided she had a moral code, and it was a stupid one.

And Kissen had played her best hand. She looked back towards Lessa to give her a piece of her mind, and instead found Aleda's sword flying towards her, hilt first. Kissen caught it in her manacled hand as Lessa then met blades with Lertes.

'You've killed her!' he cried, his bright eyes filled with fury. 'You've killed my wife!'

'You stole my ship!' snarled Lessa.

'I had to choose one of you! I chose her.'

'You chose wrong.'

Their swords flashed brightly in the grey dawn as they entered a vicious dance. A fight to the death, all trust gone, their history dead. Kissen cursed and kept to her defence, stopping anyone she could from getting close to Lessa, hopefully to save her for long enough that she would decide to save herself.

'Stop!' came a cry. The Restish delegate, Efana, had climbed down the plank that had finally been lowered from the Restish ship. 'Stop this brawl! This is madness. Lady Craier, you will be blasted with cannonfire if you do not—'

Lessa and Lertes both turned on him with some garbled combination of, 'If you fire on my bloody ship I will rip out your eyes.'

They could not open fire without destroying the *Silverswift*, but Kissen would not put it past them. There was no clean way to end this: they were outnumbered.

'Then you give me no choice,' Efana declared. 'Release!'

An arrow punched into Kissen's back with enough force to blast the air from her lungs. Crossbow. One struck Shah in the thigh as he threw himself down, and the others followed, all of them pinning themselves to the deck in a show of submission.

Kissen turned, dazed. Lertes had taken a shot to the arm, and Lessa to the hip, but they were still fighting, buoyed on by rage. The Restish had boarded now, wielding swords, reloading their bows as more of their guards spilled onto the *Silverswift*. Her lungs were not ready for this; her body was trembling now from fighting so soon after she had nearly been scalded to death, beaten and caged.

But she dragged herself to her feet.

Well, she knew she'd never die of old age. She never thought she'd die trying to save a stupid noble either, but it wasn't so surprising that she'd die trying to save a beautiful woman.

She stepped into a Restish guard who aimed his blade for her thigh, knocking it aside and ramming the bread shovel into his chest. The second, she struck with the sharp end in the throat and disarmed them before they had a chance to take a breath.

Then she heard a step behind her, and she snarled, swinging the manacle. It was Efana, and he lifted his arm, ready for her, and caught the flailing chain. Then he dragged her forward.

Kissen fell, the arrow in her back scraping, blood hot across her shoulder. She could taste it on her lips too. Red, copper, death.

'Lady Craier, stop or I will kill your veiga!' snarled Efana.

Kissen felt his blade on her neck, and she laughed. Lessa would not stop for her. More, if they had Inara, they would have threatened Lessa with the death of her daughter first. That meant the wily girl had escaped.

Kissen looked towards Lessa, hoping now, at last, she would find a way to flee. But she didn't. Instead, she stopped, holding her bleeding side while Lertes had collapsed to one knee, his blade down. Lessa could have killed him, but she was staring at Kissen with something like fear.

That was all it took. That moment of hesitation, the lowering sword. Then the Restish came. They dived on Lessa before Lertes could right himself, dragging her by the sword arm, weighing her down.

'You fucking cowards!' she yelled, not a lady any more. 'You heartless, godless traitors! You piss-stained bastards of no mothers!'

'Don't hurt her,' came another voice, nearer Kissen. 'The godkiller helped kill crew. She's the crew's to kill.'

It was Rhiyande. She spoke with confidence. The ambassador scowled at her, but he could have ended Kissen's life with a flick of his wrist and did not. Instead, he dropped the chain and stepped over her, as if she were nothing more than a bag of dirt.

'Half-arsed, saltless fucker,' snarled Kissen after him, but he ignored her, instead moving over to Lessa, who was pinned by both arms, on her knees, as the Restish patted her for weapons, finding several.

'*Silverswift* crew,' called Ambassador Mirim, who was also now descending from the Restish boat. 'See to your captain.'

Lertes, bleeding badly, was crawling closer to Aleda, sobbing.

'Leda. My foolish love. My fierce soul . . .'

Aleda was already dead, the cook's knife still buried in her chest. He put his face to her shoulder, no care for his own wounds, and wept.

Rhiyande helped Kissen upright by the back of her shirt. 'If there's an opportunity,' she hissed, 'take it. That's all I can do for you.'

Kissen froze. She cast her gaze back to the shore and the increasing energy of the Long Harbour. There were several ships on the waves now, but only one turned in their direction. Irisian, a pointed prow and slanted cross-masts, but was it Bahba? Kissen didn't dare let herself hope.

'I won't leave her,' said Kissen.

Lessa could have abandoned her, could have let her die. Could not have cared at all. She was still cursing Efana, the Restish, the crew, their mothers and their mothers' mothers.

'This is bigger than people like us,' whispered Rhiyande. 'This is big power. Nations and nobles.'

'I'm not a fucking traitor,' said Kissen.

'No, you're a worker. You weren't blessed with a bellyful and silk sheets for swaddling.' Rhiyande gazed towards Lessa. 'No matter what that woman pretends, she was. She will never be like us. She picks us up like toys. She picked up pirating, she picked up politics and rebellion. She's picked you up, but she will drop you just the same.'

Rhiyande was right. Kissen was in danger here of falling for a woman who was bound to death or glory, nothing in between. Kissen shouldn't even be here. She should be sitting at home with her sisters, in her wheelchair, hiding in some quiet corner away from the clashes of great gods, their countries, their councils and monarchs and greed.

But Kissen didn't make promises lightly. She had promised Inara that she would look after her mother. She had promised gods and Elo that she would do her best to save Middren from Hseth. She had promised herself.

She did not break promises.

The Irisian ship was closer now, crew up the mast and the ship already at full sail.

'Lady Craier of House Craier,' said Efana, his voice certain and clear, 'you are a threat to the peace of the Trade Sea, and therefore we have come to—'

Lessa growled up at him. 'You have no fucking authority over me, pissant. Stab me like the sorry coward you are and get it over with.'

No. Kissen could see clearly now. The Irisians were headed straight for them, they just needed a bit more time. Lessa hadn't seen it, she was only choosing to face death with all the pride she had.

'As you wish, lady,' Efana spat. 'If you desire no ceremony.'

He nodded at one of the guards holding her, and one of the men stood to the side, drawing his sword as the other two forced Lessa down into the blood of the deck, pressing her face to the boards.

'A beheading, how pathetic,' she snarled into the blood, defiant still. 'Scared to look me in the eye or scared of your own shit aim?'

None of them were looking at Kissen, or the encroaching ship. Rhiyande's hands loosened, letting her go. Letting her run.

And she took her moment. She ran forward. Towards the would-be executioner, drawing one of her other knives as he lifted his sword. One stride, two. He turned, eyes widening with alarm.

I'm sorry, Kissen thought, then grabbed his raised arms to stop them falling, and slammed her blade into his belly, point up into his chest.

The blade punctured leather, skin, belly, organ. Hot, red blood gushed out onto her hands. He stumbled back, tugging himself off the blade.

No time to think. Kissen turned towards one of the men holding Lessa, flipping the knife around and coming down at him from on high, ramming it into his shoulder. He let go of the lady, who turned and tackled the legs of the final guard as Efana cursed.

'This is foolish!' said Mirim, trying to be the voice of calm. 'You are outnumbered! Why do you insist on—'

A cry came from the Restish ship, a warning of some kind. Mirim looked up, frowning in confusion. Then Kissen heard its translation from Shah.

'Hit the deck!'

A whistle in the air. Then wood splintering as a cannon ball smashed across the deck, smashing a banister from the aft-deck stairs and flying on into the side of the Restish ship.

Kissen threw herself to the ground, screaming as the arrow shifted, biting against the bones of her back and ribs.

'Leave off my fucking ship!' Lessa snapped, glaring towards the Irisian vessel. It had turned side on, revealing an array of cannons on every deck. Enough to blast them out of the water.

Bahba was on the prow, glaring as if she could stop them with her eyes. Sosul stood beside her, supported by two crutches, while Aslani shouted orders.

Efana drew his own blade again, his eyes fixed on Lessa. 'I will kill the bitch now before they—'

'Hold!' cried Bahba, her powerful voice cutting through the chaos of the deck. 'By order of the Mithrik! You have committed an act of war on Irisian seas.'

'We are beyond the harbour, Mitha!' Efana shouted back, flushed with anger. 'These seas are not yours. We commit an act of piracy, not an act of war.'

'This is the Long Harbour, ambassador!' bellowed Bahba. 'You have not left it yet.'

She pointed, and Kissen turned painfully to see what she had indicated. There, a cluster of boats were moored together and covered by a sail that had been made into an awning. At first glance they seemed like just fishing boats, till Kissen saw the heavily barnacled chain that must attach them to the harbour floor. On them, sat six folk, clinging to the sides of their little island, holding pipes that had long gone out, eyes wide and terrified at the battle that had begun just near their trading spot and smoking break.

Efana looked fit to explode. He glanced at Mirim, who gave him a small shake of the head. But that did not dissuade him. 'Preposterous pedantry,' he said, striding to Lessa, who scrambled to her feet, ready to meet him, though her hands were empty. He lifted his blade. 'You cannot claim all the sea your people trade on—'

He stopped, his eyes fixed on the city, terror in his face.

No . . . shock. Awe.

Kissen dragged herself to her knees again, grunting with pain, hoping that whatever had startled him wasn't one more thing come to kill them.

A gauze of purple light, no, cloth, streaming through the silver clouds of the hazy dawn. A glitter of gold, light, curling hair, and darker, appearing out of the light.

Wings. Skedi. Still a hare's size. She heard his will, whispering, pressing not to her but everyone else on board.

You cannot stand in arms before your god.

'Yusef,' whispered Mirim, her hands flying to the red beads at her neck, then she cried something in Restish and dropped to her knees. All crew members did the same, their weapons clattering to the deck at Skedi's suggestion. The great god of safe haven descended in a ripple of rich cloth and gold, shining as if with the light of the sun. As he landed, waves burst up around the boats, blasting and setting all of them bouncing from side to side.

Kissen clung to the deck, scared to move, squinting her eyes, but then she saw Inara, clambering down from his back. She ran towards them across the deck, worry etched across every feature.

'You cannot harm the Craier family!' boomed Yusef, resplendent with power and will so vast that even Kissen found herself caught in it, feeling nothing but shame and fear till she slammed that down with her own intent.

Cannot harm, came his will like the aftershock of an earthquake. *Never harm.*

'B-but Yusef, great lord, guardian of ships and sailors . . .' said Efana. 'She is our enemy.'

'She is *your* enemy,' said Yusef. 'Gods have no enemies. Gods have no petty squabbles over monarchs and borders. Gods are gods.'

I'm fine, Kissen signed to Inara, *go to your mother.*

Inara spun to see Lessa, bleeding badly from the arrow in her arm and now a slice to her ribs, but the lady was staring at Yusef ashen with disbelief. He did not look like his old statues, even Kissen could see that. He looked like a man just out of boyhood, a god fresh from his first manifestation. Lessa was looking at her old lover, the father of her child, and he had the face of a stranger.

'Be gone,' the god commanded the Restish, 'and offer me your apologies in gold and blood.'

His will came again, like a wave, flattening the delegates into shivering prostration. The ropes holding the Restish ship snapped and broke, unravelled, sending all but the stern turning, creaking around on its anchor, pointing west. It must be frightening for Efana and Mirim to see their god as a force beyond human dignities, asking without giving, demanding without shame.

Inara was exchanging words with her mother, whispering quickly.

'If you do not,' Yusef added with palpable excitement, 'your ship will shatter on Irisian shores. It will be torn apart in the seas and storms, and no one will remember why you sailed it in the first place.' The sails billowed and rippled, and the sea shook the ships with churning currents. Yusef could promise safe haven, or he could take it, break it, crush it. Kissen got the impression the god was *enjoying* himself.

'Y-yes,' said Efana at last, his will crumbling before the force of the god's. 'Of course. We will . . . return.'

'Them too,' said Inara, pointing to the crew of the *Silverswift*. 'Take my mother's betrayers back to Restish with you.'

'N-no,' cried Lertes. 'Please, my lady. Captain. Let us stay with the ship. Gather our things . . .'

'No, Lertes,' growled Lessa hoarsely, her daughter helping her up. 'I will not risk me and mine, our fate to the north, on a traitor-fool's losing game.' She clutched her side, and glanced at Aleda. 'You have lost your mutinous wife, so I will allow you to keep your tongue.'

Kissen looked to Inara, not understanding how she had convinced Yusef to fight for them. Then she saw it. A dark band wrapped around Inara's left arm, like a manacle of writing. Kissen couldn't read it, but she knew the style of stone-struck sea-script. The script of a god of waves and land.

A boon. A binding.

'*Liln*,' she whispered. 'What have you done?'

CHAPTER THIRTY-THREE

Arren

A WEEK SINCE GEFYRTON. IT HAD BEEN A LONG, PAINFUL ride back down from the Bennites, leaving the city a wreckage of broken planks, the waterfall still bleeding through them. Much of the lands below it had flooded, and so Arren had been forced to take the army back west and south before turning towards Lesscia, leaving Tiamh to guard the Daes and prevent further attempts at crossing.

They had now paused in Yesef lands. Lord Farnhall Yesef had given over the use of his own family holdings and now the kitchens steamed all day and night to feed the king's army and a city's-worth of refugees. As soon as the final bowl of broth was consumed, the people were hungry again.

Arren had been given the lord's study, and emptied it of almost all furniture. Apart from the bed they had moved in from his travelling things, there was one lounger and a high-backed seat by the fire, both too heavy to move, and the three rickety pieces left by the desk and window. All the other furniture was for those encamped in the halls or corridors, the haylofts and the cellars, or under the tables with the hounds. Each evening every window brightened the night, and the smoke rising from each chimney darkened it.

And that was just the holding. Beyond the keep's walls, Arren's people were spreading out across the hills. Homeless, clinging to one hope, singing of it with Methsme's words. He heard them at night, the music of prayers and praises, the pleas for victory. Each lyric fluttered the flame in his heart.

Fireheart.

Methsme had taken one of the fire seats. She liked to be close to him, watching him with hawkish eyes. He let her as he read his letters: cagey offers of grain from the north, more arms from the south, coin from the west. Some were begging letters, asking him to split his army, and send them all a slice. Others were pledging undying loyalty, to their one and true king after his tainted triumph in Gefyrton. Offers of marriage, offers of children to adopt, offers of animals, sacrifices, prayers.

Absently, he put his hand to his chest. Hestra burned brighter than she had ever before. His bones and her twigs were one now, threads of sinew and branch, moss and little fires, all growing together.

He picked up the next missive. It was surprisingly short, sparse, and in Knight Commander Peta's writing. Arren put it to his nose. Citrus. He thought of Elo. It was his mother Ellac who had taught them as boys the practice of invisible writing, and they had made much use of it during the war. The scent of lemons told him that beneath Peta's terse account of losses and gains, there was a secret.

Perhaps he would invite Elo to help him read it. Perhaps it would get him to speak again. He had barely done so since he had watched the city fall.

A clatter outside the window disturbed Arren before he could hold the paper to the flame to reveal its message. He glanced out. A retinue in yellow had entered the courtyard of the fortress, their bright cloaks clean and shining in the daylight.

Bad news, said Hestra.

Arren couldn't help but agree as he saw the new Lord Yether dismount and run through a list of orders. Commander Yesef came out to greet him, her arm in a sling and her lord with her.

'Take me to the king, traitors!' Yether demanded.

Arren stepped back and briefly contemplated barring the door. Then his gaze was snagged by the stables beyond the first courtyard, which had guards at the door and mud and dung splattering the walls. The Talicians they had captured were in there, chained, and every Middrenite who passed took their turn to spit at them. Arren had stationed knights outside, well-disciplined and ready to keep them in, and the rest of the army out.

He may yet have use for them.

'Your nobles should learn respect,' murmured Methsme.

'Hmm,' said Arren, sitting down as feet hammered up the stairs.

Beloris Yether burst into the room, his blood already up and his face furious. 'My king!' he cried. 'Daesmouth is fallen!'

Arren felt Hestra burn hot in his chest. His own emotions ran wild, but he controlled his face, kept his tone serene. 'Lord Yether,' he said as Commander Yesef and Lord Farnhall also came to the door. 'Please, be calm.'

'The Talicians had already made headway on the southeastern bank,' said Yether. 'They were marching upriver, building ships! No matter what my sister said, we had to pull back to defend Lesscia.'

'You called . . . a retreat,' said Arren. He glanced up to Kyaum, who looked aghast.

'You must put a stop to this, Sunbringer,' said Yether. 'My city cannot take another battle. I beg you make some deal with them. Treat with them. Just stop this war.'

Arren looked at the man who had killed his own father at a king's suggestion. His suggestion, but he barely heard the words he spoke. Yether's hands were soft and unbroken. He had never touched a bow or sword in his own land's defence and had called a retreat against the will of his own sister.

He felt sick.

After everything they had done, everything they had lost, the Talicians would have crossed the Daes. There was a breach in their dam, and the fire was flooding through. They did not even know if their sacrifice of Gefyrton had worked, whether Hseth's strength was even slightly diminished.

'Has Lesscia run out of birds?' Arren asked icily.

Yether looked at him in surprise. 'No.'

'Then why have you come riding away from the city you say you are intent to defend? Where you were *ordered* to be.'

It was too much like Tulenne. Undisciplined nobles, too rich on trade to understand anything about war. Sending emissaries like Kyaum, Crolle and Elemni rather than take the fight on themselves.

'My sisters made an able command,' said Yether, a little bitterly. 'The elder was killed, but Captain Alianne—'

'Then what, I ask,' interrupted Arren, 'is the point of you, my lord?'

Lord Yether stared up at him, cut to the quick. 'My king,' he said. 'All my love for you . . . all the things I have done *for you*.'

It had made sense at the time, killing the irascible Lord Yether using the only one who could get close to him. It had worked. It had helped him win the game he had been playing, the game of hearts.

But the game had changed

Do not cut him away now, Arren, said Hestra straight into his mind, her fire flaring in his chest, as if she were about to break out of it. *We need him still.*

Arren focussed. He could see the shine around Lord Beloris Yether, the similar, steady, brightly coloured zeal that Methsme held. It burned about the cleric now, her face brightening at the flames in his chest. For her, he and Hestra must seem like one and the same.

And the god was right. He could not lose this faith, this glow. He saw it in his armies, his knights, even in the people whose city he had destroyed. *Fireheart. Sunbringer. Saviour.*

He could not lose the hearts he had won.

'My apologies,' said Arren, tempering his tone. 'Craier has gone to treat with Irisia and Restish, but I have received no emissaries from them directly, or I would have put them to bargain long ago.'

Yether stared at him, his mouth working, a ripple of a strange green across his colours, quickly dimming.

What does that mean, Hestra? Arren asked.

He is surprised, she answered. *Perhaps is hiding something. Though I am not so skilled in telling lies from truth. Fire hides few lies.*

Arren sighed. So even the colours he could see could not be trusted.

'I heard you made a pax with Craier,' Yether said at last, scowling. 'And others who supported her bid for power.' He looked over at Lord Yesef, whose cheeks heightened with colour. 'Who's to say she will not join the Restish and try again?'

Arren had been wondering the same thing.

She is too proud, said Hestra. *Her daughter's pride I have seen too, a candle to her mother's torch. Their ship is moving northwards now.*

Arren caught his breath. *You have a shrine there?*

Barely a thread, a symbol, a link.

Do they have any others with them?

I do not know, I can only sense their vessel.

Would she return if she had no aid? Would Craier of all people come to fight for him, when his supposed allies would not? He did not dare to hope.

'My lord Yether,' said Arren, rubbing the top of his head. It was hurting, and he could feel two lumps on his crown, as if he had struck it on something. 'Have you been to the front line? Have you seen what the Talicians do to our prisoners?'

Yether flattened his mouth in disgust. 'I have heard reports they are used as sacrifices.'

'Sacrifices to summon their destructive god. Commonfolk, some of them. Nobles, others. When they could be used as hostages, to negotiate, for reprieve or exchange. Is this an act of a nation that has any desire for peace?'

Lord Yether swallowed. 'No my lord.'

'We have prisoners too.'

This was Methsme, who had, while Arren cooled Yether's temper, moved closer to him, watching their exchange with avid eyes. 'Some of the clerics believe you should have them punished,' she added. 'Used, as they use our people.'

It took Arren a few moments to understand what she was suggesting, all bright-eyed in her white dress, clutching her lyre like a shield. 'You want me to burn them,' he said.

'It would give you power, as it gives their god power. *Fireheart.*' She glanced down at Arren's chest. 'It could release your potential, give punishment for Gef—'

'I am not burning prisoners,' said Arren, and Hestra twisted in his ribs.

She wants the god more than the man, said Hestra. *There is danger in too much faith.*

And he had already burned people. Children. A manor of innocents. Back when he thought his victory would come with swift brutality. When he thought he would have a god's power over Talicia *and* Middren. When he had been willing to commit atrocities to ensure stability.

Arren shook his head. 'Prisoners have uses other than meat for shrines,' he added.

'Like what?' said Methsme crossly.

He glared at her, and she glared back. He was starting to think he had made a mistake in elevating this cleric. She had been useful during the first weeks of the war, but her deference had given way to confidence. She spoke her mind of lords, of tactics, of him, as if she knew it all and more.

'Like information,' he replied. Tired of being questioned, he looked up at Kyaum who already stood ready.

'Have them prepared, Commander Yesef,' he told her. 'We need to know their next move now they have the Daes.'

'They want Lesscia,' interrupted Yether as Kyaum bowed.

'If that is so, then we will confirm it,' said Arren.

Kyaum did not even glance at her lord for his permission. 'Yes, Sunbringer,' she said. She had a shine about her too, a steady bronze-gold. More like sunlight than the metal, but it had the same qualities of what Hestra called faith.

'And bring the commander general as well,' Arren added. If Hestra couldn't tell a lie easily, he would need Elo's insight, and cynicism. Kyaum paused, and Arren heard Methsme mutter something under her breath.

'He is well,' Arren asked tentatively, 'is he not?' Surely someone would have told him if Elo had taken ill.

Kyaum bowed lower. 'He is well in body, Sunbringer,' she said. 'I will find him.'

Arren tried not to show how tired he felt as she left. Instead, he stood and brushed down his light blue shirt with recent flames added to its open heart. For Hestra. Showing another kind of fire.

'My lords,' he said, 'my cleric, you are welcome to join me.'

He wished they wouldn't, but he couldn't tell them that. Instead, he got up and went out through the door. The guard there stood to attention, then fell in step as Methsme, Yesef, and Yether quietly jostled to be closest on his heels.

Arren sighed. The summer heat was stifling. In the winter every stone wall here was thick with tapestries to keep the warmth in, but now they had been bared to allow for the free movement of air. During the day the castle became an oven, sweaty and close.

'Yether, your trading ships,' said Arren, feeling calmer as they walked, 'I was told six were salvaged and made it to Weild.'

They passed two servants, who bowed as low as possible. They were carrying bandages. On their way to treat the surviving wounded.

'Yes, my king,' said Yether, sidling closer as Arren turned down the corridor towards the main stairwell. This was carpeted, and the king's banner hung with the Yesef coat of arms above them. The Yesef banner was a long red stripe, its blazon a cockerel. They and the Yethers had once been one House, centuries before, but had long been rivals on the south coast. 'Three were already out for trade.'

'Well done. They will be needed,' said Arren. 'Yours too, Yesef.'

'Yes, my king,' said Yesef quietly, but Yether stayed silent.

'Beloris?' said Arren, and Lord Yether cleared his throat.

'Of course,' he said. 'You may take whatever you wish.'

Arren looked at the floor they were passing over, a tessellating pattern of fine wood. It looked like a sunburst, or a flower, with dots of brass shining between the petals. Arren wondered if it was Talician brass. How much had he overlooked the nation's power? How foolish had he been to believe their god had any need of him other than a face and a throne? He had got them into this mess.

'Are you certain you have been sent no messages of treaty?' Yether asked.

'Which of our invaders would you like to speak to, my lord?' Methsme cut in. 'Or is it their god you would like to send you letters?'

Arren bit back a smirk. When not at the receiving end of it, the effect of Methsme's cutting tone was amusing, and the gall she had at speaking back to a noble. Perhaps the two would entertain themselves and give him some peace.

A pity he could not let them eat each other. 'There has been no proclamation of war, Yether,' he said. 'The Restish have not even claimed any part in it. Unless you know something I do not?'

'N-no,' he said, his colours glimmering again.

I think . . . that is a lie, said Hestra.

Useless.

They reached the open doors of the keep, where it gave out onto what had been a garden, and was now a trampled mess of mud and water. Some of the horses were being walked here by their ostlers, giving them gentle preparation for more marching days ahead. There, the commander general was waiting on his own, gazing at a brown steed with a white stripe on his nose.

Elo was wearing a dark russet shirt of finely woven cloth, cut close to his body, with wide sleeves tied back. It was clean, but his hands were not, for they were covered in flour. He had a sheen of heat on his skin, and a scruff of beard.

'What? What are you doing here?' said Beloris, as he recognised who they were meeting under the hot sun.

Elo looked across at Lord Yether, his gaze direct, hard, empty. 'I was called,' he said.

His voice was hoarse, seared by shouting commands and breathing in smoke, then roughened from lack of use. Arren did not want to tell him about Daesmouth, did not want to cause him any more pain.

'Commander General Elogast,' Arren greeted him. 'Thank you for coming so swiftly. Beloris, you must have heard of the commander's promotion, and his work on the field of battle.'

Beloris had gone pale. It seemed neither his sister nor Peta had deemed it fitting to share Elo's new position with him. He gawped at Arren, then back to Elo, his eyes darted around, seeking help, but none came. 'He k-killed my father,' he said, pointing an accusing finger in Elo's face. 'I need protection. I want my guard.'

'Then by all means, go and find them,' said Arren smoothly. 'I require the commander's advice.'

Beloris stepped back, then towards Elo, then finally turned on his heel and wheeled towards the keep, muttering in fury. Presumably to find the favoured guard he had come with, Hafil.

Arren and the others watched him go.

'Well . . .' said Methsme at last. 'I did not like him, Sunbringer.' Yesef covered a scoff of laughter with a feigned cough.

'You don't like anyone, cleric,' said Arren, turning back to Elogast, who was watching impassively.

'Commander Yesef told me Daesmouth has fallen,' he said.

No use hiding it if he already knew. 'Yes,' said Arren. 'Two nights ago. Yether retreated.'

Elo nodded slowly to himself. He did not look devastated, only weary, and Arren feared he had gone so far inside himself that no feeling could make it through. He still gave commands when needed, advice when asked, but what was one more blow to a stone already crushed into dust?

'I will begin gathering the army,' he said at last.

'Wait,' said Arren, painfully aware that Methsme, Yesef and his guard were still with him. 'Not yet.'

Elo took a breath, and visibly straightened his shoulders, but stayed still.

'Yes, my king,' he said.

You ask too much of me, he had said. *Ask someone else.*

But he was still here.

They walked through the courtyard, Methsme staring daggers at their backs. Perhaps she wanted the god, like Hestra said, but Elo needed a friend.

'Do you know that horse?' said Arren, nodding at the chestnut gelding Elo had been gazing at. Elo did not look.

'No.'

He waited a little longer, then tried, 'I thought I called a commander, not a baker.' He smiled at Elo's floury hands, telling Elo it was a joke. Arren loved Elo's smile: it was like a burst of rain on a hot day. Refreshing, bright, softening his face and tracing furrows around his eyes.

But Elo didn't smile, he simply looked down at his palms as if just now seeing them.

'They needed help in the kitchens,' he said at last.

'Yes, I received some complaints from the cooks,' said Lord Yesef, and Arren frowned at him. The kitchen staff had been afraid of the Lion of Lesscia coming into their midst. But, despite hearing this, Arren had not wanted to take away the one thing from Elo that brought him any peace.

'They got used to me,' said Elo.

'When they realised you were better than the lot of them at baking?'

The slightest smile, a crook of the mouth. Elo had loved breads since he was a boy; pastries, buns, rounds, nameen, crispels, pies and tarts. He'd said it was because his fondest times with his mothers had been when they had cooked together. Irisians, even wealthy ones, took pride in self-reliance, while before knowing Elo, Arren had only ever set foot in the kitchens to steal food when his mother tried to starve him. If it involved flour and water and heat, Elo either wanted to eat it or make it, and Arren had adored watching him, eating what he made, teasing him for it.

The easiest way to touch Elo's heart was to compliment his skill.

The smile quickly faded, but it was there. There was a hope of more.

Arren turned them right, past the horses as the ostlers bowed to them, and towards the stables he had seen earlier.

Here, it was abuzz with activity. People carrying food, vats, brushes, barrels, shovelling shit, filling fresh bails with straw. Dogs ran from person to person, loudly begging for scraps, while a cat sat on top of one of the overfull stables, tail swishing as they watched for rats. No one wore armour: these lands were not yet under threat.

By the stable-prison, Kyaum had lined up several Yesef knights, who bowed to both Arren and the lord and then stood back.

Inside, were the prisoners.

They had captured five Talicians alive. They had been separated and bound, but four had clustered together. One was a priest. He wore a once-white cloak that had been stained by mud, blood and his own excrement to a dirty brown. His feet were bare, and his hair hung lank around his neck. The bells known to grace the Talician theocrats had likely been stolen by his gaolers, smashed or sold, but he had the smudged remnants of make-up on his face. Arren remembered that they were patterns of fake burns used to emulate the pain they wrought, rarely experiencing it themselves.

Beside him sat three foot soldiers, judging by their poorly dyed sackcloth jackets with patches at the elbows. They were young, perhaps no more than fifteen or sixteen, and were hunched over and shaking. They had fought like fiends in Gefyrton, but it was one thing to fight with an army at your back, another to sit in your own filth.

Separate from them, however, sat a man in a neater jacket, newly made and with brassy buttons. A krka, Arren understood. One of their commanders, second only to the priests. He was older than Arren by perhaps a decade, and glared at him like a wolf in a trap.

'What are your names?' said Arren in Talic, coming to the door.

One foot soldier, a boy, answered 'Tomek' before the priest interrupted.

'What need are names for the godless?' he snarled in rotten Middric, his accent so thick that Arren could barely parse it. 'What is it to be? The sword, the pyre or the rack? Torture us how you will, you will gain nothing from it. We would rather die than abandon our god.'

As he spoke, the foot soldiers looked stronger, their faint colours steadying.

'That can be arranged,' said Methsme, and Arren cast her a glance to silence her, then stepped into the shelter of the stable. He felt the knights start forward, half-panicked, but Elo came in with him and they settled

'Tell me, priest,' said Arren in Talic, for the benefit of the foot soldiers, 'do you think all leaders as cruel as your own?'

'We have heard of your leadership,' the priest retorted. 'Killing gods. Destroying cities. Beating the faithful from west coast to east should they dare worship the true god Hseth. Let alone any of those weak, other deities who turn to shades in her glory.'

Arren felt Hestra grow hot and angry in him, and the fire in his heart lit up the room. The foot soldiers cowered, twisting with fearful shades, and so did the priest. The shine was different for each of them: the priest felt fear in a shadowy blue, the foot soldiers in bloody red, and orange. Flames.

But the krka. His vision of fear was white. As white as the priest's robes. *Him*, said Hestra, and Arren came to stand before him.

'Do you think your priests are cruel, krka?' Arren asked.

'Don't answer him,' spat the priest.

'Fuck you,' said the krka in Middric, though Arren wasn't sure if it was to him or the priest. 'We are Talicians, and we are loyal. We will return with blades and fire and run Middren into dust as your ancestors did with mine.'

Arren looked at Elo, who had a hand on his sword and met his gaze. The krka's Middric was practised, clean. He had been taught. Teaching suggested wealth. Wealth suggested inheritance.

They say the commanders come from the old Talician kerls, said Hestra. *I heard them.*

'My apologies,' said Arren; he put his hand to his heart and gave a small bow. 'I did not realise the great raiding families had survived the incursion of Hseth.' The krka closed his mouth.

'There are no great families in Talicia,' snarled the priest. 'Her priests are *chosen*.'

'The king wasn't speaking to you,' said Elo.

'What do you wish to gain by tickling the ballsack of a dead line?'

The krka growled and rounded on his leader. 'The fuck did you say?'

Elo drew his sword warily. Days marched through endless roads by angry Middrenites, eating maggoty bread and left in their own filth had frayed the Talicians' nerves to snapping, as Arren had hoped.

The krka slipped into cold, clipped Talic, bearing down on his priest. *'My ancestors were questing the seas while yours were scraping molluscs from their arses, you nothing man. You loose end.'*

'Krka, *o'thoi alek*,' said one of the foot soldiers, not Tomek, another young man sitting up on his knees. *Please stop.*

'We live for Hseth, we die for Hseth,' the priest snapped at the krka.

'And what good did that do at the bridge?' came the reply. *'She destroyed us!'*

'It was a mistake,' said the priest, and then turned his ire back on Arren.

'Torture us,' he said, 'kill us, burn us. Through pain and blood these lands will be hers, and you will die screaming in her fire for longer than we live screaming at your hands.'

Arren summoned his patience, and his cunning. 'My heart is not one of fury,' he said in Middric, then Talic, to make his point perfectly clear. Not to the priest, he would take too long to break, but to his people. '*It is one of warmth and welcome, home and hearth. That is the land I fight for. I have no desire to hear you scream, priest, but you must be punished for your crimes.*'

The foot soldiers stared at him, and Elogast very carefully did not look his way. Arren could taste his own hypocrisy, bitter-white, coating his tongue. He swallowed it, then turned to the door of the stables.

'You want an execution, cleric,' said Arren, Perhaps the priest could be ransomed, but what would that do save put a few more gold coins in their pocket? What to exchange people for, if their lives were valued only as sacrifices to their holy of holies? 'Here is the one you will punish, who burns his people for the sake of a god and sends them to their deaths at her hands.'

It was a lie, Arren had sent them to their deaths, but it seemed to have stuck for the krka. What about the others? At least his own guards' colours brightened. Middren had been hurt, badly, and now they all wanted to inflict pain in turn. Anger and retribution. Lord Yesef and Methsme were much the same. They wanted so much from him.

'Have him put to the sword' said Arren, pointedly at Methsme. 'No burning. Quick, clean and public.' She inclined her head. 'Take him away.'

Two guards piled in, grabbing the priest. The boy who defended him threw himself at them but was swiftly kicked aside. The priest began screaming in Talic. '*A martyr!*' he howled as he was dragged away. '*Make me a martyr! Tell them nothing, die before you speak.*'

'What of these?' said Elo in a low voice, nodding at the youths, braced as if for impact. The foot soldiers looked so young, half starved, shaking.

Arren looked to Commander Yesef. 'Have them fed in the next stable,' he said. 'And give them something to wash with. We wish to speak with the krka alone.'

Kyaum nodded, and gave the command to two of the reluctant knights, sending a nearby kitchen boy to go fetch some food. The young Talicians had no fight now the priest was gone: they let themselves be led away.

Elo and Arren were left with the krka. The man's eyes glittered; they were a pale, pale blue in his olive brown skin, his hair black and cropped short.

'And what of me?' he said. 'Are you another fool with too much power who wishes me to kiss his arse? Or am I the one you will torture?'

Elo looked down at the krka, his expression inscrutable, the glow around him confusingly steady. Arren wondered for a moment if he also desired pain and retribution. Torture was a tool, but it took someone practice and time to discern lies from truth; it was also punishment. If that was the one thing that would heal Elo's pain, would Arren let him do it?

'Sometimes,' said Elo at last, 'the king prefers sweetness over stick.'

Was that a joke? Or just a statement to unnerve the Talician?

'We wish to know what Talicia will do to Lesscia should they invade,' said Arren.

'Burn it if they have no use for it,' the krka scowled. 'Perhaps even if they do.'

'Why do you not keep the cities you claim?' said Elo. 'What purpose is there in such wanton destruction?'

'We kept Blenraden,' said the krka, 'gave it to the Restish so they could turn a profit. But Hseth doesn't need profit, the priests say. She wishes for domination. She wishes for power. Burn the gods, burn the cities, burn their shrines, burn their king.'

He spat on the floor at Arren's feet.

'Talicia only wants your decimation. They will crush Middren into the dust you made of us and raise Hseth's banner over the Trade Sea. Restish, Irisia, Curliu, Usica . . . they will all fall, one after the other, and come to their one god.'

It was a familiar idea to Arren, who had so recently dreamed that it would be he who dominated from coast to coast, turning gods into shadows and replacing them with his image. He had wanted to claim power in the Trade Sea and show them all what he was capable of.

This is the story he had told himself. He had convinced himself that no matter what he did, it would be worth it for stability, for peace, for power. Now, he was barely clinging to any of them, and had only one thing on his mind: survival.

'Then it is not Lesscia itself that they want,' said Elo. 'Not its riches, not its port.' He looked at Arren. 'They want you. They want us.'

'If we fall back from Lesscia,' Arren said, 'with the full army . . . they may follow.'

Elo nodded, and Arren thought he saw a glimmer of hope in his eyes. 'We could draw them into open battle. Save the city.'

Could he do it? Should he? Leaving Lesscia was inviting the Talicians in, if he then could not defeat them . . .

'They will destroy you,' said the krka. 'We have the numbers. We have the god.'

'The god who burned a city with your people in it?' said Arren. He didn't care it was a lie, he would press it home, because he saw it bending the Talician's colours, turning them small. Turning them scared. 'What is your name?'

The krka looked as if he were considering biting his tongue off rather than answering, glaring Arren straight in the eye. But he broke gaze first.

'Estefin,' he said. 'My grandmother was kerl in the north. Her name was Ruoch. She was one of the first they sacrificed to bring Hseth into Talicia.'

Arren nodded. 'You will be given a room, Estefin,' he said. 'Food, and new clothes. I would hear more of what happened to Talicia in the years between the raider wars and Hseth's rise. And our part in it.'

'A room?' This was Lord Yesef from outside. 'Sunbringer, there are no rooms. Not for our own people, let alone a Talician murderer.'

'He can have mine,' said Elo softly, looking at Arren. As always, he was the one who understood him, who tempered his anger with wisdom. 'I sleep poorly on feathers, and I can join the others outside while the skies are warm.'

Arren bit the inside of his cheek. That, he hadn't intended. He had been half waiting to turf Methsme out, to teach her some humility. 'Very well,' he said. 'See it done.'

'That's it?' said the krka. 'I told you nothing.'

'It was all we needed,' said Arren. 'A way to protect our kingdom. But, if you have more to offer. . .'

Estefin clenched his jaw shut, but he had already shown his weakness: his pride, and his anger. Torture would shatter a man like that, but food and wine would run him chattering. He would press that nerve later, collect any titbits he could, even if it was the krka boasting of Talicia's superior strength.

Now, he was tired, and he had missives to write. Peta wouldn't like the idea of retreat. It was a weakness to her, and she despised weakness as much as Methsme. Hopefully, she would understand that if they met Hseth in Lesscia, they would destroy it between them. And he had had enough of destroying his own cities.

He had had enough of seeing the pain in Elo's eyes.

They left the stink of the stable behind, with baffled Estefin waiting to be escorted by a stoic Kyaum and her guard.

'And the others?' said Elo, stopping before they went too far. They both looked back. The Talician foot soldiers were sitting, chained, and scarfing down weak broth from the bowls the guards had given to them, as if they had not eaten in weeks.

I saw them once, said Hestra softly to Arren. *I pitied them.*

'What do you think?' said Arren out loud.

Elo had sheathed his sword, and was rubbing his thumbs absently over his fingers, cleaning them of flour. 'Kill them clean or let them go,' he said.

'Let them go?'

'Yes.'

They were enemies. Destroyers. Arren considered Methsme's desire for vengeance and sacrifice, and Elo's for pity, for mercy, when he had been afforded so little. Perhaps he could give him some. An offering of his own, for Hestra and Elo.

'I will see it done,' he said. 'They will be sent across the Daes, and told to go home to their hearths.'

'They may go back to the army, tell the Talicians of our strategy.'

'Let them. We want them to know.'

Elo's mouth tightened, closer to a smile again, and Arren saw a curious shade of blue in his shine. 'Is that all you wanted me for, King Arren?'

That wasn't all Arren wanted him for, but for the life of him he couldn't think of another way to ask him to stay other than *please*.

'Yes,' he replied instead.

Elo walked away, and Arren turned back to the fortress, his personal guard still at a respectful distance. He felt eyes on him still, as he passed through the courtyard back to his chambers: from the servants, the knights. He could see their shining too, out of the corners of his eyes. Their fears, their hopes, their faith, their love; so bright, so much.

It was becoming a warm blue evening. Arren looked out of the windows as he passed, taking in the vivid, endless horizon, marred only by a few smudges of dark cloud and veils of rain falling to the west.

'Wait outside, please,' said Arren to his guard as they came into the study. He was left, the door closed, and at last he was alone.

Not alone. With Hestra.

That was well done, she said. *I understand why the knight has such a hold on you.*

A compliment? From Hestra? He shook his head bemusedly, going to his desk.

Did you mean what you said? she asked. *About your heart being different?*

Was his headache because she was speaking more to him? No longer did he feel such needling pain as he usually expected from a god in his mind, but it was not comfortable either.

Is it not true? said Arren.

It is strange, she said. *I no longer have many homes but you. Our bond deepens, yet it was made by a being who abandoned us both.*

She was right. He had no home: even his own body was shared. The closest to home he'd known had been stolen moments in Elo's bakery, sharing bread, or the tents and meals on the battlefield.

You play this war like a game of faiths, said the god at last. *Perhaps it is. But I fear even with what we have wrought, Hseth's power will remain unbroken. The girl said a god more powerful was needed to win against a rage so great. Despite what she wanted, I am not she.*

'The girl?' said Arren, sitting down. 'Craier's girl?'

Hestra did not answer for a moment. *She can speak to me*, she said at last. *She tried to call me to join Middren's side.*

Inara Craier.

'What is she?' Arren asked.

It depends on who you ask, said Hestra. *There have been some over the years, some hunted, some worshipped. A halfling. A god's child.*

'Gods can have young?'

Rarely. Some grew too close to humans, wanting to experience mortal pleasures, or to claim a different kind of adoration.

This was the most helpful Hestra had ever been. Not an enemy, not a whispered voice of anger, not a pressure of will and conniving with other gods. As lost as he was, he had found himself for the first time on equal footing with her.

'Did you have any?' said Arren.

Lovers or children?

'Either.'

Hestra fell quiet for such a long time that Arren feared she would not answer. The edge of night was creeping closer, and he could hear shouting below, the gathering of forces. Ready for the execution. He should go, he knew that. But he was so weary, so lonely.

I once loved a human woman, said Hestra softly, flickering and warm beneath his shirt. *She would sing and stitch by the flames. Such beautiful music. She did not read or write as you do now, pinning songs down like sparks to the wall, but she . . .* Her voice took on longing. *She had a voice that could make gods weep. Centuries I had lived already, and I had never heard songs like hers.* She paused. *Nor have since.*

'What happened?' said Arren.

The same that always happens, said Hestra. *The same thing that is happening now. She moved away from her hearth and home, driven by war or plague, I cannot remember which. I was so angry that she left. I burned down the cottage that she abandoned. She never found another hearth, not one I could hear her in. So, I expect she did as all humans do.*

Arren put his hand to his chest. 'What is that?' he said.

She died.

'I'm sorry.'

You should get used to it, if immortality is what you truly crave. You already tried to give your heart away for power, and now you begin to see with a god's eyes.

'Surely that means I would be able to love people more, understand them more.'

The love comes from you, kingling, not from them, she said. *What is faith if not an offering in return for love?*

Arren sighed, picking up Peta's letter and holding it to his chest, where the warm flames of his heart heated the parchment, revealing what was said.

Daesmouth is lost, she said. His most loyal follower, his knight commander, the first to call him Sunbringer and mean it. *Do not trust anyone. The Restish have sent envoys to Crolle and Yether, looking for another to hold the throne. We need your power now, Sunbringer, your godhead, or all is lost. Help us.*

Arren lowered the parchment and put his head back against his chair. Of course. The Restish were not Talicians. They wanted cities, profit, control.

They wanted the Houses.

And Arren had few now left he could trust.

CHAPTER THIRTY-FOUR

Elogast

THE COLD HE FELT INSIDE COULD NOT BE WARMED BY bread or burning alcohol. Elo had tried both, and only felt the chill sink further.

He saw Benjen's smile. He heard Perin's cry as he realised his husband had died. He saw Tulenne disappear into flame and bones. He shivered with Legs's screams as he perished in the worst way Kissen could imagine.

He hoped he would never have to tell her. He'd rather crawl back to Gefyrton on his hands and knees. He'd rather be as dead as he felt his soul had become. Frozen in ice.

But Arren had tried to warm him with his small jokes, his little mercies. Elo knew he had done it for him.

So, he brought his own offering up from the kitchens through the servants' stairs to the study where two guards now stood on duty in the flickering torchlight. They stood to attention as Elo approached and allowed him to knock.

'Enter.'

Arren sounded exhausted, and Elo found him just rising warily from the chaise, his hand on the sword at his waist. He dropped it with surprise. 'Elo?'

Elogast held out to Arren the pot he had put together, covered with a thick, fluffy slice of his own herby bread, traditional to this area of Middren. 'I . . .' he began, then the door shut behind him, enclosing them together. Alone again, for the first time since Gefyrton. 'I guessed you would not have eaten.'

Arren opened his mouth, then closed it, glancing at the tray that had been brought to him earlier. He clearly had partaken of none of it save the wine. Someone had at least lit the candles in the room. Enough to cast a dim, flickering light.

Elo put down the pot on the table in front of the chaise, as if he was laying down a gauntlet. Arren stared at it for a moment, then lifted its bread and lid and peered in through the fragrant steam. Elo was happy with the stew, made from beans, fatty meat, and spiced sausages called talchet, as well as preserved lemons from the previous season. No king's fare, no prime cut. Soldier's rations.

Elo bowed, his chest tight and heavy, as if ice were growing in his ribs where he could feel the scar of Hseth's hand. He would take his leave. He must. 'Good night, King Arren.'

'Stay?'

Arren said it so softly that Elo wondered if he had heard. He paused, his back to him. He shouldn't stay. He was so angry; he was so sad. His hands trembled when he did not bake, his stomach cramped and he couldn't stop seeing the battle. Every battle. The gods, the wars, Hseth, Kissen, Canovan.

Gods, he was so lonely.

'All right.' Elogast turned back to the chaise. No, too close. He sat down instead on the heavy chair across from it. Arren smiled shyly in that infuriatingly boyish and attractive way he had, then went and poured a second glass of wine from his carafe, which Elo accepted. What else could he do?

'You made this, didn't you?' said Arren, sitting and lifting the lid of the pot again, before ripping off a piece of the bread and dipping it in. 'It smells like the hunting stews you used to cook.'

Elo remembered. Quick pots in lodges, shooting ducks from hides along the rivers and ponds in the north. They had eaten similar food the day that Elo had saved Lord Yether's prideful son from a boar's tusk. Arren was trying to make conversation, but Elo was worried that if he opened his mouth he would say something stupid.

Or just start screaming.

He shook his head, pressing down his fears. 'I helped with this batch of bread,' he said. 'But the stew was assisted by young lady-heir Geralfi, much to the ire of the cooks.'

'The talchet sausage was her idea?'

'She insisted that it was the proper way.'

Elo had found the Geralfi girl, Freia, crying in one of the gardens he had hunted through for herbs. She had looked so like Inara, had watched her people strung up on cliffsides and her entire city crash into the river she had lived on her whole life.

'She shouldn't be working in the kitchens of another lord's manor,' said Arren.

'It is better for her to be doing something,' said Elo. 'Pain will bind a person to their bones if they're not careful.' He paused. 'I lent her a horse. My horse. And he was used at . . . at the west gate.'

Legs. He had promised to keep him safe. Had kept him away from the war. For nothing. All for nothing. He blinked back the hotness in his eyes, the tears. He had cried enough.

Arren paused, then sat up slowly. 'Elo,' he said, his eyes raking him. 'I'm sorry.'

Elo tried to focus on the candle on the table, its flickering light, as he thumbed his wine. What was he doing here? Why had he come? Was it because he could not face Elseber, Ainne and Perin and the rest? Was it because he wished he had died on the bridge so that he did not have to feel again this . . . this bloodless wounding that caught his heart and seized his lungs and set his body shaking and aching? Was it because he wanted to fight Arren, blame him?

Or because he needed someone who knew him?

'You can talk to me,' said Arren. 'If you want.'

Elogast frowned down at his glass, then at last took a sip of Arren's rich wine. Almost too sweet.

'I don't know how to mourn,' he said at last. 'Benjen was barely a friend any more. I ran from all my friends and shut myself away. When my mother died, I couldn't grieve then either, I was still too buried in my own darkness.' He took a breath and looked at Arren, who had laid his life before a god's blade to save him. He had adored that face once. Studied its every detail. Now he felt like a stranger considering a statue of someone he had known long ago.

Arren's cheeks reddened slightly under his scrutiny, and his lips parted, as if he wanted to say something.

But Elo hadn't finished.

'I didn't allow myself a life without you, you know. Not a hope. Not a breath. And I didn't even see it.' He laughed bitterly. 'The cruelties of what you became. I only saw the face you showed me. And I blame myself for that. And I blame you too.'

Arren swallowed, putting a hand to his forehead as if it pained him. 'We agreed not to speak about the things that hurt us,' he said.

'So, we lied to each other,' said Elo. 'Through silence.' And not for the first time. He wondered whether Skedi would have liked it, whether those lies of never speaking were a kindness or a cruelty. 'I have never been very honest with you, Arren. Not with my love, not with my anger.' He ran his fingers over the braids that Lotta and Benjen had made, their hands firm, deft and sure. Never again.

'Perhaps I should have stayed with you,' Elo continued, half to himself. 'Perhaps I should have challenged you every day. But you held the world too tightly to see any light in it. You allowed yourself to be cruel, all in the name of doing what you "must", not what you "should". And little by little, you lost yourself as well. You became the thing that you hated. A god, desperate to cling to power no matter who it hurt.'

The pain was pouring out of him, and Arren took it. The king did not speak, did not move. He just . . . looked at Elo as he would look at a river rising, knowing nothing could be done to stop it.

'Instead,' Elo went on. 'I let myself shrink to nothing. Less than nothing. Barely existing because I forgot how.' He laughed. 'It took a killer of gods to remind me what it was like to be alive. That it was something I deserved . . . something I wanted. A woman I barely knew brought me back to myself.' He looked back at Arren, whose expression had shifted slightly into jealousy.

'I tried,' said Arren. 'To involve you. To visit you. I tried to tell you I loved you, in silent little ways, over and over.'

Elo remembered him coming, sneaking out of the palace like when they were youths, sleeping, he on the floor, Arren on the bed, hand spans apart.

'But you didn't tell me to leave,' Elo said. 'You asked me to stay, "over and over", stay in Middren, stay near you, and I couldn't bear to leave you. Even knowing that my mothers were waiting, that I had another life I could live.'

Arren's eyes slid off his, moving away, to the wall, the window.

You ask too much of me. Elo had said it in Gefyrton, and he had meant it.

'I did love you,' Elo said. He felt hot, uncertain, foolish, but sure. 'I loved you deeply, Arren, and entirely. All those days we spent at war, all those years after. And I am sorry I wasn't there for you in the way you wanted. I'm sorry I wasn't honest with you. I owed you more than that. But I didn't deserve what you did to me in return. You say you love me, but you hurt me. You became obsessed with gods and power. You broke us, and yourself. You can never take that back.'

They had crossed swords and clasped arms on a battlefield, but now here with bread and stew, by candlelight, Elo unburdened the pains of his heart, the depths of his soul. He could not live with them another day. He could not choke on the burning ash of their friendship, their love. He had to let it go.

And he felt the warmer for it.

Arren stood up, angry now. He paced across the room, around the table. Back again. 'Why didn't you say anything?' he said to Elo's surprise, accepting all of the other accusations but fixating on the one that stung the most. 'You took other lovers!'

'We both did,' said Elo. He hadn't seen this Arren in an age; energetic. Wilful. Vulnerable. His eyes were bright in the candle-light, his hair shone with golden strands. His shirt was undone from throat to belly, flames exposed to the world. 'I'd known you since we were boys. I'd known your every pain, your every rejection. How you longed for stable ground but never found it.'

'Apart from with you!' said Arren.

'Exactly,' said Elo. 'You were a prince, and we were so young. We could be friends, but even princes cannot love the children of foreign merchants, much less kings. I saw everything you ever suffered, and I could not bear to be another thing that brought you pain. Better to love at a distance than break each other's hearts.'

Arren shook his head, angry. 'You did cause me pain,' he said. 'You *left* me.'

'You wanted everyone to fit into the shape *you* decided for them,' said Elogast. He put his glass down and stood up to leave. 'You wanted me to stand quiet at your side when I should have stood there loudly. But I did *not* deserve what you did to me.'

'Tried to do,' snapped Arren.

'No Arren,' said Elo, unbuttoning his shirt, showing the livid scar. The hand of Hseth. 'Did. *You* did this. You burned people just as Hseth has. You broke my heart and called it love. You used me.'

'I have asked your forgiveness,' said Arren, coming back to him and standing face to face. 'I am trying to be worthy of your forgiveness.'

Elo almost laughed. 'It cannot be forgiven. I cannot forgive you for burning your own subjects, for turning to violence over negotiation, for sacrificing your goodness, yourself, your heart.'

'For a kingdom!' said Arren. 'For a future.'

'For power.'

Elo was right, and Arren knew it.

'Then don't forgive me,' said the king. 'Hate me. Fight me. Just don't . . .' His voice went hoarse, tightening with strain. 'Just don't leave me.'

Elo clenched his jaw, looking back to the candle, the stew, still uneaten. It was everything he wanted to say, everything he needed to unburden from himself.

'I won't leave you,' he said. 'Because . . . gods help me, I still want you to win.'

And that was not all he wanted. How he hated it when Kissen was right. He did not forgive Arren. He would not. But he felt that blossom of warmth that loosened up the pressure on his heart. In him rose the spark of life that meant, within all the pain, he could feel human again. Just for a moment.

Arren took a step towards him, eye to eye, chin proud. Elo didn't step away. His breath caught, caught quick. 'Till this is over then,' he said. 'You'll stay?'

Elo wanted to hold his face and kiss him. He wanted to forget about all the world, and all the wrongs in it. 'I'm so tired, of being alone,' said Elo, his voice barely more than a breath. 'Of killing and dying and hurting and never mourning.' His voice cracked. 'I'm so tired of it, Arren.'

Arren came to him. He wrapped his arms around him in an embrace so fierce it almost threw them both over. They held each other as they had in the old days, the best days. The simple ones. Elo's heart ached as Arren's chin fitted perfectly onto his shoulder, and Elo pressed his temple down onto Arren's head. They held each other as they would have when the world ended, and the seas rose up to swallow the lands and the gods tore each other apart.

Then Elo pulled back, and Arren reluctantly loosened his grip, sliding his hands around so they instead pressed on Elo's chest. He would feel Elo's heart beating, he would feel the want of him.

'I want . . .' said Elo. He shouldn't. He mustn't. 'I want to not care for a while,' he said. Not care what Arren had done, who he had become. He wanted the simplicity of flesh and desire, he wanted someone to know him. 'I want to be reminded what living can be.'

Love and pain are not so different.

'What?'

Elo leaned down and pressed his mouth to Arren's. It was a clumsy kiss, unexpected. Arren's mouth was half open in surprise. But then he dug his hand into Elo's shirt and pulled him closer. Kissing him hard. Harder.

Tentatively, carefully, Elo moved his hands down Arren's back, to his waist, pulling him in closer, hip to hip, and parted his mouth. He could feel the warmth of the fire in Arren's chest, the heat of him.

With fumbling fingers, Arren reached for the rest of the buttons of Elo's shirt, and Elo let him pull them open. He wanted nothing between them, nothing any more. No shame, no hate, no hurt, only the passion that they had only allowed to smoulder, never to burn.

Elo pushed off Arren's jacket from his shoulders, feeling their muscles as he did so, then reached up again as it fell, took off the king's circlet and threw it clanging onto the floor. Then he pulled up his shirt, releasing it from his trews.

The door rattled with a knock, and Elo froze, but Arren used the opportunity to push him down onto the chaise.

'Leave us,' he said, his voice deep and commanding as he finished Elo's job and tore off his own shirt, showing everything. The heavy blow of the god of war's axe had torn a diagonal line through his ribcage, caving it in and biting his heart through the cavity. Now, Hestra's nest of twigs and flame filled the space with a wall of moss and lichen, the centre burning like a smouldering egg of coal. It looked more like flesh than Elo had seen before, as if it had grown into him, become part of him.

'There can be no secrets from her,' said Arren, apologetically, seeing where Elo's eyes had gone. 'We are a part of each other now.'

As if in response, Hestra's fire licked up Arren's chest, dancing around his exposed bones and flesh. Elo touched the chasm, gently, his fingers tracing around the scar. The flames caressed him softly, not burning. It did not look like a separate god. This was a wound Arren had suffered to save him. This was who Arren had become.

'I understand,' he said at last.

Arren smiled with relief and knelt before Elo. He put his hands on his waist and kissed the centre of his chest where Hseth had burned it. Beginning with the tips of each of her fingers, he followed the scarring down, further, over Elo's heart, over his belly. Elo's breath hitched, and he threw his head back. Pleasure rose in him. Pure, thoughtless, desperate; deep.

Then Arren loosened his belt and released his trews, dragging them down till his thighs were exposed, his knees, his shins, the cloth tangled around his feet. The king grabbed the glass of wine from the table behind him and took a sip, moistening his mouth, then leaned down and pressed his soft lips to the tops of Elo's legs, gentle, gentler. Then he took him in his mouth.

Elo gasped, biting his lip to keep from crying out and disturbing the guards further. Arren drank him in, slow at first, then faster. Wanting, needing, more and more. He wasn't experienced, but he was passionate, all his pent-up adoration and loathing going into the movements of his lips, the flicker of his tongue, till Elo couldn't bear it. Couldn't bear to take without giving.

He drew Arren free, then leaned down to kiss his open mouth. Pulled him up onto the chaise with him, then dragging him down onto his back. In the candlelight, he looked fierce and beautiful, his skin bright, his expression full of want.

Elo kissed Arren as tenderly as he had yearned to do, as deeply as he had imagined, his legs slipping between his king's. Chest to chest again, heartless and heartful, burned and burning. He winced as he felt the fire, but Hestra did not hurt him, and he didn't release the kiss, instead kissing harder, leaning into the flame, pressing them down together.

Together at last.

CHAPTER THIRTY-FIVE

Skediceth

THE *SILVERSWIFT* WAS BACK ON THE SEA, UNDER FULL SAIL and with the summer winds at their stern, casting them at speed back towards Middren.

Skedi could feel the shrine Solom had made for him as a faint tug on his heart, not as painful as the one he had once felt with Inara; more like a string binding him, reminding him of other shores, other hopes and dreams.

He could go back. He had somewhere to go back to. Telle had promised to keep it for him, and bring it to Middren if they returned. Because now Solom was no longer around to keep it safe.

But first, Inara. She had insisted on returning with her mother and had threatened to summon god after god from the ocean to follow them if they left her behind. Whether she could or not, Skedi was more worried about protecting Inara from herself. She only thought of now, not the future. Not the consequences. How much more did she have to offer? Her pain? Her life? She had already wounded her flesh, cut her hair, and made a dangerous promise. Skedi didn't want her to bring herself more suffering just to push the limits of her power.

This time, he would come with her, he would be her conscience. He would make sure she didn't do anything stupid.

Though for now, he was watching her soundly beat Kissen at hitting targets.

'Fucking pirates,' muttered Kissen for the hundredth time, rubbing her wounded shoulder, though it was the Restish who had struck her with an arrow. 'Fucking gods.'

'Stop complaining because you're losing,' said Inara, lowering her bow.

She and Kissen had leaned some broken boards against the latter's door, after they had been replaced by the newly hired ship's carpenter. Kissen's half-joking suggestion that they use the shrines of gods for their target practice had not been met with approval.

Kissen now had a surfeit of knives, bought and sharpened at the Irisian markets, and Inara a new bow. Between them, they had pitted the target with holes.

One of the Irisian crew stepped around them, frowning as Inara's arrow thudded into the boards.

'Se'kes t'bliamich,' they said to Inara. *You'll blunt your arrows.*

Bahba had filled their ship with her own experienced sailors to get them back to the Middrenite armies as quickly as they could move. Smooth seas and fair winds blessed them, or Yusef did, and the journey that had previously taken a month slid by in a tenday.

'Aleyi'i alma,' Inara replied. *I have a whetstone.*

'What did they say?' Kissen asked, preparing her next throw.

'They said I was better than you,' said Inara with a wicked grin, stretching out her string and sending another arrow flying into the target's centre. She adored the bow: Skedi could tell by the way her hands shone when she touched it.

Kissen narrowed her eyes at Inara, then looked briefly at Skedi, before clicking her tongue and turning back to the board. 'Little lick of good it will do me, to ask a liar what the truth is.' She swapped hands away from her aching shoulder, targeted her knife, then let it fly. It flashed in the sunlight, slamming straight into the centre, and Kissen grinned, curling her forefinger into the base of her thumb in her 'fuck you' sign to the target. 'And you as well,' she said to Inara, flashing her gold tooth, and Inara stuck out her tongue. 'See what I can do with balanced knives.'

'I'll thank you for not exercising your colourful gestures around my daughter,' said Lessa, coming down from the helm where she

306

had been measuring their position against the sun with the sextant and advising Rhiyande where to alter course.

Rhiyande was the only one of the old crew who had been permitted to stay aboard. She had become quieter, more awkward around Kissen, Lessa and Inara, but she had nowhere else to be, and no desire to meet her other crewmates if they ever returned from Restish.

You've made the right choice, Skedi whispered to her some days, when she looked liable to cry. *Betrayal is never right.* It soothed her. Sometimes. And she knew it was Skedi giving her comfort because she sometimes poured some of her drink by his statue in thanks.

'And Inara,' continued Lessa, 'surquedry is in poor taste.'

'What the salt is "surquedry"?' asked Kissen. She had drawn another knife and was flipping the blade. She and Lessa were almost as awkward around each other as Rhiyande was around everyone.

'It means being a sore winner,' said Skedi.

'Hmm. We close?' Kissen threw the blade, and it glinted as it spun, but landed deep, point first, a few inches to the left of Inara's bullseye. She sucked her teeth, still annoyed.

'Closer by the hour,' said Lessa. They were headed towards Weild, hopefully to find out what had been happening in the war before they attempted to land anywhere that might not be so friendly. The edges between Kissen and the lady were still sharp sometimes, and brittle, but they had fought back-to-back, had watched each other brought low. Skedi already knew that Kissen always liked people more when she had seen them at their worst.

'Knives are less accurate than a bow, and their range is shorter,' Lessa said, looking at the pitted boards. 'It's impressive you've even come close to Inara.'

If Kissen had a tail, she would have wagged it. Human flirting was so strange, bickering and jabbing for weaknesses, then fluffing each other up.

'Why do you use the knives?' said Inara. The breeze had grown cooler on the sea as they moved further north, and the wind had turned more westward. She wore a wool jacket, and had braided her hair back from her eyes, much like Kissen. 'You can use a bow.'

'Briddite arrows are more useful for annoying gods than killing them,' said the godkiller. 'Knives can move quickly.' She pulled out another blade and flipped it to her other hand. 'Recognisable patterns get you killed. Especially when some gods chatter worse than any old gadgie.' She threw the blade and it hit the target just off-centre. That was her last one, save for the one she still kept by her waist. This one glowed faintly to Skedi's eyes, with colour. 'Water gods especially,' she added, touching the hilt.

'Do you want to talk to him?' said Inara, seeing the movement. 'We could try.'

Kissen crooked a smile at her, but it didn't reach her eyes. Instead, she pulled out the knife and sent it spinning towards the boards to land next to the first blade. 'We have no hold on each other any more,' she said. 'Neither should Yusef have on you, the slippery little bastard.' She looked darkly at the mark on Inara's arm.

Skedi shrank with guilt. He had let that happen, had let Ina make a promise. Yes, it had saved her mother and Kissen, but it had bound her to a god who cared nothing for her. As soon as they were underway, Yusef had disappeared in a cloud of silks and the scents of perfume.

'I can break it,' said Inara, looking at the boon on her arm, bound like a cuff. 'I've done it before. But he said he would find me again and make it a curse.'

She was attempting confidence, brashness. Like Kissen, like Lessa; but Skedi could feel the question in her statement, the slight tinge of fear. He looked at the shrines on the ship, where Yusef's statue still stood. The Irisian crew hadn't celebrated their send-off with sacrifices and drinking, but judging by the way they bowed to the shrines when they passed, they had great respect for the *quya*.

Yusef could have helped them and asked for nothing. He had enough. Bowls and bowls of love from a city that was not even his, a land that saw him as a vestige and not their true god. He could have seen Inara as his daughter and helped her, like Lessa. Like Elo and Kissen even, like all the humans he had met. Instead he had asked for more.

It was disgraceful.

Kissen wanted to lie, Skedi could see it. Wanted to tell her that of course she could protect her from the choice she had made, that she knew of a way to prevent the god finding her again.

'I'm going to give that bastard a second death,' the godkiller growled instead.

Lessa released a breath she likely had not realised she had been holding. Of course there was not another god, not one who would not ask for something too. They lived in a world of gods and exchanges, money and deals and blood. A world where no good thing was given for free.

'Perhaps he'll change,' said Skedi brightly. 'Perhaps he'll soften as he ages and learns more about humans.'

'Gods don't change,' said Kissen.

'Skediceth has,' said Inara.

If Skedi had been human, he would have blushed, Ina said it with such pride. He wasn't sure he had changed, nor that he had earned her admiration, but he basked in it all the same.

Footsteps came running up from below. The Irisian cook, who was paler even than Kissen but did not know a word of Talic or Middric, hurried across the deck to Lessa, speaking fast in Irisian.

'What did he say?' Kissen asked Skedi, who flicked his ear at her.

'If I haven't changed,' he said, 'why should I tell you?'

Kissen rolled her eyes. 'Fine, yes, you appear to have changed, you little miscreant.'

Skedi sat back on his hind legs and ruffled his fur, then he dipped his ears down again.

'He said the fire wants to talk to Inara.'

CHAPTER THIRTY-SIX

Inara

INARA RUSHED DOWN THE LADDERS, WHILE LESSA LEFT Rhiyande in charge of the bridge and followed.

'Which fire god, Ina?' Kissen demanded, clattering down behind her.

'Inara, answer her!' barked Lessa.

Several of the Irisian crew turned to stare at them as they barrelled past.

'Captain, are we under attack?' said one in Middric.

'Not yet,' said Lessa as they charged down the next deck. 'Stay at your posts.'

Inara was barely listening, but Skedi she could not ignore.

You've been speaking to her, haven't you? he said.

Not Hseth.

I meant Hestra! She is dangerous.

Inara bit her lip. She should never have let the symbol remain in the fire. Why were the gods and kings of this world so intent on making her homeless? Seemed a bit petty, seeing as half of them were about invading the homes of others.

She was starting to lose her own faith. In gods. Maybe in herself. There had been so many who had given her kindness, offered her help, even if Aan's most recent advice had been next to useless. But then Hseth, Hestra, Satuan . . . even Yusef. Especially Yusef. Inara felt unsettled, so deep in shades of grey that she was forgetting what colour looked like. Was this growing up? Or was it losing hope?

She could feel the warmth of the galley on her cheeks, smell its scents, before she reached it. Yellow peas for the evening fare. They served them mushed, dressed in anchovies, with vinegar greens, biscuit and bread. She could smell salted beef too, already red with ageing and further brightened with spice.

But under the scents as she entered the kitchen was the smell of smouldering embers, the sharp sap of pine roots, and the almost-sweetness of burning hay.

Hestra.

The woman made of twigs was sitting in the centre of the oven where Inara had previously tried to talk to her. But she wasn't all twigs. Inara had not seen her in this form before. She appeared more human-like, her hair soft and brown, though still threaded with lichen and wool. Her structure was still all branches, thickened with moss and sometimes with gleams of twig and fine bones. In size, she was the height of a child, but she did not look young. She looked like an ancient being from before time, before house and home, back when hearth might be cave and hope.

Then Hestra looked up. Her eyes . . . they were paler again. Strangely human. Soft and blue.

But the illusion shattered when Lessa and Kissen came in: the god hissed, flames brightened in her mouth, sparks flying around her teeth. *We did not ask for you,* her inner voice whipped out, lashing at the two of them.

'Tough shit,' said Kissen, the flicker of the flames brightening the red of her hair, the scars of her neck, her chin, her hands. She had grabbed all her blades and was stuffing them back in their places on her person.

Skedi flew in, landing on Kissen's shoulder, the size of a mouse. 'How is she here?' he said.

'Our sneaky little demigod has been trying to make new friends,' said Kissen, though her voice lacked sting.

'It was after Satuan,' said Inara. 'I just . . .' She was torn between Hestra and Kissen, and settled for standing up straight, hands by her side. Like her mother did. 'I wanted to help, but Hestra wasn't interested.' She aimed the last words at the god. She must have used some power to reappear in this shrine.

'Is the king dead?' said Lessa, to Hestra now, her voice unreadable. 'Is that why you're here?'

'No,' said Hestra. 'He lives, and gains strength and power. Though he also gains enemies and loses land.' Embers ran up her arms, dancing and crackling, a few flames caught. The room was warm, not oppressively hot. Comforting. 'The end of this war is coming for us. Which end, I am here to see. Did you succeed in your quest?'

'We have Irisian ships on their way,' said Lessa. 'They will be a few days behind us, archers, land army, and sea fighters, two thousand in number. Can you last that long?'

Hestra crackled, pausing as if listening. She must be speaking to the king. Inara's heart and stomach burned and tightened. So, she was back in line with Arren. He had managed to convince her. Or something else had.

'We are drawing them away from the city of Lesscia,' said Hestra. 'To open battle. Hseth is too destructive to meet elsewhere. Gefyrton and most of Daesmouth have already been lost to flame.'

'Gefyrton?' whispered Inara, and she felt, rather than saw, Kissen and Lessa exchange a glance. What had been happening since they had left? Their weeks of travel suddenly felt less like building an army and more like finding a last dreg of hope. 'Where is Elo? Is he all right?'

Hestra smiled knowingly. 'The king's knight is well enough,' she said. 'He speaks to the king's heart, and they both bade me come here.'

Inara stared at the god, and the god stared back.

'Give me an offering, girl, and I will tell you more,' Hestra said. 'I have not the power now to run from port to harbour, hearth to hearth, without something more to bind me here.'

Inara saw Skedi's wings raise. 'She has given enough, hearth god,' he said, before Kissen could. 'Ask something else.'

Skedi, you don't have to . . .

How many pieces of yourself can you give away, Inara, before there's nothing left?

But . . . it was what she could do, wasn't it? There was little else she could contribute.

'You came here on the king's power,' said Lessa. 'Use him as an offering, not us.'

Hestra turned her attention to Lady Craier, moving her twig-face into a mask of disappointment. 'If you wish for my guidance, we will both need a stronger tether to this ship.'

Lessa clicked her tongue. Inara could see the charcoal mark she had made on the oven, still there, but fading. It would not be long before Hestra could not return to the ship, having no semblance of a shrine to root herself to.

'Shrines,' Kissen muttered. 'Everyone wants a fucking shrine. What happened to just having your own built because people actually like you?'

'No one asked you, veiga,' whispered Hestra.

'Give me a knife,' said Lessa, holding her hand out to Kissen.

'You're not serious,' said Kissen. Lessa looked at her and her dark eyes brooked no argument. Kissen sighed and drew Osidisen's blade, putting it in her hand. It was as good as permission.

Lessa approached the oven and carved Hestra's symbol, the one Inara had drawn in soot: two lines going diagonally down, a straight line carved across the top, over its front. The simplest kind of hearth.

The lines she flared, turning yellow then orange. The scent of greenwood intensified, the salted stink of the beef reducing against the cracks and twists of woodsmoke and embers.

Lessa returned to Inara's side. 'Will that suit you, hearth god?'

No negotiation, no requests, no offers of bigger and better. Inara bit her lip. She had offered too much for Yusef; she knew that. She had not thought how poor Middren might be after a war, after losing a port city, half of Sakre, Blenraden, Gefyrton. The country was gutted and ruined. Her country. And she had offered the god of a foreign power a home when her own was burned.

'It needs antlers,' said Hestra, without looking, and Inara noticed, beneath the branches and colours of her hair, two little nubs were showing through, soot-dark and shaped like fungus, velveted like the tops of stags' antlers in growing season.

They are becoming more entwined, said Skedi. *Hestra and the king. It seems I am not the only god that can change.*

313

Lessa leaned in and struck two upward strokes from the hearth, like rays, or like antlers, then threw the knife point down in the boards. Done.

Hestra nodded her head. 'You must dock east, in Yesef lands. There is a small fishing harbour you can enter at high tide.'

'I'll get the charts,' said Skedi, taking off from Kissen and swooping up the stairs to find the state room.

'What of the Irisians?' said Lessa. 'They cannot load on some fisherfolk's dock.'

'There's a deep Movenna harbour not far from there,' said Kissen. 'They've been cutting in steps down to the waters so they can start a bigger port. That would take them'

'They never reported this to the king's council,' said Lessa.

Kissen grinned. 'And get taxed to shit before it's done? You should do some more walking.'

Hestra had turned her head to the side, listening again, or speaking to Arren. 'The Restish and Talicians have been spotted moving ships west. If they make land, we will be forced again to fight on two fronts, and this war will be over.'

Over. Inara caught her breath, and Hestra looked at her.

'I take it, beast, you did not find the power you were looking for?'

Inara swallowed, shook her head. 'There are no great gods that will help us,' she said. 'Not without them taking more than we can give.'

She felt Kissen's eye on her, but the veiga and her mother both decided not to comment as Skedi came gliding in, a bundle of rolled papers in his mouth. Lessa pulled them free then laid them out in front of the hearth, and Hestra opened her mouth: sparks flew out from between her teeth, drifting on the air and then landing on the map to burn tiny holes, one for the Yesef harbour, the others marking positions east.

'These points are where the invaders' ships have been sighted,' she said. 'We will need the Irisians for our sea defence, aligning with our own boats. The rest of you will meet us east of Sorin, on the Arrenon. There, the Fireheart awaits with his lion. And me.'

In a flare of heat, she was gone, and Inara let out a breath.

'Fireheart?' said Kissen. 'Pissing "Fireheart"? He is *such* an arse-hole.'

'He chose it for her,' said Inara. 'Sunbringer cut her out, Fireheart brings her back to him.'

Kissen cursed under her breath, and Inara too felt a surge of rancour. She had wanted Hestra to come to her, to work with her, undo the king from the inside. She still wanted revenge, when all of this was done. If the two were together, she might not have as much power to match him as she had hoped. They seemed to be becoming one creature, one god.

It could not be true. Arren shouldn't get everything he had wanted, it wasn't right.

'One problem at a time,' said Lessa, then leaned down to retrieve Kissen's dagger and looked at its edge before handing it back to her. 'Things in Middren are more desperate than we feared.' She put her hand on Inara's shoulder, giving her a squeeze.

'Give nothing else to the gods,' she said. 'No matter what happens. You do not owe them. You don't belong to anyone but yourself.'

CHAPTER THIRTY-SEVEN

Elogast

THE FINAL WAR COUNCIL HAD JOINED TOGETHER WHEN the godkiller returned.

The armies had united, those that had guarded Daesmouth and Lesscia, and those that fought in Gefyrton.

Elo stood by Arren, moving pieces with Alianne Yether on the maps as she explained the last weeks' movements around Daesmouth. Her older brother, Lord Yether, sat sullenly by the fire with the new Captain Hafil and Captain Faroch, who appeared to be itching to get away from them. He had given Elo round eyes when he saw him in armour and cloak, setting commands for the combined forces to be organised into shape, food, water, and shelter, ploughing the Movenna fields with their feet into dust and grass and mud.

If anyone noticed that he and Arren were acting differently, no one said a word. Still, Elo felt as if everyone knew. Every weighted look, every bow or salute. Perhaps they did. It was Elo now that Arren summoned to his right hand, to his chambers, to his war meetings. His general, his lover.

The wall more than a decade in the making had come crashing down between them, between prince and squire, between a king and his knight, between a rebel and his enemy. Now the floodgates were open, Elo could no more resist Arren's call than he could resist the rushing of his own blood, his hardening, his heartache. If these were their last hours in this bitter world, they would spend them without shame. Redemption was not possible. Forgiveness did not matter, Arren's selfish tyranny and Elo's bloody rebellion were joined in force against increasing certainty of defeat.

'I have judged the Talician numbers to still be fifteen thousand,' said Commander Yether. 'Their god is indeed smaller than when she first came to Daesmouth, but she is still uncontrollable. Each time they summon her . . .' Her voice tightened. 'It is devastating.'

Elo had first known Alianne by a different name, but her new one suited her, and her title. She was as steadfast as a leader could be having had her sister and city burned from beneath her by a god of flame. While her brother had gone to prepare their ships to sail against the Restish, the commander had overseen the freeing of the Lesscian prisoners, the evacuation of the city.

Naiala. Elo's fellow rebel must have been freed with the rest of the Lesscians. Perhaps she was there, in the army, already handing out pamphlets.

'The commander held out bravely in Daesmouth,' said Peta. 'But with Lesscia abandoned, morale is low. And the Lesscians heading west are vulnerable.'

'The Tiamh and Elemni lines have been advised,' said Elo. 'Camps are being set up across the inner towns, and Irisian support will soon be arriving.' Additional help in the battle and in the defence, and additional ships to assist the volatile Beloris Yether.

Peta glared at him. Arren had been afraid she would loathe him for ordering the evacuation of Lesscia, but it was to Elo she had turned her ire. She spoke even to Methsme with more deference, telling the cleric how much she admired her songs.

'And what has been offered to the Irisians in return for that support, commander general?' Peta said, her tone dark and full of threat.

'At present, it does not matter,' said Elo, meeting her gaze.

'I do not trust a traitor to—'

'We are long past that, Knight Commander Peta,' said Arren quietly. 'Against all odds, Lessa Craier has done what she said she would. That is more than can be said of many allies, let alone previous enemies.'

'And how do you know that she does not come with ships to

usurp you?' This was Methsme, and Peta nodded her agreement. 'You are too close to your *enemies*, Fireheart.'

Elo tried not to look at Arren, though he found the back of his neck heating through the force of her implication. Methsme had not looked Arren in the eye since he had freed the Talician prisoners, and she instead addressed his chest, and the bright fire there.

'Oh would you cease beating this drum, cleric?' said Iuri Movenna, pushing their spectacles up their nose. 'What do you say to the Vittosks? To the Yethers? The Geralfis? Who have lost land and people? That we should spit in the face of aid we sorely need, in case we lose the lands they are come to save?'

Lord Geralfi stood pale and grim by the incense brazier with Regent Graiis, another of Craier's rebels, and a Captain Graiis, whom Elo had fought in Lesscia. Lady Crolle, too, had come east, bringing forces to muster at Arren's call. Enemies rubbed shoulders with enemies; friends did not seem so friendly.

And it was him they looked to when the mood turned sour. He was the Lion of Lesscia; he had put a sword through the heart of the king; he had been there when the Reach of Sakre fell.

'Hah,' said Methsme. 'Half of you here would have throned her after she toppled our great king. Would you still choose your silly little gods of wells and rivers over he who has united you? The true god in our midst?'

She was growing bolder, to Elo's distaste, her palms freshly tattooed with the sun and flame, and a hearth and antlers inked high on her chest. Elo could smell the bitter alcohol she washed them with from half a camp away.

'Methsme,' said Arren quietly, and shook his head. She curled her lip, and gave a little sarcastic bow to Movenna, then sat down again. Arren looked towards his fractious command, his beleaguered nobles.

'My friends,' he said, 'I appreciate that there are wrongs I have done in the past, and the enmities you have put aside to be here. But please, remember what we are fighting for: Middren. Our home. We have long been the heart of the Trade Sea, the hearth where all lands gather. We know this place better than a god who has barely lived, and we will not lose any more of it.'

Silence fell. Elo broke it.

'Right,' he said. 'I take it we are all done with bickering? Can we go back to planning a war?'

Lord Yether stood up, shaking, and it took every ounce of Elo's self-restraint not to roll his eyes at the angry little man. Yether looked at Alianne, who ignored him, then at Arren. Then, it seemed, he decided against an argument, made the Sunbringer salute and went for the door, Captain Hafil quick on his heels.

'Lord Yether,' Arren called him back, and he stopped, looking hopeful, as if Arren were about to beg for his forgiveness. 'Are your ships prepared?'

The lord's face fell, and he made a bow. 'Of course, my king.'

He looked over to Faroch, who hadn't moved.

'Captain Faroch,' said Yether. 'Come.' He pointed to his side.

'Apologies, my lord,' said Faroch tightly. 'I am no sea captain, and I can offer my assistance on the field. If you will not stay, then I will continue with the House of my own blood. Yesef.' He nodded to Kyaum, who smiled in return.

Yether's mouth worked, but then he turned on his heel and left without another word.

'Anyone else?' said Arren, and he looked at Peta, whose jaw hardened, her teeth grinding together. She believed in him, had believed in him fervently during Blenraden and all that followed, unlike Elo.

'No, Sunbringer,' she said, breaking eye contact and gazing down at the map, to which Iuri was now adding lines of information.

'There's a hidden valley down here,' they said. 'Where the canals join at the dam and the Arrenon river, before it connects with the Roan.' With a charcoal piece, they marked the map. 'The ridges here are steep.' The notation was less neat than Arren might have liked, Elo could guess from the king's slightly pursed lips. A dam was marked with a hard line of black.

'It's not an easy retreat,' said Graiis, coming over to look. 'And we do not know how fast the Talicians can link their north and south forces. They may do so before following us.'

'They won't.' The krka, Estefin, spoke up. He was permitted to sit in the tent, quietly by the brazier, and given a healthy supply of Curlish wine and the king's food. In return, he had given them crumbs of information – some lies, some truths, but Elo and Arren had learned some more on Talician tactics, weaponry, planning. 'They will think you are running, and they will follow. They have twenty thousand, not fifteen, in Daesmouth. There is barely anyone left back home.' He glanced at the map, no remorse in his face. Home it might be, but his anger at Hseth's priesthood had eaten his loyalty into scraps. 'And you're right, they always follow the riverlines. They have no maps of Middren.'

It seemed Estefin much preferred being an imprisoned courtier than a krka under priest-generals.

'Knight commander,' said Arren, 'how many do we have?'

'Nine thousand at last count,' said Peta. 'Twelve hundred horses, fifteen hundred knights, two thousand trained guards; the rest are commonfolk; soldiers, mercenaries, armourers, blacksmiths. A few new recruits. Our losses have been heavy.'

There had been six thousand commonfolk soldiers in Arren's parade on Lesscia, and their army at Gefyrton had another two. That meant over two thousand had died. Two thousand souls lost, and that did not include the knights, whose deaths had tallied even greater.

'How are we preventing desertion?' said Graiis. He had brought with him a strong number, including Craier guards and many other recruits from his land.

'The old ways have held,' said Peta. 'Runaways caught have their non-dominant hand removed, the burn sealed shut with the king's brand, and are put on the front line. I recommend we turn instead to hanging.'

'It is brutal enough as it is,' said Elo, before another round of questioning could begin. Instead he looked to Gods Commander Hovan, the supposed leader of the godkillers who had signed up to the king's battalions. He was a big man, in a fine blue cloak with the veiga symbol on it, but he did not seem to have any opinions to volunteer, only sounds of affirmation if Peta spoke.

'Have you any proposals on how we undo Hseth should she be summoned, Commander Hovan?' Elo asked. 'Assuming she will be summoned, we will need a plan to protect ourselves, damage her, kill her if we can.'

The veiga cleared his throat, looking at the canvas ceiling, the map, then to Peta for support. She gave him none. 'Briddite doesn't hurt her,' he said at last.

'It stops her,' said Elo. 'It sticks to her.'

'That's not enough. She does not act like a god, like she has will or intention. She acts like a demon.' He shivered. 'If we can't use briddite, there's nothing the veiga can do. I have been directing them as soldiers under Commander Peta's advice. We can only hope they don't summon her. Or that the message of Gefyrton spreads and the Talicians start to doubt her.'

'What a load of shit.'

A voice from the doorway made them all look up, and Elo saw a sight he had hoped for in all the weeks since she had left.

Kissen stood at Lady Craier's side, wearing a fine cloak of green with fresh-sewn pockets all up the inside, pockets filled with knives, chains, and trinkets, judging by the heft of it around her shoulders. The freckles across her cheeks and nose had intensified with the sun, her burns shone pale. She wore a chestplate of Irisian scaled leather and metal. Just as enthralling and dangerous-looking as when they had first met.

'Ho, baker-knight,' she said.

'Talician,' whispered Peta, hand going for her sword as Arren's heart flared bright.

'Oh piss off, stick up your arse,' said Kissen.

Elo took two steps towards her and threw his arms around her neck, all decorum lost to the rush of terrible, overwhelming relief at seeing her here, in Middren. She had come back. He felt another piece of tension ease.

'You should have stayed away, you lunatic,' he said as she returned the embrace, tipping back to almost lift him off his feet. She felt thick, muscular. And, even after the little time they had spent together, like home.

'And let you get yourself killed? You know that's not my way.'

He laughed, stepping back, and saw Inara standing behind them, Skedi in his smaller, meeker squirrel-size in his usual place on her shoulder. She smiled shyly, but he went to embrace her too and she laughed as he picked her up.

Oh, to be so overjoyed and so unutterably sad at once. He didn't want to put her down, he didn't want Inara to look between him and Arren and tell immediately what he had done, how close they were, when he had hurt her so badly. He wanted to explain, apologise, stop time and ask her not to hate him.

She had every right to hate him if she chose. Kissen too. Though it was possible she'd just give him a knowing nod and a clap on the back.

He couldn't decide which was worse.

He put Inara down at last and looked down at her mother.

'Don't even think about it, commander general,' she said. 'I am not in a hugging mood.' There was a touch of humour in her voice, but she had slight bruising across her nose and eyes, and a split lip that looked barely healed. Kissen too, beneath her new shine, looked more than a little worse for wear. So, their journey had not been as smooth as they had hoped.

Lessa looked past him, towards the war council. There was a moment of pause, a pulse of fear, like the prickling sensation before lightning struck. Then she moved past Elo, and went to one knee, bowing her head.

'Thank you for your patience, King Arren,' she said towards the ground. 'The Irisians have sent a fleet to your aid, and have been advised of your commands. We have Mitha Bahba, Mitha Sosul and Mitha Aslani to thank for their help. The rest of the council . . . took some convincing. But they are now in agreement, and broke the treaty of Belhaven to offer Middren their assistance.'

She didn't move from her knee, and Elo heard some muttered approvals from other council members. The look on Alianne Yether's face, in particular, was one of admiration.

Then Elo realised. Bahba. It was not an uncommon name in Irisia, but . . .

'Your mother is quite some woman,' said Kissen quietly.

'She's on the Mithrik?' he muttered. 'But she's a trader. She calls them pompous asses.'

'She wouldn't be the first one to say one thing and do another.'

Elo looked at her sideways, and she gave him an innocent smile.

'What have you offered in return, Lady Craier?' asked General Elemni suspiciously.

'New trade deals at the expense of Restish,' Lessa said, still on her knee. Elo looked at Arren, realising she would not stand till the king told her to. 'They will have a large section of the harbours of Weild and Blenraden, which will be re-established as a port and its remaining gods cleared or remedied. Given offerings enough to survive.' Methsme, Peta and Elo looked towards Arren, who did not blink, did not approve, but did not deny. For a moment, his eyes found Elo's and slightly, almost imperceptibly, he nodded. 'An Irisian–Middrenite blockade will be formed on the western pass of the Trade Sea,' Lessa continued. 'All goods are to be taxed at Wsirin, the profits split.'

To have come in so ready for dissent, she must have been listening for the right moment. Or, more likely, Skedi had. The god looked well. Softly groomed and steady, his antlers gleaming white, the offerings on them shiny and clean.

'Also . . .' she said, though Elo detected some degree of reluctance. 'A shrine. To be built to the god of safe haven.'

'No,' said Methsme. 'No new shrines. We need no god of the Restish traitors. One god belongs in Middren. One.'

Lessa levelled a gaze at her. If she recognised Methsme as one of those who had killed Tarin, she said nothing. Inara, however, scowled ferociously; Elo had no doubt that she had made the connection. Still, the girl guarded herself better than Elo expected her to. She did not appear intimidated by this great gathering of Houses, generals and king, but it seemed she had learned some wisdom on her journey.

'I did not realise,' said Lessa coolly, 'that the king had grown another mouth.'

'Methsme,' said Arren, 'if you have nothing to offer but spite, you may leave.'

She whirled on him, her face flushed bright and angry. 'You dismiss me? It is my songs that make your story, Sunbringer. My voice. *Mine*. Not your Houses, not your pretty knights, not your generals and maps and planning. Me.'

'You forget yourself, cleric,' said Arren. 'Do not climb further than I raised you.'

Methsme shook with anger and humiliation. 'You are no god

yet,' she spat. 'Before you are whole, do not forget those who have been most loyal to you.' She glowered at Elogast, then strode straight between him and Kissen, her stained white skirts floating out behind as she marched out of the door. Peta stared after her.

'Charming,' said Kissen.

'Lady Craier, thank you,' said Arren, and Elo knew that despite how much he hated her, he meant it. 'You may rise. I owe you a thousand debts for this great service.'

Lessa stood gracefully, and she and Arren looked at each other, eye to eye. Arren's expression was somewhat beseeching, and Elo knew he was wondering how to ask her to absolve him of what he had done. Lessa's face was inscrutable, her poise complete. Whatever Arren offered her in return for her forgiveness, he would never have it.

Lessa turned, and went to acknowledge the other Houses in the room. Arren watched her go, his expression closing. Then he turned to Kissen.

'Veiga,' he said.

She blinked, surprised at being addressed.

'You know a way to kill the fire god?'

The gods commander scoffed. Kissen smiled at him. Dangerously. Her gold tooth flashed.

'Kill her?' said Kissen. 'No. But we can fight her. Big gods, you see, aren't so bright. And new ones have few tricks.'

CHAPTER THIRTY-EIGHT

Kissen

WELL, SHE WAS COMMITTED NOW.

Kissen didn't miss the stink of an army. Nor the foolishness of a fine-blooded, saltless 'gods commander' who had barely scratched out a few little shrines before being handed the title. At least she could make herself useful.

'Ah, Elo, petal,' she said softly to her friend, in the quiet spot they had set up a fire together. 'I could see it in your face.'

It had been days of organisation since they had arrived, moving forces across plains and roads, setting up their plans, and waiting. Waiting for Talicia to come close enough to fight.

They weren't far from this valley of death that they were about to consign themselves to, and the Middrenite armies were arrayed across fields that till recently would have been filled with sheep regrowing their wools for winter. Over three leagues away, as the crow flies, the scouts had finally passed back word that the Talicians had been spotted.

'I'm so sorry, Kissen,' said Elo.

Legs. Elo had spun her a story of an arrow and a swift end. And, though she could sense a delicate whispering from the god of white lies, Kissen had let herself be lied to. The night before battle was not for weeping and lamenting. Kissen didn't need an imagination to suspect the depth of pain behind Elo's tales. That Benjen lad, Gefyrton, Legs. Elo had about him the determined and unfettered air of a man who had gone beyond the edge of himself and returned.

Inara was crying quietly, rubbing the backs of her hands across her face. Later, Kissen would find a proper way to mourn her most loyal friend. Tears would come when she needed them. But now, she took a long draught of bad ale from a worse mug as Elo made oval rounds of bread and put them on a hot stone in the fire.

'And what of you and the king?' Kissen said.

Elo paused. 'What of it?' he said.

Kissen snorted. 'I knew it.'

'Knew what?' said Inara sniffing and stirring the edges of the stew pot to stop it burning. Her face was puffy and raw, and she looked at Elo. 'Knew what?'

'They've been – ah – together,' said Kissen, before remembering how close Inara had come to ripping out the king's heart. Elo closed his eyes, looking ready to disappear into the fire itself.

Inara almost dropped the spoon. 'He tried to kill you,' she said. 'Elo, how could you still like him?'

'He's telling himself lies,' said Skedi confidently.

'Don't we all, for a bit of a tumble?' smirked Kissen.

Elo cast her a vicious look. 'It's . . .'

'If you say "complicated" I'm going to throw the spoon at you,' said Inara.

It was the first time the four of them had been around a fire since they had been together in Blenraden. It felt strangely familiar, even though that journey had been so brief, and had ended so badly. It had bound them together irrevocably.

'I know there is no future,' said Elo. 'I know this is stupid. But . . . I was just . . .' He looked at the fire, a tremor in his hand as he put it to his chest. 'I was so tired,' he said.

Inara looked baffled, horrified. Skedi turned towards her, and presumably said something soothing, because she cursed under her breath and went back to stirring. 'He doesn't deserve you,' she muttered at last. 'He deserves a long walk off a short plank.'

'Ina!' said Elo, surprised. 'Honestly, Kissen, what are you teaching her? She's thirteen.'

'Blame her mother, not me.'

'Oh, so it's never your fault?'

'No. And your bread is burning.'

'Shit.'

They had cooked a fresh red stew with ginger root, zither, and fragrant seeds that Kissen didn't know the names for, made in a pot with a stock that Elo had requested from the king's cooks, still swimming in chicken bones. On top, he had broken eggs which were starting to poach in the bubbles from below. A true feast. Apart from the bread, he was baking a long, doughy fruit with yellow skin, wrapped in thick leaves that Inara had brought from the lower decks of the *Silverswift*. A gift to Elo from his mother.

Kissen held out a cloth in her hands for Elo to put the slightly charred breads on, and they began to deflate as the steam escaped. Inara smirked; Elo must be really troubled to forget about his bread.

As last meals went, Kissen thought it would be a good one.

She was equal to death. She had faced it many times, accepted it almost as many. But, looking at Inara, she really hoped this time she would escape it. She wanted to see the girl grow up. She wanted to see Telle and Yatho's ambitions and family grow out of all shape and reason. She wanted to grow delightfully fat and old beside the hearth of her loved ones. Elo would visit, hopefully find someone other than Arren to warm his bed. Someone who loved him gently. Inara would come, and even Skedi, and tell them of their adventures.

Kissen had never thought she would grow old, but she was starting to think she might like to.

'Here.'

Elo was holding out a bowl of the broth dotted with a slice of sheep's cheese and laid with round slices of the yellow fruit, without its peel.

Well, maybe she would warm his bed if he kept making her food like this. But then . . . Lessa's face poured into her mind like wine from a cracked cup.

She blinked and took the bowl, glad that the evening covered the reddening of her cheeks.

Elo filled another bowl for Inara, then offered a small helping to Skedi.

'I don't need to eat,' said the god, looking down at the ceramic dish the baker-knight had placed beside him, complete with its very own crust of bread.

'It's more so you can share,' said Elo, serving himself. 'Think of it as an offering.'

Inara pulled out a spoon of the stew, still looking cross, and—

'It's hot!' warned Elo as Skedi's ears flattened.

It was too late; Inara had put the whole steaming spoonful onto her tongue and then squeaked as Kissen started laughing. Elo passed her a gourd of water, and she took it without protest, gulping it down. Skedi looked at the stew as if it had burned *him* instead.

'It's . . . it is delicious,' said Inara with streaming eyes. 'Sorry.' She swallowed, laughed at herself, then said more seriously. 'Sorry.'

'So am I,' said Elo.

Kissen took a more considered approach, using her bread to dip in the stew first and then the egg second, then blowing on it to cool. The red, thick sauce tasted spicy in her mouth, a welcome change after so long on ship's bait and boiled-down peas.

'The hearth god,' she said after a minute. 'Whose side is she really on?'

'Her own,' said Elo, without pause.

'No surprises there,' muttered Skedi. He was sitting by his bowl and had even leaned down to nibble on some bread. Kissen wondered if he had taken it as an offering, or if he was just trying to be polite.

'Arren is her best hope at survival. Together their power is . . .' Elo shook his head. 'People treat him like a god. People ask him to touch them, bless them, warm them. And Hestra brightens with it.' He swallowed. 'People sacrifice animals to him, bury bones beneath their campfires before they light them. That cleric woman has been composing songs, and people sing them as they march.' He broke his bread in one hand, throwing its burned edges into the fire, while Kissen ate hers.

'And you're still fucking him?' she asked.

'Kissen!' said Inara, shocked.

'What?' said Kissen. 'I know you know what it is.'

'He feels different when we're together,' said Elo. 'He feels like himself. Like a human.'

Kissen kept any further crude jokes she might have made behind her tongue. The look on his face was pained, dark.

'You can't save him, you know,' said Skedi. 'You can't undo the things he's done. To Inara. To you.'

'I know,' Elo said. 'Some people can't be saved.' He paused, then looked at Inara. 'And you'll be holding to that thought in the morning, won't you, Ina?'

Elo said Arren had asked about her, he was not stupid, but that he had convinced him her gifts were not strong enough to be worth alienating Lessa.

Inara sucked her tongue and took another grumpy bite of stew. 'I still think I could help,' she said. 'I could stay on the cliffs with the archers. I could call gods.'

'And offer them what?' said Skedi, in a tone that sounded as if he had had this fight with her many times already.

'I don't know,' grumbled Inara.

Kissen and Skedi exchanged a look, and she lowered her guard enough for his will to sneak in and speak to her. *She will do everything in her power to fight,* he said.

I know, she replied. They had another plan. One that only she and Lessa knew, for they were the only ones who could hide it from her.

'Maybe you would look good bald,' Kissen said out loud, keeping her tone light, her sadness buried down deep inside her.

Inara looked at her with round eyes, considering it. Then she burst out laughing. They all did.

'Imagine,' Inara said, spluttering. 'Sitting on the edge of a battle-field trying not to cut myself with a razor.' Elo snorted, and Skedi's wings hunched up around his shoulders in confusion.

'Honestly, Ina, if I'd seen you the first time, I'd have thought you cracked,' grinned Kissen. 'Sitting on a horse, hacking off your hair in the street.'

'Why are you all laughing?' said Skedi, looking around at all of them. 'It's not funny.'

This only served to make them laugh harder. Elo was wiping tears from his eyes, and Inara was cackling into her broth. Skedi had one ear cocked and was standing on all fours as if he was about to bolt.

'Humans are so strange,' he said.

He did not yet understand that a laugh could be a lie too. Because Kissen didn't want to say goodbye to Inara knowing that she might not live. Knowing she wouldn't be able to teach her to throw knives, or how to skin a deer she had shot, or what fungi tasted good. She would have to learn all of it by herself.

So, she laughed. And later she would drink some courage and would barely sleep at all and hope that Hseth decided she didn't really want to kill them all anyway.

'Here,' said Kissen, drawing open her cloak and pulling out a familiar dagger. She flipped it in her hand and gave it to Inara, who looked at it, frowning.

'Osidisen's dagger?' she asked.

'Won't be good for shaving, but it'll do you for stabbing, threatening, or annoying sea gods.'

Inara snorted, but took it, turning it over in her hands. 'You don't want to keep it?'

'He can do me no good. And every girl needs a good knife. Anyway, I know you wouldn't like one made of briddite.' She nodded at Skedi, who had settled back down at his stew. He twitched his whiskers back at her.

'I thought I'd managed to find a haven away from the drunkards and merrymaking,' came a voice, familiar, soft and deep. 'But here you are cackling like fisherfolk at a festival.'

Inara looked up, tucking the blade into her belt. 'Mama, try some!'

Lessa was dressed in a mail tunic fitted with a light cuirass from throat to hip, along with bracers and greaves. Covering it was a tabard of green and silver, and with her sword at her waist and her long black hair braided around her head, she looked like a warrior from an old tale.

'I've eaten, thank you,' said Lessa, though Kissen suspected from the way Skedi fluffed his fur that it was a white lie. They all faced battles in different ways: some fed the nausea in their bellies; some starved it. She could hear drums now, and singing, some raucous, some tuneful. She wondered if someone was making a sacrifice, hoping for good fortune.

'I'll have some,' said another woman, stepping out of the dark behind Lessa. She was tall, with dark skin that shone warm in the firelight, and thick, tightly coiled hair that she wore in fine plaits that had grown out some, and were now tied on top of her head with patterned cloth.

'Naiala,' said Elo, standing.

Kissen didn't recognise her, but she clearly knew Elo. She signed to Inara: *Who?*

Inara replied with a combination of two words: 'fight back'. *Rebel.*

The woman didn't look like a rebel, she looked like a healer, a wealthy one. Something about her warm eyes.

'I'm so glad you're all right,' said Elo hesitantly.

After a moment, Naiala managed a smile and reached out to him. Elo clasped her hand in his, firm and warm. 'They said you campaigned for our release,' she said. 'Thank you.'

'I'm sorry it wasn't sooner.'

She gave him a sad, soft expression, then glanced at the food on the fire and her eyes widened. 'You have plantago?' she said, looking at the long, doughy fruit. 'How?'

'My mother sent it with the Craiers. Please . . . sit.' Elo gestured to the logs and half barrels they had gathered around for seating. 'My lady, you are welcome as well!'

Inara patted the bench next to her, and Lessa came to sit down. Damned woman made even a muddy log look like a velvet throne.

'Are you wearing that cloak to fight?' she asked Kissen.

'What's wrong with it?'

'Not enough protection, and too much flash. That cloak was for show till you had all those pockets sewn in.'

'I like pockets,' said Kissen.

Lessa sighed, but then Inara pressed her bowl into her hands insistently. 'Try it,' she said.

Lessa looked at her daughter, then affectionately chucked her chin, and took the bowl.

'Anyone in the gaols was recruited,' Naiala was saying. 'Some joined the clerics' singers, but I work managing food distribution. Most of the inkers weren't caught. Nor Canovan; I haven't seen him since. Faroch did what he could for us. After you and the king disappeared, everything was chaos.'

All these names meant little to Kissen, apart from Canovan, whom she heartily hoped had suffered a long and painful death, and that his bitch-god had abandoned him.

'I'm so sorry, Naia,' said Elo.

She took the bowl he offered her, with a generous helping of plantago. 'And here you are,' she said. 'Back at the king's side. Wearing my grandfather's armour still.' She looked at the scratched lapis lion on Elo's chest. She sounded tired, not accusatory. 'Why? You said you would kill him.'

'He tried to,' said Kissen, before Inara piped in. 'I stopped him.'

'Kissen . . .' said Elo.

'Oh.' Naia seemed to look at her more intently. 'You're the veiga?'

Kissen nodded.

'You *stopped* him?'

'I thought you were the rebel against violence,' said Kissen. 'Isn't king-killing a bit messy?'

'He attacked my city.'

'Aye, I heard. It was my city too, and now we're all here in his army.'

The rebel woman pressed her lips together. 'I didn't have a choice.'

'Nor did Elo. It was kill him and bow to a fire god, or bow to him and fight back.'

'Kissen . . .' said Elo. 'I don't need you to defend me.'

'Well, you're shit at doing it for yourself,' said Kissen with a shrug. 'You should get to eat your dinner before your ethics are questioned.'

'Coming from you?' said Elo, the fire dancing along his jaw. 'You've insulted me over unbroken bread more times than I can count.'

'Well, I'm special,' said Kissen.

Naia looked at Elo, then at the bowl in her hands, and laughed hollowly. 'You're right,' she said. 'My city is lost – everything I tried to protect – and now I join an army to fight for a king I don't believe in.' She turned the bowl in her hand, then used the flatbread to pinch up some plantago and vegetables. 'I would like to quibble with you, Lion of Lesscia, if we survive. For now, I'm glad you lived.'

They sat talking till the fire burned low. Inara and Lessa shared pieces of her bowl, till Inara fell asleep with her head on Skedi's back, and Lessa took her away.

They spoke of Irisia, Bahba and Wsirin, which delighted both Naia and Elo. Some of Elo's other comrades joined them briefly, bringing wine or hipgin and thanking him for sending them some of the plantago fruit. One had braids that were similar to Elo's, and he and her knight held hands for a sad, long moment, before they departed.

Kissen even had some visits from veiga she had met before in Blenraden, most but not all wearing the colours of the king's bloody 'gods' army', to tell her the stocks they had for their plan against Hseth. Kissen drank some bootswill, feeling the burn of the alcohol drip into her cheeks.

The rest of their army's sea of flames and lamps was still thick with the sounds of making merry. The scents of smoking herbs, alcohol and the sharp burn of bile from emptied stomachs mingled together with mud, cookfires and bodies. There was an active sector of tents with red-lit lanterns, for people getting in their last fucks before they could fuck no more. Kissen had considered it, though now it was just her, the knight and Naiala, and she was waiting for the teacher-rebel to leave so she could proposition him.

'Commander General Elogast.'

The moon had risen, round and full. Their fire was low, and a runner had come.

'The king requests your presence,' she said, a young woman who looked as if she had recently been crying. Or carousing. Likely both.

Someone else had beaten Kissen to the proposition. Elo paused, looking up at the runner, then glanced across at Kissen.

'I'd better go,' said Naiala, standing. She was a bonny one, Kissen thought, but didn't look as if she had any desire to dally.

Elo looked uncertain, apologetic, but if he were to share one more night with someone before a battle, she knew who it should be.

'Go on,' she said. 'I'll finish this flask, then find my tent.'

Still, he hesitated. That was flattering at least. 'Piss off, knight,' she said, pointedly this time, and Naiala grinned.

'It's nice to meet you, Kissenna,' she said, then moved away into the dark.

'Tell him I'll be there soon,' said Elo.

The runner nodded and raced off.

Elo stood up and came towards her. Flames glimmered over his braids, across his cheekbones. He really was one of the most beautiful men she had ever met. And he seemed more comfortable in his skin, in his life, his choices. He had accepted everything that he was, the bad and the good, and there was freedom in that. Power.

He knelt before her and put his fingers to her chin. Then he leaned in, giving her a long, tender kiss before breaking away.

'For luck,' he said, and smiled. 'I'll see you tomorrow.'

Then he stood, and left Kissen alone in the dark.

'Bastard,' muttered Kissen, touching her hand to her lips. She used to like solitude. Wandering, fighting, hating, loving. It had been a good life. One she had been proud of. After a few minutes, she held a flask up to the fading embers.

'Fuck you, fire god,' she said. Then, as she took a swig, she realised she wasn't quite as alone as she had thought.

Lessa Craier had come back. She stood, haloed by the silver moon, while Kissen sat bronzed by flame and gold. They looked at each other in silence.

'I was wondering if you might help me out of my armour,' said the lady at last.

Kissen's heart burst into action, slamming hard against her ribs.

'Tarin would usually do it, and I sent the armourer to rest, I didn't think . . .'

'Of course,' said Kissen. She got to her feet using her staff, then tucked it under her arm and followed in Lessa's wake to her tent, which looked similar to the first one Kissen had met her in. Small cot, table, chair. A lantern gave them soft warmth, and a bit of light. The night was warm, the air tense with the apprehensive quality of a brewing storm.

'Did it work?' Kissen asked, taking off her cloak and draping it on Lessa's chair.

'She won't stir,' said Lessa. 'I have not used sless seeds before. Skedi is watching over her.'

Sless seeds. Sleeping seeds. Lessa had used some sleight of hand to ensure that enough were tucked into the food she had shared with her daughter.

'Good,' said Kissen. It felt bitter, to have lied to Inara as her last choice. She didn't tell lies. It wasn't in her nature. But then, she'd said she didn't kill people, and she had done so. That she hated gods, and she no longer hated them all.

It seemed she did break promises.

'The children's guard will take them to the coast,' said Lessa. 'She should be far enough away by the time she wakes that she won't be able to come back. I just . . . wish I could have said goodbye this time. Properly.'

It was the softest thing Kissen had heard her say. Inara deserved a mother. Deserved someone.

'Maybe you shouldn't fight at all,' said Kissen.

'I have many faults, veiga, but I am loyal to my land.'

'And you won't give the king the satisfaction of calling you more of a coward than him.'

'Just so.'

She began unbuckling her gauntlet, and Kissen leaned her staff against the table then took her hand from her, undoing it herself, slipping the leather from her hand. Lessa's nails were short, the ridges of her palm and thumb calloused from ropes, swords, her fingers marked from bowstrings. Kissen wanted to put her lips to her wrist, her fingers. She wanted to feel her tremble with it.

She resisted. Instead, she took off the lady's tabard and unbuckled her chestplate at her ribs, her neck. Lessa watched her, her skin glowing in the heat and flickering light, as Kissen moved in front of her, opening up the metal and lifting it free. She was careful. After setting it down, she was careful as she went for her bracers. She wouldn't let her touch come too close to the lady's skin, the soft crook of her elbow. She had not been asked.

'Lift your arms,' said Kissen.

Lessa did, and Kissen pulled up the mail, lifting it over her

pinned braids of hair, taking the weight of it from her shoulders
and into her own hands. She laid the mail out on the table, ready
for the morning, its links clicking into place, one after the other.
She breathed in, and released it, then looked at the lady, who hadn't
moved. Her padded jacket beneath the mail was cotton-white, stark
against her shining skin, her dark brows, her hawk-like nose. She
could undress herself now, if she wanted.

'Is that all, my lady?' asked Kissen.

Lessa lifted her chin slightly. Her look was a challenge. 'You
know it is not, my godkiller,' she said.

Kissen swallowed. Could she? Should she?

But if she died tomorrow, could she not have tonight?

She stepped closer to Lessa and reached up, pulled a pin delicately, carefully, from her hair. Then, another, another. The braids
fell down around her shoulders in a river of thick, shining black.
Lessa tipped her mouth up higher. A kiss. She wanted Kissen to
kiss her. What miracle was this? Kissen didn't care if she was being
used, because right now there was a beautiful woman standing
between her arms, wanting to be kissed.

But Kissen wouldn't give in that easily. No, she was not one to
be commanded here.

Instead, she pulled at the threads of Lessa's padded jacket. One
after the other, she tugged them loose, opening the cotton, then
unlaced the shirt beneath till she found the softness of her breasts,
the brown of her belly. Lessa's breath quickened.

Kissen put her hands around Lessa's waist to support herself,
and slowly, surely, descended to her right knee, shifting the heavy
weight of the prosthesis beneath. Here, she could kiss the bottom
of Lessa's ribs, between her breasts, but she put her mouth instead
to the top of the lady's trews and, with her teeth, took the draw-
string and pulled it loose. Then, she slid them down Lessa's thighs,
past her boots, to the floor.

She looked up then. Lessa was breathing fast, staring down at
Kissen with a look of hunger, and Kissen met her eyes. Then she
slid her hands up, slowly, over her waist, her ribs, then ran her
fingers over her breasts, featherlight. She moved the shirt aside
with one hand to tease her dark nipple.

'Do you want more, Lady Craier?' said Kissen. She didn't like to kneel, but she liked to see the flush of the pirate's face, the trembling of her lips.

'Yes,' Lessa said. 'Please.'

Kissen smiled and brought her hand back down, slipping her fingers between the press of Lessa's thighs, stroking her gently. There: the tremble. 'I'm going to make you very glad you didn't cut out my tongue,' she said.

CHAPTER THIRTY-NINE

Elogast

ELO WOKE IN ARREN'S ARMS AS THE WAR HORNS BLEW.
The pressure in the air was intense, heavy. His king had a leg draped
over Elo's calf, his belly to his back, and his left arm wrapped tightly
around his chest.

But Elo's spine was starting to burn.

Wake up.

Elo jumped upright at Hestra's voice, and Arren's eyes shot open,
disorientated for a moment as he looked at his knight, a sleepy
smile forming on his lips.

Then a horn sounded.

'Shit,' said Arren.

They both looked at the ceiling, but the light coming through
was grey. It wasn't an emergency. It was just the dawn summons.

The end of their war.

'My king,' came voices at Arren's tent door. 'We're here to make
you ready.'

'Fuck,' hissed Elo, looking around. His shirt and trousers were
scattered from wall to floor, and he was stark naked. Both of them
were. Elo had thought returning the evening before that Arren
would be angry with him, jealous perhaps of the time he had spent
with Kissen, Inara and Skedi. But he had only wanted them to
hold each other for one more night.

I haven't earned the right of jealousy.

It hurt when he said things like that. Made Elo think Arren had learned something. But was he so calm because Elo always came to him, in the end, and because he thought he always would?

Still, Elo had intended to leave by morning.

'Commander general, we are here for you too.'

He and Arren looked at each other, and Arren chuckled.

'It's not funny,' Elo hissed.

'It's not like they don't know,' the king said. 'I am not the first monarch to love a knight.'

'It's . . .'

'Come in!' said Arren, as Elo whisked up the bedsheets to cover himself. There was no time for squabbling, and when the armourers came in, they already had his gear with them, from padding to mail, to cap and helm.

'Sunbringer, we have what you requested,' said a broad man, who, with another, was carrying in golden armour. Elo recognised the showy plates that Arren had worn for the march on Lesscia, its helm covered with antlers and rays. Heavy and unyielding.

'It's not practical,' said Elo, while Arren stood shining and naked, hands on his hips, the flames in his chest bright and strong. When they were together, Hestra was there too, warmth and fire, blood and lust. She had entwined herself with Arren's will, becoming more a part of him than ever. Elo had managed not to let it unnerve him. 'And it makes you a target.'

'Exactly,' said Arren, and nodded for the armourers to come forward before leaning down to grab his cotton braies and pull them on.

Elo's stomach was turning already. He dropped his sheet and pulled on his hose, then went to the washstand to splash his face with cold water. It had ripples in the surface; a thousand fighters, animals, cooks, blacksmiths, were shaking the earth with their movement.

The tent door opened again, and Methsme entered with Knight Commander Peta, looking proud and haughty in her white dress, though this time she wore a breastplate over it. Peta herself was in full armour, her gleaming briddite longsword at her waist. Both entirely ignored Elo's presence.

'What is this, knight commander?' said Arren. 'If you are trying to convince me to stay back from the field, I—'

'Cleric Methsme requests,' said Peta, 'that she may join you.'

Arren looked at her, frowning as his leggings were pulled on, and his gambeson tugged over his shirt. 'A field is no place for weaponless clerics.'

'I wish to see you face the fire god,' said Methsme, with a bow, her eyes on Arren's flaming chest. 'This is the day of your ascension. What kind of cleric am I, if I do not stand at your side?'

Arren looked at Peta questioningly. 'And what do you think?'

It was idiotic, Elo thought, though he would not particularly mind if the fool-cleric got herself on the wrong end of an arrow. He yanked on his shirt, and his own armourers came forward with his padding.

'Fireheart,' said Peta, 'I must admit, I have known cleric Methsme for some time. Before you showed us the flame in your chest, the god that you are, she and her clerics were already singing for you.'

Elo frowned. He knew it was strange that those women had known how to overwhelm the knights on the *Silverswift* and hide their knives. But what could he do? They had worked so hard on creating unity, consistency, trust. He could not cry foul now and send a knight commander into the stocks on the edge of battle. Nor could he throw accusations at popular clerics. He wanted Arren to deny Metshme, stuff her back in a tent and keep her away, if only because Elo did not trust her.

'Why did you not tell me this before?' said Arren to Peta gently. The commander cleared her throat.

'I feared you would think the songs of commoners and soldiers . . . beneath you,' she said.

Elo gave Arren a sceptical look. *Don't do it*, he tried to say with his expression. *Don't let them coddle your pride, don't let them near you.*

Arren shook his head slightly, as if to say *too late for that*.

'Methsme,' he said, 'despite our differences, you have done great work for me. If you wish to join us on the battlefield, you may be fitted with armour and a knife.'

The cleric dropped to her knees, pressing her face to the floor. 'Thank you, Fireheart,' she whispered.

'Knight Commander Peta.' The older knight bowed low and deep. 'Tomorrow we will discuss honesty in our council, agreed?'

She breathed out in relief. 'Yes, Sunbringer.'

'Then go, I'll be out in the field shortly.'

Once they were gone, Elo sighed. 'That was a mistake,' he said, as the armourers fitted his chain mail. 'What if she trips on her stupid ribbons. Or her antlers fall down?'

Arren laughed. 'What harm can one cleric do? She can lift a knife, but not a sword.' He shrugged. 'I could see the colours around them, the emotions they have. Those two are so bright it's blinding.'

It's faith, said Hestra, and Elo flinched at her voice in his head, though it sounded softer than it had before. *It consumes them.*

They were out and onto the fields before the final waking horns had been blown. The reports said that the Talicians were moving as expected, and that Estefin had proved useful after all. They likely knew by their own scouting that Middren had set the pitch for battle, and they had committed to it nonetheless. They were as confident as the krka had said, with their tactics of brute force and a powerful god.

A horse was brought to Elo, saddled. A grey, thank the gods, not another brown with a flash on their nose. Elo mounted swiftly and followed Arren as they rode out into the field.

The armies were moving, obeying the calls of their commanders. The colours of each House appeared more sporadically now: either the surcoats had become dirtied, or the fighters had lost their interest in representing their House over their king. Most of the spaces they passed reeked of sour beer and strong spirits, and he saw many worse for wear, their eyes red, their skin sallow.

At least they had not run.

Arren nodded at those he passed, the grid of his face open, showing that this time he was fully present. This time, he would be fighting alongside them.

Elo kept behind him, looking around, checking that the formations were moving as they had been ordered. He saw the gleam of russet hair in the sun, a green cloak. Kissen commanding a contingent of veiga, despite her deep distaste of any kind of group activity. She saw him, and he caught the flash of gold tooth as she threw him a cocky smile. Her idea was mad, desperate, but it gave them a chance. An opportunity to break their enemy's faith completely.

Arren looked across at Elogast. It was time for them to part.

'Ride well,' he said. 'I'll see you on the field, commander. Elogast.'

He smiled. If there was worry in his blue gaze, he hid it well. All this waiting, all the fear, all the pain, it would soon be over. Elo relaxed his shoulders, his seat on his horse, and nodded. No last kiss, no soft words, no final dismissal. All that had needed to be said between them had been said, most that they had desired and buried had been dragged into the light. And, though he was afraid of each hour that pulled itself over the eastern horizon towards them, Elo would no longer run from the future. Or himself.

He knew exactly who he was.

CHAPTER FORTY

Kissen

THE VEIGA GATHERED IN THE DIP OF THE VALLEY WHERE the river rushed. The worst disadvantage, the lowest ground. But Kissen knew what disadvantage meant. She knew how to make it her own.

Talking to veiga was worse than herding damned cats. They all thought they were smarter, better, and brighter. Kissen preferred the older ones: Gannet, a woman Kissen had never met before, Pruro whom she knew by name, and Erl who had put on weight and power in his older age.

And as soon as the veterans were on board, the rest fell into line. Older veiga were worth their weight in gold: only clever bastards fuck with gods for years and still win.

Half of the others in Arren's gods' army were barely brushing twenty, having taken up briddite and the veiga stamp with the hope of good pay and glory. Few of them had done more than trash a few shrines or whip the feet of pilgrims, and taken a pretty penny for doing so. Idiots.

But at least they were idiots that had to back her up.

'The stage already set then?' asked Gannet, chewing on a wad of leaves that stank something awful and turned her teeth yellow; she nodded to the huge contraptions that had been raised around them.

'Let's hope so,' said Kissen. There was little breeze down in the basin, but the high winds of the sky were moving fast, and the pressure in the air swelled with stormthreat.

The woman cackled and tucked the wad behind one of her teeth, and pulled out a sickle of briddite, spinning it on its leather thong.

'This is the last time veiga should get involved with kings,' said Erl.

'You're the one wearing his sigil,' said Gannet, nodding at his cloak, which was indeed pinned with a stag's head backed by rays.

'I enjoy wearing the head of a dead god,' he grinned. He had two front teeth missing. 'And it's spare briddite in case I run out.'

'What are you going to do, throw it?'

'B-briddite doesn't hurt her,' said Hovan, the gods commander, for the hundredth time, where he stood in his thick armour and the colours of House Spurrisk. He looked liable to shit his pants. Fair play to him, as long as he did it in the right direction.

'It doesn't need to hurt her,' said Kissen. 'It just needs to hold her.'

'We-we're all going to die, aren't we?'

Kissen glanced at him. They were in the pit of the valley, a godless river oozing past their boots.

When the Talicians came, their little force would be directly in their line of sights.

The king, however, came clipping down the slope, carefully arrayed in shining armour, followed by a large command of knights in blue and gold at his back, on foot. Even his cleric was coming, bright white amid the blue, walking by the silver-haired Commander Peta, ready for her god to win. Sunbringer versus flamebringer, fireheart versus wildfire.

Kissen glanced around the armies hidden in the valley. Lessa Craier she could recognise by the silver and green she wore, the same as her cloak. Kissen relished the memory that shivered through her, the taste of the night, the tangle of the sheets. Her lady's mouth, hands, fierceness, filling her up with pleasure.

'Everyone dies,' said Kissen softly. Then she shook herself, raising her voice. 'Everyone dies!' she yelled. 'People and gods, lions and sheep. Storms pass, winds howl, the sun sets, and the night grows dark. We all go to dust and nothing. Everybody dies.'

They were looking at her, an army she never asked for, for a king she never wanted. Her sisters gone, Inara safe, Elo and Lessa ready to ride into death.

'But we choose!' Kissen bellowed. 'We choose how to live!'

CHAPTER FORTY-ONE

Elogast

HE HEARD THE BELLS AGAIN FROM WHERE HIS CAVALRY stood at the lip of the valley, facing the oncoming enemy.

Bells and drums, bells and drums. He wondered what Kissen must feel at the sound of them. Did it scare her as it scared him? He could see Benjen's face as he turned towards the flame, hear the screaming of Legs as his tail and mane caught fire. He could smell the burning of flesh and wood, the steam of water. He could see gold and red, the bellow of the god of war. The terror was still there, it still shook his hands. Pain shot down his back, curdling in his belly.

But he knew it, he felt it, he lived it.

He drew his sword as the Talician army crested the hill ahead of them, the sun at their backs. They were in red, the first of the flame, with white priests dotting the ranks.

Then, at the edges he saw cavalry, with armour of dark leather: Restish.

The Irisians Elo's mother had sent had been split between the land and ships, supplementing their ranks and given to the defence of the coast. They were practised archers, masters of the heavy longbow, and he had arranged a strong line of them behind the Middrenite cavalry. He wished he could see his mother again, thank her, and apologise for every hurt he had caused her.

The Talicians let out a cry, and a bell rang. They had seen their shining line of riders, the morning sun gleaming on their armour as they stood arrayed. The warfront. The rhythm of the bells and drums grew louder, booming over the warm wind as the incoming army picked up pace to meet them.

'Steady,' said Elo, as he felt the shifting of his own cavalry, the stamping of hooves. The Talicians spilled over the hills and down, thousands of them in a great mass turning the green to red. At the same time, clouds were rolling in on the swift winds of the south, bringing shadows from the sea. Elo breathed in, tasting the rain on his tongue.

The storm was ready to break.

Me or them. Death or survival. The lion on his chest, the sword in his hand. Warrior. Lion. Irisian. Middrenite. Commander, baker, lover, lost.

He smiled. The hills he had grown up on were gilded now in stormlight, and he felt it warm him, the distant mountains, the wild forests, the fallen cities, the people who made homes for gods. Little hopes, all for this green land, this centre of trade. Middren. Fear? It served him, quickening his breath, beating his heart and lending strength to his muscles, clarity to his thoughts. Hope? It took root in him, shoring up his spine, tightening his fists.

At last, as the enemy flooded closer, he saw plumes of smoke rising around glimmers of brass. It gusted black at first, then grew into hot tremors in the air, barely visible against the darkening sky. Not one shrine to Hseth, many of them, already being lit with hot coals.

Good.

'Perin,' said Elo, looking to the sergeant who was seated on a horse beside him. 'Get word to the king: they will have war weapons that can move down the slopes. Deepen the ditches if they can, move the blockades further up.'

Perin nodded once, his eyes hollow, his jaw set, then dismounted and went to find one of the battle birds to send the message down to the king. The more they were prepared, the better.

Elo could see cavalry more clearly now in the Talician lines, picking their way across the fields in between the groundsfolk. They were cautious, with all the light on Elo's command, they wouldn't be able to tell if they were a hundred or a thousand lined up together. Nor would they be able to see what they hid behind them.

'Archers!' cried Elo. 'Test their mettle!'

The order was passed on by horn, in Elseber's hands this time. Though she was still healing from her hip wound, she had refused to be left behind. From where they sheltered behind great wooden shields held by squires, the Irisian archers flamed their arrows, two for each bow, and drew. Elo could almost hear the stretch of the gut, the bend of the wood. Then, the hiss of the shafts being released, the smell of hot pitch and cloth as they broached the air above them, over them. A hundred or more, flying over the grass of the field and hitting down, perhaps fifty strides shy of the encroaching army, further than any standard bow, still blazing.

Flames roared up from the dry bales they had placed there, set with stags' antlers from the previous shedding season in a long line along the fields. It spread along the field, roaring up, and the breeze that carried the storm swept it around towards the Talician front, obscuring their vision.

They weren't the only ones who could use fire for their god.

Perin returned, leaping back up onto his horse, ready to fight. Return fire skittered far short of them, confused by the fire and smoke. Perin looked over at Elo. 'For our loves,' he said. 'My life, my blood, my heart.'

Elo nodded, and put on his helm. 'For hearth and home,' he said. 'My life, my blood, my heart.'

Time to move.

'Forward!' Elo called. 'For Sunbringer! For Middren!'

'For Middren!'

Their cavalry began their march as the fire burned brighter along the field, fierce and wild. Forward, veiled by thick smoke, each House, all their guards, together for a final cause.

The flames were burning low. Just enough, just a little more. Elo blinked the smoke-sting from his eyes.

There.

They could see the Talicians, closer now, clear through the haze in their red. Elo could just glimpse their expressions, the horror at how near they had come.

'Now!'

The mounted Middrenite archers had already been aiming, ready for his command, and they released. The arrows flew, unlit this time, into the Talician ranks. Few of them were knights in helms; few had shields or the protections they needed. Those who still had crossbows fired them haphazardly, glancing off their plate armour and chain mail.

'Charge!' Elo cried.

Their cavalry leapt over the dwindling flames. They did not hit the enemy head on, instead charging southwards first, then swooping around and targeting the edges of their army with spears, halberds, longswords, and scattering the foot soldiers with the thundering of their horses, the whirling death in their hands. They inflicted as much pain as possible, as much fear as they passed through.

'Break!'

The Middrenite charge broke away before the Talicians could rally, following up with the far strikes of the Irisian longbows, confusing the enemy as the horses raced away, making a large circle before looping around to the north, and beginning another charge.

Finally, an order came with the ringing of a bell. The Talician ranks exploded, and Restish and Talician riders came out to meet Elo's force and head off their assault. They rode chaotically, the only thing binding them was trajectory. And lack of awareness.

They did not expect the second charge of the Middrenites.

Captain Graiis led his riders around from west to east, slamming into the enemy riders, splitting their force, while Elo's command swung back for their next assault. Elo gritted his teeth to keep them from rattling, holding on to his horse with his legs as tightly as he could to keep from being shaken in his armour from its back His eyes were streaming with the black smoke, arms already aching from the first assault.

'Break!' Elo heard.

The Graiis riders had not come off well in their clash with the Restish cavalry, who were fast and strong, bred on the Usican plains, but they were now close enough to be hammered by arrows.

'Cover fire!' Elo commanded. 'Charge!'

The Graiis charge retreated, while Elo's own riders re-formed into a spearhead strike. The mounted and Irisian archers aimed to support the Graiis, giving them a chance to escape as Elo's horses thundered past them. Hooves pounded on the burned grass, sending sparks up into the storm-heavy air. Elo lifted his sword, yelling out his fury, as they slammed once more into the Talician army.

Elo was at the forefront. He hacked down a spear that tried to fell him, then sliced his sword across a snarling face, thrust it into another chest and felt their ribs crack with its weight. Flame was reflected in his blade, blood flew up into the air. Gold and red. The colours of the dead god of war.

The terror had him, but he was the terror.

He twisted his shoulder and struck through the throat of one of the mounted Restish who had fled back to pursue them, then wrenched his sword free and hacked once, twice, through the point of a halberd that nearly struck him off his horse. He was in a knot of screams and bodies, heat and sweat and fury.

'Break!'

His turn now to command a retreat before they became swallowed and taken down by sheer numbers. His voice was rough with smoke, his head swimming, but he was too embroiled in innocent horses and guilty bodies to be able to extract himself. With the next strike, he ripped through the arm of a Talician woman, and an arrow glanced off his helm, another off his pauldron, a sword sliding over his back. His horse was trying to buck and whinny, to push out, push back, animal instincts kicking in. *Danger! Away!*

At last, the pressure around them released as the rest of Elo's cavalry heeded his order. He reined his horse free, peeling away once more as thunder rolled across the sky.

This time the Talicians were better prepared, responding with hard crossbow fire that slammed into horses and riders as they raced back towards their archers and their shields. Elo heard a yell as one of his own warriors fell, then the heave and shriek as a horse collapsed with bolts in its flank, sending up a volley of grass and dust. The poor beast rolling over, mad with pain and fear.

The Middrenites spread thin and wide, racing back between their own shielded archers, and the crossbows soon tailed off. The invaders were running low on bows and bolts. Estefin the krka had told them the crossbows were bought, not made, and they lacked the knowledge to fletch new arrows to fit well.

So, they would soon run out.

Their Irisians, however, had plenty. As Elo and his riders passed their shields, they returned a rain of arrows towards the enemy line, who screamed even before they struck.

But there were still so many more coming.

Elo was hot, so hot in the warming morning. The mail over his arm had been torn, some blood was leaking through, though he had not felt the strike that had pierced his flesh. He still could not. Sweat dripped into his eyes, down his neck. He wanted to tear his helm from his head, relieve the press on his braids and skin, but he knew better.

The Talician force was close now. They had narrowed their attack to an arrowhead formation, pushing long weapons to the outside more easily to defend against the next charge, which came again from Graiis, as the enemy reached and passed the blackened streak of burned straw that had struck a line across the field of play. Elo winced as they lost several riders and two more horses while he gathered his own force, Perin and Elseber still at his side, breathing heavily. Their only luck was that one stallion charged straight into the oncoming force in a panic, ploughing a swathe through them before it was taken down.

Still, Elo led their horseback sweep once more into the pikes and crossbows ordered forward by the warrior priests. The storm had reached the skies above them, churning across the sun like a fist, rays gleaming around it, before the light was blotted out in an eclipse of black.

Rain met them as they charged again, a veil of cooling grey turning the ground slippery and flattening the last of the smoke. The Talicians could see their numbers clearly now as they crashed into their formation, trying to take down at least three foot soldiers for every horse they lost to a pike.

It was a losing game. The enemy knew what they were defending against now. Their brief advantage was lost. A volley of arrows came up from the red ranks, sparser this time, but better aimed. Two knights fell, then a third.

'Scatter!' Elo cried, ducking and turning his horse away to present a smaller target of its leather-covered haunches, giving one last strike beside him to a running boy who thought he would get lucky with a knife. Two arrows hit his saddle, but didn't strike flesh.

His knights ran in all directions on horseback, or foot, if they had fallen, throwing off the aim of the Talicians and coming back to the line of shields and archers for shelter as the enemy force made chase.

The krka had been right about another thing: they were vastly outnumbered. Even without the full force of Talicia's northern regiments, even supplemented by the Irisians, the amassed number of the invaders was greater than anything Elo had seen.

And his cavalry had now lost the element of surprise.

'Sound the retreat!' yelled Elo.

Elseber put the horn to her lips and made the call for escape, all of them turning back from their aborted charge and rushing for the safety of the shields. But the archers there also began to pick up and run, the squires carrying the shields onto their backs and speeding into a downpour of rain.

The Talicians and Restish made chase on hoof and foot, their ranks loosening as they drove on, tasting victory. Elo looked back, seeing the faces of the army that had come to destroy them, and he saw their triumph, heard the screams of their jubilation as they ran in ragged clumps, set on chasing down the horses that had harried them and turning the clash into a rout.

Fools. They had learned nothing since Gefyrton.

'Turn!' cried Elo.

The mounted archers, those Elo and the Houses had selected carefully and scattered along the two cavalry lines, gripped with their thighs and twisted on their mounts, facing back.

This was no true retreat.

'Loose!'

They fired, surprising their pursuers, who had mounted no defence. The Pinethian shot. A faked rout, a turn, a strike that ruptured the over-committed Talician and Restish forces. For they had arrows in plenty.

Elo's command continued for the valley as the Irisian ground archers and the Middrenite squires dived down the slopes, rushing to their designated shelters. The horses reached the tipping point of the crest and spilled over its edge, but not before turning once more and taking down another row of the Talicians.

Forcing them to give chase.

CHAPTER FORTY-TWO

Arren

ARREN STOOD BEHIND THE MAIN PHALANXES ON A hillock. It had previously been an islet in the river that usually flowed through this valley, rushing and quick. But the water was gone.

All was going to plan.

He could see the Gods Army ahead on another few knolls, almost two hundred. They were a messy knot, led now by Elo's foul-mouthed veiga. Sunk into the mud were the trebuchets she had requested, dismantled and then built again at the valley's base as the water dwindled. The clunky machines were designed for bringing down walls, not gods, but seeing as she had felled Hseth once before, Arren had little choice but to trust her. It helped that she was, somehow, the reason they were all still alive.

She and the gods.

Perhaps Arren should have loosened his grip, gone back to the gods, asked them for help, or acknowledged that he could no more kill them than kill the sea or the sky. Perhaps so many would not have died fighting each other rather than preparing for this war.

But he could not, would not undo what had been done. He would face the god as the king he was. With his army, and their faith. They were ready. He could see the glow of his people pooled around the valley basin, gathered up its slopes, waiting for their signals, believing in him. He would try to be kinder, better. He would try to earn it.

'Here they come,' whispered Peta at his side.

Elo's vanguard made its planned retreat, breaching the lip of the valley and sweeping down it under a veil of rain. Arren caught the blue of Elo's lion, saw the stride of his horse, and breathed a sigh of relief.

Then, the Talician army came down after them: tens, hundreds, racing over the edge.

Too late did they see the arrayed armies below: Irisians in their scaled armour and perfectly arranged phalanxes, Middrenites in mixed units of knights and land army with their swords. Too late did they realise they had been led into a trap.

Hearth and home, flame and heart, Hestra whispered. *We know this land better than she who has barely lived.*

Lady Craier led the second wave, covering the backs of Elo's riders. She came with her command along the valley sides, slamming into the narrowed spearhead of the Talician onslaught.

More kept coming, spilling and stumbling over the hill in the now pouring rain. The Restish thundered down, losing formation and footing, their horses falling into the spiked pits the Middrenites had spent days digging. Other northern allies fell to arrows from the Middrenite archers positioned all around the crests of the valley, led by Iuri Movenna. The red invaders were easy to pick out, and slid like drops of blood down the green slopes.

Thunder rolled and lightning cut across the sky. Arren couldn't hear the sound of the bells or the call of horns over the rattle of rain on armour, and the distant screams of the dying. He stayed where he had to, watching his war be fought.

Eventually, the enemy's momentum slowed. Their commanders must have conferred on a different tactic that would not haemorrhage them so many fighters.

What now?

Then, he saw them beneath the belly of the storm. Statues of brass, dull, then bright as the lightning struck: fifteen gleaming statues of Hseth drawn to stand at the edge of the valley, all twisted in different shapes of beauty, dark metal binding them.

This was what Elo had warned him about. In response, Arren and Peta had moved their unoccupied shield blockades forwards, hoping to slow their advance.

The rain thinned, and Arren blinked away water as the storm edged away, and light burst down from the sun, sliding already past noonday. All the statues were hot and glowing, the grilles of their mouths bright with fire.

'Hold steady!' Peta bellowed with all the force of her lungs. 'Await your orders!'

At some unseen call, the statues of Hseth's flame and terror were shoved down the slope.

What would have been frightening on any field of battle was terrifying from the bottom of a valley. Fifteen giants of incandescent metal came careering towards them, trailing sizzling steam and smoke as they smashed down, tipping and rolling on the rocks and the slopes.

One fell into a ditch after only a few metres, but continued to roll and bounce, breaking open and sending shards of coal and broken metal shooting into Arren's warriors. Two more made it further before their wheels shattered. One simply stopped, still flaming, while another rolled further, faster, and veered off course, taking out one of the Irisian units.

The blockades of shields buried in the muck were enough to break the wheels of two more that set fire to the grass where they fell, but that left eight. Eight huge statues churning through, their coal-filled mouths open like a scream, or a howl of war. Anyone unlucky enough to be in their path was obliterated. Arren could just imagine the heat of the metal as they came close. Unbearable.

The mud of the riverbed stopped them before they hit the veiga, but the impact of the idols was devastating. The Crolle battalion was in disarray, and two others were barely kept under control by their captains and commanders. Some sprinted for the valley sides, and Peta blew on the horn harder, stronger. A warning not to run.

They fear, whispered Hestra. *I fear.*

Arren gritted his teeth. His head ached beneath his helmet, and his absent heart felt fit to burst.

Fear is not the end of all things.

Then he heard a call coming from the veiga, the gathering of godkillers. Not for him. Not for Sunbringer.

Hseth. Hseth. Hseth. Hseth. Hseth.

CHAPTER FORTY-THREE

Inara

HER HEART WAS POUNDING AS SHE CAME TO, HEAD SPINNING.
Her mouth tasted rank and dry and strange. Too sweet.

She was moving, her body shifting and tilting, and she could
hear the sound of heavy rain hammering down above her. Not
against tent cloth, but against wood and board.

Sleep had dragged her so strongly into its arms, down and
down, quicker than she had wanted. Quicker than she had thought
possible.

'*I love you.*'

She remembered her mother whispering as the darkness took
her.

Inara sat up, throwing Skedi right off her chest with a squawk
of indignance.

Finally, he said into her throbbing mind. She groaned, putting
her hands to her temples. *I was starting to worry.*

She was in the back of a carriage, on a soft couch of feather
cushions. Sitting across, there was another girl whom she vaguely
recognised, staring out of slitted windows, and two boys even
younger who were gawping round-eyed at Skedi. The woman with
them was pressed back in the furthest corner, staring at the god
as if he might bite.

'Where are we?' said Inara.

'On our way to the coast,' said Skedi.

'But I said to Mama I would stay back,' said Inara, massaging her eyes. Gods, even her *eyeballs* ached.

'Seems like she didn't believe you,' said the girl in the window. She wore finely woven cloth and her brown hair was tied back in a hunter's tail. Last Inara had seen her, she had been sitting on a throne of budding branches: Lady-heir Geralfi. 'They must have fed you sless seeds for you to sleep like that.'

'*Fuck*,' Inara hissed. Of course they did.

'Please!' said the older woman. 'Not in front of the children.'

Inara looked to Skedi, who was sitting small and guilty. 'You don't sleep,' she said, accusing.

'They . . . didn't want you to watch,' he said. 'If it went wrong. And they knew you wouldn't leave on your own.' He looked up. 'I'm not sorry Ina. I should have protected you better from fighting and war, from the gods and what they would want from you.'

Inara shook her head and staggered to her feet, too bleary to be angry with him. In truth, many of the tactics they had discussed had gone over her head. What would she have done, sitting back with the archers and watching them all fight, other than get in the way? But didn't they want her to see them win? Didn't they want her there to hold Hseth back, in case the god was too strong?

She braced herself against the ceiling and moved closer to the girl to peer out of the window. They were in cattle lands, and she could see a sliver of churning blue, dark through the gap in the hills.

They had already made it to the sea.

'You're Inara Craier,' said the girl. 'Aren't you? I'm Freia Geralfi.'

Inara looked at her. Months ago, she had been seethingly jealous of the young Geralfi, at her father's side, celebrated and given jobs, given respect. 'I've seen you before,' said Inara. 'At Mutur.'

'You've been . . .' Freia's throat moved, swallowing. 'You've been to Gefyrton?'

Inara nodded. 'I'm sorry for your loss.'

'That's how you pity someone who lost a relative, not a city.'

'Then I'll pity you later,' said Inara, looking around at the padded doors. Tightly closed now, they would open straight onto the road. 'How do I get out of this?'

'You want to go back?' she said.

The sun is high, Inara, said Skedi. *It all began hours ago.*

'I just want a better look,' Inara grumbled at both of them. Though it was in part to see how far they had truly gone from the battle.

'You are both to stay put till Weild,' said the woman, whom Inara suspected would be the wet-nurse for the younger boy, who could not be more than a year old.

Inara looked pleadingly at Skedi. *Just for a look?* he said. *Of course.*

He sighed disbelievingly, and pushed his will towards the nurse's colours. 'No harm can come from a look.' *No harm. No harm can come.*

'You can get to the roof,' said Freia, jerking her chin up at the hatch in the ceiling. 'I'll help.'

Inara cast around, but Skedi had already landed exactly where her new bow was, and its quiver. Osidisen's knife was strapped to the outside. She grabbed it as Freia unbolted the hatch and opened it to a storm-bruised sky and a deluge of water.

'You're letting the rain in!' said the older boy.

'Quiet, Arren,' said Freia, and the boy pouted. He was named for the king they'd all put their hope behind. Even Elo.

But Arren didn't deserve Elo's love. He didn't deserve anyone's. Fear of Hseth had blinded them all into accepting the past they could not change. But Inara would not forget it, not if Arren lived a hundred lives begging for forgiveness.

She made a jump for the hatch from the top of the bench and climbed on top of the sloped roof. Rain flattened her hair in heavy, tender drops, but the world outside was bright with sunlight, gleaming across her skin, the number of other carriages in their caravan, the carts, the civilians, picking out glints of wet wood and leather, the shine of metal and wheel.

Behind them, east, the clouds were darker. Lightning raked across them like lace swept across velvet, but the rain that fell on them was blown from the south.

Inara turned. The summer storms were sweeping in from the sea, carried on the warm, southerly wind. The skies were all light and darkness, the next storm rising up to blot out the sun, casting them in shadow, while in the distance the waves were tipped with silver.

As Skedi fluttered up to land on her shoulder, Inara heard a distant boom. But this was not thunder; it didn't crackle, it was short and sharp. Again it came, and she had known it recently enough to recognise the sound.

Cannonfire.

Across the radiant foam, Inara could see ships on the water: Middrenite, Irisian, sailing together to meet an array of Restish and Talician ships and prevent them from making land.

Then, orange flashes burst from their sides, soon after followed by the staccato booms. But it was not the Restish who were firing yet . . . it was the Middrenite ships striking at their own blockade, Irisian and Middrenite alike, while flying yellow flags.

Inara gasped as an Irisian ship's sail caught flame.

'Lord Yether,' said Skedi, understanding as well. 'He has turned on Arren and the alliance. If they help the enemy make land . . .' He dug his claws into her shoulder and shrank. 'They could trap our army from behind.'

Inara set her jaw, crawling to the front of the roof.

'Ho! Driver!' she cried, down at the hunched body and its hat below. They looked up in surprise, blinking the water from their eyes.

'Get back inside, you little menace!' A woman. She pulled down her masking scarf. 'You'll get yourself killed.'

'Look!' Inara said, pointing to the sea battle. The effects of the sless were fading fast now: she felt alert, and scared. The driver followed her finger, seeing the shadows of the distant ships. 'Does this train have a messenger? We need to warn the army if Talicia makes land.'

The driver paused, frowning at the sea. 'The Yether messengers are prepared at the cliffs,' she said. 'Go back inside.'

'Yether has defected!' said Inara. 'See the colours? We need another way!'

'Ah, come, girl,' said the driver, looking sceptical. 'You don't know one thing about sea battle, and Yether is as loyal to the king as they come.'

Her eyes landed on Skedi, and with a sneer of distaste, made a Sunbringer salute on her heart. 'Get back inside, Craier-whelp,' she said. turning back to the road. 'For all I know you'd be as like to spread rebellious nonsense as give our Fireheart any help at all.'

Inara narrowed her eyes, and she felt Skedi sigh. *I guess we're going back then*, he said.

Forward. If they don't want me there, maybe I can help the Irisians.

Safely?

Safely. She looked at him. *You don't have to come, Skedi.*

Oh, I'm coming. He looked down at the driver, gathering his power. Then he willed towards her one tiny lie: *Attack?*

The driver whirled around, looking for aggressors and giving Inara the chance to jump from the roof onto the seat beside her and shove the woman off it. She hit the ground with a screech, just as Freia Geralfi poked her head out of the roof hatch to see what was happening.

'Left front mare!' said Skedi.

'Inara Craier!' came Freia's surprised cry, as the driver cursed in the mud of the road. Inara didn't pause, she jumped from the seat onto the shaft that held the horses, then used it to launch herself onto the front left brown. She was unsaddled, but had a bit and a bridle with reins.

Head still pounding, Inara took out Kissen's knife and used it to cut the reins loose from the cart and traces, freeing the mare. Skedi whispered to the animal, soft calming words that Inara could just hear breathing at the edge of her mind. *It's all right. It's a game. This is fun.*

He knew exactly what she needed.

The driver had found her feet and was livid with fury. 'Oi! Stop, you—'

The mare was free. 'Go!' Inara cried, digging in her heels, and slapping down the reins. 'Go!'

'Craier!' yelled the driver, and several others in the train looked out.

There's no harm in letting her go. Skedi forced his power back to them. *It's not your job. It's not your problem.*

Inara spurred the horse on, heading seawards towards the storms and ships, the bright water and dark sky. She gritted her teeth, holding on to Osidisen's dagger. She understood now why Kissen had given it to her. Why Lessa and Skedi had conspired to send her away.

They didn't think they would all survive, and they hadn't wanted her to see it again: the things she loved burning to ash.

She was close enough to the coast now that she could smell the salt of the sea, see dunes and white sands rolling away from her, the long grass waving like another body of water. No one made chase, but Skedi flew at her back.

She struck the dagger across her arm, hissing through her teeth as it hurt.

'Inara!' Skedi protested.

'OSIDISEN!' she called.

Surely, he had to come. Surely, he had to help. He had sent Kissen here, had warned them about the Talicians. The rain came cascading down again, heavier, plastering her clothes to her skin. She hoped it rained Hseth to death. She hoped it bit her like a thousand needles.

Who is it that calls me now from so far away?

His voice came quiet as a hum, soft as the retreating tide. Inara reined in the horse and Skedi landed on its head as she held the dagger out before her. Its grey stone was not like this sea, deep and gleaming like a dark sapphire. It was the grey of the wild north.

I am Kissenna's ward, said Inara. *Her sister, her child.*

Kis-sen-na . . . Osidisen whispered her name softly, like the hiss of waves between stone. *Born on the love of the sea. I loved her father deep, but he loved her more, his sea-born girl. And so, I loved her too. In my own way.* Inara felt his sigh in her bones . . . *She called me. I remember that. After all those years.*

Inara's heart fell. She had heard havering such as this before, from Scian, and the weaver-god of Blenraden, their minds broken with their shrines.

Inara thought she was summoning a great god, the god who had helped kill Hseth in Blenraden.

She was wrong.

363

Kissen's in trouble, she tried, hoping that would rally him. *She needs your help.* She could feel his presence, like a droplet in her heart, a twist of salt and blood.

Alas, little fin, he said, his voice drifting into her mind, then away. *I can help her no more. I am weak. I am . . . faded.* The stone of the dagger gave the faintest glimmer. *No one loves the sea any more. They do not love the water for what it is, only for what it can give them.*

Inara breathed in, shuddering. Glanced back at the ships. She couldn't tell who was winning; she couldn't tell who was sinking.

I can give you power! she said. *My blood that called you here, I can give you more.*

'Ina, please—' hissed Skedi.

You have a totem from my most precious shrine, the one I used to watch her. Used it to cut your flesh and offered me pain. And it is barely enough to keep me present.

My blood is powerful!

Not powerful enough. Osidisen's voice was so soft she could barely feel it. *It's not enough.* His voice drifted away, then, a last, mournful whisper. *I wish I could help her . . . I wish I could see her before I die.*

He fell silent, and Inara was left with a bleeding arm and nothing to show for it. That wasn't supposed to be how it went. Osidisen was supposed to come roaring in and smash the Talician and Restish ships to nothing.

'He wanted to,' said Skedi sadly, as if reading her mind.

'He loved her,' said Inara, and she looked at her other arm, wrapped as it was in her father's demand. 'She was not his, but he loved her.'

It angered her, the mark Yusef had made on her. He was so powerful, but had offered her nothing without taking. And now she had a power that she could not use, because everything worth taking from her had been stolen. All she had was a promise to a father who would never claim her, and a mother who had gone to die.

She rubbed her hand over the mark, feeling for its colours. It was a manacle, a bond of desperation. She had been used. Kissen said the writing of gods took on the nature of their will. Yusef's was sea and stone, soft and hard, and purple-rich.

'I have to go and warn them,' said Inara. 'But Skedi, it's time for you to be free. Go to him, or to your own shrines. You don't need me any more.'

Skedi shook his head. 'I choose you,' he told her. 'I chose you in Blenraden, in Lesscia, in Wsirin. And I will choose you again. Over and over.'

Inara felt tears rising in her eyes. He gave her love. Without expectation, without limits. He loved her.

'I won't be bound to him,' she whispered. 'I don't want his mark on me. I want to be my mother's daughter, not my father's mistake.'

'Then take it off,' said Skedi.

'What if he comes for me? For us?'

'My girl,' said Skedi, and tipped his antlers forward, resting them against her brow. 'I would fight the world for you.'

Inara swallowed, and nodded.

She dug her fingers into the colours of Yusef's boon, the shining purples and golds, the wealth and riches, and *pulled*. She dragged it out of her own skin, and it hurt, but not like a knife wound, like a splinter, a poison, drawn out, out, out.

The colours came with it, stretching, snapping. Broken. She tossed them into the long grass where they fell apart like a tangle of threads. *Fuck you.*

She was not his to bind. She was her own, and she would choose her own path.

CHAPTER FORTY-FOUR

Kissen

'HSETH, HSETH, HSETH.'

The name was bitter in her mouth. The statues had taken out great sweeps of the Middrenite army, including one of their trebuchets and several veiga, and there might yet be more of them. Kissen could still smell hot death on the wind.

Taking the lower ground felt less wise than it had originally seemed, but Lessa launched a counter attack, taking her foot soldiers up the edge of the valley bowl to enact a pincer movement with Elo's knights. The rain was playing in their favour, turning their ground muddy, sliding and uncertain. The allied invaders fell and tumbled down the slopes, some falling into their traps, others crashing into the scorched furrows left by their burning shrines.

She wondered how long it would take them to realise the next stage of their plan.

The veiga kept their chanting.

'Hseth. Hseth. Hseth.'

The Talicians used Hseth to overwhelm their enemy, but what if the Middrenites summoned her first?

The ground beneath Kissen's feet was flooding. She and her veiga stood spread across the raised knolls of grass that made islets in the water, but there was little they could do to predict how a river would move when its dam spilled over.

They couldn't blow it up: that would have decimated their own force, and it appeared that Arren had finally understood that winning a war didn't need to be achieved by destroying the very ground they fought on.

Instead, they had blocked in the overflow days before, and redirected the canals to fill the lake's basin so it would quickly fill to the top, and spill over.

Kissen kept up the chant. *Hseth. Hseth. Hseth.*

She could see no Talician priests, no shrines. If they were calling to the god themselves, sacrificing to her, it must be further back from the top of the valley. That would benefit them the most, having her fall on them from above. A weapon with a mind of her own.

The veiga called her name, and they made offerings. Not offerings of blood and bone, not flesh and blood; but prayers. Ones she was not usually offered.

Kissen had sourced quite a few in Wsirin. It hadn't taken more than two conversations with Skedi at her side to find a veiga's street in the market behind closed and shuttered doors.

And the god of white lies had helped her find the best prayers. Wishes to other fire gods for warmth against a coming winter, to healing gods for sickness and fever to be burned away. To gods of war, begging for an end to skirmishes in Usic with woven beads of perfect glass, bargaining for their family's safety with offerings of children's bracelets, little shoes. It broke Kissen's heart to buy them, but she did.

And then she had the veiga and the clerics go through the Middrenite camp, finding every offering they could, both legal and illegal. Prayers, so many of them. Prayers to Arren, prayers for rain, prayers for home. Prayers of mourning, prayers of love, of sex, of wine and freedom from ill. Hopes by the thousand.

Would their prayer-offerings outweigh the sacrifices, the burning, the pain? No. But it didn't need to. All they needed was temptation, something special, something new, votives stolen from other gods.

Exactly the kind that Hseth liked.

Hseth, Hseth, Hseth.

Their offering, too, held out the sweet temptation of Arren's fighters turning towards her, loving her, desiring her. A god of all things.

The water was spilling around them faster now, rising up their ankles. The Talicians had committed over half their force to the fighting on the slopes. Kissen couldn't see Lessa any more, or Elo. She knew the king was behind them, standing between the waters, as bait.

The rain intensified once more, hammering down on the field. Thunder boomed across them, lightning crackling down and silhouetting the fighters on the slopes, shining metal and red cloth, blood and helmets, hands and bodies, torn and bloody.

Hseth, Hseth, Hseth.

Then, she smelled it. The scent of childhood terrors. Flame, blood and coal, oil and sweat. The machinery of war.

The fire god came in a flash of lightning, a glimmer in the air, a twist of fire, vivid with light. Not for her people, not for her priests. For herself, she manifested above the fallen statues at the valley's base, still whole enough to be a shrine, her war skirts flaring out around her like a bell.

And the Sunbringer's heart flared brightly in response.

CHAPTER FORTY-FIVE

Elogast

ELO HEARD THE SCREAMING OF THE TALICIAN PRIESTS AS the god appeared before they had called her. They had been drawing out a final shrine to the very crest of the slope where they desired her to descend. Too late. Elo smiled through chapped lips and bloody teeth. Hseth had come, but at the summoning of the Middrenites. The veiga had her attention now.

Elo felt the heat of the god behind him, smaller than she had been before, slightly taller than human. He saw the confusion of the Talicians and Restish, seeing the flame down by the floodwater that deepened the broad basin of the valley.

But she was Kissen's quarry. He had his own.

'Keep going!' cried Elo. 'Do not give up! Charge!'

The Middrenites and Irisians fought well against the tide of Talicia, but their front lines were exhausted. Elo's body ached, his horse was faltering, sweating, and stumbling, blood dripping down its flanks. And the Talicians still came, their numbers overwhelming, managing to keep the momentum of the high ground.

They needed the reinforcements if they were to keep up their front. Yether and Tiamh fighters were gathered to the southwest, ready for when the veiga made their move. Elo filled his lungs and blew his horn. Sharp blast, then long. *Request for aid. Request for aid!*

No horn sounded in response. Had they not heard him over

the thunder? He brought his sword up and down, cracking it into the skull of a Talician who had stumbled as he looked around. Elo's fighters were run ragged, Lessa's cavalry too, and the Irisians, were close to being overwhelmed. But if they faltered now, the veiga and the kings' guard would be overrun before they could succeed.

They needed more time.

CHAPTER FORTY-SIX

Kissen

HSETH ROARED INTO BEING OVER HER FALLEN STATUES.

What is this? Her voice whipped across them, a burning behind the eyes. *This offering?*

Her voice was cracked. Metal veins dripped across her body from her chest, dull and grey. Briddite. Hseth twisted as if weighed down with it, but she was still mighty, the rest of her flesh burning ember armour.

And this was Hseth weakened? Hseth small? True, she was smaller than she had been in Blenraden, a tree rather than a behemoth. Her hair was wild and golden, the flames around her heart blood red.

Kissen prepared her lungs, took a deep breath. 'Look what we have for you, god!' she bellowed. Gannet and Erl stood by her side, elbows to her elbows. 'Our king gives you all his offerings in return for leaving our land alone.'

All the veiga, she hoped, were controlling their colours as best they knew how. They hid their lies with their will, sending instead their fears, their hopes, their fierceness towards the god as she contemplated the great pile of prayers they had presented on a raft. It floated now on the water, which had deepened to a few feet, pooling at the valley's base.

The god looked up towards where the king waited on his islet with his battalion behind him, golden and bright, his chest aflame.

Fire dropped from her feet as she drifted closer, boiling the river where it touched.

'These offerings are not pain.' Hseth seemed almost curious, childlike, then her mind-speak cut through their heads. *Not screams? Not death?*

Kissen winced. The god's voice seared like hot wires, cracking through her defences as easily as a hammer crushed glass.

Just a little closer, they needed her a little closer.

Hseth tipped her head. Her presence was heating the air to steaming, and Kissen's lungs ached. 'Do other gods get such quaint little things?' Her smile was dangerous. Even not in its full force, her presence made Kissen feel like her flesh was peeling away from her bones.

'They're for you, Hseth,' she said. 'Take them.' She gripped her throwing knives inside her cloak. 'Middren wants you to give them safety.'

Hseth looked at her, and Kissen felt her heart twist in her chest, trying not to show it in her colours, in her face. Would she know her as the girl whose family she burned? Would she understand this was the woman who had killed her last incarnation? But there was no recognition in those eyes. Hseth did not know who she was.

'My priests are calling for me,' she said, sparks drifting from her mouth as she floated above the water, looking to the white robes on the slopes. The slow flood was past Kissen's thighs now. Enough. It had to be enough. 'They tell me to be afraid.'

Kissen took a shaking, hot breath. She could feel the burn scars on her neck, chest, hands tighten. She had killed this god, and she had returned as something else. Something worse.

'Were you born for fear, great fire god of the north?' Kissen tried.

'I was made . . . for others to fear.' Hseth's hair burst up in corkscrews of flame, tearing up like a beacon to the sky. 'I was made to destroy. I was made in pain.'

The flame shuddered around her chest, licking around the brid-dite that cracked around her. For the first time, Kissen felt some pity for the god that had come to kill them.

'I *am* pain,' said the god. She bared her teeth: broken rocks, stones and metal. Her skin ran from red to white, hotter. Hotter than a brand. She came closer. 'I need not your puny offerings. I need not your squalid gods and your weak little country.' She reached forward, not for the offerings, but for Kissen, who held her nerve. 'All I need is death.'

Well, it was worth a try, but she knew a god used to blood would desire nothing less. And she had come close enough.

'Now!' bellowed Kissen.

The veiga at the mechanism had been aiming while Hseth was distracted. Chains of briddite weighted with stones fired, wrapping around her. Perhaps it couldn't hurt her, but if it was a part of her, then it could touch her. It could weigh her down.

The god stumbled, shrieking as her feet sank below the flood-plain.

'Go!' Kissen cried.

The veiga on the wings began swinging their own chains over their heads, throwing them across the god, wrapping her chest, her arms, her neck, dragging her down, down towards the river.

'W-wait!' Hseth cried. 'What are you doing?' *What are you doing?* 'Priests? Priests!' *Help me.*

'Fire!' Kissen roared.

Middrenite crossbows now. The hard bolts with iron tips flew through the god's flame as she tried to avoid them, but dragged behind them briddite chains that bit into Hseth's flame flesh, and stuck there.

'Pull her down!'

Because what *could* hurt her was water. Kissen and the other veiga took the ends of every chain they found and dragged the shrieking god down, down into the flood. Then they used the stakes they carried with them to pin the chains down beneath the water.

Hseth was dragged bodily into the current, deep enough to cover her as she shrieked, sliding over her flames and heat. Her inferno sputtered, diminishing. Faltering.

'Run!' Kissen cried. 'Fucking run!'

She grabbed the staff at her feet and waded away, as fast as she could. The other veiga did the same, quick, quick, as she heard the Talicians begin to scream.

She looked back as she reached the bank. In the water, she could see Hseth's twisting, writhing flames as she struggled against her bonds. It would have been enough to kill her in her previous life, though back then she would have been too smart to fall for a trap like this. It had worked on the god of war only long enough to hold him in place for spears; but spears wouldn't kill Hseth.

No, this was about faith.

The Talicians had seen their great god dragged under a lake of water, her fire winking out of existence. The fight they had been dragged into had been hard, confusing. Their numbers had counted for little.

They just needed a final stroke to shatter them into terror and send them fleeing. Kissen looked up. She saw the Middrenite and Irisian cavalry and the standing army were scattered into small units, churning in desperate melees. Exhausted, all but overrun. Elo's horn was blowing for his reinforcements, the master blow.

No one had yet come.

Kissen's heart dipped, then rose again, as there! She saw them! Along the valley edge came a string of riders and foot soldiers in the colours of Middren's Houses. Indigo, blue, grey, green, and red, and Irisians charging in their lightweight armour. There were supposed to be more, in Yether yellow, but there were only two: Captains Alianne and Faroch.

But it was enough. The Talician army saw them too.

It was the Restish who broke first. They had taken the heaviest losses, and their biggest advantage had disappeared into the waters, screaming and bound by briddite. They would not stay for another charge.

So the Restish fled, mud flying up from the hooves of their horses as they clambered for higher ground. Priests who had gathered at the lip of the valley were shrieking after them, but even as the veiga watched, some red cloaks began to run.

Panic spread. There. Kissen noticed Lessa making chase of the Talicians.

There. She saw Elo and his blue lion. Still alive, scrambling up under a press of bodies, still on his horse as he cut down the enemy's main attack.

A cheer broke out from the Middrenites, the final battalions of the army that surrounded the golden king. Fire burst out bright and brilliant from his chest as their faith in him increased a thousandfold, making a beacon beneath the storm-lashed skies.

The heart of a god-king. Fireheart. Sunbringer. Faith triumphant.

And the Middrenites called him.

Sunbringer. Sunbringer.

Fireheart, firehearth.

Our flame, our home.

Kissen breathed out. They had done it. Broken the faith of thousands, harried the greater foe until they fled. Would it be enough? Would it kill Hseth, as Kissen had hoped? The water and the broken faith?

But the god did not diminish. Hseth felt the loss of their fair-weather love. She felt the faiths turn towards Arren, ripped away from her. It hurt. It had to hurt.

And Hseth was unused to disappointment.

Her flames burned hotter beneath the water. Wilder. Angrier. The flame of a wrathful god.

It seemed she had remembered what fire could do.

'Shit,' Kissen hissed.

Flame burst out at the top of the slope, a flare, tall as a beacon. The larger shrine from which her priests must have planned to summon her. Hseth used her power to tear it into a flame that ripped all her priests away with it, their robes setting alight, their hair burning. She was making her own sacrifice, consuming her faithful.

Because gods loved martyrs, and pain was an offering. Pain gave her power.

The water was boiling hotter now where Hseth had been bound. The hillock that had protected the king and his battalion, an island in the current, had now the potential to trap them.

Kissen could see the glow of the briddite chains as Hseth melted them. Her arm broke free, blazing like a brand into the air, and then the rest of her followed, surging up above the water in a cloud of steam and terror.

Kissen was already running, calling the others to follow her as the god returned in a body of flesh and licking flame, hot briddite dripping everywhere. She flung her arms wide, and a spray of molten metal went flying towards the valley heights, striking enemies and allies and burning cloth to flesh, flesh to bone.

Kissen's eyes were seared. She lost sight of Elo, of Lessa, could barely feel the ground beneath her. Hseth's brightness was almost too much. Blindingly hot, white-hot flame.

But Hseth had no interest now in the little veiga who had attacked her, only in the king who stood before her, his fire mirroring hers.

CHAPTER FORTY-SEVEN

Arren

ARREN SAW THE GOD RISE FROM THE WATER.

This would be the end of them if he did not face her. The veiga had already half-retreated, and too few cavalry had come to help Elo. Far too few to fight a god. It seemed many Middrenites had fled before they had come to join the battle.

But Arren still had his heart. His body. The faith of his people. He could feel it, surging in his blood. His skin glowed with it, warm, bright, welcome. Shining with his and Hestra's power.

'Raise your spears!' he commanded.

The king's knights did so, lifting their spears and pointing them at the god, steadfast. Their colours vivid, their love immaculate.

It filled him. Them. He and Hestra. One will. One purpose.

'Die, flame of terror!' he cried towards Hseth as she turned down on him. He drew his sword. 'Die fire of death!'

Die, said Hestra with him, *god of war and madness. I was weak for you.*

'*I was weak for you,*' whispered Arren.

'*I let you guide my heart,*' they spoke together, '*and choose my ways.*'

I let you turn me cruel, said Hestra, *and lose my faith.*

Arren had lost his faith. He had lost it in his people. He had lost it in his land. His loves.

No more.

The fire god rose, a burning pillar of flame, and Arren dismounted.

'Sunbringer?' said Peta, but he ignored her, moving across the hillock to stand before his knights.

'I have found my faith again, fire god!' he roared. *'And you cannot break it in me.'*

The god moved closer. She was larger again, fuelled by her martyred priests, and he could hear the flames of her body, roaring and wild with fury. Beneath her floating feet, the river broiled, and steam billowed up in great clouds.

'Fear me,' she hissed, 'and beg for your life.'

We can fight her, said Hestra, burning in his heart of hearts. She poured flame out of his chest, across his armour. It did not burn. It was his.

He tore off his helmet. He needed to be light. To be free. As he did so, he felt the nubs of antlers on his head, beneath his hair.

'I fear no gods,' Arren snarled. 'I am the only god this nation needs.'

'Not yet.'

He heard Methsme's voice before he felt it. A strike, burning through his back, breaking through his armour, striking out from his chest. Dull metal. A knight's sword.

Briddite.

Hestra screamed. Arren turned back, and saw Peta staring at him. Her sword was through his chest, where his heart had been. She and Methsme watched, expectant. Waiting.

'Become a god, Sunbringer,' the cleric whispered. 'Show us your power!'

Then her face fell. In Arren's chest, his fireheart faded, and he felt his flame go out.

CHAPTER FORTY-EIGHT

Elogast

ELO HAD COME RUNNING DOWN THE SLOPES WHEN HE SAW the god rise again, driving his horse over bodies and wreckage. The Talicians weren't the only ones held together by strings of faith and hope. If she tore out their centre, destroyed the king, she would kill them all.

He blew his horn, reinforcements again. *To me! To me!*

But every part of the army was fighting its own battles, chasing down the Talicians and the Restish. Or they were running at the sight of Hseth returned and furious. Racing up the slopes with the Talicians, away from flame and water.

Would no one help him? Would no one be brave enough to face the god, and save their king?

A horn. A cry of response.

Lessa Craier, true to her duty, had summoned another array of horses. They rode hard down beside him, following at his back, charging at his side, straight for the god at the valley's heart.

Gods.

Elo could see the flame of Arren facing Hseth, his brightness a match to hers, one nation's faith against another. Arren's fire was the light of a flame on a cold night, the light of a sun rising in the autumn. Elo saw him rip off his helm, the bright blue of his eyes, the twists of his hair, the antlers that just showed above the curls.

Fearless, he stared up at the god who had betrayed him, died and then lived to kill him.

And then he saw Peta draw her sword. He saw the cleric, Methsme, whispering at her side.

'Arren!' Elo screamed. 'Arren, no!'

He saw the strike, true in his heart.

CHAPTER FORTY-NINE

Skediceth

SKEDI FLEW BETWEEN STREAKS OF SUNLIGHT AND STORM, rain and gusts of wind into utter chaos. He flew as the gulls flew, wet and ragged, his button and his jade bracelet shining in his eyeline.

He could see the lake overflowing the dam, spilling with flood-water into the valley beyond. He saw, too, the flat flood at its base, the mud, black and blood of its sides. The clashing armies, Talician, Restish, Irisian and Middrenite. No sign of Hseth, just water and lightning, thunder and nothing.

The reds were fleeing the valley. Running for the high ground, chased by riders in the king's colours.

They're winning! he cried to Inara, racing far below him on her stolen horse.

The sun was lowering now, sinking long into the evening. Colours arced across the sky, the hues of sunset and the shine of rainbows, turning everything shining bright. Like the shades of human feeling.

Then, white flame. Skedi was blasted upwards by a wave of heat that curled his feathers. He felt Hseth's power like a pulse of lightning, and saw her drag herself out of the water.

What is it, Skedi?

In the valley, the knights in blue clustered with fear. Skedi could see Craier colours too, green and silver, gathering around a knight on horseback on the valley slopes, charging down to face the great god of fire.

Then, another, golden fire came from the centre of the flooded river, before the knights, deep in the valley. A challenge. For a moment, Skedi had hope, bright as the blaze for a beautiful moment, warm and radiant.

Then it winked out.

Skedi?

CHAPTER FIFTY

Kissen

KISSEN REACHED THE ISLAND FIRST, WADING THROUGH the slick river, dragging her metal leg through the water with a pain that felt as if the increasing current was trying to rip it off her.

Commander Peta's hands were still on the sword sticking out of the king's chest. The other knights were in shock, frozen, unsure what to do. But terror grew on their faces as the god-king's flames dwindled, then disappeared.

Kissen dragged herself onto dry ground, pulling out a throwing knife and flinging it spinning towards the sour-faced Commander Peta. It went through her neck, sending her spinning into the mud, but the cleric didn't seem to notice.

'Fireheart!' Methsme cried, her eyes on the king as he stumbled to his knees, cloaked in stormlight. She dropped too, her hands out before him, as if welcoming him into an embrace. 'The king who must die, so the god can live!'

'You fucking lunatic!' yelled Kissen. 'What have you done?'

Methsme did not hear her, and pointed her shaking fingers up at Hseth. 'Fire god, be gone!' she howled. 'Be gone before the true god comes to kill you.'

The king fell on his side in the mud The nubs of velvet antlers were poking through his hair. It had worked. He had almost managed it through will alone. To become a god. Powerful enough to face Hseth. Powerful enough to kill her.

But his own faithful had decided it wasn't enough.

Hseth stared, baffled by this little cleric who did not seem to realise she had just had her 'true god' destroyed.

'He was too tied to the world!' cried Methsme, beseechingly at anyone who would listen, though her voice was beginning to falter. No one did. Some knights had realised that all was lost, and began struggling past her, away from the flame. 'To his loves, to his flesh and bone. Gods do not need affection; gods do not take lovers! Gods love their priests and commanders! Gods—'

Kissen should run. It was too late now. She had no more tricks, and there was nowhere to run but the water. Nowhere was safe. And Hseth smiled because she knew it.

'Let me show you,' she snarled, 'the power of a true god.'

She reached down, pouring flame across her arm towards the earth, and the cleric screamed as it struck her. Methsme's antlers caught fire first, her hair all rushing up in a burst of heat and flame. Then her skirts, her skin. Her very voice was burned to smoke, and then she was songless. In an instant, all her attempted power, all her hopes, were ash.

Kissen threw herself back into the water to avoid the fire, and saw a blaze of light, heard the screams. Felt the heat.

But it was not the heat that came to kill her; it was the thudding of fleeing knights and their frightened feet. She tried to push herself to the surface, but the crack of a boot on her leg forced her back down into the water. Another. Kissen tried to yell as she was forced down, but only bubbles blew out of her mouth. Where was her staff? Her strength? She had no grip on anything. Another knee hit her head; a hand pushed her away as she tried and failed to grab a body to pull herself up.

They didn't care. In their terror, they didn't notice her at all.

Water was in her nose, her throat, as she struggled to rise against the crush. She was weakening, her lungs straining, and her vision swam, darkened. She had tried to kill Hseth by drowning, and now she was suffering the same fate. *What a shitty way to die.*

Then she felt a hand grab her cloak, pull her up. She surfaced, gulping for breath, retching water.

All the world was aflame. The water was hot on her face, and she found herself clinging on to Lessa. The lady had found her by her green cloak, and wrenched her to the surface.

'Are you all right?' she asked.

Kissen didn't answer. She was not fucking all right. None of them were.

And ahead was Elo, a shield raised against the flames, throwing himself back onto the island, towards the fallen king.

CHAPTER FIFTY-ONE
Elogast

ELO REACHED ARREN ACROSS THE BLACKENED GRASS AND ash. The king was curled in a ball. There was not much blood, for his heart had been lost years before. Now, there were just embers, flickering and sparking in his chest.

'Arren.' Elo dragged him up. His armour was hot but, almost dead as he was, Hseth had not bothered with burning him.

'Elo?' Arren choked. He was still alive. Just. But beneath the burning metal of his grand armour, his skin was turning cold. The army was a mess, scattered, split and leaderless.

They had failed.

I cannot do it. Hestra's voice was weak in Elo's mind, barely a prickling of flame. *She did not end me, but I cannot fill another rift without his power. They believe in us, not him, not me. I cannot mend him.*

Here Elo was again, in his worst nightmare, with Arren dying in his arms. The last of his line, the last god of Middren.

'The . . .' Arren was trying to speak as fire rained down about them. He reached up to touch Elo's face, 'The . . . only one. Elo. You were the only one. Who truly l-loved me.'

You're the only one who ever loved me, Elo, he had said last time he was dying. *The only one who ever believed in me.*

'I'm s-sorry,' Arren said. 'For wasting it.'

Elo held him tightly. The fire was drying the tears on his cheeks

386

even as they fell. A surge of flame came near them, sweeping over the grass, but didn't quite reach them. Not yet.

It would come.

Elo closed his eyes and bent over his king. His friend. His love. His enemy. Arren's breaths were fading. His body, so long sustained by a god's will, was dying. The fire was closer now. Hseth was dancing after the fleeing knights, throwing fire after them up the banks of the valley.

'We could have changed the world,' Elo whispered to him. 'You and I.'

The world will change without us, said Hestra. She brightened in his chest, one last moment, and then she went out.

The god was gone, and Arren died in Elo's arms.

The burning reached them, turning the world hot and orange. It came roaring down from Hseth, and Elo closed his eyes, waiting for the end. Alone again.

The end didn't come.

He looked up.

'Kissen,' he said hoarsely.

The veiga stood with two fallen shields on her back, yelling as they burned her through her wet clothes, but standing high enough that the fire spilled around them. Lessa was with her, taking shelter from the fire. She looked grim, bleeding from a burn on her arm, the flesh seared and black.

'Run!' cried Elo hoarsely. 'You have to run.'

'It's too late for that, baker-knight,' said Kissen. The fire passed, and she threw down the half-melted shields as Hseth turned her attention elsewhere. 'This isn't sacrifice. This is love.'

Lessa stood up with her. She had a knight's blade. A briddite sword. Kissen did too.

'Inara is safe,' she said. 'That's all that matters. All that matters is our hope.'

CHAPTER FIFTY-TWO

Inara

THEY CAME TO A HALT AT THE TOP OF THE ARRENON valley where the path turned rocky, and Inara dismounted. Their warning had no one to go to. Their words were lost to nothing.

The battle had turned. Hseth had burned it back into her own favour. The rain had stopped, the sun uncovered and spilling, fresh and golden, across the devastation of the valley. But the fire god, glutted on pain and sacrifice, was raining flame down upon the tattered centre of the king's battalion, tearing through swathes of soldiers as they fled.

And there, at the centre, the lightless body of a man in golden armour, the flames of his heart gone out. A man in silver, holding him, his colours shining blue.

'Elo,' murmured Skedi from her shoulder.

And behind him, facing the fire, facing death, were two women who knew how to hide their fear from gods.

Lessa and Kissen, swords in hands.

Can you find an escape? Inara said directly to Skedi.

He looked at her, his wings raised, but could not deny her the lie. With a press of his paws, he took off into the air, swooping around in the setting sun, the fading light, the encroaching dark. Inara stood and watched the last of her loves below, still fighting, unafraid to die.

She knew now why her mother had not wanted her to watch. *Anything?*

Skedi's silence was his second lie. He didn't want to say no. He didn't want to tell her they were too late. There was no way off the islet without falling into the water and suffering death by boiling instead of burning.

Her family had already chosen the way they wanted to go.

No. She wouldn't let them. Not when she had some power. Something. Anything.

She pulled out Osidisen's knife again. Its blade was still dirty with her blood.

It won't work! said Skedi from above.

A roar of heat from the valley had borne him higher. High enough not to stop her? He had a shrine; he might be all right.

Ina, it won't work.

She shook, terrified. Could she? She lifted the blade, put the point to her chest, between her ribs.

Only death can match Hseth's strength, Hestra had said. *Perhaps yours would do. Would you offer me that?*

'Gods love martyrs,' she whispered. She hesitated, frightened. Frightened of it hurting. Frightened of dying. Not like her mother below, like Kissen and Elo who were facing death standing.

Perhaps she was just a child after all.

She tightened her grip, took a breath. Point facing in. Her heart's blood, to summon a powerful god, surely it would be enough.

Skedi was diving down towards her. *Don't you dare, Inara Craier!* he cried. *It's not enough. Pain is not enough!*

'I have nothing else!' she cried. 'All I have is me! And I won't let them die! I can't.' She choked on a sob. 'I can't let them die.'

She remembered looking into the valley of her home, seeing it burn. She remembered watching Kissen fall, flaming, into the sea. She remembered encouraging Elo to fight, putting Telle in danger, watching the rose god die.

She put both hands to her blade and closed her eyes.

There were still gods in Middren. Somewhere. There had to be. *There is another way.*

Inara opened her eyes, infuriated. 'Don't lie to me!'

But he was no longer diving towards her. Instead, he was swooping down into the valley. Towards the fire.

Sacrifice me.

CHAPTER FIFTY-THREE

Skediceth

THERE WAS ONLY ONE CHOICE. HE WOULD NOT LET INARA give her life away, and she couldn't stop him now. He was certain that he had gained enough of his own power, his independence, that what bound them now wouldn't hurt her if it was broken, because it was love alone that kept them together.

Skedi, no! He felt the whizz of an arrow as she dropped her blade and picked up her bow, then tried to knock him down, aiming for his wing, another for his leg. But he eluded her. *Stop!*

He did not stop. There was no other way to save the others. With every blast of flame, they came closer to death. And he was close now to Hseth. The heat curled his whiskers, singed his feathers. The string that held Inara's button burned, and it flew away. The beads, too, scattered. At least it wouldn't be wet. He hated being wet.

Don't leave me, Skedi, her voice still reached him in his mind, but he couldn't see her any more. *You're my family too.*

His eyes filled with flame and light. He hoped she would close hers, that she wouldn't watch. His brave, powerful, strange little human.

Use me, he said to her. *It's all right.*

For only love was greater than pain.

I don't want to lose you.

Gods are never lost if there is someone who still believes in them.

Heat consumed him. He was a god of white lies, a god of hope and a god of tales. And he had already lived longer than he deserved, with the love of a girl who had chosen him.

I love you, he said.

And he flew into the flame.

CHAPTER FIFTY-FOUR

Inara

INARA SCREAMED AS SKEDI FLEW TOO FAR TO STOP, TOO close to Hseth to survive.

She had to use it, or lose him for nothing.

Gods! she called, using her will and binding it to Skedi's as he turned to a small point of darkness within Hseth's flame. *I offer my love to you.*

She could see the shades of her own intent, her own power. Skyblue, bright and shining. And with it, the brightness of her love. Her offering. Skedi's offering.

Aan, Hestra, Lethen. Yusef, Kelt and Osidisen. Gods Sali, Daefer, Faer. Gods of thieves. Gods of the towns and cities, the trees, the waters and the wilds. Come to me! Take the god who has diminished you.

She couldn't see Skediceth. Not the shape of an antler, nor the curve of a wing. It was too bright. But she heard him.

I love you.

Then she saw the blaze as the flame took him, flaring him into light, then colour, then gone.

Hseth did not even notice him die, but Inara felt her heart explode with him, turning her world into ash, and her will into power.

Gods of Middren, she called with her broken heart, *come back and claim your land!*

The power was so bright, it flew out of Inara and into the sky, the earth, the air, the water. It tore into the heavens and ripped the storms and skies apart.

First, the river moved. It poured over the dam in a rush of green water, flooding in a wave of water gods. Hundreds of them. Aan took the lead with Sali of the Gefyrton falls, cloaked in steel and ice. With them came others, beings of cracked stone and teeth, moss and green and water lilies, snow and ice and deep black power.

Then, from the heavens came the winds, dragging lightning down behind them. The goat god danced down from the storm, breasts bare to the wind and a mask cut to roaring. Others flooded down, howling across the hills as seabirds, rainbows, storms and summer heat.

The earth of the hills cracked, and from their bowels came bones and riders, death and hunters, deer gods, forest gods, gods of shadows and gods of music and song. The little creatures of broken sandals or silver gossip, the wisps and demons of Lethen, the cracking golden limbs of gods of fortune dressed in cloaks of spices and green leaves.

Inara dragged them all up with her will and Skedi's offering, and they dived upon Hseth like hounds to their prey, tearing her flame apart. No great power, no great gods, just thousands of little secret faiths, of small shrines and precious prayers.

Wave after wave, the hidden gods of Middren dragged their enemy down into the water, deep into the earth, where she was extinguished in the land she had tried to destroy.

All for the love of a little god of white lies.

CHAPTER FIFTY-FIVE

Kissen

NOT FOR THE FIRST TIME, KISSEN OPENED HER EYES, surprised to be alive.

Her heart was still beating as she stared at a gloaming sky. Empty of fire, lit by the sinking sun.

The gods of Middren had come, and they had torn Hseth apart.

Only one power Kissen knew could have summoned them.

'Ina,' she croaked.

She turned, dragging herself to her knees, her feet. The flood had diminished, the fires were all burned out. The surviving Middrenites were picking themselves up and groaning. The Talicians left on the field were dead or dying. The rest had fled.

'Inara!' Kissen yelled. 'Skediceth!'

What had Inara done? What had she lost to save them?

Elogast was picking himself up, wounded and burned, but alive. Arren lay lifeless, his chest empty. Elo met eyes with Kissen, but Lessa was already up and running, trying to find a horse, trying to find her daughter.

'Inara!'

They spread out over the battlefield, crying out her name, trying to find a lost little girl who had saved them all.

Kissen threw herself up the slopes, her legs trembling with pain, hauling herself to higher ground.

They couldn't waste a moment. If Skedi was not flying to take them to her, then he must be afraid to leave her. The gods had disappeared back to where they had come from, exhausting whatever great strength had brought them all so far from their shrines.

Then a ribbon of water threaded itself up through Kissen's feet, a trail up the green, the black and the mud. Shining through the bodies, slightly crisped with ice.

Aan. Aan, who still had Inara's hair.

Kissen followed the ribbon, half sobbing, half panting through her blistered lips. 'Inara . . .' Even to her, her voice was weak. Ina wouldn't hear her. She just had to find her. Up to the crest of the southern slope she dragged herself, up over the rocks and the bodies.

There. She saw a small form in green, curled in a ball.

'Inara!' Kissen limped towards her over the sodden ground. 'Inara!'

She reached her. Where was Skediceth? Where had that bastard gone, leaving her all alone in danger? Kissen pulled Inara upright, checking for wounds. The child was shaking so badly that Kissen could barely keep a grip on her. There was Osidisen's dagger on the ground, but its gem was cracked, the blade gone dull.

'Ina what happened? Are you hurt?'

Inara opened her eyes. They were red with crying, but there was no bleeding, no obvious wound.

'Ina . . . Where's Skedi?'

'I loved him,' she whispered, then a sob shook through her body. 'He knew how much I loved him.'

Kissen began to understand. She gathered Inara to her, holding on to her as the child's heart broke, her whole body shuddering with her loss, and Kissen found her own eyes filling with tears.

Skediceth, that little god, the liar, the rat, the pest.

Kissen buried her face in Inara's hair as tears spilled over her eyes and down her face, her scars, her wounds.

For the first time in her life, the godkiller wept for the death of a god.

EPILOGUE

Inara

INARA DIDN'T WANT TO LET ELO GO.

'Careful, little one, you'll crack my ribs,' he said softly. Still, she didn't release him. 'I'm coming back,' he assured her.

After a few more moments, she stepped back, tripping on her formal skirts as she did so.

They had returned to Sakre's harbour, and the *Silverswift* awaited its new guest. The ship had taken a beating in the battle of the southern waters, but the sudden appearance of Osidisen, god of the north sea, and Yusef, god of safe haven, had tipped the fight against the fire god's allies. Osidisen, too far from home, weakened as he was, had disappeared, his shrines shattered. Kissen never said what she felt about her second father's death.

It was nothing against the loss of Skedi.

'Do you promise?' said Inara.

'He'd better,' grumbled Kissen. 'He's bringing my sisters with him.'

She stood beside them both on the stone wall of the harbour. Dark cormorants wheeled in the bright spring sky, excited by the new ships that were docking in Sakre's port and looking for mates to nest with. Irisian vessels, mainly, some Usican, Pinetish, Curlish. Even one from Restish, which annoyed Inara no end.

'You sure you don't want to come with me?' said Elo to Kissen. 'My mother says she wants twelve more tales from you.'

'Bah, tell her yourself,' said Kissen, then grinned, and ran her hand through her curls. 'Make me sound good, though, will you? I've work enough to do here.'

She put her hand out towards Inara, who took it, squeezing tightly. She wasn't sure whether Kissen had stayed for her or for, as she professed, making sure 'those cleric bastards' didn't start some king-cult and 'those shrineless fuckers' in Blenraden didn't hamper efforts to rebuild.

Elo wore a gold and green cloak sewn with lions and birds along the hem, with a tree sprouting up its back. An ambassador's cloak, complete with a sigil ring on his fourth finger. He looked proud and calm. Ready to go home.

Inara still found herself listening for Skediceth's voice. She mourned the tug on her heart she had always felt when he went too far away from her, his snide little asides, the way he cocked his head when he didn't understand people's strange whims.

And now she was losing Elo too. To finally visit his mothers' home, to mourn, and heal.

'Goodbye, godkiller,' said Elo to Kissen, who smiled crookedly, then put her hand on his chin and kissed him full on the mouth.

'For luck,' she said, and he laughed.

I wish you could see this, Skedi.

Inara received no answer, of course. Perhaps she never would.

After the *Silverswift* left the harbour, she and Kissen climbed on a carriage to take them back to the Reach.

The old Regna stronghold had been shored up and was slowly being rebuilt, its walls hung with the colours of all the noble Houses, united. Even Yether. Lord Beloris had been forced to hand his power to his sister, and was banished for ordering his troops to defect to their enemy. Many had fled before the final fight when they saw the yellow-clad guard retreating, but Faroch, Alianne and Movenna had managed to keep the rest together. They had survived on sheer luck, it felt. And sacrifice.

Lady Craier was in the first courtyard as they entered, assessing an array of scrolls with a trade ambassador while being assailed with petitions by several greater and lesser nobles.

'Regent, the wine and olive yields were too low last year . . .'

'We have no one to till and plant the crops. We lost too many to the war, and then the winter was so hard . . .'

'How are we going to pay for the building work—'

Kissen paused, and Inara looked up. The veiga was watching Lady Craier, a strange expression on her face. Not for the first time, Inara wished she could see her colours, know what she was thinking. She did not know what had passed between Kissen and her mother, but she could hazard a guess.

'Kissen?' said Inara.

Kissen blinked and smiled. 'Bloody typical,' she said. 'Pirate, noble, rebel and regent. We just got rid of one god-king and now we have a half-god princess.'

Inara shoved her playfully. 'I'm not a princess.'

'Not yet.'

Lessa found them with her eyes, and the hard line of her mouth softened slightly, warmth coming into her face. She wore a silver circlet across her brow. No antlers to be seen.

'If it's my blessing you want,' said Inara, looking from Kissen to her mother, 'I'll give it to you.' She could think of worse things than two people loving each other.

Kissen smiled and ruffled her hair. 'Come now, *liln*,' she said. 'I'm no fool, and kingdoms are not in my future. All I need is a warm fire, good ale, crisp bread, and people who love me.'

Ina sighed. 'I love you.'

'I love you too. Now, how about we practise some swordwork?'

Inara bit her lip. Tempting. But she shook her head. 'There's something I want to do first.'

Kissen nodded, glanced once more at Lessa, then headed towards the garden paths. Strong and proud, with a staff for her balance. She still wore her cloak full of pockets, and her blade of briddite. Her new scars had blended in with her old.

Inara didn't follow her, instead going past the courtyard council with bows and polite greetings, then heading towards the receiving hall.

The king's hall had been all but ripped apart inside, the blackfire damage shorn up with wooden beams and buttresses of stone. There were shrines again, the first welcoming of gods under the new regency, showing its aims and desires: a god of learning from Curliu, discovery brought over from Lakaii, and healing, from Middren itself. There was a shrine, of course, to Yusef, measured palm for palm to be larger than his Wsirin-based temple, and not a hair more. It had a locked gate before it, directing people to offer no tokens. Some still did. But Inara's boon was fulfilled, and he had no right to challenge it.

But there was another shrine at the back of the room, where the throne had once been. There, the dais had been lowered, and there was no throne, no deer, no rays of sun. There were still some who worshipped Arren the Sunbringer, Fireheart, but Lessa was determined he be remembered as only a king, sacker of Lesscia and Blenraden, burner of his people, not the winner of their war.

For he had not won it.

In the space where his throne had been, a small but grand shrine had been raised. Its walls were panelled in etched brass, showing green leaves, patterns and feathers, and its totem was white marble, beautifully carved: a hare with a stag's horns and a bird's wings.

His eyes had been set with amber, his fur detailed so meticulously it looked as if he might spring up and move at any moment. Offerings had already been draped on his antlers, pooled in the bowls before him. Libations, incense, sweets and wine.

Inara's offerings were different. They were written notes on long thick pages. Inked stories of what he had been, what they had done together. She had one tucked in her pocket, ready to read aloud. His history, and hers.

It was a greater shrine than he had ever dreamed, etched at its base with his name:

Skediceth. God of hope and telling tales.

ACKNOWLEDGEMENTS

HOW TO BEGIN WHEN WE HAVE REACHED THE END?

These books, I have each dedicated to my family: my father, my mother, my brothers and my sister. They have been my shield and armour at every turn, and have loved me through every time my heart broke, and every time I put it together again. We choose our families, and I would choose them over and over. Thank you.

To my husband, my heart. I chose you too. Thank you for the adventures and inspiration. Thank you for being the wind that fills my sails. Thank you for being my haven and home.

To Juliet, my agent, and an inspiring and extraordinary woman, we finally did it! A whole trilogy, and what a ride it has been. You've been my north star, showing me there is land ahead if we can only keep going. Thank you.

To the rest of the Mushens Entertainment team: Liza, Alba, Rachel, Catriona, Emma, thank you for championing my work around the world, it has been incredible to reach readers and publishers everywhere, and I couldn't ask for a better team.

To HarperVoyager on both sides of the Atlantic. To Rachel, Jane, Julia, Natasha, Chloe, Jes, Deanna, Catherine, Susanna, Siobhan, Fleur, to the design and sales teams, to the copy editors and authenticity editors and countless, countless others. Thank you for giving these books shape and beauty, thank you for putting them in the hands of readers, thank you for seeing them to the end.

To Tom Roberts, for the most exquisite art, for your attention to the smallest details and your epic, extraordinary imagination. I can't imagine this journey without you. I'm so sad it is over, and I'm so glad it happened. Thank you.

To my friends, my loves, there are too many of you to name: incredible writers, school friends, hill walkers, taste testers, sea swimmers, night sky chasers, fire starters, adventurers and pioneers. I owe so much to you. You all inspire me to be the best I can be.

To the writers and advocates who have made it possible for stories like this to exist. To those who broke through the ceiling, and lowered the ladder behind them. I hope I can do the same.

To the booksellers and librarians who connect stories to people, and people to stories. Thank you for loving and sharing this series, thank you for welcoming me and stocking these books on your shelves. I still feel like I'm dreaming all of it.

And to my readers. Thank you for joining me in this world, on this journey. I hope you will come with me on another.

The end is also a beginning.